Between
Two Abysses

Between Two Abysses

PART 1 OF A TRILOGY

Samuel Lewin

Translated from the Yiddish by Joseph Leftwich

Cornwall Books
New York • London • Toronto

All characters in this book are fictitious.

Cornwall Books
440 Forsgate Drive
Cranbury, NJ 08512

Cornwall Books
25 Sicilian Avenue
London WC1A 2QH, England

Cornwall Books
2133 Royal Windsor Drive
Unit 1
Mississauga, Ontario
Canada L5J 1K5

The paper used in this publication meets the requirements of the American National Standard for Permanence of Paper for Printed Library Materials Z39.48-1984.

Library of Congress Cataloging-in-Publication Data

Lewin, Samuel, 1890–1959.
  Between two abysses.

  Translation of: Tsvishn tsvey thomen.
  Contents: Between two abysses—Dark mountains and blue valleys—Shining through the clouds.
  I. Title. II. Title: Between 2 abysses.
PJ5129.L47T713 1987   839'.0933   85-22377
ISBN 0-8453-4795-0 (alk. paper)

Printed in the United States of America

Contents

Foreword:
Samuel Lewin

by Rudolf Rocker

It is a special satisfaction for me to say something about Samuel Lewin. There is a comic flavor to it, because of the race-anti-Semitism that became prevalent in Germany in our time. For I am a German and not a Jew, and it fell to me in Germany to introduce this East European Jew to a gathering of German Jews.

I had the opportunity of living among East European Jews for about twenty years. I got to know the Jews from the small towns of Eastern Europe. I got to know the Ghetto in London, New York, and other places. I must say that getting to know them produced a complete change in my way of thinking about Jews generally and the East European Jews in particular. I believe there are antitheses not only between Jews and Christians, but also between German Jews and East European Jews. The German Jew who lived in Germany for generations, and obtained his entire culture, knowledge, and view of life in Germany had very strange and, I am sure, completely wrong ideas about East European Jewry.

If we draw a distinction between culture and civilization, and we understand by civilization man's desire to organize only his material life, while culture is the higher force that tries to tame the material and to lift it to a higher spiritual plane, then I would say that we have absolutely no reason to look down on the East European Jew as though he were an uncivilised being. The East European Jew has culture. His culture is different and unique—it is not the culture we have in Germany and other countries. But it is a strong and vital element, and I consider that it has a great future.

I experienced the whole development of the modern Yiddish language. I can remember the time when men like Mendele and Shalom Aleichem wrote Hebrew, and only later, when the spirit came upon them, they realised that it doesn't do to write in a language that the mass of the people does not speak, and that they must write in the language that the people understand, in which you can reach the soul of the people. That was when the new Yiddish literature began to grow, and with the literature the Yiddish language developed and flourished. Yiddish is in that sense one of the youngest languages, but it has achieved important things, and much of it has gone through translations into German and other world languages.

When I first met Samuel Lewin he wanted me to read a Yiddish manuscript of his. To tell the truth I didn't expect much. It was his "Visions." He revealed himself here as a poet who was trying to give shape and form in a work of art to the catastrophe of the First World War. It was strange, but till then very little had been done in literature to give expression to that great world tragedy. It seems to me that in this regard the poet is in the same plight as the historian. The man who has grown up in the midst of the calamity is too close to it to explain it. The poet must have time and distance before he can give shape and form to his material.

When I read "Visions," it was clear to me that Samuel Lewin is a poet, one of those poets who write because they must, because the stuff is in them and must come out.

We feel with Lewin that he grew up in a small Polish town, far from what we call education and culture, but he knows the depths of life in those Polish small towns, and knows the Polish Jews.

The urge to write came to him when he was already a mature man. He dug deep down into the human soul. His creative faculty developed under the worst material conditions, but no hardships and difficulties could curb his creative desire. I felt that when I read "Visions." Many of the pictures he painted still haunt me. I found one particular feature of Callot in Lewin's "Visions." One who has seen Callot drawings has seen the frightening abyss that was the Thirty Years War. Not only man, but the animals and all nature breathe war. It is the same with Lewin's "Visions." Every scene that Lewin has drawn in "Visions" hits you like a spear plunged in your body. What this one man has felt in his soul is the general feeling of humanity.

There is an astonishing scene in "Visions"—a battlefield; clouds chasing across the sky. Pain and anguish. Weeping and wailing. And in the midst of the death and destruction a broken cannon pointed at the sky.

It made me think of Goya, that great painter of war scenes. He did not give you war as an epic poem, a heroic saga. He saw war is cruel and brutal. Not noble and grand, but the expression of the beast in man. Lewin has in my opinion completely succeeded in conveying this in his "Visions."

But Lewin is not a pessimist. The great disaster is followed by a rebirth, a resurrection, a human renaissance. Out of the boundless woe and grief something new arises. It seems that all great art, all new great culture is born of pain and suffering. We can hardly believe that without the suffering and pain we could possibly have that great thing which has no name, which shakes our soul to its depths.

If we consider all that Lewin has written, everything of his that I have read, including the things he has only just sketched out for working on, I would say that there is in his work a great idea in many variations, each different from the other, but always returning to the one idea.

In our time of folklore and technical civilization, in our time of generalizing our entire psychic and spiritual life, in our time when even cultural ideals fall increasingly under a general concept, in such a time Lewin believes that it is possible to be born anew. This resurrection is for him an awakening to a renaissance of a great religious idea and a deeply religious feeling. But there is a difference between what Lewin understands by religious idea and religious feeling, and what is generally known under these terms. There is a difference between believing in God and religion.

It is perhaps useful to quote in this regard a phrase from the materialist philosopher Ludwig Feuerbach: "Man makes his God in his own image, yet he may still be religious." When Feuerbach said this—he was repeating what a Greek philosopher had said 2,500 years before him—he was dreaming of founding a new religion, the religion of man.

The religious idea was to Lewin primarily what rouses the sense of community in man. Where there is community in a man's soul it draws to itself a second soul, and where man joins with man in the depths of feeling, there is community, there is religiousness. Religiousness is thus man's sense of responsibility, the revelation of man's individual qualities, which are based on the sense of community, of spiritual belonging.

The idea finds expression in every one of Lewin's works, in all that he has written. It makes him perhaps one of those poets who are born before their time and therefore cannot become popular. At a time like ours when only the practical and the material are valued, in which religious feeling is not given much regard, at such a time it is very hard to deal with a poet who has taken it into his head to want to liberate the world through religious feeling. Lewin is full of the religious feeling of the faith of his people.

It is the idea of the Prophets in the Old Testament—they speak through him. Lewin realizes that the religious feeling that manifests itself deep down in a man is the same in all its forms. The forms are different, but at the heart they are all one. What raises man higher, what makes him understand his fellow man, this deep ethical idea, this religious feeling is not restricted to only one certain religion—on the contrary, we may say that where religion is stultified in dogmas, there the living thought that comes from the depths of the soul, the thought that speaks from man to man, which is possible through what is generally described today by the word *religion*—is pushed into the background. The stream must come pouring out from the soul.

Lewin understands the old Prophets of his people in all their depth. His social sense, his sense of community, the ideal of a community as he conceives it, has nothing whatever to do with any modern conception. Yet this ideal is always new, always modern, because it streams from the depths of the soul, and because it can't be surpassed in simple humanity.

In his novel "The Song of the Generations" Lewin—so far as it concerns the external, the scaffolding—pictures a Jewish small town as he knew and lived in it. We see the Christian element, the large Jewish community, the various groups in it, the different characters, from a common thief to a Rebbe and a Rav, to whom the Rebbe's wonder-working is repugnant. We see all kinds of small-town people. It is all so skillfully, plastically molded that each separate figure stands out clearly before our eyes. Everything is exactly right; you feel that it couldn't be any other way.

Take the old thief, Wolf Itzik. A remarkable figure that no poet could have invented. He must have known him, lived with him, before he could have given him artistic shape. The whole wonderful milieu of the back turns the whole time around the one and only pole, around the question of a religious renaissance of his people. Strange, but in the soul of the young thief, the old thief's son, there is a deep mystic sense. The father, the old thief, in spite of his trade is a Chassid of the Rebbe of the town. He takes his son every Sabbath when he goes with the other Chassidim to the Rebbe's table, to hear him expound Torah and to join in the holy meal. The young thief sees the Rebbe's youngest daughter, a girl of sixteen or seventeen, and falls in love with her. It starts a struggle in him. He stops being a thief, becomes an honest man, in order to win the privilege of marrying the Rebbe's daughter.

Here Lewin achieves a remarkable synthesis. When it comes to the religious idea, irrespective of whether it is Judaism or Christianity, he does not mean church or synagogue, but the deep inner feeling of faith.

Every scene in this book stands out—whether it is the Chassidim drunk with religious ecstasy, drinking the words of their Rebbe expounding Torah to them, or the Rav holding forth to his followers about the errors of the Chassidic Rebbe's ways, leading to a clash between Chassidim and Mithnagdim—each scene is a manifestation of the inner psychology of a certain group in a particular surrounding. The psychology of any one group, say, the Chassidim, is resolved in the individual psychology of a single person. Lewin does not lift up one section to thrust down another. We see the deeply human everywhere, both in ordinary everyday affairs and in the common religious life. Everywhere, in every scene of the novel, there is a wide range of difference in human character and feeling.

In his drama "Galuth" Lewin shows us the decline of the small town, and you know that he has lived through it, and felt it with all his being. The town goes through all the experiences of the war. But the Jewish population suffers most. First it is the Cossacks, a cruel people led by brutal instincts. We see how terribly they treat the Jews, who live segregated in their own quarter, as once in the Ghetto. When the Cossacks withdraw with the Russian army, the Germans enter. It makes things no better for the Jews. The Jew is always the victim. Then the Germans have to withdraw, and the Poles take over the country. That starts a new series of troubles for the Jews, no longer at the hands of the Russians or the Germans, but of the Poles. Humiliation and suffering.

But it would be wrong to think that Lewin is trying in this drama to show us the sufferings of his people during the war. All these sufferings caused by the war, the degrading of the women, the prostitution, murder stalking the streets, smuggling, greed—they are all the background of the drama. He shows us the animal lusts not only of the body but of the soul. What he wanted to show is what lives in the depths of his people, what lived there and was being gradually destroyed. He wanted to show us how the economic position in which the Jews in Poland were forced to live, and their own peculiar conditions, affected over the course of time their spiritual life. It destroyed their religious feeling—material desire took its place in their souls. The Jews in Poland endured not only murder and sin, but the tragic destruction of Judaism.

What Lewin shows us are the spiritual wounds, the wounds in the heart, the blood dripping from the wounds. That is what Lewin shows and what we see in each of his works. The writer's whole life, his religious feeling, turns around this problem.

Will it have any influence in bringing about the renaissance he wants? That question is hard to answer. I don't consider myself prophet enough to attempt to answer it. What I feel is that even if it should succeed, it would not take long before the same old state of affairs returned.

There is a painting by Rembrandt in the Kaiser Friedrich Museum, a clergyman with a broad-brimmed hat on his head, standing in the shadows, his eyes lighted up with religious ecstasy. He is speaking. The Bible lies to his right. A burning candle sheds light on the Book and on the clergyman's face. A simple women of the people sits before him. The clergyman is speaking with fervor and zeal. The words come from his lips, and through the shadows reach the ears of the Woman. She receives them with simple naiveté, like a child. Here we feel the tragedy. Between the clergyman's lips and the women's ears lies a mystery. The profound things he says she understands quite differently. The old diplomatic quip that language is given us to conceal thought is very true, not only of diplomacy. We are always being tripped up by the impossibility of bridging the gulf between the said and the heard. There lies the great mystery, which will no doubt also face the readers of Lewin's works.

The question is unanswerable. All we can say is that we hear in Lewin's work the voice of a true poet, who does not barter great ideas for the small coin of our materialist time, but tries to penetrate into the depths of the human soul, and particularly to understand the people of his own folk. It is not a simple art. It is fed with the writer's own heart's blood. The poet founders, that his ideas illuminate the darkness like a star for his readers, to show them the road to go.

Author's Introduction

We are living in a time of extreme, almost medieval intolerance. That applies also to our Jewish social life, especially in the field of the spoken and the written word. It started after the Bolshevik victory. The cry of the Bible, "Who is on the side of the Lord?" has been sharpened to "Who is not with me is against me." The result is that public opinion has ceased to respect the right of man to have his own idea about the problem of Socialism, not only according to the Party line, and refuses to have any understanding of his individual view of the problem of social morality and ethics in the way our Prophets of old saw it. It has a deadening effect on spiritual life, especially on the creative word.

The foundations of Judaism and Jewishness are, in my opinion, the Exodus from Egypt, the going out from slavery to freedom, and all the other social, moral, and ethical laws and commandments. That is what the Prophets always stressed and demanded from the Jewish people. Justice and righteousness are the essentials of the greater part of our religious postbiblical literature, beginning with the Talmud, up to the latest moralistic rabbinic work. And these moral and ethical laws and commandments were of course formulated according to the most progressive ideas of those times. The underlying motive in our secular, worldly literature is its continuation of the earlier principles of social justice, morality, tolerance, and liberty.

This essential Judaism never ceased to live in the souls of many, a great many Jews. It lived in all periods of our historical existence, sometimes among only a few Jews, sometimes more and sometimes less powerfully. This Judaism of "from slavery to freedom" and of social justice that glowed in the hearts of our Prophets, and which they never stopped proclaiming with poetic force and glorious vision, and demanding from the rich and powerful, from the oppressors of the poor—this Judaism lived at all times in the hearts of all those who fought for freedom and social justice. Of course, the language, the conception, and the method of the struggle kept changing all the time, according to the changes in social-public life.

Since the rise of modern capitalism and with it the rise of the proletariat in our present-day sense, we have created quite new conceptions of social justice and new

13

methods of conducting the struggle in the economic and political sphere. The proletariat began to organize, and the word *Socialism* flashed out on the red flag, which
became a pillar of fire in the battle for a just, free, spiritually elevated world. Under
this flag, in partnership with the Socialists of all nations, we Jews provided what was
proportionately the largest element—in every sphere, theoretical, propagandist
and in actual fighting on the barricades. The reason why we provided the largest
element is understandable from our historic condition, from the economic and
political state in which we lived in the various countries as aliens, in exile.

Those of us who held a high place in the history of Socialism included the sons
and daughters of rabbinical scholars. It was generally said that what brought them
to Socialism was their emancipation from religion, their going over to freethinking.
That is nonsense. They came to freethinking and to Socialism by way of the Bible,
by seeing how far the spirit of Judaism, which the Prophets preached and demanded, was from the official Judaism of the life around them.

The battle for freedom and justice, the struggle for Socialism went for a long time
almost unnoticed in our worldly, secular literature. First Weissenberg, then Bergel-
son, Horontchik, and several less-known writers began to picture this struggle.
They painted artisans, factory workers, the lower classes generally, conscious organized workers, and those still unaware of their place in society, unorganized, radical intellectuals, strikes, demonstrations.

In America the subject matter of Yiddish worldly literature was from the beginning Socialist-revolutionary, and so it remained till the end of the First World War.
Then a great change came. The Introspectivist movement arose, and presently—as
a reaction—a kind of symbolism and mysticism, like Leivik's "Golem" and the
"Redemption Comedy."

In Poland and other East European countries after the First World War increasing numbers of Jews fought in the ranks of the different Socialist parties. The struggle grew more bitter, more violent in the twenty's and thirty's. The reactionary
governments in the ostensibly republican democratic lands—in reality they were
Fascist or semi-Fascist—acted ruthessly against these fighters for Socialism.
Thousands were arrested and kept imprisoned for years; some were sentenced
to death and executed. Many were flung into concentration camps like Kartuz-
Baroza—in this regard Poland anticipated Hitler by several years. Yet the fight was
not stopped. People continued to sacrifice their liberty and their lives for their
convictions, for the idea they held sacred, in the same way that religious Jews were
always ready to sacrifice their lives for their faith.

The Holocaust of the Second World War—the most terrible in our history—cut
short not only Jewish lives, but also our Yiddish literature. From that time the pulse
of Yiddish literature began to beat more feebly in America too, and in all other
places. It was reduced largely to a literature of the Destruction and a literature of
memories. That is only natural. Most of these books pictured the pre-Destruction
life of the Jews who were massacred with a halo of sanctity. It almost looks as if all
those Jews were saints, angels. It is from one point of view understandable. For
these six million Jews, of whom a million were children, were wiped out in the most
atrocious manner. The reaction in America and in other places where Jews live was
to idealize the victims, to generate a great love of everything Jewish, and to look
back on their life and their ways of life with nostalgia. Religious Jews, and many

who were never religious, who had long ago thrown off the burden of Judaism and have no connection with it now, used the opportunity to call "Back to the Synagogue," back to the earlier, religious, traditional Judaism.

Both trends, the nostalgic love of Israel and of all things Jewish, and the propaganda for a return to traditional religious Judaism, have given almost the deathblow to the worldly-secular Yiddish literature as it existed till the Second World War. An author who has realistically treated Jewish life in the old home before the Second World War, as it was, with its lights and shades, has tried to be objective about it—as far as it is at all possible for an artist to be objective—will find that all the doors to publication are closed to him, both the private publishing houses and those run by communal and social bodies. If he wants his book published, unless he is one of a few famous writers, he will have to publish it himself. They won't take it even if he pays all the costs himself. The excuse given is that the life is pictured in such a way that "it does not fall into line with the books we publish." I stress the word *line*.

This state of almost medieval intolerance in our public life today is in a certain respect what might have been expected. And we might have expected too as a natural development the campaign that Socialists of all kinds conduct against the Communist Parties in the so-called free countries everywhere, and especially against Bolshevism in Russia (though it is strange to consider that they are thus allies in the cold war of the capitalist and often reactionary governments). We can understand it because the idea of Socialism, which was the finest, the noblest hope of all Socialists for redeeming man from his material sufferings and spiritual humiliations, is being brutally trodden down in the Communist countries, stifled with lies and drowned in blood, and instead of freedom there is slavery in the Communist countries.

There is no equality, but there are castes of dictators, with the supreme dictator on top. Instead of brotherhood there are prisons and concentration camps, from which few return. It is a bitter disappointment from which every honest militant Socialist has suffered since the Bolshevik victory.

Yet we must overcome this, we must make every effort not to lose our grip on commonsense, not to throw out the baby with the bath water. I mean this—we must not identify those who have fought for Socialism in the Communist Parties with the Bolshevik Government and its helpers in the existing Communist Parties (outside Russia and her satellites). The honest fighters for Communism in the period between the two wars outside Russia were double victims—they were convinced of their idea, of their ideal. They fought and suffered and sacrificed themselves for it.

One more thing that we must not forget—we must look at historical events in the light of history, including this present tragedy of a human ideal. Let us remember the two greatest events in the last two thousand years, the first at the beginning of our present era, the struggle for Christianity. What has become of this great religious-social idea for which so much blood was spilled? The second, at the end of the eighteenth century, the great French Revolution. What became of that noble ideal of liberty, equality, fraternity?

It seems to be one of the laws of history that an ideal for which men fight bears little resemblance to what they fought for when the victory has been won, or what remains of it is so distorted, so mutilated that it is impossible to recognize it as the idea for which they fought. It is a travesty, a monstrosity. Indeed, it seems that the finer, the nobler and more elevated the idea, the less of it remains, the uglier and more repulsive it becomes—the very opposite, the antithesis of what the idea was.

Yet what is left of the idea after the revolution is another link in the chain of progress. Its results are more often indirect than direct. A revolution is never only local—its effects are felt far beyond the frontiers, often over vast distances. Not immediately. Slowly, gradually the effects of the revolution reach distant countries and achieve significant results. Without the revolution nothing would have happened. Evolution is as dependent on revolution as vice-versa. Evolution and revolution are Siamese twins. Gustav Landauer says that in his book *The Revolution*, about topia and utopia. Revolution is the work of men and circumstances. Therefore, so it seems, it is not possible to know when a revolution is to take place and how it will achieve the results for which people fought. "Man makes history, and history makes man."

If you consider it, you find it hard to say that man is the master of his actions. Goethe put it well: "We think we are pushing, but we are being pushed."

Between
Two Abysses

Part One

1

The Ruined Town

The rectangular marketplace had been the heart of the town. Almost every house had contained a shop, large or small. But it had all been destroyed in the first year of the war, in 1914. Many houses had been consumed by fire. There were strong, solid, two- and three-story houses of which only black charred walls and chimneys were left. The wooden houses were just heaps of ashes. The Town Hall in the middle of the square was not destroyed, but its life had fled. It stood dumb and silent. So did the church, to the left of the Town Hall, just off the great highway. It was undamaged, but empty—no worshipers. The gilt brass cross on top of the tower, witness much earlier of man's inhumanity to man, looked down, surveying the scene of destruction. Inside the church, immediately you entered through the great door, hung a painting of the Virgin Mary kneeling before Christ on the cross, her face hidden in her hands, weeping for the destruction.

Only the walls of the Synagogue and the Beth Hamedrash, both in the poorest part of the town, had remained. A great many chestnut trees, limes, and acacias were burned and charred and pitted with shot.

Like the arteries of a living body connecting all parts with the heart, the streets and alleyways spread from every part of the town to the marketplace. The great highway cut through the town, connecting it with Warsaw and Lublin. Other roads linked it with other cities, towns, and villages. A bridge over the river led to the Jewish graveyard and the Christian cemetery.

It had been a town of artisans and traders, and of factories, which had been put up early in the twentieth century. The factories had been destroyed, leaving only charred walls, with holes that had once been windows, and tall dead chimneys and broken machines.

On a fine evening in early autumn, when the air was already cool yet still mild, some people thought they could feel the breath of those dead lives, destroyed by bullets or bayonets. Their death still hung in the air. Birds circled round, twittering, looking for their nests.

It was only a few days since the last battle had flared here. The population had twice been driven from the town. Now the Russian army had been chased a long way off and the refugees were beginning to return. But their homes—mostly in the poorer quarters, where artisans and factory workers, small shopkeepers and village peddlers lived—had been largely destroyed. Kalman the tinsmith's old-fashioned house, with a big kitchen and a baking stove that looked like an altar of olden times—this house that people used to call the Fortress—nothing more remained of it than the fire-resistant walls. That was where several homeless women had now assembled; together with Kalman's wife, Rachel, they had collected sticks and straw and dry dung and had made a fire, on which, over iron plates laid on bricks, they were boiling big black pots of water.

Of all the things the people had left behind when they fled, nothing remained except what wouldn't burn and what the looters didn't think worth taking.

The fire in the kitchen wouldn't burn. It only smoldered and smoked. Rachel blew into the glowing embers. Dressed in tattered rags that were stiff with mud, and wearing a cloth round her head, she looked like a great black stone and part of the fitting of this old-time kitchen.

The sooty, fleshy face was listless, the shoulders hunched, and the hard black hands and twisted fingers raked the fire till the smoldering glow burst into flame.

The women round the fire, none better clad than Rachel, looked as though they had turned to stone. Their sallow faces were pinched with hunger. Their eyes, which had seen so much death and destruction, were hard, and aged not with years but by terror and horror.

They put on pots of water to boil. But they had nothing to cook in the water— neither barley, groats, nor peas. Not even potatoes. There was nothing yet that you could buy in town. The shops that had been left fully stocked had been cleared out. The peasants in the villages round about had fled to the forest, and had started coming back only when the shooting stopped. They had not yet come to town to sell anything.

Very likely they had nothing to sell. Both armies, the Russian and the German, had emptied the barns and carried off everything they found in the villages and towns. They had broken into all the hiding places and confiscated the secret hoards.

Most of the women at the fire hadn't had a taste of food all day. Their husbands had gone into the villages and the adjoining towns that had escaped more lightly, hoping to earn something by work or trade to buy some food to bring back. Their grown-up sons and daughters were idle, like most of the artisans and factory workers in all the destroyed towns. There were no chedars open yet, so their children ran wild and hungry. They poked around in the ruins—searching the fields for potatoes, for empty bullet shells and shrapnel, and for iron from broken rifles.

The women round the fire hoped that God would take pity on them and that their husbands or one of their children would bring something home to put in the pots.

Itte, Abraham the tailor's wife, said with a sigh: "My husband went with our boy Noah to one of the villages. He heard that the peasants had come back there; so he thought he might get some sewing to do, mending and patching. He took buttons and packets of needles with him and a few other things that he managed to save when we were driven out of town. And more that he had bought in Warsaw. I do hope he gets a little money. The peasants always need needles and buttons. Somebody said this village wasn't even touched by the war, so he may bring some food back, cereals and potatoes."

The pots on the fire were beginning to boil. The women went on talking about their troubles, all they had gone through in their two evictions from the town, plodding with their bundles on their backs towards Warsaw—all that had happened to them and their husbands and children, all they had seen and endured, both from the armies on the road, who beat the refugees, robbed them, and often left them crippled, and also as homeless wanderers, exposed to the elements, sleeping in the fields, and always hungry. Every now and again one of the women, overcome by the recollection of her sufferings, burst into tears; she made a list of all her belongings that she had left behind for the looters or had lost on the road.

They spoke of children and relatives and friends who had been killed or had died on the road. The angel of death had visited every one of them. He had reaped a rich harvest not only on the battlefield. He had other weapons that he used besides guns and swords. He also slew with hunger and disease.

Jochabed, the scribe's wife, started talking about her misfortune. "My husband—," then she stopped. She suddenly felt that she would be profaning her husband's greatness and his sanctity by talking to anyone about him. She just sighed from her heart.

The sun was setting. The fire in Kalman the tinsmith's kitchen was going out; the women had stopped adding wood. The children, who had been running wild all day, were coming back, looking for their mothers.

"So you've turned up at last!" the mothers grumbled; the children only said, "I'm hungry!"

The children looked thoroughly miserable, faces sallow, pinched with hunger, sad frightened eyes. And strangely old. Children suddenly aged before their time, weighed down by the troubles and cruelties of life. In rags and tatters; filthy with the dirt and exposure of being out all day in the open, without a home. Their eyes darted hungrily toward the black pots of water in the kitchen.

Now the men came along, the husbands of the women, the fathers of these hungry children. They looked hopeless, doomed, sad-eyed, with bent backs. They got together in little clusters, and from the snatches of talk they overheard, the women gathered that they were talking about God. They were saying that God is a beneficent Father, and He would not forsake them. He would help.

These unhappy people clung desperately to their religion, the only consolation they had left. Yet some didn't say a word; they stood there dumb.

Mechel Greenzweig, who before the war had been a broker, and who, because he knew all about world politics, was known as "The Politician," stuck to his point, that "the world is not going under yet."

The most dispirited were the aritsans. There was Itche the cobbler, with a straw between his teeth, to make him feel as though he had a waxed thread there. He spat, and flung out his arms.

"Of course, people must have boots. They can't go barefoot. But—where does one get a workshop, with bench and lasts and tools? We've only our bare hands. Not even a room to live in. All right, we'll make do, and live in the workshop. But where does one get a workshop? Half the houses in the town went up in smoke, or they were shot to bits. Those left standing will be repaired—trust the rich house-owners to look after their affairs. But how are we poor folk to find a home? They wouldn't rent us a room even before the war. They wanted six month's rent in advance. And winter's coming."

This was the great worry of the poor; they had always been poor, and they had always had troubles. But now they were destitute and had absolutely nothing. Not only the artisans, but also the shopkeepers, the small traders, the village peddlers, the agents and brokers. The same with the Hebrew teachers, and the students who had sat in the Beth Hamedrash all day over the sacred books.

The people standing round the naked, fire-resistant walls saw Reb Yossele (or Panie Fuksman, as many addressed him to win his favor) approaching. Before the war Reb Yossele had kept a big haberdashery business. But like all the other shops and businesses in the town, it was smashed.

Fuksman's nickname in the town was "Twister." He had several other business-men with him, one-time householders, and also Reb Isser, the hermit. They had all just arrived in the town, returnees after the flight. They broke up, and each disappeared down a different street. Reb Isser was left standing by himself.

The hermit had never had a home. He had always lived in the Beth Hamedrash. There wasn't much he needed. A crust of bread was enough. And the pious women of the town used to see to it that he got that. They sent it to him in the Beth Hamedrash, where he sat all the time studying. On Sabbaths and Festivals the best houses invited him to be their guest, especially his own associates and friends, the Chassidim, among them Reb Mordecai Goldblum, the factory owner.

Reb Isser never worried. He had no difficulties about his livelihood. So he was always contented and cheerful, more so than the richest man in town. In that way he was really the richest of them all. Having had nothing, he had lost nothing.

Left alone in the middle of the empty marketplace, he looked round with his little, bright, childlike eyes. He saw some Jews standing near Kalman the tinsmith's ruined house, so he walked slowly toward them. They all looked sad and dejected, especially the women. He smiled at them like a child: "Why do you look so worried? All your ships sunk?"

"It can't be so bad," he went on. "You haven't lost your last boat. That can never sink! Never! Not even in the worst storm. God Almighty is always here with us—He always was and He always will be. There's nothing to worry about! You surely haven't lost all hope, God forbid! No, I can't believe it of you! A Jew never loses hope in God. Never! He mustn't! It's the most terrible sin! It's a transgression against the very foundation of our religion!

"Things could have been worse," Reb Isser continued, "much worse. But God rules the world with mercy and justice. As the Psalmist says—'Through Thee we push down our adversaries. Through Thy Name we tread them under that rise against us.' There's nothing to worry about! Lots of Jews have come back already. Reb Yossel has come back, with his wife and children. This very moment. And Reb Yechiel Leibish and his wife and children."

Mechel Politician cheered up at this.

"What? Reb Yechiel Leibish is back? I mean Panie Bernfel and Reb Yossel—Panie Fuksman? Both back? Ah, now we shall be able to make a living, my friends. No more need to worry. We shall be all right now. We shall make money. Doing the same as other Jews do; and the Christians too. In all the other towns."

"What?" people asked him.

"Smuggling!" Mechel cried excitedly. "Smuggling! Pan Bernfel will see to that. He was always hand in glove with the authorities. Those daughters of his. . . . You'll see! Everything will go well now. We'll trade! We'll sell things to Warsaw!"

Hope began to shine in many woebegone faces. Women who had been looking at their husbands reproachfully, accusingly, demanding money and bread, suddenly became gentle and forgiving, trustful and loving, as in the old days. The children too became quite jolly.

Presently they heard Kalman the tinsmith calling from somewhere far away, "Come here, Rachel, my Queen! Come here, Rachel! Look at this!"

He appeared, almost running, his coattails flying. As soon as he was near enough he stopped and pulled a lot of things out of a sack that he had been carrying over his shoulders.

"Look at this, Rachel! Bread! Barley! flour! Potatoes too. What's more—you'll never guess, friends—onions! Garlic! And a horseradish as big as a German's head. All who are hungry, come and eat! Go cook a meal, dear wife! Don't stand looking like a stork when the frog has jumped out of reach. The world isn't going under! We're alive! What does the prayerbook say—'As long as the soul is within me.' Get a meal ready and let's eat! Let the rich worry! We've got four daughters and five sons, thank God! Our daughters are provided with dowries—they've got lovely red cheeks. And bright flashing eyes. And something besides—no, I won't say it. There are respectable people here."

"Time you did shut up," his wife, Rachel, silenced him.

Then Kalman saw Reb Isser, and greeted him warmly.

"Reb Isser! Glad to see you here! Shalom Aleichem! I hadn't noticed you. Look, there's Abraham the tailor, with his little boy. How many needles has he sold, I wonder."

Abraham's wife, Itte, welcomed her husband effusively as he joined the group. She hugged and kissed their little boy.

"Did you do well in the villages?"

Reb Isser broke in: "Time for Mincha!"

Everybody suddenly turned to look toward the marketplace. Three tall German militiamen had appeared there, in long gray-blue field uniform, with spiked helmets and rifles over their shoulders. Mirel, Malke's eldest daughter, was walking between them. Mechel Politician ran toward the German soldiers.

Reb Isser reminded them again: "Time for Mincha prayer!"

2

Youth in the Dark

The air was still fragrant with the breath of a fine autumn day. A gentle breeze brought from time to time the moldering smell of fallen leaves, the carrion stench of dead animals lying unburied behind the town, and also the sweet scent of pine trees in the wood nearby.

A crowd of young people squatted on the ground, outside the half-ruined town. They were the worst sufferers from the war, not only because it was the young who fought and died on the battlefield. Those who were at home had their special worries too. What was the outlook for them? What was their future? The factories where many of them had worked before the war had been destroyed. Nobody had thought of rebuilding them. Except for one, the factory owners hadn't even returned. Not only the workers among them, but the artisans too had no work and no likelihood of getting it. And work meant more than just earning enough for room and board, especially to young people.

Those who were more aware of things were now busier than even before the war with ideas about Socialism, which had been maturing in their heads. Now these young people sat here full of thought, staring into the night, trying to find an answer to their questions.

There was a buzz of conversation. But the talkers were few; most sat silent, as though waiting for something. Many of them hadn't eaten any supper. Some hadn't eaten all day. Yet these felt better than the rest; they had a kind of special courage. They could see in their imagination great events coming; they could already foresee what would happen after the great war. These young men and young girls sat here dreaming of heroic deeds, which they would rise to when the time came. The hunger in their bellies was like dynamite to their souls.

Jacob Lichtenberg, one of the scribe's sons, came up with several comrades; he brought with him Pearl, Reb Mordecai Goldblum's youngest daughter, and Isaac Lehrman, one of Kalman the tinsmith's sons. Pearl walked between Lichtenberg and Lehrman. They brought food with them—bread and apples. The "heroes" who had been glorying in their fast felt a little mortified as at a profanation of their

24

abstention from food, which they had come to think of as deliberate self-denial for the cause. But one look at Jacob, with his kindly, shining eyes mollified them. His eyes were so gentle, sincere, friendly, and comforting that they awoke fresh hope in their hearts, and renewed devotion to their cause. The pieces of bread and the few apples that were passed around were like a symbol of light in the dark night.

Jacob Lichtenberg was physically an ugly man, thin and hunched, but standing there in that group under the moonlight he looked to many of them like a great, heroic figure. Those who had been fellow students with him in the Beth Hamedrash and had afterward become factory workers or artisans like him looked up to him with respect and even affection. Even those who were more to the Left, and called him the Beth Hamedrashnik, gave him grudging admiration. Perhaps it was because he didn't always agree with them. He was always with them, belonged to the same illegal organization in the town, but he had his own way—nothing new, but one that somehow brought together all the different roads that led toward justice and right, like a bridge joining two shores. The comrades respected him, as almost the whole town respected his father, the scribe.

One of the comrades, Aaron, Itche the cobbler's son, held his piece of bread in his hand and couldn't decide whether he really ought to eat it. Wasn't he taking the bread out of the mouth of someone hungrier than he was? He had an oversized conscience. He was sure that Jacob's younger brothers and sisters, or Isaac Lehrman's needed the bread more than he did. He was always sorry for the little ones. He held the bread in his hand and looked at Jacob.

Jacob felt his glance and read his thoughts.

"Eat it," he said. "Too much conscience isn't good for one. It's like putting honey on sugar."

Everybody laughed. A few comrades who had come late and were looking for them in the dark heard them laughing and called out: "Where are you? We can't see."

Guided by the sound, Comrade Hersh came up with Comrade Feiga and several others, and exploded angrily:

"We arranged to meet by the river, didn't we? And you're talking and laughing too loudly. Have you forgotten the German militia!"

Isaac Lehrman spoke up:

"As far as I know the Social Democratic Party in Germany is legal. It plays an important part in German life. Has its members in Parliament."

Comrade Hersh Krumholz answered with pride: "Yes, of course. The Party is very important in Germany. In other countries too. All the same, it's best to be careful. Here our movement is not legal. Not yet. I'm going to put in an application to the Commandant this week."

David, Abraham the tailor's son, lived in fear of the German militia; he complained to Comrade Hersh: "They've been making too much noise!"

"We mustn't be too scared, either," said Comrade Feiga, calmingly. "Mirel is very friendly with the militia. With the Commandant as well."

"Only Mirel?" David sneered. Then he suddenly burst out: "Other women, and girls too! They go out with the militia, and with the Commandant."

"Yes," added others. "They're busy smuggling. They're opening the shops now. Mirel is starting a café. Or a restaurant. For the German soldiers. And for the smugglers. Things are beginning to hum in our town."

Feiga's brother Aaron repeated the word *hum*, stressing it significantly, bitterly.

Bluma, looking up at the moon, put on an innocent face, and remarked:

"They say that Pan Bernfel has got the Commandant in his pocket—I mean, his daughters have."

Comrade Hersh didn't like this kind of talk, and flared up: "That's enough! That's not what we came here for!"

Comrade Jacob Lichtenberg felt offended because Comrade Feiga had made nasty insinuations about Mirel, his prospective sister-in-law. So he got a dig in at her: "But who started it? Wasn't it Comrade Mickenshleger!"

Bluma turned her blue eyes up to heaven again, and said as innocently as before, with the air of a dreamy angel, as though she hadn't heard either Hersh or Jacob:

"But Reb Yossel Fuksman the twister's young daughter, with her holy, pious face, has got all the three German militiamen under her white apron. And Mechel" (she suddenly remembered that Mechel's daughter, Dinah, was sitting there with the rest of the comrades, next to Aaron, and she stopped).

But Dinah (Comrade Greenzweig) didn't let it pass: "What about Mechel?"

"Nothing!" said Bluma. "I didn't mean anything. Your father is a contact man."

"So what?"

"Stop it!" cried Hersh. "That's enough!"

In the dark night, outside the half-ruined town, squatting silently on the ground in an empty field, they all looked lost and forlorn, like something left in the middle of the road.

"Let's start," said Hersh, clearing his throat as in the old days when he was opening a meeting, held secretly, like this one. Only then it was different. There were more people there. There was big activity then, both in the trade union field and politically. Hersh was at that time the chairman, the leader of the Party in this town, till his arrest. He spent time in prison; then they deported him to Siberia. He escaped and went to America. He had come back just before the war.

"Right. So we are taking up our trade union work again, and our political activity as well," he began, speaking quietly but firmly.

The more serious ones hung on his every word. When he had finished, some expressed disapproval. Jacob and Aaron, shrugging their shoulders, asked him:

"Trade union work, did you say? What can we do in that field now when the factories are all smashed and nobody is at work? And politically—"

"There will be a lot of activity politically," Comrade Hersh broke in very excitedly. "You forget, comrades, that our Fatherland Poland is occupied by a foreign power. We must free it from the invader. Make it a free Republic!"

"A Socialist Republic!" Abraham added.

Comrade Krumholz then began to outline his plan of action:

"We shall link up with our Polish comrades here. I have already discussed it with Comrade Strzelkowski."

Most of the Comrades agreed with that. Feiga, her brother Aaron, Jacob, and Dinah spoke; they expressed their opinion, and they made proposals. David also spoke, timidly, in a quiet, frightened voice. He buttered up Comrade Krumholz and Comrade Feiga.

Abraham, Bluma's brother, launched into a flow of revolutionary rhetoric. It was his first meeting with the rest after a whole year, and he wanted to show off what an important man he had been in Warsaw. He said he had been Secretary of the Leather Workers Union there. He was also trying to impress Dinah. He had taken his seat next to her, but he kept looking furtively at Pearl Goldblum.

Isaac Lehrman had kept quiet all the time. He finally plucked up courage, and asked if he might say a word:

"You will all please forgive me. I am like a stranger here. I spoke to my friend Jacob today. And to you too, Hersh. You told me to come here, and to bring Miss Goldblum. You said it was about opening a school."

"Yes, of course," Hersh agreed, with enthusiasm. "The Jewish school where you used to teach had a lot of children of factory workers and artisans. A school is very important, most important."

"Especially now," said Isaac, "when all the Chedarim are closed, and the children are running wild."

"Better than having them in Chedar," Hersh interrupted him. "At least the children are out in the fresh air, and they don't get their ears stuffed with nonsense, as my father used to stuff them with it, and would like to do again. We all went through it."

"But what sort of a school?" Abraham asked. "It must be like all our schools."

Lehrman tried arguing that a school must not be run on Party lines. That started another discussion that nobody had expected. And it grew very heated, because Pearl Goldblum supported Lehrman in his point of view:

"Education has nothing to do with politics," she said.

"Why not?" Hersh asked. "A school is a place where the child is trained to become a member of society. We don't teach it only grammar and arithmetic. We absorb politics from the moment we come in contact with life."

"What politics?" Comrade Aaron wanted to know. "According to what Party?"

"What Party?" Hersh and Feiga both asked together, surprised.

"Our Party! Our Party," most of them shouted, Abraham loudest of all. David too. They all seemed to have forgotten that they had to keep quiet.

Aaron felt that something here was not quite right. But he couldn't be sure what it was.

Jacob suggested a compromise: "No Party, but Socialism. Which means justice, and hatred of capitalism. That's what we must teach the children in the school, Isaac."

Pearl was flabbergasted.

"You say that, Jacob? Teach children hatred? I never expected to hear you say that!"

Dinah couldn't contain her dislike of this superior intellectual, this young daughter of the rich factory owner, any longer. So she said cuttingly:

"I didn't pass through all the classes at school, like you, Panna Goldblum, but I do know, with my little commonsense, that in Chedar they teach the children religion and to go in fear of Him who sits above and spits down on them below; and in the universities, which are only for the rich, they teach obedience to God's anointed. They teach them that the bandits who make wars and spill our blood— the blood of the common man, which has no value—that they are heroes! They teach hatred, too!"

"That's true!" a lot of the others agreed, David and Abraham loudest of all.

Several girls who had worked in Goldblum's factory before it was destroyed, and some of the young men too, especially Aaron and Jacob, were surprised at the animosity that Dinah showed toward Pearl. They all knew that Mechel Politician, Dinah's father, had always earned good money from business contacts that he brought to Pearl's father, Reb Mordecai Goldblum. The girls who had worked in Reb Mordecai Goldblum's factory felt no animosity at all toward Pearl. On the contrary, they liked her. And she had now come here to help them by teaching the working-class children. She was herself poor now, like all of them.

Pearl was apologetic:

"Please forgive me, all of you, for having spoken. I came here with Lehrman and Lichtenberg because I want to be a teacher at the school."

"Don't apologize! It's quite all right," Hersh and Feiga tried to assure her. "It's quite all right. You're a welcome visitor here."

Then they returned to the discussion of political activity.

The young people who had met in the big meadow outside the ruined town were still there, squatting on the ground in a circle, discussing serious problems. The thin crescent moon shed a silvery light on their faces. Their parents slept, but they were awake, with all the burden of responsibility for the future of the world on their shoulders. The fate of the world was their fate, and they wanted to master it. They were sure that all of them together, united by a common desire, would overcome all obstacles.

A dog with a white body and black legs came up to the circle, peered anxiously into every face, and waited with pricked-up ears for someone to call him by name. No one did. But Abraham clicked his tongue, and the dog moved toward him. He stood by him for a while, but as Abraham made no move he went over to Dinah. Dinah pretended that she was scared of the dog (perhaps she was) and turned for protection to Abraham and Aaron who sat on either side of her. Then the dog nuzzled Pearl. She stroked him, and her fingers met Jacob's; he was stroking the dog from the either side. She didn't know that Jacob was afraid of dogs and was stroking it only because he saw that she was. Lehrman sat on the other side of her. Since her return to the town she had seen much more of Lehrman, and she was beginning to have a warm feeling for him. She knew that Jacob was in love with Rabeh, Malke's youngest daughter.

Some of the young people were beginning to feel the chill, sitting so long on the ground. Also some were getting sleepy. The discussion was petering out.

3

*Reb Yossel Fuksman Says His
Prayers*

Reb Yossel had once started with a little cheap merchandise, cretonne and muslin, "just rags," as he himself used to say. But he had gradually worked his way up.
And then people had begun to have respect for him, though they still thought of
him as a "twister." Afterwards, when he grew rich, they made him Chairman of the
Community. He built a big house, two floors, all brick, in the same row as all the
best houses in town, with an entrance from the marketplace. When he returned
after the second flight he found the house very little damaged. The poor folk said:
"The rich have all the luck."

It was true. Because the whole rich district, "the green road," as it was called,
where the wealthy people (almost all Christians) lived, had escaped unscathed. As
though the cannonballs and shells had been told: "Don't damage the property of
the rich. Do what you like with the poor."

Reb Yossel, Pan Fuksman, as he was now called, moved back into his old house,
with his wife and three children. Everything he had left locked up in the cellar,
furniture and crockery, had gone, as with everybody else. But he had money. So he
started trading again, in the way of the new times, to which he adapted himself very
quickly.

It was a lovely day in late autumn. Reb Yossel didn't get up so early as he used
to, because he didn't have to go to the Beth Hamedrash now since it had been
burned down. He put on Tallith and Tephilin at home, in the big room, and there
said his prayers to God. Because the house hadn't been completely repaired yet,
the big room, which was the dining-room, was also Deborah's bedroom.

She was an only daughter, so her parents spoiled her, and let her sleep late.
Deborah was seventeen. But Reuben, too, the older son, a grown man, was also
still asleep. And certainly Ozer too, the baby of the family. Their mother, Broche,
didn't want to wake them. "Let the children rest," she said to her husband. "Sleep
is as good as food."

Reb Yossel's head, with the Tephilah in front like a black crown, and the silver ornamentation on his long woolen Tallith drawn over it, kept turning over one thought—"Must have a talk with the Commandant himself. Talking to the gendarmes, and even to the Commandant's secretary, isn't the same thing. Must go to the boss himself. But who is to go to him? I? It wouldn't get me anywhere. Waste of time!"

He knew it from the experience of other people. And he had Bernfel's example. Bernfel never went himself. Even when the Russians were here he used to send his daughters to the officer in command.

But Reb Yossel didn't like sending Deborah. He was afraid. Suppose Broche, his wife, went? No, that wouldn't do, either. The thought had plagued him all day yesterday and the day before. He had gone as far as to suggest it to Broche. She had blushed, and dropped her eyes. He had a vision at that moment of the Commandant taking his wife by the hand and drawing her to him. He hadn't slept all night because of it.

"No", he decided. "I won't send Broche!"

He raised his voice in louder prayer. He beat his breast, and he remembered that he had already said that part of the prayer.

He started the Hallelujahs. Then he stopped again, and began to think:

"I'll send Deborah. She's a sweet innocent child. She'll do nothing wrong. She's very lovely. How she has grown, bless her!"

Reb Yossel had almost come to the end of his prayers, which meant that his plans had already matured in his head. He had decided that there wasn't much to be done now in his own line of business. Where would he get haberdashery, and who would buy such things now? Who had money for such things? It was a better plan to try to get a concession for supplying pork. The German soldiers wanted pork. The Commandant was sure to give him the concession.

Reb Yossel turned his eyes up to the ceiling, and started saying "Our Father, our King!" His lips moved silently, but his brain was working fast. "A concession to supply the army.... But a Jew mustn't deal with pork. Very well, then, he would take a Christian partner, as a cover."

He continued praying: "Our Father, our King! Inscribe us in the Book of Prosperity!"

"I must outdo Bernfel," he said to himself. "Such things happen. It can be done. The wheel turns. Look at Reb Mordecai Goldblum—he had a big factory. He was almost the richest man in town. He's lost it all. Now it's my turn."

Deborah called to her mother. Would she let her have her dressing gown. It was lying on a chair by her bed, but she didn't like stretching out her bare arm to get it while her father was in the room. Her mother handed her the dressing gown, and stood in front of her to shield her from her father's eyes, while she got out of bed. Deborah left the room to wash.

She found her elder brother already at the washbasin. She was even more bashful in front of him then in front of her father, because he hadn't been living at home the last few years. He had been in Warsaw, working as a bookkeeper, and coming home only twice a year, for Passover and Succoth. He was a Warsaw dandy, a cavalier, a gallant even to his sister. He washed quickly, and went out of the room.

He came back almost immediately, to ask Deborah if their father had finished saying his prayers. Would she please not mention at table that he had only just got up? He knew that neither his mother nor his father would question him whether he had said his prayers. They knew he didn't say his prayers. He had stopped that long ago. He hadn't even got his Tephilin any more. But he didn't want the subject brought up at the table by any chance remark by his sister.

Deborah used her brother's scented soap that he had left lying by the wash basin. As she washed her neck and shoulders she remembered her dream of Boruch. She had never dream of him before. Boruch an officer! She laughed at the idea. But if he put on uniform, with brass buttons, epaulettes, and a sword and spurs, then he would really look like an officer!

But Boruch didn't suspect that she was in love him. And he probably wouldn't care for the idea. For who was she, and who was her father? Yet when he saw her in the street, and he was alone, he raised his hat to her, and stopped as though he wanted to talk to her. But her heart always started thumping, and she dropped her eyes and walked away.

As she was thinking of Boruch, she suddenly saw the Commandant's figure in front of her. She had seen him several times in the street. Why was she so frightened of him? She could hardly breathe. She pressed both hands tightly to her breast. She tried combing her hair, but the comb dropped from her hand. She couldn't get her hair to go right. How should she wear it? She tried two long plaits hanging down. They looked too long. They made her look like a girl of thirteen. Today she wanted to look older than she was. She coiled the plaits round her head. That was better. She looked a lady now. But she tried another style, arranging her plaits round both ears. In the end she decided to wear the plaits in a topknot.

Which dress should she wear? The blue costume with the white blouse? Should she put powder on? She didn't like to very much. But she would use a little perfume. She loved the smell of lilac.

The table had been laid, and her parents and both her brothers were already seated. Deborah didn't want to be late for going to the Commandant. Hadn't her father said she should go first thing in the morning? She said she wouldn't wait for breakfast; but her father told her there was no hurry. "He's at the office till one o'clock."

As he said grace after the meal Reb Yossel looked at Deborah, and he felt sure that in a year's time Bernfel, the rich man of the town, would come to ask him to let his son marry his daughter, Deborah.

When Deborah rose to go to the Commandant, Broche threw a desperate, appealing glance at her husband. Don't let the child go! But Reb Yossel kept his eyes averted, because the same thought was in his mind.

The sun already stood over the cross on the top of the church tower. The whole atmosphere that autumn day was one of melancholy. The clouds chased across the sky—big jagged patches, some like great mountains, others like small hills, and animals of all shapes. And all sorts of colors—gray, brown, black and puffy white. They chased across the sky like mad, now hiding it completely, now revealing bright streaks of blue, and a golden sun. Now wind, now warm and still, now very cold. It added to Deborah's fears. She felt that everything was telling her to go back, yet she went on. Not because her father, whom she loved, had sent her, but because she herself wanted to go. Something had drawn her to the Commandant ever since her first chance sight of him in the street. Perhaps because he had looked so strangely at her, and his gaze had seemed to pierce right through her. She had never seen such blue eyes before. He was tall and slim, and looked very young, though his hair was turning gray at the temples.

Long threads of spider web floating through the air settled on her face. She laughed gaily at first as she removed them. But the more she removed, the more settled on her face. She grew frightened; she took it as a bad omen. A web was being woven round her. That was how she felt about it since her father had first spoken to her yesterday about going to see the Commandant.

At that moment a bird flew over her head, quite low. Such a pretty bird. It chirped almost into her ear. It flew off, but it soon returned, and chirped into her ear again. It was flying in the direction she had to go. As though calling her: "Come!"

Deborah was smiling now, as she walked on. She took her small mirror out of her handbag, to see what her hair looked like. She bit her lips to make them look more red.

A girl she knew passed her, and threw her a wanton glance. Deborah felt a stab at the heart. She had always known the girl as quiet and decent and religiously observant. But she had turned wanton since the Germans had arrived. In that short time! Deborah thought that the glance meant to say: "I know where you're going. You'll be like me soon!"

The sound of a shofar from a house quite near suddenly frightened Deborah. She stood still. That was the shofar, a warning to her from the Rabbi! Shouldn't she go back?

She saw that a big butterfly had alighted on her blouse. She put out her hand to touch it and it flew away. But like the bird before, it kept returning, fluttering round her—in the direction she had to go.

4

The Little Heroine

The streets, even the little back streets in the poor quarter, were full of people. Things were very different from the first days, when the refugees had started coming back home, and now when they were already nesting. Not very long, yet such a difference. The ruins were still the same—the same charred walls with tall black chimneys, the same burned houses, the same piles of broken bricks, the same heaps of ashes and rubble from the wooden houses.

But a new life had started. In some of the undamaged houses people had opened shops and customers were queueing up. They were waiting with their cards for bread, which was doughy and uneatable. Yet they fought to get it, because the rations were not enough for even one meal. The rotten potatoes were worse, and the moldy barley and groats, and the oily runny stuff that the Germans called margarine, that stank and turned your stomach. The prices—it was like buying at the chemist's.

People queued in long lines, hundreds of them, mostly women, old men, and children. They shoved and pushed. Everyone wanted to get in front, to get into the shop first. Because they knew that a voice would soon call out from inside the shop: "All gone!" Useless then to go running to another shop, to be last in the queue there. Besides, the inhabitants of the town were registered according to districts.

People grumbled: "German order!"

A woman prayed to God: "Let them sink into the ground with their order! Let their order make an end of them, dear God!"

She asked the people near her: "What are you staring at me for? If He who lives eternally wants, the German will go to hell with his order!"

Without stopping talking all at the same time, moving a few steps at a time, everybody pushed and shoved, tried to get ahead of the others, cursed and swore and fought, till the soldier keeping the queue in order bawled at them: "Polish swine! Dirty pig-Jews!"

One old woman was talking to herself: "We're pigs ...? They get into other people's gardens, like pigs, into other people's countries."

"I've stood here since daybreak," one man grumbled.

"Since daybreak?" another echoed. "I've been here since midnight. Some people have been standing here since yesterday afternoon. Those who have money don't have to stand in the queue. They can buy everything of the best. Fresh butter, hot rolls, sugar—everything. They don't eat bread with sawdust and chalk and other junk. Those rich Jews! Pan Bernfel, Reb Yossel, Reb Henoch, Pan Buxbaum, beautiful Mirel! There's a new life starting for people like that! Smuggling! They're having a fine time!"

The people suddenly pricked up their ears. "There they come again!"

Marching along the great highway from Warsaw to Lublin came German military with heavy guns, "Big Berthas," field hospitals, field kitchens, baggage trains. The German army went through the town, with bands playing and all the youngsters in the town running behind. Grown-ups too walked over to the high road where the soldiers marched, drawn by the music. At such moments people forgot their misery, and their feet kept time to the music. They fell into step, and followed.

A gang of street kids started playing war games near Bernfel's house. Stones flew. A window of Bernfel's house was smashed. Bernfel came rushing out, along with the Commandant, who happened to be with him.

The gang fled.

Bernfel said goodby to the Commandant on the porch and went back into the house.

Before the big power factory was put up in the town Bernfel had not been a rich man. He had been a dealer in scrap iron, and was known as Yechiel Ox. But then he started getting rich, and the townsfolk said: "He hasn't made his money out of scrap iron!" They now called him "The Upstart." It didn't take long and people began to have respect for him, and then they called him "Panie Bernfel." He became an important person in the big houses of the local nobility and gentry and with the police and government officials.

Bernfel had returned to the town later than everybody else. He had left before everybody. He had found his house undamaged, and all his things where he had left them, in the cellar, which was protected against fire and had a heavy steel door that no one had been able to open. The war had made Bernfel richer.

Now the Commandant himself had come to his house to give him a concession for supplying scrap iron for smelting to Berlin. This wasn't the concession Bernfel had been hoping for. This one had seemed to him a dead certainty. For who else was there in the town to get it? What he wanted was another concession, to supply the German army with meat and flour and other provisions. He knew there were a lot of other people in the town who were after this concession, like that stuck-up nobleman Krzewicki and other landowners, who could supply all these things more cheaply from their own farms. There was also Reb Yossel. Bernfel had heard people talking about it in the town, and now he had seen that young daughter of his going to the Commandant, all dolled up. Bernfel had watched her as she passed his window. He had leered at her, licking his sensual lips: "A real beauty! An unopened bud!"

He scratched the soft pads of his left hand with the thick hairy fingers of his right. Big, coarse hands. He found it delightful at certain moments to scratch the soft pads on his palm. He was glad that he had such big, broad, powerful hands.

Women loved them, loved kissing them. Even his own daughters Bella and Helena, loved his big powerful hands, loved kissing them. Only his youngest daughter, Chelia, didn't like them.

Bernfel was thinking that when the Commandant had been seated at his table now, between Helena and Bella, all sipping Benedictine, he had come not so much to hand him the concession in person as to see Chelia. The Commandant had taken a fancy to the girl when he had seen her out walking one day.

Bernfel found his wife, Rivka, sweeping up the broken glass from the window the youngsters had smashed, and clearing away the bottles and glasses and plates from the table. She wore a sheitel, like all pious wives, drawn down to her eyes. She was always grumpy—and she moved slowly, just crawling along. Not because of age, or because she was ill, or her body was heavy, but because "What's the hurry? I've got time." She was always grumpy, annoyed with everything and everybody, without any cause or reason. As she saw it she had nothing to be happy about. She was rich? So what! She wasn't Itche the tailor's wife, or Dobbe, the cobbler's wife, or Rachael the tinsmith's wife! She had a husband? Women have husbands! Children? A woman with a husband has children. Her health was good? Why not? Let others be ill!

She groaned because she was discontented, because she enjoyed groaning, because she enjoyed being unhappy. Just as she loved keeping busy all the time with housework, though she had a maid. It gave her an excuse for groaning and grumbling and shouting at the maid because she didn't do it, taking her money for nothing.

"Well?" she asked her husband, in her dull, inarticulate voice.

"Very well!" he answered, feeling highly pleased with himself. He clapped his hands like a Sultan summoning his women, and called: "Helena! Bella! Chelia!"

None of them came.

"What do you want them for?" his wife asked him.

"What do I want them for?" He took his wife and led her very respectfully to the door of the adjoining room.

"Go in there, and lie down for a bit on the couch, Rivka. You're tired."

He closed the door behind her, and again clapped his hands: "Bella! Helena! Chelia!"

Bella came in, and asked irritably:

"What do you want? What are you calling me for? I heard you the first time. It isn't me you want! I'm no longer young. and I know it!"

She was wearing her finery, and her face was flushed. Her father wasn't sure whether it was because she had been drinking (she liked a drink) or because she was wearing her new red dress and the tight corset that she had bought to make her look slimmer. He took her by the hand, sat down in a chair, and held his daughter between his knees, as though she were still a child.

"You're talking nonsense, my daughter," he said, pretending to be angry. He took a hand-mirror from his waistcoat pocket, looked into it, stroked his little Franch beard, then handed the mirror to Bella.

"Look," he said, letting his big hands rest on her big hips, and regarding her affectionately, "You can still put the loveliest girls in the shade. You're a woman! A fully blown woman! If I were a young man, not your father—" He drew her toward him, and kissed her. She fondled his hand, the big soft pads of his palm, and grumbled:

"I spoke to him yesterday about the second concession. He gave me no answer. He said he would speak to you today, when he came with the concession for the scrap iron. But he didn't say anything to you, because he really came not to see you, but to see Chelia. He noticed her in the street one day, and asked me who she was. I told him she was my youngest sister. Since then he has changed completely toward me. He's no longer the same man. The German officers are no gentlemen, as the Russians were. They drop you very quickly. Particularly now, when everybody sends his daughters after concessions, or even his wife, if she is young and good-looking. Don't send me to him! Send Chelia! Chelia can get you the concession!"

At that moment, Helena entered the room.

"Don't send her!" Bella cried excitedly. "Don't send Helena! She's become the lady!"

"I have no intention of going," said Helena, who was wearing riding breeches and brown riding boots with spurs, and flicking her riding crop against her boots.

"You're all dressed up like that for Jan, aren't you!" Bella sneered.

"Yes, because of Jan," Helena answered haughtily.

"That drunkard! The chemist's son!" said Bella, with a bitter warning. "He'll drop you like a hot brick! He'll use you as long as he feels like it, and then he'll drop you! He'll use you as the Commandant would, only we'll get nothing out of him!"

"I don't want anything out of him," said Helena.

"Nothing but love?"

"Nothing but love!"

"That's enough!" their father broke in.

Helena flicked her sister playfully with her riding crop. "I've told you several times, Bella, learn to ride! There's nothing so enjoyable! Papa! I'll talk to you later, when I come back. I don't know when I'll be back. Don't wait dinner for me. Bye!"

She put her arms round her sister, and kissed her.

"D'you love me, Bella?"

Bella kissed her. Helena wasn't satisfied: "Speak! Tell me that you love me! I want to hear you say it!"

"Yes! I love you!" Bella cried aloud. Helena kissed her again, kissed her father, and flicking her riding crop, walked out of the room, almost dancing with joy as she went.

Her father called after her: "Don't forget to tell Jan to put the whole of the corn away for me! Tell him to speak to Krzewicki. I'll take the lot from all of them, as much as they can give me. I'm going to have the concession to supply the army! Me! Nobody else! You can tell him that I've got it already!"

Helena blew her father a kiss through the window, called out "Bye!" again, and disappeared.

"She's a little devil!" Bella muttered, running to the door. With her hand on the knob, she turned to her father and said:

"I'll get you Chelia if I have to drag her in by the hair! She'll have to go to the Commandant! I had a lot to drink before, when we were at the table, but I didn't miss you watching Reb Yossel's daughter passing. That Chassid means to outbid you. He always wanted to be the richest man in town. It's his turn now, he thinks. Because Deborah is very beautiful, and young, and innocent, the Commandant is sure to fall for her. She's just what he wants! I know! I know him! Chelia is the only one who can compete with young Deborah Fuksman. She's the same age, and she's just as lovely. Only Chelia won't go! Unless you make her! I'll get her for you!''

Before Bernfel had paced the full length of the room Bella was back, dragging Chelia by the arm.

"Here she is! But she says she won't go!"

Chelia tore herself free from Bella's grip with such force that she nearly fell.

"I won't go! You're not going to make me what you made of her, and what you've made of Helena!"

That infuriated Bella.

"You're a nice one to talk! What about your Juziek! Fine fellow you've found! The hunchback carpenter's son, a common bricklayer, without a decent pair of trousers to his bottom. A Socialist! Are you a Socialist too? You'll be working against us, against your own father! You speak to her, father! Now you know it all! It's the truth! I didn't want to tell you before!" She ran out of the room, slamming the door.

Chelia, in a tight-fitting red-brown dress, buttoned from the neck down, with a narrow red belt that made her childishly slim figure seem even slimmer, stood in the middle of the room, facing her father defiantly. Her face was pale, and she kept her blue eyes fixed on him, waiting for him to speak. She had her hair cut short, just down to her shoulders, with a fringe over her forehead.

Bernfel didn't speak. He took his daughter's hand and stroked it affectionately, and kissed her. He put his heavy fleshy hand on her shoulder, led her to his chair, sat down, and tried to sit her on his knee. Chelia slipped out of his grasp and stood facing him like a child expecting to be punished, but determined to stand her ground.

Bernfel looked at her dress admiringly, and said:

"It suits you, Chelia. But why did you have your hair cut, and why the fringe? Is that a new hair style you saw in Warsaw? It suits you—but I've got to get used to it."

"You're a pretty girl," he went on, "much prettier than your sisters were at your age. Much prettier than the loveliest girls I saw in Warsaw. Why are you so defiant? Have I ever laid a hand on you! Have I ever hurt you? Why are you so stubborn? Is it true what Bella said?"

"Yes!"

"You're in love?"

Chelia didn't answer.

Her father's voice rose angrily:

"You have turned Socialist? Have you joined the Party?"

She still didn't answer. He got hold of her and shook her.

"So you're against me! You're against me!"

Chelia wrenched herself free, and screamed at her father:

"Yes, I'm against you! I'm against everybody like you!"

Her mother, hearing the row in the next room, came rushing in: "What's going on here?"

38 SAMUEL LEWIN

Chelia ran out of the room, banging the door behind her so hard that the bits of glass left in the smashed window fell out. That brought the two sons, Boruch and Notte, and Bella as well into the room. Bernfel was muttering to himself:

"She's against me! That's the way she repays me! I love her more than all my other children! I gave her everything she wanted! What has she against me? Didn't I help everybody I could—all the poor of the town, the Sick Fund, the Talmud Torah, the Society for Dowries for Brides? Everybody who put his hand out! I never grudged money! I saved so many people who were in trouble! I intervened for them with the authorities, I gave them money—I gave a lot of money—because that was the only way I could save them!" He shook his fist at the door through which Chelia had gone. "I'll show them!"

Boruch tried to calm him.

"It isn't the first time Chelia's run away. She'll come back!"

It wasn't the first time Chelia had run away. Her father was right when he said she was stubborn. Even as a child she had often refused to do what she was told, and when she was reprimanded she had run into another room or into the street, and they had to go and look for her. The explosions usually happened at meal times. Not because she wasn't hungry, or she didn't like the food, but as a protest. Protest without any reason, against her father or against her sister Bella, or against her brother Boruch. She hated and despised these three. Her mother, Helena, and Notte left her cold and indifferent. She never got worked up about them. She had wanted to be fond of them, to love them, especially her mother, but she had never been able to do it, only when she was quite small. The older she got the less she liked them, and the less she had to do with them. It brought her closer to her young friends. Unlike most Jewish girls of her circle she had friends of both sexes. But she didn't have many friends. She was very careful whom she chose. She didn't take to people easily. "Chelia is a strange child," her father used to say, telling the family to give in to her in everything. He really loved her most of all his children, with the result that her sisters and her brothers hated the sight of her—they resented her attitude toward them.

Her feelings for her father alternated from love to hate and contempt. Hate and contempt always went together with her. When she loved him she kept asking herself how she could ever hate and despise him, as she often did; and when she hated him she wondered how she could ever have felt any affection for him.

Out in the street Chelia's temper began to cool, and she wondered: where should she go? She was no longer a child to be run after and dragged back home. And she wasn't going home on her own! No more! So where was she to go? "I'm not hungry now. But what will I do afterward, when I do get hungry? I can't just dump myself on one of my friends, and expect them to feed me, like at home!"

It was the first time she had thought on such practical lines on any of her flights from home. Where was she going to live? She wasn't quite clear in her mind why she had run away from home. She had some vague ideas about justice and injustice, about poor and rich, moral and immoral. But she had never thought deeply about them. She only knew that there was something at home that wasn't right, that repelled her.

Chelia was on the high road, where she often went for walks. There was no park in the town to walk in, perhaps because fifteen years ago it had been such a small place, and because the high road served the purpose of a promenade, being planted on both sides for miles with oaks and lime trees and acacias, even pear trees and nut trees.

Chelia stopped. What was the use of going farther? She must make up her mind where to go. She had flung herself out of the house with no hat or coat on. And she wasn't going back! She wasn't going back to live the way she had been living. It was a rich, comfortable home, with all her material wants satisfied. But her soul had rebelled against it. She wanted something different, something that would satisfy her spirit! If only she had learned a trade, to earn her own living, to have her own roof over her head! But what could she do? Unless she went as a maid, or took a job serving behind a counter, or became a governess or a children's nurse. But where in the town could she get such a job?

She burst out laughing. Her situation was beginning to look comic. Then she felt someone watching her. It was Deborah Fuksman.

Deborah was not one of Chelia's friends. But at the moment Chelia felt that she wanted to be friends with her. She smiled, and started to walk toward Deborah. But Deborah dropped her eyes shyly and walked away.

Why shouldn't she go to Juziek? Chelia wondered why she hadn't thought of that before. She needed someone to talk things over with. He would be able to advise her.

Why hadn't she thought of him before? Perhaps because she hardly knew him. She had been out walking on the high road. And he had been walking on the high road, with some of his comrades. He had left them, and had come over to her, taken his cap off, and had spoken to her like a gentleman:

"I wouldn't go walking about here alone, if I were you," he had said. "There are German soldiers around . . ."

She hadn't thought about the German soldiers till then. But at that moment she began to be frightened. He had bowed to her politely, and said: "Perhaps you would allow me to walk back with you."

They talked as they walked. He told her that his father was Mateusz, the carpenter. He had charmed her with his good manners. And he was so well informed. He spoke so beautifully. He was serious. He had brains and he was handsome.

"A beautiful young lady like you mustn't be out alone on the highway. It isn't safe these days. There's a war on."

She wanted to look in her mirror. Then she realized that she hadn't brought her handbag with her. And she hadn't a pocket in this dress even for a handkerchief.

He had told her he was a bricklayer, only a poor working man. But he was so pleasant and charming. It was because she had found him so pleasant that she had resented so much her father wanting to send her to the Commandant. For the first time she realized what it all meant, and she hated her father more than ever before.

What had Bella said?—"A common bricklayer, without a decent pair of trousers to his bottom. A socialist!" Chelia pondered that word *Socialist*. She hadn't given much thought to it before. Now she considered it—"He is a Socialist."

Going through the narrow streets of the poor quarter, hoping that she might meet Juziek on the way—he had asked her to call him Juziek, not Pan Strzelkowski—she saw the destruction the war had made. There was a good deal of war damage also in that part of the town where she lived, but she had hardly noticed it. It was really nothing compared to this. Chelia watched the people going in and out of the ruins, and she asked herself how people could live in such places, with the roofs and the walls tumbling about their ears. The air was foul. It made her feel sick. She wanted to put her fingers to her nose, but she resisted the urge. She wondered why all the people here looked old and ill. "Are there no young people here?" she asked herself.

She had never been in this district before. She hadn't realized that people were so poor. She had sometimes seen a poor man or a poor woman, but the extent and the depth of the poverty in the town had till now completely escaped her. She didn't know any of these people, though it wasn't a large town with a lot of people. But most of the people here knew her, knew whose daughter she was, and they watched her curiously and wondered what had brought her there.

Though she met no young people of her own age in these streets, Chelia saw a lot of children, ragged and starved. It brought tears to her eyes. She felt ashamed, and she wanted to run away. Where should she run? Hadn't she come here to look for Juziek? She didn't know where he lived. He hadn't told her. She could ask some-one where Mateusz the carpenter lived. Then she thought—perhaps Juziek was a married man, living with his wife and children, not with his father. She wondered why the thought hurt her. What difference did it make to her if he was married or not? Why was she going through these streets, looking for him? She hadn't seen him more than twice. And what could he do to help her? She was going to tell him that she had run away from home? What would he do? He would shrug his shoul-ders and wonder why she had come to tell him about it.

Then suddenly she saw him; she saw the handsome young Christian coming down the street with Jacob Lichtenberg, deep in conversation.

Chelia didn't know who Jacob was. But when she recognized Juziek she hurried toward him, calling him by name. He turned red when he saw her.

5

The Everlasting Struggle

Mateusz Strzelkowski, Juziek's father, was known in the town as the Hunchback Carpenter—his trade and his deformity. He lived in his own house, in a street where both Jews and Christians lived. Because he associated with Jews the Christians called him "Jew," and because he was a Christian the Jews called him "Goy," though he loved using Yiddish words. This Gentile took Reb Saul, the sick scribe, into his home.

He let a room to the Jew. But the word *let* was a euphemism; Mateusz did it out of ordinary humankindness. The scribe had been left literally in the street, with his wife and children, after their return to the town. He had no money to pay rent for even a corner of a room, to have a roof over their heads. The Jewish householders who found their homes intact or only partly destroyed wanted high rents for every inch of space. The returnees quarreled and fought for every corner of a room, outbidding each other for it. Two and three families moved into one small room, into a cellar. The Jews may not have noticed that the scribe, whom they all respected, had been left homeless.

Mateusz went up to him in the street, and said:

"Panie, man of God, you haven't anywhere to live. Move into my place. I've shifted my workshop into the living room. I can work there just as well. So that leaves me with an empty room, a nice room with a stove in it. My Juziek is a builder, a bricklayer. He's done it up. And you don't have to pay me now, if you haven't got the money. Pay me when you can."

So the scribe moved into the Gentile house. Then he took in Gronem, the melamed, who had also been left in the street with his wife and children, and could find no home and had no money to pay rent.

"You'll pay me when you can," the scribe said to the teacher, using the same words the Gentile had used to him.

Afterward the two women, the scribe's wife and the melamed's wife, took in an unhappy young woman who had been raped by soldiers in the flight, while her husband—they hadn't been married long—gave his life on the battlefield. Tzippe,

41

who was all alone in the world, couldn't get a corner anywhere—because she was "defiled."

The scribe in the first flight from the town had lost one of his children, a little girl who had died on the road. On the second flight his wife, Jochabed, had borne him another little girl, in the open field. So again he had four children. They called the little girl Nachma, which means comfort.

The melamed had a big family. His first wife had given him six children. But two died before she did. One son was killed at the front, and a daughter had emigrated to the Argentine. So he had been left with only two children of his first wife, both sons, Hersh and Yoske. His second wife, Henia, had only one boy. But she was pregnant again, and she had had two still births and she had buried two children.

The scribe's room wasn't very spacious. The flooring was rotten, full of cracks and holes. The landlord would have mended it if he had any boards, but he was too poor to buy any to repair the hovel. He did what he could, and he didn't charge them for his work. He only asked for what it cost him to buy a few bits of wood.

"Empty pockets," he told them in Yiddish. "The dealers have hearts of stone. Won't give you a piece of wood on credit."

Then he said to Reb Saul: "I've got two tables. You can have one."

One day he turned up with a handsaw, a hammer, some nails, and two thin planed boards. He went into the half-room on the right, which had a window with three blind (cardboard) panes because there was no money to replace the broken glass. This was where the scribe lived. At night it was properly partitioned off, with bedcovers drawn across on wire.

"Panie Saul," the carpenter said to the scribe. "I see your holy books lying around. I know that's a sin with you. I've got some wood from a box."

He set to work, and as he worked he talked:

"Panie, man of God. You are a scholar. You know everything. I'm a plain simple carpenter. I never went to school. I'm a poor man, with a pack in front and a pack at my back."

He drove another nail in, and stopped. He wanted to say something, but didn't know how to say it. He found it very hard. Besides, the scribe was sitting over one of his books all the time, hardly listening to him at all. He didn't want to interrupt his studies.

"Am I disturbing the Pan?" Mateusz ventured. "I'm a common man. But I want to know—why must a man of God like you—never sinned—why must you suffer? Why so much punishment for a man? Are all men bad? Always punish, punish! The Lord God does nothing but punish people. They don't sin that much!"

He banged a nail in angrily, a second and a third. He stopped again, boiling with rage.

"I can't make it out. We Gentiles eat swine's flesh, go to war, sin!"

He laughed at the words *Gentiles* and *swine's flesh*, and went on:

"But you Jews—you don't eat swine's flesh, you don't work on the Sabbath. You are always praying to your Lord God. You are His children. Yet you suffer more, are punished much more!"

He started work again, and stopped again. He was breathing hard. His small head with almost no neck peeped out between his hump and his high, pointed shoulder-blades, as from a hiding place. His big watery eyes, usually dull, were now bright and shining:

"The priest in the church says the Lord God is punishing us. But why does He punish only the poor and not the rich? Their houses have remained whole, all of them, not one burned down. Bullets and cannon balls didn't hit them. Pan Krzewicki, Pan Gnilowski, Pan Woikow, Pan Zaremba—all rich—suffered no damage. Pan Mordka Goldblum suffered. His factory and his house burned down. Now he's poor, like us. But Pan Fuksman, Pan Bernfel, Pan Silver, Pan Buxbaum—all rotters—they were unharmed."

The scribe had to break off his studies. He lifted his sad eyes several times from the page, looked at his landlord, and couldn't understand what he was trying to say. His thoughts were elsewhere. But the Goy confused him. The scribe had told himself several times that his landlord must be one of the saints of the Gentiles. He wanted to show him his gratitude for the many kindnesses he had done him. But how could he answer his questions? Enter into a discussion with him about the ways of the Creator? Besides, he had himself said that he didn't understand these things, that he couldn't even read and write Polish, had never been to school. Yet some answer he must give him. Reb Saul realized that if someone asks a question—even if he isn't a Jew—if someone wants to know about the Holy One, blessed be He, and about His ways, you mustn't leave him without an answer.

So the scribe answered the Gentile as any religious Jew in his place would have answered. He said:

"There is a higher Reason. Nothing happens just so. All that God does is right. His ways are hard to understand. But He does not punish if one has not sinned."

That infuriated Mateusz.

"You mean that you, Pan Saul?..."

The scribe went pale, and muttered: "Perhaps—"

"Impossible!" Mateusz protested. "I don't believe it! You're always sitting over a holy book, or praying. You, Pan Saul, write the Holy Torah. I know Pan Saul never done anyone harm. Never taken a thing from anyone, always kept all God's laws. No, Pan Saul not sinned—never!"

The man fell silent. He fixed a stern gaze on the scribe, as though seeing him for the first time now, or as if he were trying to look into the Jew's soul, to discover once and for all what sort of people these Jews are. You live with them together in one town, in one street, in one house. The town calls you "Jew," yet you don't understand the Jews—not the religious Jews.

Because he did understand the others, the modern ones; they were like his own, especially the young. Like the sons of both these Jews to whom he had let this room.

Mateusz felt suddenly triumphant, avenged.

"Pan Saul's son—quite different from you. Like my son Juziek. Both Socialists. Both want a Revolution. Want to turn the world upside down. No more poor and rich. They want to chase the Germans out, these dogs who have come into our country, and are taking everything away. We shall be free. Then the Jews ..."

The door opened, and the scribe's son Jacob came in. Mateusz was delighted.

"There's your son! Let Pan Saul question him!"

He drove in the last nail, picked up his tools, and went out.

Reb Saul was sitting down, pale, breathing hard and rapidly. There was perspiration on his face. Jacob saw that his father was upset and angry. He was afraid that he might have an attack. He wondered if Mateusz had been asking him to pay the rent, which he hadn't got. Yet he felt that his father's anger was not against Mateusz. That he was angry with him. Why? It didn't occur to Jacob that it was the same old story—that his father was worried and upset and angry because he, Jacob, didn't go his own straight road. Jacob thought his father had already got used to it—it didn't enter his mind that it was this that upset his father.

"Where's mother?" he asked. "Where's Benjamin? And Meir? Where's everybody? Nobody here at all, not even Gronem and his wife? Left you all alone! What did the landlord want?"

The scribe didn't answer.

Then Jacob saw the new bookshelf.

"I see—he made that for you! A shelf for your books. Very kind of him! He's a good man."

The scribe looked up at his son, and said angrily:

"Where have you been?"

"Where have I been?" Jacob repeated the question, uncomprehendingly. After all, he was no longer a schoolboy for his father to question him about his movements.

"Been running around with the sheigetz (young Gentile)?"

The word infuriated Jacob. "What did you say, Father? Who took you and mother and the children into his house, and gave us a roof over our heads? The Jews took no pity on you, though they know you're a sick man. They left you out in the street."

The scribe didn't want to listen to that. "You were out with the sheigetz?" he insisted.

But Jacob kept to his point: "The Jews here all know you. They're supposed to have respect for you. They call you 'The Scribe,' 'The scholar,' 'The great Chassid.' They can't say about you and about mother and the children the things they say about me. Yet all these Jews whose houses escaped destruction, many of them religious Jews, have let rooms to all sorts of people, but they left you out in the street. Only because they know you can't pay."

The scribe didn't say anything. And Jacob went on:

"If they had taken you into hospital, or into a warm room at least, with a bed to lie in for a few days, you wouldn't be in this state now."

The scribe murmured: "God sends healing for the sick."

"Look at Reb Isser," Jacob continued his indictment, "one man, all alone in the world, who hasn't an apostate son as you have; he has nowhere to stay either. He spends his nights between the bare walls of the Beth Hamedrash ruins, sleeping on the ground."

"I'm not accusing anybody. That's the way things are," Jacob said. "But don't say "sheigatz,' and don't say "Goy.' There are still a few good people around, Jews and Christians."

The scribe kept silent for a while, then he said with an effort:

"I don't want to quarrel with you, Jacob." He passed his hand over his forehead and groaned: "Sin leads to sin.... And I have been punished; punished because ..."

He drew his hand down across his face, took hold of his black beard, and said:

"I'm not going to quarrel with you now, Jacob. But what are you? I want to understand you. What do you and your people mean to do? Abolish poverty, you told me once. The Goy said the same. But that doesn't make sense. How can you do it?"

He flared up: "You're going to do this? You, with your own hands! Not God, but you!"

He controlled his temper, and went on more calmly:

"How are you going to bring it about? There are crowds of you. The melamed's son is one of your crowd too, isn't he?"

"Yes."

"Two Messiahs in one room," the scribe muttered to himself.

Jacob couldn't take his eyes off his father's face. He had such a beautiful face. Even now, when he was so ill, his color was fresh and rosy, and he was fragrant like a cherry tree. He had beautiful hands, with long, delicate fingers. His lips were full and red. Not like a sick man at all. And his eyes were like deep wells on a moonlit night.

Jacob looked at his father and wondered what he could say to him. His father would never understand him because he did not want to understand him. He would be afraid to.

So he asked him another question: "What were you saying about sinning? About having been punished? You've never sinned, Father! Never!"

The scribe pondered. Hadn't the Goy just said that? Strange that his son should repeat it. He looked at his son:

"We'll talk about that another time. What I want now is that you should answer my questions."

"Yes, Father, on one condition. That you will let me be frank. Because I shall have to say things that you won't like me to say."

"About?"

"About God."

"About ... No! I don't want you to talk to me about God! You're an unbeliever! You don't believe in God! Then why do you want to talk to me about God? Why don't you answer my questions? I asked you something else!"

"You asked me how we were going to do it. With our own hands? 'Not God, but you!'"

"All right, then! Say what you want to say!"

Jacob looked for a while closely at his father. Then he began, with a heavy heart:

"Our religion consists of two parts."

"Two parts? What two parts? Our holy religion is one, whole! It has no split! All is One! God is One! Israel's Torah is One! We have 613 commandments. We have thirteen fundamental Principles. But the faith ..."

Jacob agreed: "Then Between Man and God and Between Man and His Neighbor is one."

"They are two different things!"

"All right, then! Two!" And dropping into the old Talmudic sing-song, Jacob continued: "What if one keeps all the commandments about loving God, but not those about loving your neighbor?"

Reb Saul wrinkled his brow. He looked at his son searchingly, as if trying to discover what he was getting at.

"The laws about loving God.... One must believe in Him with a perfect faith, love Him with all our heart and with all our soul. That's how it is written. A Jew says three times every day: 'And you shall love the Lord your God with all your heart and with all your soul.' You know that, Jacob. You are a Jew. You learned it. About man and his neighbor, there are laws, many laws, which must be obeyed."

"Doesn't it say, 'Love your neighbor as yourself?'"

"Of course! Only as yourself. Not with all your heart and with all your soul. It means that you must love God more than yourself. You must sacrifice yourself for Him, martyr yourself, if necessary, for His Name's Sake."

"Good," Jacob smiled. "'Like yourself' means, according to Hillel, 'Don't do to your neighbor what is hateful to you.'"

He paused, then turned to his father:

"I don't want to argue with you about texts, Father. You know the Talmud—you know every book of it, you know the revealed and the secret, the first and the last. I'm talking about something else, I'm not a scholar, not in the way you are. And not about scholarship. We're not just trying to best each other. This is a matter of fundamentals. You know that without justice, without truth, without righteousness—I'm talking about loving one's neighbor—you know, that without this, religion is no religion. Do you agree?"

The scribe considered it, then he shrugged his shoulders. Jacob continued:

"God almost destroyed the world with the flood because the people were corrupt. Afterward there was Sodom and Gomorrah. All because there was no justice, because people were wicked. The Jews lost the First Temple, and the Second. They fell under the enemy's sword. They were driven into captivity. The Prophets admonished and warned, they proclaimed God's word: 'Bring no more vain oblations. It is an offering of abomination to me!,' and 'When you make many prayers, I will not hear,' because 'Your hands are full of blood.' God tells us through the mouths of the Prophets: 'Cease to do evil. Learn to do good. Seek justice, relieve the oppressed, judge the fatherless, plead for the widow.' Isaiah, Jeremiah, Ezekiel, Joel, Amos—they all scolded and rebuked us for the same sins."

His father agreed: "True! But you and your crowd don't believe in God and His justice!"

"Father," said Jacob, "Justice punishes if we sin against her. Always. From the beginning. She has her Prophets, who warn beforehand. But the sinners refuse to listen to the warnings. Till the punishment comes."

"You"—his father asked sarcastically—"you and the melamed's son, and the sheigetz, you are the Prophets?"

Jacob saw that his father was beginning to boil again inwardly and, fearing for his health, he pleaded with him:

"Father, I am no Prophet. None of us is a Prophet. Yet no one knows whom Justice selects as her Prophet. She finds her Prophets—sometimes a shepherd, sometimes a workman, sometimes the son of a Priest. And their prophecy is fulfilled."

Reb Saul stroked his beard, searching his son's face.

"Tell me," he asked, "do you believe in God?"

"I believe in Justice."

"In God in Heaven?"

"In Justice."

"In God's Justice?"

"In Justice."

The scribe jumped up: "Get out! Get out of here!"

Jacob dropped his head. But he did not go. He didn't want to leave his sick father alone.

But when his mother came back, with Benjamin and Meir following her, he moved toward the door.

At that moment his father's voice rang out like a gong, as in the old days, "And God spoke to Moses . . ."

When he was studying the Holy writings aloud or when he was saying his prayers, his voice always rang out with the old force. It was in ordinary talk that his voice was weak and broken.

He faced the east, and aloud, word by word, said the Mincha prayer. It meant that the two younger boys were to join him in the prayer. And Benjamin and Meir did that, while Jochabed busied herself with the baby in the cradle.

6

Love and Conscience

That day Jacob felt powerfully attracted to Pearl. But he fought down his longing for her, as he always did. He waged a desperate struggle against himself. He confessed to himself that he loved Pearl; he also realized that the more he fought against it, the stronger became his desire for her. But his conscience kept him bound to Rabeh, Malke's and Reb David Joel's daughter. His conscience kept a check on his love for Pearl, and admonished him sternly: "You can't, you mustn't let down Rabeh. It would be a mean thing to do, and it would kill her!"

They had so many common experiences, and they were bound by all their common sufferings. He had accepted the blame for her sufferings, even though he couldn't see what blame there was. After all, he had suffered just as much. But these sufferings they had borne together had united them.

United? He asked himself this question over and over again. He didn't recognize any other force to unite a man and a woman except love. But he no longer loved Rabeh. Perhaps he had never loved her. Yet he knew that there are other forces that can unite a man and a woman, not only love—responsibility, conscience, common sufferings. These things too united a man and a woman—not in the way love does, but they unite.

Jacob wanted to be clear in his own mind about his feelings for Rabeh. He reminded himself how he had come to fall in love with her. It was a long time ago, when he was still a little, naive, Beth Hamedrash boy, who had just begun to be a disbeliever. At that time he had looked up to her. Perhaps because she was a student at the High School, and because her brother was a poet. He had forgotten Pearl by then. He had been only thirteen when he fell in love with Pearl. But that evening, when they had been together with the crowd at the secret meeting outside the town, and his hand had met hers on the dog's back, his boyish love for her had reawakened.

Jacob felt his reawakened love for Pearl. And neither his conscience nor his knowing that his friend Lehrman loved Pearl, and that she liked him, could keep him away from her whenever he got the opportunity.

So now, though he was terribly upset by his quarrel with his father, he found himself going to see Pearl. Hersh met him on the way:

"Where are you off to, Comrade Lichtenberg? Up to the skies? Up to the clouds?"

Jacob stared at Comrade Hersh Krumholz in surprise.

"And where have you been?"

"You'll never guess! I've been to see the Commandant. To ask permission to start an organization for our comrades. He refused to see me. His secretary said the Commandant wouldn't allow any Socialist organization here. I told the secretary that we belong to the same Party that the German authorities in Warsaw have legalized, and that this Party is in the same International as the German Social Democrats. Then the secretary flew into a temper:

"'German workers belong to an International gang of conspirators! There's no such thing in Germany!'

"He bawled at me in real Prussian fashion: 'Polish swine! Jewish bandits!'

"So I left. What else could I do? But they make no difficulties about granting all sorts of concessions for taking everything out of Poland to Germany—flour, milk, meat, sugar, potatoes, timber, our last bit of leather, every scrap of iron. The young women and the girls know how to get these things out of them. Usually women from good religious homes. Very well! We'll have to find some other way of getting what we want!"

With that, Krumholz walked off.

The short autumn day was breathing its last. Jewish men and women, young and middle-aged, hurried through the streets with packs, slinking along furtively. Jacob knew these were smugglers, making their way to the carts waiting for them to drive out of the town immediately after dark. He didn't waste much time thinking about them. He preferred to look at the artisans, like Itche the cobbler, back at their honest toil. He recognized one whom he held in high regard, and stopped to speak to him: "Good evening, Gershon!"

Gershon was busy trying to put his big weaving loom into working order. He was binding parts together with bits of wire and string. Or he was nailing in a piece of wood in a gap. Then he sat down and worked the pedals. He let the shuttles fly. He seemed pleased with the way the loom was working. And most pleased of all that he hadn't in his wanderings from town to town lost the knack of his trade. "She's working well," he said, "but not as well as she used to. She creaks. But she'll do. I only hope I'll have work enough."

He was speaking aloud, because he wanted his wife, who was busy in the corner with a lot of boxes and bundles, to hear what he was saying.

There was a baby lying on a big straw sack, covered with a lot of rags, and a little girl of seven or eight standing near.

"Why don't you answer 'Good evening'?" his wife said reproachfully. "Here's the scribe's son coming in and saying 'Good evening,' and you don't answer. Put your work away now. You've done enough for to-day."

"Good evening, Jacob!" Gershon said. "You're a very welcome visitor. How is your father?"

"Is this where you're living now?" Jacob asked, looking round gloomily. "You're going to spend the winter in this place, with the children?"

Gershon's wife burst into tears. Gershon explained:

"Two of our children died—Feigel and Sarah—they were eleven and thirteen. One in the first expulsion, the other in the second. Both while we were on the road. They were never very strong, always coughing."

Gershon finished with a burst of coughing himself.

"Please leave the loom alone now," his wife begged him. "There's no air in here," she went on, speaking to Jacob. "And his chest is so bad. He keeps coughing all night. I have the door open all day, to get a little air and light in. We have no window."

"I'm going to knock a hole in the wall over there," the weaver told Jacob, "and put in a window. And I'm going to get an iron stove, to heat the place. As soon as I get working and earning. I hope that my old customers in the villages haven't forgotten me. They'll bring me their flax, and I'll weave the linen for them. God will help us. Thank God, my loom is not damaged. I left it in this very room. I took it apart. Anything could have happened to it. It could have been burned to ashes with the house, like so many other houses, like most of the town. Thank God that didn't happen to us! So we have a place to live in. It's only the cellar, where we used to store our fuel, and lumber. But it's a roof over our heads. Lots of people are worse off than we are; no roof over their heads. Take Reb Mordecai Goldblum. He was a rich man; owned that big factory, had the finest house in the town. A Chassid, a scholar, much more important to God than I am. Now look at him ..."

The mention of Pearl's father gave wings to Jacob's feet. Luckily for him, Gershon suddenly said: "It's getting late! And I haven't said my Mincha prayer yet!"

He walked over to the can of water in the corner, washed his hands, put his muffler round his loins as a girdle, and started saying Mincha.

"Time he gave that old loom a rest," his wife remarked to Jacob. "He's been tinkering at it all day. He hasn't had a thing to eat."

"Mummy, I'm hungry," the little girl cried. The baby was asleep.

Jacob found Pearl alone at home. It was quite dark by the time he arrived, and the house too was dark. She hadn't lit the oil lamp yet. She had been sitting in a half-doze, from which Jacob's footsteps and his "Good evening" roused her.

"Who's that?" she called out.

"Me," said Jacob at the door, not daring to venture inside because it was so dark that he couldn't see his way.

"Who's me?"

"Jacob Lichtenberg."

Pearl jumped up.

"Jacob!" she cried happily. "I'm so glad you came now!"

"Now?"

"Yes, because I'm all alone now. Father's gone out. I don't know where. As a rule he goes to his ruined factory every day, first thing every morning. He may be there now. He rummages around among his broken machines, among the burned walls. He can't keep away from it. The factory was half his life. And that half has been destroyed. Believe me, Lichtenberg, my father was not like the other manufacturers, whom you and your comrades call the bourgeoisie, just as your father is not like all the other religious Jews here. Money wasn't the most important thing to my father. I don't think you need me to tell you that. You knew my father when he was a rich man. You came to our house when you were still religious, still studying at the Beth Hamedrash. You used to come to us every Sabbath with your father for the Shalosh Seudah, and sing with all the other Chassidim. I remember you sang very beautifully."

She laughed, a little coquettishly, but also as if anxious and worried.

"I'm letting my tongue ran away with me," she said, "leaving you standing there in the dark. I was half asleep, dreaming in the dark. I'll light the lamp."

"Don't light the lamp yet, Pearl", said Jacob. "It's pleasanter to sit and dream in the dark."

But Pearl had already lighted the lamp.

"It fits in with the way we live now," she said. "In fact, it's too good for this ruin. A torch would be more fitting. Like in the days of the cave dwellers. Just as well our electricity doesn't work. It would make the desolation look worse. Come in, Jacob. Sit down, and let's talk. I'm feeling so sad."

They sat down at the round table, which had once been a precious piece of furniture. Jacob remembered it standing in an alcove against a big window and two smaller windows opening into the garden, that made the alcove look like a balcony inside the room. There had been green damask chairs and a green damask couch there, and a lot of flower-boxes that turned it into an orangery. This had been Pearl's favorite spot. The idea of the alcove had been hers. She had sketched a design for it. She had not dared to tell her father that she had got the idea from a Christian house she had visited.

The boxes in which she had planted shrubs and flowers still stood there, but the shrubs and the flowers were dead. There were broken flower pots and broken vases on the floor.

"I haven't the heart to throw them out," she confessed. "These plants were living things to me. It would be like throwing dead bodies into the street."

The dim light of the lamp cast sadness over the room. Here and there the signs of former wealth only added to the gloom. Except for this one room the house was almost completely destroyed—and in this room too there were holes in the walls, and the ceiling bulged as though it were about to collapse. Most of the windows were smashed, and had been boarded up clumsily. The holes in the walls had been partly bricked up by unskilled hands. The walls still showed where costly tapestries had hung. Heaps of stones and bricks lay round the door. These at least had been gathered up and arranged in heaps. Reb Mordecai Goldblum and his daughter Pearl had done that themselves.

"You must do something about this place," Jacob said. "Else you'll have the ceiling and the walls tumbling down on top of you. I know your father has no mind for these things now. So you must do it. Get a builder in; ask him if it's safe to stay in this house as it is."

"This is all that is left of my father's riches," Pearl said, with a sad smile. "We're lucky to have this one room left, so that we have a roof over our heads. The factory is a total loss. We're covered by insurance, but the insurance companies are not paying out, not now. Who knows if they ever will. And the Russian government doesn't pay my father for the goods they bought from him. He carries a lot of securities and other papers and bills around with him, but they're worthless. But that isn't the worst of it. I wouldn't worry so much if we had only lost our money, and we were poor. Sometimes I think my father welcomes being poor. When we came back to the town and we found our house in ruins like this, he cried out: 'Praise God! Thank God, that this burden has been removed from me. Now I shall have more time to serve You, as I always wanted to. I didn't dare to cast the burden off myself. I said that if God chose me to carry this weight of wealth and of business, I must not renounce it. I am Your servant, and I must do Your will. Yet more than once I wondered if it was not the evil one who would not let me give up my wealth. More than once I stumbled on my road, though I tried to walk upright, not to take a penny that was not mine, to pay my workers what was due for their labor. I used no false scales. I did not cheat with the quality of my material. I did not price my goods higher. I gave charity with a full hand. But money is an idol. Therefore I thank You, God, for having freed me from it!' Those were his very words. Tell me, Jacob, do you call a man who speaks like that a bourgeois, an exploiter? Is he that, Jacob? And I? You know Dinah Greenzweig's attitude to me. She hates me! You remember that night with the group outside the town. Perhaps she was right. Perhaps I shouldn't have come to the meeting. Perhaps my place is not with you all."

Jacob took hold of both her hands.

"Don't speak like that, Pearl! Don't speak like that about your father. I know your father, and I respect him. But you can't get away from the factory. He had a big factory. He was an employer. He was a rich man. That is a social problem. That's why people feel the way they do."

"Don't let's talk about it now," Pearl broke in. "I don't worry so much about our being poor. I wouldn't mind if we were even poorer than we are. But when a rich man becomes poor he is doubly poor. It isn't the loss of the factory and the money that is so hard for us. There are worse things. We have no idea where my brothers are, and my two sisters, and their wives and their husbands and their children. They fled to Russia. God knows if they got there safely. God knows if we shall ever see them again.

"Don't you remember them, Jacob, all our big family sitting round the Sabbath table! All the Chassidim who came on pilgrimage to the Rebbe came to our house for Shalosh Seudos and Mlave Malkes. . . . If only my mother were alive!" She burst into tears.

Jacob was embarrassed. He didn't know what to say or do.

Then at last Pearl composed herself. Jacob thought it would be best to talk about other things, to take her mind off her father's troubles and her own.

"The year I started putting on Tephilin," he began, "I went every morning to the Beth Hamedrash carrying the Tephilin under my arm, and I stayed there till noon or later. I don't remember for sure if I was still religious, or whether I had already begun to doubt."

"But you were already sixteen when you still came to our house every Sabbath for the Shalosh Seudah. I thought you were still religious then!"

"No!" Jacob said smiling. "By that time I had long been a disbeliever. I was pretending, as many of the young men at the Beth Hamedrash pretended."

"So you're used to pretending!" Pearl teased.

"I still said my prayers very devoutly," Jacob said. "Do you know why?"

"Why?"

"Because of you. I was in love with you."

Pearl blushed, and giggled.

"Because your father and your brothers and your brothers-in-law were all religious, and because you were all rich, and I was the poor scribe's ugly son."

"Ugly? A man is not expected to have looks. You're not ugly."

"You were the most beautiful girl in the town," Jacob exclaimed. "You still are!"

"I wanted to be a Rabbi," Jacob explained, "I thought it would give me more chance. After prayers I sat and studied Talmud. On my way home I stopped and hid in a house in your road, to see you pass. You never noticed me. Each time I wanted to come out and talk to you, but I didn't dare. Once I met you in a narrow back street, deep in snow. I wanted to make room so that you could pass. But in my confusion I kept stepping back and coming forward again, till in the end you drew back to make room for me. I was so ashamed."

"I remember that," Pearl smiled.

"Why hasn't he come yet?" she suddenly went on.

"Who?"

"Isaac—I mean Lehrman."

"Are you expecting him?" Jacob's voice dropped.

"Yes, he should have been here half an hour ago."

Presently Isaac arrived, and the two friends, Isaac and Jacob, greeted each other warmly.

7

The Commandant and the Rebels

Comrade Hersh was one of those people who insist on their rights. So with the consent of the more important of his comrades he submitted an application to the Commandant demanding the rights which the German Government had given to the German Socialist Party. This time the Commandant received him.

The Commandant, Major von Wolfensthal, was in a good mood.

"Show him in," he said, when Hersh was announced. "No, no file. I know what it's about." And mentally he added: "I know the Polish population and the Jewish population here through and through."

He followed this up with a string of oaths, expressing his utter contempt for Poles and Jews alike, without being quite sure which of them he despised most. But this question of Jewish workers in Poland who were Socialists and demanded recognition as Socialists worried him. He didn't know enough about the subject. "I must find out more about it." He decided.

Major von Wolfensthal had a habit in certain moods of slipping his military coat over his shoulders, and hunching into a corner of the plush violet couch in his office, with the tasseled hilt of his sword sticking out through the slit of the pocket.

The room was large and bright, with two windows looking out on the street. They had double curtains. The waxed floor had two rugs arranged crosswise. He had three portraits on the wall facing the door; one could see that he thought more of Frederick the Great than of Wilhelm II. And more of Bismarck than of Hindenburg or Ludendorff. The tiled stove was so regulated that the room temperature was kept at an even 68 degrees.

The Major played with the tassels of his sword and with the hilt, and hunched back, his head deep in the high fur collar of his military coat. He found the feel of the fur comforting. He hardly ever took the monocle from his eye. Waiting for his visitor to enter he ran over in his mind what he could remember of the German Labor movement.

He knew a great deal about Poland. He had made a thorough study of Polish history, her economic development, her industry and agriculture and trade—even her folklore. More than that, he had learned a good many Polish words and Yiddish words. He knew the geography of Poland from end to end. But he didn't know the Jewish Socialist Labor movement in Poland. He reproached himself—"I should have known it!"

"Pleased to meet you!" the Commandant greeted Hersh, without shifting his position or looking up at him. But he was observing him closely, though Hersh was not aware of it.

"Now tell me, Mr. Krumholz, what is this all about? Do you really mean to say that there are working people among the Jews? What sort of work do they do? On the land? In the coal mines? Are they factory workers?"

He suddenly looked up at Hersh, who was still standing at the door, and said: "You can speak in Yiddish. I understand."

He listened attentively, following every word, every syllable, marking the resemblances to Middle High German, which had been one of his subjects at the University.

He didn't show it, but he wondered at this young Jew, who looked so different from the usual run of Polish Jews. It annoyed him that here was a young Jew who looked just like any Polish or German workman from Mecklenburg or Saxony. He stretched his legs out in front of him, so that the spurs jingled. He intended to indicate by this nonchalance his utter contempt for the Polish Jew, who was a Socialist on top of it.

The Commandant lit a cigarette, leaned back and, blowing smoke rings, started an exposition of his own to show the representative of the Jewish Socialists how thoroughly versed he was in Socialist theory and Socialist history. He spoke of Marx and Engels, and of the English and French Socialist thinkers and leaders, and even of Russian Anarchists. The Commandant was a well-read man, and he remembered what he read. He knew his German literature, Goethe and Schiller and Heine too, and the contemporary writers. He had studied Schopenhauer, Nietzsche, and Fichte. But his greatest joy was in Frederick the Great and Bismarck and von Stein. Yet he was not really an anti-Semite, he despised Jews no more than he despised Poles and Russians.

He sat thinking for a while. Then he said to Hersh: "There will be no Socialist movement permitted here, where I am the Commandant. You want a Labor organization? What for? There are no Jewish workmen here. There are only a few artisans, and they don't employ anybody now. They work on their own, if they have any work at all. The factories are all destroyed. So you see there is no need for such an organization, except for political ends. That's right, isn't it? And your political ends are directed against Germany, of course."

He laughed. "You say you want it for cultural purposes? You know very well that cultural matters are the province of the Jewish religious community; they belong to Mr. Bernfel and Mr. Fuksman. and the Rabbi, of course."

He laughed again at the idea of having separate Jewish and Polish Labor organizations, and without waiting for Hersh to speak he rose impetuously, and drew his coat round him like a toga. He fixed Hersh with a stern eye, and warned him not to think of taking any illegal action. "I know all the methods of conspiracy," he said, "all the methods used by the Russian conspirators."

He walked over to the window, with his spurs jangling, and stood there looking out. It was the signal for Hersh to go.

Comrade Krumholz reported his second failure to his comrades.

"I find it hard," he said, "to tell you the kind of man this German Commandant is. He spoke about Marx and Engels, and about their works, and about someone called Moses Hess who wrote a book 'Rome and Jerusalem.' He asked me if I had read the book. He spoke to me about Bakunin. He knows a lot, this German. Real German thoroughness. Listening to him you would think he was a Socialist, with all he knows about Socialism. But I saw through him. He kept me nearly two hours. But no permit. Not even for cultural work. Bernfel must have had a word with him before I came. We shall have to go very carefully."

Hersh was proud of having been received by the Commandant, who had discussed Marx and Engels with him. He reported it all with full details to Feiga, and he grew in stature to her. Abraham and the others too, except Aaron, Jacob, and Dinah, looked up to him with increased respect because of it. Yet he smarted under the unconcealed disdain with which the Commandant had treated him. He remembered that the Commandant had kept him standing the whole time, hadn't even deigned to look up at him from where he had lolled on the couch, and that when he had decided that he had had enough he had just got up and walked over to the window, ignoring him.

Hersh also reported his interview, especially the bit where the Commandant had said that he couldn't see the need for separate Jewish and Polish Labor organizations, to Comrade Juziek Strzelkowski, who clucked his tongue, and said:

"Yes, he's a real friend of ours! Wants us to unite ... He's an educated man. With a bellyful of books."

Then he started bombarding Hersh with orders. "We're going to start work at once! Propaganda ... War against the invader, against the foreign foe! We must suspend the class war for the time being. I'm going to see Jan. We already have the nucleus of an army. We are in touch with Pilsudski. Call a meeting of the comrades! First a small meeting. You send out the notices. Let me know when it is. I'll come too."

Juziek laughed: "He knows all the Russian conspiratorial methods, does he? Does he know our Polish methods too?"

The German military gendarmes kept rounding up men in the streets, men between eighteen and forty-five. On the first day of the German occupation army proclamations had appeared in the streets telling all men who had served in the Russian army, who had got cut off from their regiments, and reservists to report within twenty-four hours to the Military Command, on penalty of being shot. Those who reported were sent to Germany as forced labor in the coal mines and the munitions factories.

More proclamations had followed. All arms had to be handed in to the Military Command. All gold, silver, brass, copper, zinc, all horses, cows, pigs, corn, potatoes—everything had to be given up. Then the requisitions started, in the villages and in the town, in every house, in every room. The German gendarmes requisitioned everything they found and sent it all to Germany, together with the men whom they kept rounding up in the streets. People began to hide everything edible, everything of value. Men, especially the younger ones, tried to keep out of sight. Smuggling started, and spread like the plague. It was the one salvation from the famine and starvation caused by the German occupation. But it was a "salvation" like that of a drowning man clutching at the blade of a sharp sword. There was fierce anger against the invader. The soil became fertile for the Socialist agitation conducted by the group of young people who had met that night outside the town.

Jacob suggested to Hersh that they should hold their secret meetings at Lozer's.

"Who's Lozer?" Hersh wanted to know.

"Red Meir's son. You never knew him. But you knew the father. A poor man, with lots of children. They're all in Warsaw now, I think. Lozer was a simple fellow, like a shaggy bear, and as strong as an ox. He wore a long coat and top boots and a big colored scarf round his neck. He never learned a trade, and when his father turned him out of the house he went to work in Goldblum's factory. They drafted him into the army three years ago. He had only another year to serve when the war broke out. He was badly wounded in the fighting round Lodz, and they sent him to hospital in Warsaw. He came out minus a leg and an arm, just at the time of the second flight from the town. He joined in the flight with his parents. Now he is back here. Alone. His parents died of typhus. He's a changed man. He lives in a tumble-down ruin on the road to Czernokota, right in the middle of a derelict field that hasn't been ploughed or tilled since the war started. There isn't a living thing to be seen on that road. Not even a stray dog. I've been there often.

"All that Lozer brought back with him is his army coffer, a couple of army shirts, a little underwear, a towel and a few books. The army taught him to read and write. The war opened his eyes. Pearl and Lehrman got him a bed and some bedding and crockery and cooking pots and a table and chairs. Pearl goes down there most days to cook for him. I don't know where she gets the food from, because her father is as poor as we are now. She does his washing and mending and keeps the place clean. And she isn't a Socialist!"

"I know what you want to say, Comrade Lichtenberg," said Hersh. "But that's philanthropy. That's not Socialism."

"I don't agree with you," Jacob burst out. "We'll talk about this and other things at the meeting. I'll bring Pearl with me and Lehrman, though they don't belong to the Party, and don't want to belong to it."

"All right! Bring them along!"

Juziek Strzelkowski went off after his talk with Krumholz to see Jan. Jan was a man of mysteries. His father was the apothecary of the town, a bit queer in the head and a drunkard. Most of the time he was in a bad temper, but he liked making vulgar jokes and guffawing into his bushy whiskers. The Jews never knew if he was a friend of the Jews or an anti-Semite, because he used to say the most dreadful things about Jews, swear and curse at them, and say that they ought all to be killed.

But when a Jew or a Jewess came to have a prescription made up, and he knew they had no money, he wouldn't take payment for the medicine, and even gave them some money out of his own pocket to buy a chicken for the sick person, or butter or wine.

His son, Jan, an only child, was very much like his father. He was no longer a young man; he had studied everything and everywhere, in Warsaw, Petersburg, Cracow, Vienna, Berlin, Paris. He had started with medicine, had switched to pharmacy, then he had taken up engineering, and after that philosophy. In the end he became an army cadet, but gave that up too to take over the administration of an estate that his father had inherited. The estate was still being managed by the old farm bailiff, because Jan had no idea of either agriculture or administration. The only difference was that the bailiff now paid the revenue from the estate to Jan instead of to his father. Jan squandered the money, roistering with his friends and having a good time with women.

But that was only one side of Jan, just as he had two names. He was Jan to his comrades in the Polish Socialist Party in the town and round about, and to his women and his friends. To everybody else he was Gnilowski. He played a dual role, one with his comrades in the Party and the other with his fellow landowners, with whom he hunted and had all sorts of business dealings.

But the boundary between Jan Gnilowski's two selves had lately been largely obliterated, because both groups with whom he associated were now dominated by the same interest, Polish patriotism. His Socialist comrades said they were just as ready to sacrifice themselves for their Socialism, but their Fatherland was equally important. The landowners of course were interested only in their Polish patriotism. They had no use even for social reform. But at this time, when their country lay under the yoke of a foreign power, they were all revolutionaries, and ready to work together with the Socialists and the common folk.

Juziek found Comrade Jan just getting up, though it was long past noon. When the servant announced Juziek, Jan couldn't quite take it in. He had been up late drinking with his friends, and he was still befuddled.

"Who?" he repeated. "Who the devil is he? All right! Send him in!"

The servant hesitated, and said apologetically with a glance at the unmade bed, "I asked him to wait in the library. The bed ..."

"The bed? What's wrong with the bed? Who slept in it?"

"You, sir!"

"That's all right then! Show him in!"

By the time Juziek entered the room Jan had shaken off some of his stupor. He gave Juziek a welcoming grin and took his hand with a firm grip. He looked a true proletarian, with his shirt unbuttoned, showing his bare chest, and his shirtsleeves rolled up, and his trousers held up by a belt.

"I had a meeting till four this morning," he apologized, "with the patriots. A stormy meeting. A historic meeting. Things are going well. I must say they showed a real Kosciuszko spirit. True revolutionary nationalism. I hadn't known that our Priest is a partisan of 1863, a bitter opponent of any sort of compromise with the Germans. He hates those Prussians like hell. He's going to be a great help to us. He can fire the people from the pulpit. We'll even be able to store arms in the Church. We've got plenty of money. Our nobles give freely. Count Zaremba alone gave us a tidy sum. I didn't get to bed till five. And we've been drinking hard. I couldn't find my way to the bed. We were all so worked up. We're going to start work right away."

Juziek took it with a grain of salt. He had no illusions about his friend Jan, nor about the revolutionary ardor of the patriot nobles. He knew something too from Chelia about Jan's private life, as she knew it from her sister Helena, who was having an affair with him, and from her father's business deals with him. But Jan was useful to the Party because of his connections with the camp of the patriot nobles.

Juziek sat on the edge of the bed, next to Jan, and told him what Hersh had reported to him about the Commandant. He proposed calling a meeting of the "Secret committee," only those people whom they could trust absolutely. He ran over the names, most of them old revolutionaries going back to 1905, and the others who had come in later, all people who had been long tried and tested in the underground conspiratorial movement. They included a few bourgeois intellectuals, an official of the Town Administration, a woman teacher, a factory bookkeeper, a veterinary surgeon, and several intelligent working people.

Jan agreed to such a meeting, but not as Juziek wanted it, to stand only on patriotic propaganda; he thought they should lay the most stress on Socialism.

"This is an industrial town," he said, "even if the factories have been smashed. It's a town of workers. That's point one. Point two—there are lots of peasants in the surrounding villages who are still serfs. Some of them are fierce revolutionaries. Point three—this is 1915, not 1863. We are living in a time of revolutionary ferment. Point four—This is war. Famine. Bread means more now than the Fatherland does. You understand? Point five—The Germans are carrying on a very clever policy. They are promising us national autonomy. They've taken the wind out of our sails, as you might say. Point six—Propaganda means promising more than the Germans do, promising everything, firing the imagination of the people. I could give you several more points, but these will do. You've got the idea now."

Strzelkowski looked keenly at Jan, and said to himself, "He's not sobered up yet." He added aloud: "We'll deal with these things at the meeting."

As he left the room he said: "Don't drink so much in future."

"And you," Jan replied, "you see to it that our comrades learn to shoot. There'll be plenty of guns for them!"

8

Love and Responsibility

Jacob spent an extremely pleasant evening at Pearl's, especially after Isaac Lehrman had arrived. They got into a heated discussion about Socialism, in which Pearl vehemently disagreed with him, and Lehrman was on Pearl's side. Lehrman made Pearl feel more sure of herself; it was now two against one, instead of herself alone to combat Jacob's agreements; and Lehrman knew the subject much better than she did. He had read a lot of Socialist literature, which she hadn't. She spoke from the heart, as a humanist, while he based himself on his wide reading of the most important Socialist theoreticians. He opposed to Jacob's arguments the views of the great utopists and moralists, among them the Hebrew Prophets. Pearl was elated, triumphant. Because she found so much identity with Lehrman, their outlook was so similar—she felt that they could understand each other. They approached the problem from the same angle. She, the daughter of the once-rich manufacturer shared the idealism of the poor tinsmith's son. He spoke as though he was putting her thoughts into words. And this made her very happy.

"Not class," he said, "not proletariat, not physical force." Yet there was one argument that Jacob brought forward that he could not answer—that the downtrodden worker had never started the fight, but had always been forced to defend himself against cruelty and oppression.

When Reb Mordecai Goldblum came home Jacob and Lehrman left together, not because Pearl's pious father had found them there with his daughter, but because the man looked so utterly wretched and miserable and brought such an atmosphere of sadness and despondency into the house that they couldn't stand it.

They stayed on for a few minutes, thinking that Reb Mordecai might want to say a word to them; but he didn't open his mouth, and Pearl too had lost her tongue in his presence.

It was all so oppressive that it drove them out of the house. They stood in silence for a moment outside the door, too depressed to speak. Suddenly Jacob made a move toward his friend, meaning to put his arm around him, but he stopped himself. Lehrman must have sensed it, for he gripped Jacob's hand with more than usual warmth. They looked into each other's eyes and walked away silently.

Jacob was now convinced that Pearl was in love with Lehrman. He didn't feel like going home, so he decided to go see Rabeh.

There were two thoughts in his mind that brought him to this decision. The first was that he must now forget about Pearl and think more about Rabeh. The other was that he must interest Rabeh in Socialism.

But he didn't go to see Rabeh after all. His exaggerated sense of honesty kept him back. It didn't seem fair to him to walk out of Pearl's house and go straight to Rabeh.

As he walked about the streets (for he didn't go home either) Jacob thought the whole thing over. "One must be very severe with one's own emotions, because your heart can so easily lead you astray. Yet the mind too can mislead you. You must keep a tight rein on both. But the heart has something richer and more rewarding than the mind—the heart has conscience and responsibility. True, but what had conscience and responsibility to do with his wanting to put Socialism into Rabeh's mind? Why must Rabeh think the same as he did? What strange will drives a man to want somebody else to share his ideas and his feelings, to make somebody else like himself? Harmony?"

When he had come home and was lying on his bed, which was made up on the floor, a bed that he shared with his two young brothers, Jacob couldn't get to sleep. Eleven people in one room ... The air was so fuggy. Impossible to keep the room clean. And his father coughed and groaned all the time.

But the thought that was most in his mind was Rabeh: "Does she love me?"

Then he reproached himself: "Why am I asking myself this question? Only because I'm not sure how I feel about her."

But the thought nagged at him all night. Did Rabeh love him? His mind went back to the start, to the time when he had first felt himself falling in love with Rabeh. He was seventeen. For three years he had not dared to do more than hold her hand when they went walking together, sometimes to stroke her hand. They used to come separately, each by a different road, to meet in the woods or in the fields outside the town, so that they shouldn't be seen together. Their relationship had been so naively innocent. But looking back now he was glad that it had been so—it had been very sweet and clean and beautiful. His whole approach to her had been that of a shy and bashful boy who was transported with happiness just to look into her eyes. He spoke to her about the advanced books that he had started reading then; he had already lost his faith by that time, had become a disbeliever. And she showed him the poems that her brother was writing.

Till her cousin arrived one Friday from Odessa. Jacob still remembered that Friday. He had come home from work, washed, changed into his Sabbath best, and gone to see Rabeh. He found her with her cousin, wrestling playfully to see who was stronger. He looked like a city fop, in a white suit, white shoes, panama hat and a gold signet ring. He held Rabeh tight, her breast against his, and he was chaffing her—"You can't get away from me!"

But Rabeh soon tore herself loose when she saw Jacob arrive.

"Meet my cousin," she said. And she went on, very much flustered and embarrassed: "You remember Jacob, don't you? The scribe's son. He was still studying at the Beth Hamedrash when you went to Odessa, Herman. He's a clicker by trade now."

Jacob had come, as he came every Friday, to see Rabeh while her father was at the Friday night Sabbath service, to arrange with her where they should meet after the Sabbath meal. When he asked her now, she said she wouldn't be able to go out that evening. Her mother was keeping a strict eye on her. Besides, her head ached and she wanted to go to bed after they had eaten.

Jacob didn't believe her. And after they had eaten at home he went out and saw her walking with Herman.

Herman had stayed all that summer in their town. Every time Jacob came to the house Herman was there, or he was out with Rabeh. But he still loved her, perhaps more than before. But his love was no longer so pure and innocent. It was much more passionate. And when Herman returned to Odessa and Rabeh and he went for walks together again, they no longer behaved so innocently. Rabeh did not repulse him. Then one day she told him she was pregnant. How far gone? She didn't know.

Jacob went cold all over. Mostly because he couldn't help suspecting that Herman was responsible for it, not he. He tried to fight down the suspicion. He called himself ugly names because of it. He told himself that he was mean and despicable, that he was only trying to get out of the responsibility for what he had done. But Rabeh's uncertainty about dates had planted the suspicion in his mind, and it went on growing.

He suggested asking the midwife in the town. Rabeh wouldn't hear of it. She said the midwife would tell her mother, and she would tell other people in the town. She wouldn't be able to hold her head up.

She suggested that they should go to Warsaw. Her brother, the poet, lived in Warsaw, and she wouldn't be afraid of telling him. He believed in free love. He was sure to help her.

Jacob agreed to go with her to Warsaw.

"I'll tell my parents that I've got a better job in Warsaw; that I'll be earning much more money there."

Jacob tossed on his bed. He saw the darkened room where Rabeh was lying on a couch, and he on his knees beside her, holding her hand tight. Her cold hand in his. The midwife was busy with Rabeh. He was kissing Rabeh's cold lips. The sweat stood on her face. The room smelled of ether and disinfectant.

"It's a four-month foetus," the midwife said, showing it. "Look!"

Jacob felt sick. Suddenly Rabeh had a hemorrhage. There was blood everywhere. The midwife got frightened and telephoned for the doctor.

When Jacob fell asleep at last, he dreamed of people being slaughtered.

Jacob remembered nothing of all this when he awoke in the morning. But afterward the whole thing come back to him. He could still see Rabeh, lying on the couch in that darkened room, bleeding.

His father, the scribe, was still asleep. It was quite early, and he had been awake most of the night, coughing. The window panes were frozen over. The room was stuffily warm, though there was a heavy frost outside. Only his mother was awake. She got out of bed when she saw Jacob was up. He poured water over his hands, and dabbed his face; that would do just now. He dressed quickly.

Before he left he looked around the room in which eleven people had to sleep; most of them were bedded on he floor, and he had to step warily not to tread on them.

The cold outside was refreshing. He hurried off to work. He was now working half days at his trade.

All day he kept thinking about Rabeh, and his heart melted with love and tenderness and pity for her. He thought of all that she had gone through both in Warsaw and afterward, when they had returned home. The story had leaked out, of course. Everybody in the town knew about it. Rabeh wouldn't show herself in the street for a long time. People pointed their finger at her. But her mother had been very kind to her. Rabeh had told him how kind her mother was to her. She hadn't said a single word to reproach her. Jacob felt very grateful to Rabeh's mother. And he put Herman completely out of his mind.

When Jacob came into the small room that Mirel had set aside for her parents behind the café and restaurant that she ran for the German military, he found Rabeh's father, with his skull cap on his head, sitting over a sacred book that he was studying.

Reb David Joel used to spend several months each year with his Rebbe, unconcerned about his wife and children. But since the Rebbe had become ill and was living in Warsaw, he stayed at home. He returned Jacob's greeting in a gentle soft voice that said, "Receive everyone kindly."

He knew that the scribe's son had come to see his daughter Rabeh. He knew the young man was a heretic and a disbeliever, and a rebel against the State. But he pretended that he knew nothing, just as he pretended not to know that there was a war on.

He shut his book and said to his wife in a voice like a cooing dove:

"Do you think I could have a glass of tea, Malka, please? and a biscuit? I've got such a sinking feeling. I'm quite faint."

"It's that leg of mine," he explained to Jacob. "My right leg. I can't lift it. It drags behind. I can't walk properly. Can you let me have a glass of tea, Malka, please? With four lumps of sugar. They say sugar cleanses the blood. And a biscuit, please."

When Malka had left the room to make the tea, he went on: "And how is your father? How are you? Keeping well? That's the chief thing. That, and work.... Earning your living. God won't forsake us."

Malka came back with the glass of tea and the biscuit, and placed them before her husband. Immediately he was oblivious of both his wife and Jacob. He took the glass of tea, holding it with both hands, then he tilted it, put it down, and stirred it very carefully.

"Four lumps of sugar?" he queried, and when his wife answered "Yes," he stirred the glass again with the spoon, said the blessing for a drink, and sipped the tea. Then he said the blessing before partaking of any food, and bit into the biscuit.

His wife, who knew something of these things, had once reminded him that if he said the blessing for food first it would cover both the food and the drink. His answer to that had been that if you could thank God twice, why thank Him only once. Why stint your praise and your gratitude to God? There is a reward, he said, for each blessing you repeat.

Physically, Malka was the opposite of her husband. He was a broad, solid man, below average height, like a square block. She was no taller, but thin. He walked slowly, careful not to overdo it. She seemed to be always running, hardly touching the ground, and she spared herself no hard work—she was the breadwinner.

Her husband looked well-fed and well cared for. His face was round and healthy. His broad black beard had a lot of fair hair mixed with it. His eyes were black. He had a thick neck. Her face was small and thin and lined; she was all skin and bone, but agile and vivacious, like a young girl. Her gray eyes twinkled, and she had a wise, rather skeptical smile. You could see through her sheitel that her hair under it was gray. Except for a stump or two she had lost all her teeth.

But she was full of life and as active as though she were seventeen or eighteen. She had a happy and cheerful disposition. There was a joke for everybody, and an apt proverb, often rhymed.

She had pretended not to see Jacob when he came in. But after she had given her husband his glass of tea and a biscuit she beckoned Jacob over into her corner of the room, where she had been busy working.

"Sit down, Jacob; sit on my bed."

She took his arm affectionately, and guided him to the bed. She was very fond of Jacob, not only because she regarded him as her son-in-law, but because she felt he was nearer to her than her own son in Warsaw.

Now she took up her work again, but all the time she fired questions at Jacob.

"Have you come from home, Jacob, or from work?"

Jacob wasn't feeling very happy, and he was hungry, besides. But Malka always put him at his ease. She made him feel at home. She put him in a good mood. So much so that he began teasing her.

The bed was heaped high with old clothes—trousers and shirts, sweaters and underwear. Jacob knew that Malka had gone about with Kalman's wife, Rachel, collecting these garments from the people in the town to distribute among those who had nothing to wear. She was busy now mending them. He pretended not to know this.

"You going into the old clothes business, Malka?" he asked.

"Yes. Why shouldn't I? It's a good business."

"On your own, or with a partner?"

"A partner, of course—a rich partner."

"Who, if I may ask?"

Malka pretended to be annoyed: "No, you mustn't ask! I asked you a question first. Answer that! Where have you come from now, home or work?"

"Does the business pay?" Jacob persisted.

"Yes, it does! I'm making pots of money! Tell you what? I'll give you all the money I make out of it. Now will you answer my question? Have you come from home or from work?"

"No! Before I tell you that, you tell me where I have to go for the money you're giving me. The next world, I suppose?" He threw a significant look at her husband.

"You're a scamp!" Malka said reprovingly. "If you want it, I'll give you a bill for it. Anyway, he didn't hear a word you said. He doesn't hear a thing when he's got his book in front of him, and a glass of tea and a biscuit. But you're not answering my question. Have you come here from home or from work? Because if you have come from work, it means that you haven't eaten, and you've got to have a bite.

"I've told Rabeh that you're here. She's busy inside, and she can't come out right away. The place is packed. Soldiers, most of them. But there are some Jews, too. Go and sit at the table. If you want to, wash your hands. It won't hurt you!"

"No, I'll go inside myself and order something to eat there. I did more than half a day's work today."

Malka barred his way. "You stay here. You have something to eat here. That's no place for you in there! You're not a German soldier, and you're not a smuggler. Sit down and eat!"

When Rabeh came into the room all Jacob's sad looks disappeared. His eyes lighted up. He became almost handsome. For Jacob had a special smile when he was feeling happy over something that was brave or kind or humane. It made his face shine. That was how it was now, when he saw Rabeh.

There was also some shamefacedness in his look, a sense of guilt because he had let himself play with the idea of being in love with Pearl, and he was now contrite and wanted to plead with her to forgive him. All that was in his eyes, and it gave softness and warmth to his face. He had never spoken to Rabeh about Pearl and it was on his conscience.

Rabeh didn't know of course what thoughts were passing in Jacob's mind. And he couldn't tell from her face whether she was glad to see him, or quite indifferent. No, she wasn't indifferent. She couldn't be!

Rabeh's eyes were very much like her mother's, but without her mother's warmth and radiant laughing wisdom. Jacob felt there was a frightened look in Rabeh's eyes, and an accusation. He thought too that he could detect lust in those eyes, but he knew from experience that this was not true. Was Rabeh a clever girl? He had often thought she was much cleverer than he was.

Malka came in from the café in the next room. She never liked staying longer than she could help in that café of her daughter's. She had stopped there for a little while, only to give Rabeh a chance of getting out to see Jacob. And she was impatient to get back to her work, mending the old clothes. For another thing, she wanted to be with Jacob because she liked listening to him talking.

He was in an argument with Rabeh, and she soon caught the drift of it.

"He's right, Rabeh, Jacob is right!" she interposed. "No man can live for himself alone. Nobody can.

"Take your father, now," she went on, illustrating what she had to say with an example, which was a habit of hers. "He's not very bright, you know. Now he's got that trouble with his leg. What would he do on his own?"

"That isn't what I meant," said Rabeh.

But Malka wouldn't listen.

"I'm his wife, of course," she went on. "Mirel and you both work hard so that we have somewhere to lay our head, and something to eat. But half the people in the town have no work, and don't earn anything. Many haven't a shirt to their back. What are these people to do?"

"What are they to do, mother? You know that you and Kalman's wife, Rachel, are doing quite a lot for them. It will tide them over, and they'll start earning again, as they did before the war, working or trading, as they used to do. Some are doing quite well even now, better than before."

"You mean the smugglers?" said Jacob.

"Yes", said Rabeh. "I mean the smugglers. What difference is it what they do? So long as they make enough to keep themselves. They are not robbers! They don't go about killing people!"

Jacob winced. "Rabeh," he pleaded, "how can you speak like that? Let's look at it this way. There are seven people living here. You are all one family. Suppose each of you acted on your own, without any consideration for the others, against the good of the others, the way those people do!"

"That's all very well," Rabeh insisted. "But don't my own sister and brother-in-law exploit me as much as they can!"

"They keep me at work from early morning till late at night," she went on. "They are getting rich. I—I have food, and a place to sleep and if I want something I can buy it. But it's their café! It's their restaurant! And if I were in their shoes I'd do the same!"

She saw that she was hurting Jacob by what she said, but she wanted to vindicate herself. She wanted to show him that she was right.

"Look at Bernfel," she said. "Look at Reb Yossel. And the rest. The workers? The poor? If they got the chance they'd behave just the same. Your friends Abraham and David and several of the others have also turned smugglers. Even Hersh. I tell you, everybody thinks of himself first.

"You talk of the world, the whole world. I don't know the whole world. I only know the people who live here, and I don't even know all those, only a few. Even those I know mean nothing to me, just as I mean nothing to them. Do you want me to work myself up about people in whom I have no interest?"

"Rabeh, my child," her mother interposed, "why do I understand what he means?"

Jacob felt embarrassed. He never liked to argue to score a debating point and to get the better of his adversary, especially when it was Rabeh. He was always ready to acknowledge it when his opponent's argument seemed to him better than his own, and to reconsider his position as a result. But what Rabeh was saying now, and what most people said, was wrong. They were arguing from the point of view of the kind of people that circumstances had made them, not the kind of people they could and should be.

Jacob saw that there was nothing more that he could say to convince Rabeh. Nor was there any further opportunity, because her sister Mirel was calling impatiently from the café in the next room that Rabeh should come back to serve the customers.

It was quite dark by the time Jacob left the house. He went to Juziek, to tell him where the meeting would be held, and he found him with Chelia, sitting on a high green-painted chest. The room was dark, because Juziek's father, Mateusz, had hung up the small kerosene lamp on a nail just over the window, to give him enough light for his work, and there wasn't much light for the rest of the room.

Jacob loved the smell of wood that hit his nostrils as soon as he opened the door. He scooped up a handful of shavings, and said: "These are trees. This is a forest.

Do you hear the birds singing? Look how blue the sky is!"

"You're quite a poet, Comrade Lichtenberg," Juziek said with a grin.

Chelia, who was holding hands with Juziek on top of that high chest, laughed at the way Juziek seemed to be poking fun at Jacob. She didn't like Jacob. He repelled her. Not only because he was ugly, except for those fine eyes of his. She just didn't like him. She couldn't say why, but he filled her with dislike and repugnance.

How different he was from Juziek! Juziek was so handsome and distinguished-looking, with his fine open face, his noble, severe features, his firm chin, and his shock of hair. Jacob was a little weedy fellow, with a humped nose, a protruding lower lip, and big teeth. She looked away from him with a shudder of disgust to her Christian lover, pressing his hand affectionately. Her eyes flashed, and her blood began to boil. At that moment she felt the same dislike and repugnance for her whole Jewish people that she felt for Jacob. She despised and detested all Jews. And because she loved Juziek she loved all Poles.

"What do you say to our Comrade Chelia?" Juziek asked Jacob. "She is no longer Panna Bernfel. She is Comrade Chelia. Say, isn't she beautiful?"

Jacob went straight to the point. He had come there to tell Juziek when and where the secret meeting was to be held. He spoke in whispers, because Juziek's older brother was asleep on a bed in the same room, with all his clothes on.

There was another smell in the room besides the smell of wood—the smell of cooking. Juziek's mother was boiling pork and cabbage and potatoes for supper. She stood over the stove, stirring the pot with a big wooden ladle. Though Jacob had been coming into this room quite often, he still couldn't stomach the smell of this un-Jewish food.

The old lady's white hair was bunched up on the back of her head. She was a thin little toothless woman, with a friendly smile like her husband's. Her husband liked teasing her. He left his work now, and walked across to her by the stove.

"Cooking something nice?"

"Yes, very nice."

"Good," said Mateusz, giving his wife a kiss.

The old lady had in the course of years, bending over her stove and her washtub, and bowed down with poverty and cares, become quite hunched, so that she now seemed to have a hump like her husband's. He made fun of her for that. "Isn't she just like me?" he sniggered. "We've both got humps. You wouldn't have believed it when she was young. She was a straight, beautiful girl. As beautiful as your Panna Chelia," he called up to his son, who was sitting with his sweetheart on top of the high chest.

Juziek gave Chelia a resounding kiss and laughed aloud.

The old carpenter took off his coarse blue apron, and said: "I've done enough work for today. I'm hungry. And that's good food we've got. We've been lucky today. Old Cizik, the rich farmer, died, and his son told me to make the coffin. I said I wanted a side of pork for it and a bushel of potatoes and a few heads of cabbage. He agreed to that. So we've got some real good food."

He walked over to the chest, and looked up to his son and Chelia: "Come down, you two, and eat!"

"When are you two getting married?" he went on. "Have you told your sweetheart who your grandfather was? My father," he boasted, "fought against the Muscovites. The Cossacks caught him, and whipped him, put him in chains, and sent him to Siberia. He died there. My father was a hero!

"You, Juziek, and you Jacob, and you Chelia too, see that you fight against the Germans as my father fought against the Russians. Drive them out of our Poland! I'll fight with you! I'll get a gun and shoot. I know how to march—one, two, three, four! March!"

Chelia jumped down from the high chest, and laid her arm affectionately around the old man's shoulders:

"We'll fight together against the Germans!" she cried.

"All of us together," Juziek backed her up.

Juziek picked up a book that Chelia had left lying on the chest, and showed it to Jacob:

"Do you see what she reads, Jacob? None of your sentimental poetry stuff, and no novels either. She reads real books!"

Jacob picked the book up. It was "The Communist Manifesto." Chelia snatchd it from him:

"That means more to me," she said, "than Slowacki's and even Mickiewicz's poems!"

"You will fight with us, Jacob, won't you?" old Mateusz cried to Jacob.

Jacob smiled. Chelia threw him a contemptuous glance.

"He won't fight," she said.

"He'll fight all right," the old man stood up for Jacob. "He is one of us. He is with the poor. He is a poor man himself. His parents are poor, and I know how poor they are. His father is a poor sick man. Dear God, how that man suffers! And he's such a wise, learned man! A good man! He once said to me: 'There is a higher Reason. Nothing happens just so, just so!' That's very wise talk! He's an honest man! And Jacob takes after his father. Jacob is an honest man too. And he's got learning. He knows their holy books. There is a lot of wisdom in them. I didn't study. I got no learning. But I know!"

The old lady woke her sleeping son.

"Get up, Caspar. Supper's ready."

"He was on duty all night," she explained for Jacob's and Chelia's benefit. "He's got to be on duty again tonight. He's in the militia. He volunteered for it after the Russians left, before the Germans came. And he stayed there."

She went to the corner where the holy lamp burned between the pictures of Jesus and Mary, crossed herself, and prayed.

"She's religious," Mateusz remarked. "That's the way it should be. Everybody should believe in his God. Everybody should have a religion."

Caspar, who was up now and pulling his clothes straight and combing his hair, sneered:

"Your God! Your religion!"

He went to the corner where the holy pictures hung and crossed himself.

The old lady was serving supper. Jacob moved toward the door.

"Stay and eat with us," said the old man.

Juziek laughed at that: "Don't you know he doesn't eat pork?"

"Then why does Panna Chelia eat with us?" the old man asked. "I know that you've dropped your religion, Jacob. You don't have any objections to eating pork."

"Let him go!" his son Caspar growled, with an ugly glance at Jacob and Chelia. But Jacob was already at the door, with his hand on the knob, and walked out.

9

The Meeting

Pearl and Isaac Lehrman were the first to arrive at Lozer's. But Pearl came there most days anyway, to do what she could for the cripple, and now she felt like the hostess awaiting the visitors. She wanted the place to look not only tidy but attractive. So she had made a curtain out of an old muslin dress of hers, and hung it at the window. She had been toying with the idea of making a few paper flowers, and putting them on the commode, the best article of furniture there, which really seemed out of place among the rest of the junk. The commode had once stood in Pearl's own room, and she had discovered it there under a pile of bricks and rubbish, almost undamaged.

"It's just what you need, Lozer," she had said when she came there with Lehrman and Jacob, who had carried it for her. "You can keep your underwear in it, and your books and your pots and cups and plates on top."

She had decided against the paper flowers, because she loved real flowers too much to want artificial ones.

Lozer hobbled on his crutch over to a sack in the corner. "I've kept a little coal here," he said, "for such an occasion. We could light a fire now."

Jacob and Aaron arrived next.

"This is Comrade Mickenshleger," Jacob introduced Aaron to Lozer. "And this is Lozer, Comrade Eibershutz."

Jacob and Aaron shook hands with Pearl, who asked Aaron if his sister was coming.

"Yes," he said. "She's coming with Comrade Krumholz. They'll be here soon."

But they didn't come soon. Krumholz came with Feiga Mickenshleger, the very last, after Juziek was already there with Chelia.

Chelia Bernfel, who had been brought up in a rich home, felt quite lost in this hovel, and kept close to Juziek, frightened of it. She also felt uncomfortable among all these people, not only because it was the first time she was at a working-class meeting, but because they were Jews, and she felt a revulsion against all Jews. She

70

disliked the Jewish workers even more than she disliked Juziek's brother Caspar.

"My brother Caspar is an anti-Semite and a reactionary," Juziek had told her, and had gone on to explain: "Anti-Semitism is the Socialism of fools. Bebel said that. I would go farther and say that anti-Semitism is a poison with which the reactionaries inject the proletariat. There is no difference, Chelia, between Christian workers and Jewish workers. They are both equally exploited, and they must both fight together against capitalism."

Every word Juziek said was holy to Chelia. He was her teacher, not only her friend and her lover. So when he spoke against anti-Semitism she wanted to fight against the anti-Semitism she felt in her own heart. She tried to convert her dislike of Jews into a hatred of the rich.

Abraham came to this meeting not with his sister Bluma, as the last time, but with Dinah. He hadn't wanted to bring his sister to another meeting; but she came all the same, with David.

The fire was now burning in the stove, and the room was warm. Juziek and Hersh both expressed satisfaction with this new meeting place.

"It looks safe," Hersh Krumholz said. "Anyone who doesn't know would never think this pile of broken bricks was inhabited. And the trees shut it out. You must search for it. No German gendarme would think of looking for us here."

Juziek wasn't so sure. "You may be right," he said, "but we must be careful. Not more than two at a time, and dressed to look like peasants from the surrounding villages."

Hersh Krumholz opened the meeting.

"Comrades," he began, "we have a number of important items on the agenda. We shall have a discussion first, and then we shall adopt decisions for renewing our activities, with strict discipline, and the utmost loyalty and devotion to the cause. We shall fight the new enemy as resolutely as we fought the old. We shall try to increase our membership, to wage the struggle, to enroll new forces for our fight, all those who do not yet know that we are renewing our activity. Our Party must grow larger and stronger. We shall elect an administrative committee to carry on the work."

After all the discussion there were proposals to start cooperative workshops, to organize strikes where work had started again, and to compel the employers to take apprentices; there were proposals about cultural work, to start a library, and to appoint Pearl and Lehrman librarians, though they were not members of the Party, and to get them to lecture on geography, history, and other subjects. Finally, after all who had put down their names to take part in the discussion had spoken, Jacob spoke. He launched into a very long and learned-sounding discourse on clericalism and on ways to end the war.

He went on speaking—on and on—, and did not notice that except for a few like Pearl and Lehrman, and to some extent Aaron, nobody was listening to him. Almost as soon as he had started David entered into an animated discussion with Bluma about his plans for the future, Feiga had demonstratively begun a loud conversation with Hersh, Abraham and Dinah were whispering together, and she made jokes about Jacob's philosophy. Chelia was trembling all over with anger and annoyance. She knew now why she had felt such antipathy to Jacob from the outset. She wondered why Juziek put up with him at all.

Part Two

10

Anything for a Living

Some time had passed, and conditions in the town had changed. Many of the war wounds had healed, but the old settled life had gone completely. The life of the factories was destroyed. There was no more noise from the machines. No sirens sounded. No smoke belched from the chimneys. No workers went hurrying to the factories and hurrying back home. There were no trucks of finished goods being taken through the streets to the railway and coming back with raw materials.

There was no more big business done by rich merchants, no new shops being opened by the shopkeepers, no new houses being built. The artisans had nothing to do now, not as in the old days, when they were always up to their necks with work before one of the Festivals.

There were no more market days every Tuesday, with the town full of noise and bustle, peasants and their wives coming in from all the villages round about, neighing horses between the long shafts of the peasant carts with arched covers over them. The town had been alive with squealing pigs and mooing cows and crowing cocks, stall-holders shouting their wares, beggars and tramps asking for alms, barrel organs playing, people singing and whistling, and children blowing toy trumpets. All that had gone, and with it had gone all the old Jewish festival life, the joy of wedding feasts and of other happy events, the packed Synagogue and Beth Hamedrash, the full-hearted singing of prayers, and the yearning sing-song of Holy study.

A new life had begun, sorrow and woe to it, as most of the Jews in the town expressed themselves. The new life was based on smuggling. Everybody was in it, young and old, men and women, boys and girls, people who had always made their living in trade, and scholars and carters and thieves, even youngsters who were still at Chedar. There were agents and contact men and go-betweens, even go-betweens for bigger go-betweens, people who arranged things with the German gendarmes and the Polish militia and the smugglers. It was real corruption.

The authorities knew of course about the smuggling, but they were bought by two kinds of payment, money and "love." People lost all shame; they stopped hiding things. Many young women and girls who had been modest and chaste became simply prostitutes. Pious Jews started dealing with swines flesh, desecrated the Sabbath, secretly at first, then quite openly. Chassidim, respectable citizens, sent their wives (if they were young and pretty) and their daughters to the German Commandant and his aides to get a license out of them for engaging in some shady business.

There was a new profession now, "leaders," touts, mostly small boys who led the German and Austrian soldiers arriving in the town on short leave, or passing through it on their way elsewhere, to shops hidden away in cellars or in back-street stores where they could buy all the things that the military forces were taking out of the country—food, tobacco, salmon, sausage, ham—and the boys had grown expert at it. A youngster of ten, eleven, or twelve had only to look at a German soldier to size him up and know immediately what he would want.

The best "leaders" were Berke Petzer, Osher Lekech, and Black Godel. Behind these dragged Yoske, Gronem the melamed's son, and Ozer, Reb Yossel Fuksman's youngest. The other boys couldn't stand Ozer.

Berke Petzer wanted to know: "What made you become a 'leader?' Doesn't your dad make enough money?"

Osher Lekech took the cue: "His family are starving, poor things! His dad's busy talking to God all the time, and uses his daughter to make millions. I mean Deborah!"

Berke gave him a punch in the ribs. "Keep your mouth shut! They say she suffers under it.... And we don't go for people who suffer.... Tell me. Ozer, is it true that she is the Commandant's...? You're not saying? You're right! What made you become a 'leader?' You're not short of money. And you don't take any commission from your father! I don't want you to take any customers to your father! None of us do! Never! You know the sort of person your father is! The skunk!"

Ozer got frightened. "I won't take anybody to my father! I'll take my customers anywhere you say."

Osher looked Ozer up and down.

"Yes," he said, "if you hand over to us all the money you get."

Ozer agreed.

"Give it to Godel!" Berke ordered. "His mother is a sick woman. His father isn't working. There are a lot of mouths to feed. And the only breadwinner is his sister Reisel. She's a good girl! She doesn't go with the German soldiers, like the others. And you, Godel, you must share with Abish. His people are really starving.

"Another thing—none of you is to take any customers to Shlomo's whore house. His wife thinks she can fool us! After I had been bringing her customers all last week she tried to pay me off yesterday with just enough for a shot of brandy and a quarter goose. That finishes her! There are plenty of other places where we can take our customers. There are new young girls there every day. From the finest Jewish homes!"

Ozer began to show off: "You know Reb Henoch's wife," he bragged. "Sure as I'm alive, after I had brought her an officer, she said to me—'Would you rather

have money, or'—I couldn't make out what she meant at first, but she undid her
dress, and showed me.... I swear!"

"Well?"

"It was my first time."

"How old are you?" Godel asked.

"Sixteen."

"That's a lie!" said Yoske. "He's much younger."

Berke cut the discussion short.

"It's worth knowing! But be careful, boys! Those women can give you a disease.
They don't go to the doctor."

One of the new occupations was keeping cafés and restaurants, where the
German soldiers came for "a bit of amusement." They had tea with rum, coffee
with cream, good German cognac, and "a nice girl" to go with it.

The place was also frequented by the smugglers, the go-betweens, and the
"leaders."

The most famous café was Mirel's. She also had the Exchange there. Her café
and restaurant was in a huge building, with a great drive-in courtyard, which took
the biggest carts that could travel for miles along the high roads. The older people
remembered when the building had been a brewery. It had belonged to the local
big landowner, who had leased it to a Jew who also had an inn there.

The house stood at the crossroad where several highways met. It had escaped
damage in the war, and Mirel had rented it. The entrance was through a big glass
door in front, to which three small flights of stairs led up. The windows looked out
on the great high road on one side and the market square on the other.

There was an enormous buffet at the far end of the large room, with two doors
behind it, right and left. One led to Mirel's private rooms, including the room she
had set aside for her parents; the other led to the kitchen. It was a huge kitchen
with twelve stoves; big iron pots and pans and kettles boiled all the time. The ovens
were full of chickens, geese, ducks roasting, and all kinds of meats, beef, veal,
mutton. The stoves were never allowed to go out. The ovens never went cold. Mirel
bought no bread or cakes—she did all her own baking. She had cooks and maids,
but she supervised everything.

The buffet was loaded with good things that excited the appetite—poppy-seed
cake, flans and tarts and pies, bagels and rolls, salt herring and pickled herring,
sardines and smoked salmon, olives, and every kind of fish, gefilt and sweet and
sour and fried, all sorts of meats, stuffed tripe, stuffed necks, livers, and calves'
brains, calves'-foot jellies, and all varieties of sausage.

There were tables and chairs, mostly ranged against the walls. And the main
door kept opening and shutting the whole time, as customers came and went. The
place was packed with smugglers, dealers, and all sorts of people. There was a
continuous babble of talk. The smoke from bad tobacco got into your eyes. The
smell of alcohol mingled with the smell of food and of sweaty bodies and sweaty
clothes.

Several pretty waitresses and Mirel's sister Rabeh were busy serving at the tables. Mirel herself served too. She was the brains and the heart and soul of the place, not only of her café and her restaurant, but of everything that went on there. She bought and sold anything that was going—tobacco, cloth, leather, gold, anything. She often fixed the prices not only for the different kinds of goods, but also how much to pay the gendarmes and the militia for letting the goods through, and how much to pay the frontier guards on the way, and the agents who brought the business, the go-betweens, the contact men, and decided who should be admitted to the trade and to any particular deal, and who shouldn't. Because there were hundreds of people in it, the buyers often resold the goods without even having set eyes on them. There were agents acting for agents and go-betweens who represented bigger go-betweens. Mirel had her finger in every pie. She knew her way about in all these deals. And she was not afraid of speaking her mind. She had no fear of being denounced to the authorities. She knew who was likely to turn informer, and to whom the informer would go. She felt quite capable of dealing with them all. She settled disputes between the different parties. And she tried to prevent anyone from being fleeced.

"That will be enough!" she said. "You mustn't charge more. There's a lot of poverty in this town."

Everybody loved Mirel; everybody accepted her ruling.

She handled things like an expert. She was quick on the uptake. She would take several orders together, and bring everybody what they had asked for. She generally served only the big shots, letting the waitresses serve the others. But she made out all the bills and took the money for all of them. She didn't trust that even to her sister.

Her husband stood behind the buffet, in a long black caftan, with a cloth cap on his head, busy and perspiring, taking money from his wife and from the customers eating and drinking at the buffet. He kept pulling out the big till crammed full of money, paper and coins, Germans marks, two- and three-mark pieces, half marks and quarter marks, ten pfennig pieces, and five pfennig pieces, two pfennigs, and ones.

His cap was pushed back on his head, not so much because he was perspiring as to show what a fine forehead he had. His caftan was unbuttoned because he wanted everybody to see how long and thick his gold watch-chain was, stretching across his fat stomach.

The carters and cabbies and their like called him a fool and a ninny. But he took no notice of them. He considered himself a cut above them. And he consoled himself with the thought—"Never mind! They're customers! So long as they bring their money here!"

But he was also hard of hearing, and didn't always hear what they said about him.

He was very fond of his wife, Mirel. He worshiped her. And she thought him a handsome man, and said he was lovely.

Mirel made all her calculations in her head, with never a mistake to her loss. She was pleasant and coquettish, but not to everybody—only to the gendarmes. She was still a young woman, extremely good looking and full of vivacity, though she had a son of Chedar age and a little girl, and was now pregnant with her third.

The little girl was always getting under her mother's feet. Then the mother would catch the child up against her breast and hug her and call her darling, and kiss her chubby cheeks and drink in the smell of her body. "Lovelier than roses and lilies," she cried rapturously.

The regular customers, especially the carters and cabbies, loved pinching the baby's cheeks. Itzik, one of the cabbies, tickled her tummy and guffawed: "You don't look a bit like your father!"

The people who frequented the café had their own separate groups, people with the same background, and according to their past or present status. In the old days the criterion had largely been Torah learning and religious devoutness. Now it was money.

At one table sat Reb Henoch Malach, a fine old-type Jew, with a long beard and a high forehead. He wore a long silk caftan and a silk hat. He was considered a scholar, but not everybody was so sure about his religious observance. Some people defended him, saying that he was a Cabbalist. But others accused him of reading heretical books, like those of Moses Mendelssohn and of Nachman Krochmal. Reb Henoch had never been a rich man. He traded in anything and everything. He could get you whatever you wanted. He had no shop, and he kept no goods at home. But if you told him you wanted this or the other he got it for you, from some precious antique to the most ordinary article of common use. That had been his way of old, and that was his way now.

Around him crowded a lot of other Jews who wanted to be in his set; they included Mechel Politician, the go-between.

Reb Henoch was holding forth, talking about the war in phrases filled with mysteries and double meanings.

"The Russians won't win," he said. "Why not?" winding his long beard round his left hand. "I'll tell you. The Russian is like a bear. But his emblem is a two-headed eagle."

He smiled: "What put the idea of the eagle into his head? Because he has under his rule perhaps half the Jewish people, which is likened to an eagle. But the bear didn't let the eagle take him on his wings and soar with him in the heights. Instead, he persecuted the eagle. Therefore he will lose the war.

"As for the Prussian, though he looks now like having almost won the war, having occupied so many countries, he too will lose. Why?"

Reb Henoch unwound his beard, and stared into the distance:

"The German emblem is a one-headed eagle. The normal way. Jews have their rights in Germany. They can rise high in the State. There is great learning and wisdom there. But the eagle is arrogant, therefore he must fall in his flight. England will win, because England is destined for a mission in this present war, a mission assigned by heaven."

The Jews at his table were transported:

"Assigned by heaven? What is that mission?"

Reb Henoch pondered. Then he answered:

"It is too soon to reveal the mystery." And he went on to speak of the end of days, of Messiah. He quoted the Zohar, he brought in Gematriah; he calculated figures, and he concluded that the time was no longer distant.

"But first," he said, "there will be terrible troubles, such as we can't possibly imagine now, especially for Jews."

He wound his beard around his left hand again, and spoke very quiety, as if to himself alone:

"The blood in a war means that the accumulated injustice in the world is so great that it has reached to heaven. Most of those who fall are not themselves guilty, but neither are they altogether guiltless. For we are all—we too—witnesses of wrongs and injustices. And we did nothing to help the wronged and the suffering. Indeed, we helped those who wronged and oppressed them. But the blood of the war can't wash away all these great sins. Therefore a second war will come, a greater war than this, the war of God and Magog. And then . . ."

Reb Henoch got up, and walked out.

At another table sat Shimmele Lotterinek, also a respected Jew in the town, but in quite a different way from Reb Henoch. He was tall, and his beard was red, seeming to consist of five parts—two under his earlocks, two lower down, and one over his chin. Before the war he had sold lottery tickets, which gave him his name. He used to go to every house in town, and almost everybody bought a ticket. The rich couldn't refuse, and the poor believed him when he said they were sure to win. Now he frequented the café like everybody else, bought and sold any kind of goods for smuggling, goods about which he didn't know anything and which he never even saw. Around him sat or stood other Jews like himself, decent, religious Jews, who were not overscrupulous about what one may or may not do, what is good and what is ugly in making money.

What is a man to do? One must earn a living!

That one phrase was supposed to answer all questions, and to quiet one's conscience.

Shimmele was not talking politics, and he was not talking about Messianic times. He was talking about what was happening around them, in their town. He was talking about Bernfel's youngest daughter, and the Christian bricklayer she went out with; he was talking about the Socialists in the town, and about Reb Yossel's only daughter.

"He's got it coming to him. They say that daughter of his will turn Christian and marry the Commandant. Not now. When the war is over."

"Reb Yossel Fuksman is a religious Jew. He's getting richer every day. Through his daughter. But in the end he'll find himself left only with the money."

"And with a broken heart," somebody at the table chimed in.

"It's not as simple as that," said the Lotterinek. "I've heard another story. That the girl is ill."

Somebody whispered, "Be careful! Her brother has just come in!"

Shimmele and the rest looked around. There at a table sat Reb Yossel Fuksman's son, the bookkeeper from Warsaw, with Itzik the cabby's son, with Abraham the tailor's son, and a few others, girls too, the Socialists of the town. They were talking and drinking beer.

Some of the thieves' gang, among them Motte Katz and Lemel Gaver, were standing at the buffet. They too had lost their old occupation and taken to smuggling. They were drinking brandy with the carters, including old Itzik, who would be driving that night to Warsaw.

There were several Christians, too, in that crowd of smugglers, young men and girls, and middle-aged men and women.

They were drinking, and had lost all count of how much they had been drinking. By nightfall the café had emptied. But then the German soldiers arrived.

The sun was setting. Its last rays were mirrored in the gilded brass cross on the dome of the church in the market, and lit a flame in the windows of those houses still standing undamaged.

In the small narrow streets where the Jewish poor lived, and the devastation of the war had not been covered up yet, it was already dark. The smugglers, who mostly lived in that quarter, were just starting their day, like bats. And that is what people called them, in fact.

The boys who led the German soldiers to the places where they could buy ham and sausage and women were going home now. Their day was finished. On their way they met Reb Isser, who had been to see the scribe, and was now going to the Beth Hamedrash for Mincha-Maariv. They thought they would have some fun with him. They crowded round him, flinging questions at him:

"Where do you live? How do you get your food? You don't do anything for a living. Whom do you sleep with at night? The Queen of Sheba?"

Reb Isser smiled his usual childlike smile, which people in the town took as a sign of senility. He smiled at these young louts because it wasn't the first time they had bombarded him like this, and he found that the best way to get rid of them was to smile and pretend that he was feeble-minded. Otherwise they might even throw stones at him. Older people passing by would look the other way. Some might even stop to enjoy the scene. There had been times when they had joined in and helped to persecute him. Rarely had anyone ever come to his help. The best way was to humor them.

"Where do I live? In God's world."

"God's world?" they jeered. "God's world is in heaven!"

"No," said Reb Isser, "God's world is everywhere."

"Go on with you! Everywhere, indeed! And where do you get your food?"

"Kind people give me food. I don't need much. A piece of bread, a potato. And if nobody gives me anything, I fast that day. It doesn't hurt. It'll only be less for the worms and more for the soul."

"Why don't you do something?" one of the gang called out. "Why don't you do what everybody else is doing? Why aren't you like the rest of us? Why must you be different, a saint, a holy man?"

"The boy is right! Absolutely right! Why isn't he like the rest of us?" chimed in some of the men and women standing at their doors, waiting till it was quite dark to go out with their smugglers' packs.

The boys, encouraged by it, took up the cry:

"Whom do you sleep with at night? The Queen of Sheba?"

"He sleeps with a cow!" one of the gang shouted, and all the others took up the cry: "He sleeps with a cow! Everybody knows that! Wasn't he caught one night kissing the cow in the middle of the marketplace? A man who does that deserves to be stoned! Let's stone him!"

Reb Isser recalled that night, the cow, and Jacob, and the barking dogs, and he thought to himself: "They are all God's creatures!"

He felt sorry for the hooligans, and smiled at them benevolently. "Poor, ragged little boys!" But at the same time he was afraid of them.

"Have you gone back to Chedar yet?" he asked them. "Has the Chedar reopened? We shall be saying the Song of Songs soon. Look, the sun is almost gone down. There was a lot of sunshine today. Summer'll soon be here."

He began to chant with the melody of the Song of Songs: "Lo, the winter is past. The rain is over and gone. The flowers appear on the earth. The time of singing is come. And the voice of the turtle is heard in our land."

At that moment a stone hit Reb Isser in the back and he staggered. More stones flew at him. But luckily for him, Reb Henoch Malach—also on his way to the Beth Hamedrash for Mincha-Maariv—passed then, and came rushing up to save Reb Isser. The other people in the doorways now started shouting at the hooligans to clear off, and Reb Isser continued on his way to the Beth Hamedrash with Reb Henoch. He had escaped, with only a few stones.

By now night had fallen. Out of the broken-down shacks came figures, men bearded and beardless, heads sunk in their collars, hats pulled down over their faces, and women and girls wrapped in big shawls to hide their faces. Singly and in pairs they slunk along against the walls, slowly at first, then suddenly quickening their pace till they disappeared into the night with their packs and sacks and baskets.

11

A Jolly Journey

Spring had already sent out its advance guards to combat the winter. The smugglers, traveling in their carts late at night, far from any settlement, felt and saw the spring approaching. They couldn't sleep, despite the fact that they were tired and exhausted and the rolling of the vehicles should have lulled them. They kept closing their eyes, then jolting back into wakefulness. The breath of spring, though it was still chill, kept the young people awake. They kept yawning, rubbing their eyes, sitting up and staring at the sky and at the fields stretching in front of them. Most of them kept their eyes and hands also on their packs, so that someone else's hands shouldn't get hold of them.

Five carts followed one behind the other. At first everybody was silent; nobody opened his mouth. Then they all started chattering, the older folk loudly, the younger ones, the boys and girls sitting together in couples, whispering and laughing.

There were three rows of seats in Itzik's cart, three people in a row, and two more in front, where Itzik himself sat, driving. His daughter Bluma sat in the middle row, between David and a middle-aged woman. Her brother Abraham was in the row behind them, with a Christian young woman and a Jew of about fifty on either side of him. Facing Bluma, between two religious young Jews whose once-rich parents-in-law couldn't go on giving them their promised keep, sat a young Christian named Stash, who had once worked in a slaughter yard killing pigs, and had now taken to smuggling.

David always tried to sit next to Bluma on these smuggling expeditions.

"Whom should I travel with and give him my fare if not your father?" he had said to her the first time. She had smiled, but she had wanted him to tell her openly that he loved her. She was hungering to hear him say those words.

"You don't have to consider my father," she had said. "He's not short of fares. He could fill the cart without you."

David spoke to Bluma in the way all lovers do. He behaved like a cavalier to his lady. He spoke of the moon and the stars, about the spring that was coming, and about their sacred Socialist ideal, and about his plan—which was to make money now, as long as it was possible. He would then rent a fine house, buy good furniture, and start a workshop, with several people working for him. That wouldn't stop his being a Socialist; on the contrary, it would help him with better means to fight for Socialism.

He spoke on and on, but he never said what she wanted to hear. His body ached for her, he wanted to embrace and kiss her, but he didn't dare; it seemed disloyal to him to behave like that to a comrade whom he respected as a comrade. He wasn't just a tailor's lad to lay his paws on a girl.

Bluma sang Polish songs and dance tunes, quietly, softly, humming with closed lips.

Stash thought himself lucky to sit there, facing the pretty young Jewess. He wore a knee-length fur coat. Without much hesitation he drew the ends of his fur coat over Bluma's knees and touched her knees under it with his.

"You must be cold," he said. "It would be a pity to let a pretty girl like you freeze."

Bluma laughed, and went on singing, looking yearningly up to the sky, to the moon and the stars.

Stash tingled with the warmth of her, and pressed his knees against hers, till finally he opened out his legs and drew hers in between them. He was thinking of starting to explore with his hands, but he checked himself when he saw David eyeing him. Was he perhaps her sweetheart, or even her husband? No, he couldn't be, or the girl would have withdrawn her knees, and shown some anger. His hands were itching. He couldn't sit still. He wanted to touch the Jewess's knees with his hands.

He hit on an idea. He took off his fur coat, and with a bow to Bluma, said:

"I hope the young lady will not object to keeping herself warm under my coat."

He spread the coat carefully over Bluma's legs, and over his own legs, up to her breast, and up to his, and immediately their hands met under the coat.

Bluma saw that he was a handsome young man. He had such lovely blue eyes. And she started humming a Polish love song.

David saw what was going on and was burning up with jealousy. Yet it only made Bluma even more attractive to him. He put his arm around her waist. But he was still burning with jealousy.

There were two carts ahead of Itzik's in the caravan, and two following behind. A German gendarme with a rifle sat in the first cart, and another in the last cart. They were paid, of course, to act as the armed escort of the party. It was no guarantee though that the smugglers would not be stopped by the frontier guard.

The gendarme in the first cart had seen Bluma traveling with the party in the third cart, and he wanted her. In the end he jumped down from his own cart while it was in motion, ran back, and jumped onto the third cart. There he saw how Bluma was placed, and he jumped down again and onto the fourth cart.

At the same time the gendarme in the fifth cart jumped down, and he too came onto the third cart. So did several other young men, including the two thieves, Motte Katz and Lemel Gaver.

Not that they hadn't any young women in their own carts who wouldn't object to a kiss or a hug. They were more worried, those young women, about keeping an eye on their packs and baskets. They would lose much more if these were stolen. Motte and Lemel had simply tired of the same girls and young women all the time; they wanted a change.

Most of the people in the carts were laughing and giggling and singing. Only the few religious Jews went through a terrible time, sitting there and seeing such shameless goings-on.

Tzippe, the young widow who had been raped several times by soldiers and cossacks on the roads during her flight from the town, sat in the fifth cart. She wouldn't allow any man near her, except one or the other of the two German gendarmes. She didn't laugh or giggle or squeal like the other women. And because she was sitting with a gendarme nobody in the cart dared to speak a word against her.

The second German gendarme who had jumped onto Itzik's cart thought up a trick to get hold of Bluma. He yelled an order to Itzik: "Faster! Gallop!"

That was interpreted to mean that he had caught sight of a frontier guard behind a tree. He even fired a shot in the air to make it seem real. All five carts set off at a gallop.

Then the gendarme went and stood between Bluma and Stash. His legs jostled Stash's knees away from Bluma's. Stash tried resisting, but the German gendarme barked at him: "Polish swine!"

The passengers were shaken up and down and from side to side as the cart rushed along; they tumbled over each other, held on to each other. The German gendarme fell into Bluma's lap, and he stayed there. The girls and young women in all the five carts squealed and giggled and laughed, because the young men kept falling on top of them.

"Turn left, to the woods," the gendarme ordered Itzik, signaling also to the leading cart.

All the carts stopped in the woods.

The drivers climbed down from their carts. They welcomed the chance to stretch their legs. Also the horses needed the rest. Their flanks were runnings with sweat and heaving like the bellows in a blacksmith's forge. The drivers wiped them down with sacks. Then they fed the horses, hanging bags of oats and chaff over their heads.

Most of the passengers jumped or crawled down from the carts. But some of the older men and women decided to stay where they were, including the widow and the elderly Jew in Itzik's cart. The younger people were excited, worked up by the gallop at which they had been driven, and glad to have escaped what they thought would have been a hold-up by the frontier guards.

They were also beginning to feel hungry, and they decided to have a picnic in the woods. One of the girls spread her big shawl on the ground, and they all brought out their food and put it down on the shawl, squatting around it in a circle. Some of the young men produced bottles of brandy from their pockets, knocked the corks out, and set them down on the shawl. The two gendarmes unfixed their bayonets to use them as knives for cutting up the loaves of bread and the big sausages. The gendarmes took the first drinks, and then passed the bottles around. Everybody ate hungrily, leaving not a crumb. Then they sat and chattered, laughed and told stories. The girls and the women giggled and squealed.

Somebody said it was cold. "Well, it isn't summer yet," some of the others agreed. Then somebody suggested making a bonfire. They all started collecting wood for the fire, and some couples got lost in the woods. Stash took hold of Bluma's arm and tried to drag her along with him. She resisted. She reminded him that her father and her brother were there. They would miss her and come looking for her. But Stash wouldn't let go. He kept kissing her and pressing her against himself. Then David arrived, just the way Bluma would have wished. She stretched out her arms to him to help her. He took hold of her and drew her toward him. Stash wasn't going to let David get away with that. He raised his fist and punched David in the jaw. David reeled. Stash's blood was up. He was going to jump on David and kick the guts out of him when someone gripped him from behind by the scruff of the neck and flung him down on the ground. Stash sprang up, a knife drawn from his boot in his hand.

It was the German gendarme who had knocked him down. "Drop that knife!" he ordered.

Stash didn't understand German, but he understood the tone of the gendarme's command, and dropped the knife.

Most of the people were still sitting around the bonfire, talking and flirting. A girl's blond head rested on a masculine shoulder. Another girl was singing a sad, wistful, Polish song. Then one of the girls started a gay, rollicking folksong.

So the mood kept changing, sad to gay, till finally the gay mood prevailed, and groups jumped up from the ground and started dancing around the bonfire.

A few religious Jews, with the exception of the elderly man who stayed with the widow, and including the two religious young men, withdrew from this profligate scene to say the Maariv prayers. They would have loved to have had a congregational service, but there weren't enough for a minyan.

So they prayed separately, quietly pouring out their hearts to Him who lives eternally and is everywhere whenever one turns to Him. They wept and cried to Him because of the evil that had come upon them so that they had to engage in this dirty business for their livelihood, and had to sit together with such dissolute company and keep their mouths shut.

They moistened their hands in the wet grass, and munched their dry bread, and said grace after food, lingering over the words "For all this, O Lord our God, we thank and bless Thee." With broken hearts they repeated "And rebuild Jerusalem, the holy city, speedily, in our days."

They shook their heads when they came to "May God grant us an honorable livelihood." Then they conversed quietly among themselves till they were told to get back in the carts.

12

Deborah Is Disillusioned

Not all the journeys were such fun. Only the braggarts told everyone that they were making money out of smuggling. The others, especially those who did make money out of it (some over a long period and some only for a short while), played it down. Their idea was that the fewer the smugglers, the better. But people couldn't help seeing that they were prospering, that they were buying up houses—broken-down houses, which they restored, and houses that had escaped serious damage—and sites where the houses had been completely destroyed, smashed, or burned down, and even half-ruins, which they patched up a bit and let to poor people—often people who had previously been well-off but were now impoverished.

There were many among the newcomers to the ranks of the smugglers who had held off as long as they could before finally deciding to engage in this dirty business, as they themselves called it. Their feeling was that smuggling degraded them to the level of common thieves, like Motte Katz and Lemel Gaver, as did mixing with all that scum. Yet they couldn't resist the temptation, things being so bad, of trying to make some sort of a living.

More people kept going into smuggling, but many who had taken it up gave it up after a while, because they found that instead of making money at it they lost everything. But the number of smugglers didn't diminish. Others soon took their places. It wouldn't have been far off the mark to say, as people did say, "the whole town is in the smuggling business."

It was indeed the main occupation, except for those few artisans and workmen who had employment and were earning their bread by the sweat of their brow. But the fact was that even these benefited indirectly as a result of the smuggling, because without the smuggling nobody would have had any money to pay for their work.

The Commandant gave orders that those who were caught smuggling should be heavily punished. He put more guards on the roads. It only meant that the smugglers had to pay more money in bribes, for there were more guards to be bribed and more informers to be paid hush money. It made no difference to the smuggling.

More cafés and restaurants opened and more prostitutes made their appearance. More women and girls took up the trade. There seemed to be no border line any longer between decency and vice. People got used to what was going on and just shrugged their shoulders. "The world's turned upside down," they said.

The world had indeed turned upside down. People who had been rich were now poor, and people who had been poor were now rich, and were throwing their weight about, much more than the others had done in the days of their wealth. For those others had dignity, and decency, and restraint. These newly rich were loud and noisy and immodest with their big parties and their lavish displays of food and drink.

It was the last year of the German occupation of Poland. There was little food for the population, because most of it was sent to Germany, requisitioned for the German army, in return for worthless money or no money at all. It brought scarcity and rising prices. Money lost all value. There was famine. People starved. Typhus broke out. And then came the Spanish flu and other epidemics, carrying off thousands upon thousands of victims. There was not enough medical help, or rather few could afford to pay the doctor and the chemist, who took advantage of the opportunity. Even so, the doctor, the chemist, and the medical treatment could do very little to stop the epidemics, It was like trying to stop malaria at an infested swamp by using mosquito nets.

David Joel's Malka, Kalman's Rachel, and several other dedicated women, and some men too, did all they could—much more than they could. They took bread and clothing to the poor, and fuel, and whatever they could. They sat up all night with the sick. But it was like a drop in the ocean.

Things grew desperate. The worst of it was that almost everybody had become infected with a mad lust for pleasure. On top of the physical epidemics there was a moral epidemic—cardplaying, dancing, dissolute revelry. Even the poorest sat up through the night playing cards for small stakes, or for no money at all, just to satisfy the gambling lust. They went dancing in ragged clothing and torn shoes. It was like a drug to most of them, to drown their sorrows and forget their troubles. With others it was a step farther down in the corruption and decay that had set in with the war.

There were big balls and big gambling parties at Bernfel's, in the mansions of the landowners and the gentry outside the town, and in the big houses of the rich Christians who lived in the green belt.

It was winter. A big ball was being arranged at the Krzewicki's. All the best people had been invited, even the Commandant himself. Deborah, Reb Yossel Fuksman's only daughter, or Diana, as the Commandant called her, was expecting to be there. Her parents wanted her to go. It wasn't only that they had grown rich, and wanted their child, if not themselves, to be accepted in the best society; there was also a feeling of guilt because of what they had made of their child.

Deborah hadn't been looking well. It frightened her mother. What was wrong with the girl? Was it T.B.? Her own sister had got galloping consumption and had died so quickly. She told her husband what she feared. "Nonsense!" he said. "The girl doesn't even have a cough."

But it had scared him. He called in the doctor. Then both parents went to Warsaw with Deborah to see a specialist. He said there was nothing wrong with her lungs. Yet Deborah wasted away. The mother watched her anxiously. She had been feeling very unhappy about those visits to the Commandant, from which her daughter had come back first with one and then with more concessions for her father. It changed the girl completely. She had grown more sophisticated, she had developed a sense of dress, she had taken to wearing jewels and finery.

Why not? the mother had thought to herself at first. Why shouldn't a young girl dress well, why shouldn't she want to wear nice clothes? She was a good-looking girl, and good clothes helped her looks. It was only right that a young woman should make the best of herself.

Then she started worrying because Deborah was getting fat. She wondered if— No! She had no right to think such things of Deborah.

All the same, she spoke to her husband. "You know, Yossel," she said, "we ought to be thinking of getting our Deborah married."

But when Deborah's face grew thinner and paler, and the fresh pink of her cheeks drained away like wine from a cracked pitcher, the parents got really frightened.

"What is wrong, my child? What has happened?"

"Nothing, mother! Nothing has happened!"

"Tell me, dear. I'm your mother. You can trust me."

Deborah looked straight at her mother, with so much grief and fear and accusation in her eyes that the mother had to turn her face away.

But Deborah did not say what was wrong. Deborah said nothing at all. She hardly spoke a word now at home—as though her tongue had gone, together with her youthful happiness.

The parents were in despair. They knew very well what was wrong with their daughter, but they were afraid to say so, to admit it, even to each other. But in the end it had to come: "She's in love!"

Only Yossel and his wife were not altogether agreed about it. The mother said she didn't believe that Deborah was in love with the Commandant. It was the Commandant who was in love with Deborah, and the child was worrying herself to death, because she didn't know what to do about it.

"She doesn't want to hurt us," she said to her husband. "She's making herself ill over it. I must tell her not to take it so seriously. These are not normal times. This is war. The Commandant is here to represent a conquering army. We are all his captives. We can't do a thing against him."

"No!" Reb Yossel said, tugging at his beard. "It isn't that at all. The Commandant wouldn't do a thing like that. The Kaiser wouldn't appoint anybody to be his Commandant. A man who holds such a position wouldn't fall in love with a young girl who doesn't even know his language, and has a completely different upbringing. He needs someone from his own background to be his wife. For all we know, he has a wife in Germany. And children. Deborah could easily be his daughter. No, a man in his position wouldn't play fast and loose with a young girl like Deborah. Besides, he's a Christian!"

"So what?" said his wife.

"So what? He wouldn't fall in love with a Jewish girl! That's why I think—"

"That Deborah is in love with him?"

"Nonsense!"

But Brocha felt in her heart that her husband was right. They decided, both of them, to speak to their son Reuben, who was educated in the modern way, and get him to find out from his sister what was going on. But Reuben already knew that his sister was in love with the German Commandant. He didn't blame her. He didn't blame his parents, either. He threw all the blame on the Commandant. And he wanted to make him pay for it. That brought Reuben to the Socialists.

Even when she was getting ready for the ball at Pan Krzewicki's Deborah still didn't know if her lover, Major Richard von Wolfensthal, the Commandant of the town, wanted her to go to the ball with him. He had once mentioned the ball to her in the midst of a lot of endearments, thinking to put her in a more cheerful mood, because she had been coming to him lately looking very sad and dispirited. His mention of the ball had made her a little happier. She had come back home chattering gaily about the ball to which she had been invited. Her mother was so delighted to see the girl happy again that she had hugged and kissed her.

"It's going to be a grand ball," Deborah had told her. "The best people will be there. I am so happy!"

The mother was happy for her child's sake.

"We must get you the right clothes for the ball, Deborah," she said—a new dress, and dancing shoes, and a new coat. I want you to look your best among all those fine ladies and gentlemen."

"Yes, mother! It's going to be a masked ball. A New Year's ball!"

"A masked ball? Then you will have to have fancy dress. We can't get that here. We'll have to go to Warsaw. We'll go to one of the big stores in Warsaw. I'll tell you what! We'll go to the Bernfels, and talk to Miss Bella or Miss Helena, and see what they say. They are sure to be going to the ball themselves!"

"No, they haven't been invited, mother!"

"Then we'll go to Warsaw ourselves. They'll advise us there."

Brocha took Deborah to Warsaw the same week. She felt as happy about it as if she were buying Deborah's wedding outfit. But Deborah's mind was full of doubts. Had he really invited her to the ball? He hadn't said so. He had only mentioned that there was going to be this ball. He hadn't said that he wanted her to go there with him. She wasn't so sure now. He was always promising to do things that he never did. He had said that he would take her to Warsaw, and to Berlin. He had said that he would become a Jew to marry her. Then he had told her it wouldn't be necessary, because he was already a Jew—his grandfather had been a Jew. His mother was a born Jewess. And that made him a Jew.

Mother and daughter returned from Warsaw with a huge case of clothes for Deborah. Brocha had bought the material for the dresses and the coats from Menassah Schwartz, the big cloth merchant in the Nalewki, and she had got them made up by one of the best ladies' tailors in Warsaw.

It was like a wedding trousseau. The ball dress and the fancy ball dress. And lingerie of the finest silk, so soft and clinging that you hardly felt it in your hand.

Corsets and brassieres and gloves and perfumes and jewelry. Her mother had spared no money to make Deborah attractive and desirable, to make her the belle of the ball.

She also spent a lot of money on herself, and she bought a great many gifts for her husband, Reb Yossel Fuksman.

Unpacking that huge case was a long, slow process. Mother and daughter brought out article after article, each separately, held it up to the light, examined it, admired it, fondled it, laid it first against one cheek and then the other to feel how soft it was. Then they tried the things on, to see how beautifully they fitted.

Every time Deborah tried on a garment or an undergarment her mother cried delightedly:

"Wonderful! You look like a princess! You're the most beautiful girl in Poland! With your looks and the big dowry your father means to give you, you should make a marvelous match. Not Bernfel's son, Baruch. Not if Bernfel himself comes to ask on bended knee! No! You will marry a young man from Warsaw, a Rabbi's son, or a doctor!"

She led Deborah to the big mirror: "Look at yourself, my child, how beautiful you are!"

Each day mother and daughter brought out all the new dresses and other clothes from the wardrobe, and feasted their eyes on them.

The house had been largely rebuilt and more rooms added; it was painted and done up, and with the new furniture they had bought it looked like a mansion. Brocha was very proud of her home.

But as the night of the ball came nearer, Deborah grew desperate, because the Commandant had not said a word yet to her about her coming to the ball. True, he had been very attentive to her again recently, especially since her return from Warsaw. He called her his "Dear Diana." He had kissed her hand. But though she had hinted several times about the ball, it was as though he hadn't heard.

Brocha saw that her daughter was unhappy, and tried to comfort her:

"It will be all right, my dear. He takes it for granted that you're going. He knows you went to Warsaw specially to buy the clothes for the ball. He gave you the permit himself so that we could both go by train to Warsaw. You told him what lovely things you had bought in Warsaw. So he considers it settled. Look, Deborah, if you really want to know, put on one of your ball dresses, the red silk, or the lilac-colored velvet, with a coat over it, and go immediately after dark to show it to him. Ask him how he likes it for the ball."

But Deborah, with a heavy heart, said: "No!"

Brocha hit on another plan. She spoke to her husband:

"Next time you see Krzewicki, say that you would like him to invite Deborah to his ball. Why shouldn't he? If Bernfel and his daughters Panna Bella and Panna Helena are going, why shouldn't our Deborah go? She's much younger and more beautiful! She's a lovely girl!"

Reb Yossel Fuksman agreed that his wife was right. He went along to see Pan Krzewicki, who received him, as always, in his tiny office in his big mansion, and shook his hand vigorously.

Reb Yossel held his ivory-handled walking stick—without which he never went anywhere, especially when he went to see one of the big landowners—in his left hand, together with his hat. He wore a rich sable coat, which he had put on because he knew from experience that unless he was so impressively dressed, the maid would think it was only some poor Jew wanting a favor, and would leave him standing on the doorstep while she went to ask the master if she should admit him. But when he came in his fine fur coat she asked him into the hall, and said the master would see him at once.

Pan Krzewicki clapped Fuksman on the back:

"There's a great time coming, my friend! The Prussians and the Austrians are finished. They have been stopped at the Marne. That's the end of them! It's only on the Russian front they can still hold their ground, and that's because there's nobody there! The lousy Russians are running away. They've started fighting among themselves. They've got a Revolution on! And a jolly good job, too! Serves them right! They're paying for the sufferings they inflicted on us all these years! Let them kill each other! And then we'll go for them! Only we must get rid of the Prussians first! We'll chase them out of our country! Out of our Polish Fatherland! The dirty German swine! I tell you, Panie Yoske, we shall together chase them out of our Poland—the Jews and we! With sticks and with rifles. Then we'll settle accounts with the Russians! We'll drive them all the way back to Kiev and Odessa! We shall build a great Poland, stretching from the Oder and the Dnieper, and the sea at Danzig! *Jeszcze Polska nie zginela*! Poland is not lost! *Nie zginela*! And you Jews will live at peace with us in Poland! All together! In unity!"

After that Pan Krzewicki turned to the business Reb Yossel Fuksman had come to talk to him about. He twirled his Kaiser Wilhelm mustache, which many Poles had adopted since the German occupation in place of the old Polish heavy-drooping mustache, and said in a tone of regret:

"Sorry! There isn't much that I can sell. My estate is a small one. And Pan Silber was here yesterday. And Pan Buxbaum this morning. The occupation forces take most of what there is. You know that yourself, Pan Yoske. Pan Bernfel, who is the Commandant's right hand, the Imperial supplier, knows just how much there should be for the army. You can't fool him! If there is anything over, he pays a good price for it himself.

"Pan Zaremba, Pan Woykov, all the landowners around here won't do business with old believers like you, with Jews who wear your traditional Jewish dress. You know that as well as I do.

"But if you give me ten percent more, Pan Yoske, I think we might do business, after all." He winked. "Pan Bernfel wouldn't get a look in! I've bought up everything there is in all the estates round here. I've hidden it, so that nobody can get hold of it. I've bought up everything there is. Even from Gnilowski—my best friend, Jan. He won't give a thing to Leibush, not even though his daughter, Panna Helena—"

This was what Fuksman had been waiting for. He dropped the subject of business, and began to talk about the ball that Pan Krzewicki was giving.

Krzewicki guessed immediately what Fuksman was after.

"You have a lovely daughter, Panie Yoske," he said. "A very beautiful girl! She doesn't look like a Jewish girl, she doesn't look at all like our daughter. She's like a princess! Why don't you bring her over here some time? I've seen her about several times." He kissed his hand: "She's much more beautiful than Panna Helena, my friend Jan's ..."

"I hope the Commandant brings your daughter with him to the ball. We shall all be very happy to see her, my wife and I, and the guests too. We've invited the Commandant, of course, and every gentleman has been asked to bring his lady with him. We didn't invite any ladies separately. But I'll tell you what! Why don't you come to the Ball, Pan Yoske, and bring your daughter with you? I invite you both to the Ball!"

"Me?" Reb Yossel tried to laugh it off. "Me, with this beard!"

Pan Krzewicki put his arm affectionately around Reb Yossel's shoulder:

"You've got a fine beard, Panie Yoske, a fine long beard. And you wear ear-locks. You've a pious Jew, Rev Yoske, not like Leibush. I prefer Jews like you, Panie Yoske! My guests will like your beard and your earlocks.

"You know, I'm having a masked ball, Reb Yoske. Everybody will come dressed up. You come dressed up as a bear, Pan Yoske."

He drew his arm through the Jew's, and took him into the great hall, where the dancing was going to be. The walls were hung with tapestries and hunting trophies, pistols and rifles and horns, and the skins of bears and boars and stags that Krzewicki had shot. This room was his pride.

"You can wear this bearskin," he said to the Jew; "you can wear it for my ball. My grandfather ..."

Reb Yossel was fuming inside. He didn't dare release the angry outburst that was boiling up in him, but he couldn't keep altogether quiet.

"Yes," he broke in, "your grandfather used to make a Jew dress up in a bear-skin, and dance to amuse his guests and be beaten by them. That's what you want me to do! No, thank you!"

"God forbid!" cried Pan Krzewicki. "I only want you to dress up for the masked ball, Pan Fuksman, because all our other guests will be dressed up!"

It was the first time he had called the Jew by his surname.

"If you don't want to have your competitor Leibush here, I'll tell him not to come."

"No, thank you," Reb Yossel said. "I won't be coming to your ball."

It was the day before the ball. Deborah hadn't seen the Commandant for nearly a week. Every time she had come, the lieutenant who was his secretary had said that the Commandant was busy on official business, or he had been called away to some other town.

She had tried to believe that the secretary was telling her the truth. But there was a nagging fear at her heart that the Commandant had tired of her and didn't want to see her any more. She had suspicions about Krzewicki's eldest daughter, Panna Florentina. She had been jealous of many women since she had fallen in love with the Commandant; she had been jealous of every young woman she had seen with him, and several times she had reproached him about it. He had always laughed her suspicions away, and she had always believed him when he said that these young women were the wives or daughters of people he had to be nice to as the Commandant of the town. But she had not been able to get rid of her suspicions of Panna Florentina.

"I must see him today," she said to herself as she set out now on her way to the Commandant's office.

Again his secretary barred her way.

"I'm sorry; the Major is engaged on important business."

Deborah left, but she did not go far. She stopped in a doorway where she could see the office. And her suspicions were soon justified, for presently Panna Florentina came out of the office.

She went straight back to the Commandant's office, proud and angry, an outraged and deceived woman, going to tell her false lover what she thought of him. But before she got to the door her anger had gone.

"No!" she told herself. "There is nothing between Richard and Panna Florentina. She only came to make sure that he will be at her ball!"

Her jealousy melted completely when, ignoring the secretary who had jumped up to receive her, she walked straight into the Commandant's office and found him at his desk busy with his papers. He rose as soon as she entered, looking radiantly happy, as though he had been waiting for her. He kissed her hand like a young gallant.

"I am so glad you came, my dear!"

She at once forgave him everything. And she reproached herself for having had any suspicions about him. She smiled tenderly, her eyes shining with love. And it brimmed over into the Commandant's heart and soul. She enfolded him warmly, snugly in her love, so that there was spring in his heart, though it was winter and frost outside.

He led her to the lilac plush couch, and sat down with her. He had forgotten his wife in Germany. But only for a moment. Because suddenly she was there, standing accusingly before him, tall, majestic, proud, the daughter of Baron von Spitzberg, a cold, hard beauty.

The next moment, with Deborah's warm hand in his and her fingers twined in his, all thought of his wife went out of his mind. Deborah was warm and lovely, and she was utterly devoted to him.

He took off her Persian lamb coat. Deborah looked beautiful in her new gray silk and wool dress.

"New, isn't it? You brought that back from Warsaw?"

It was a lovely dress. It set off Deborah's figure. She seemed more beautiful to him now than when he had first seen her. She was indeed more beautiful. For her womanhood had ripened, so that she was more attractive now to a man than the innocent, inexperienced young girl of their first meeting.

Deborah had not chosen for this visit to her lover any of the dazzling dresses that her mother had selected in Warsaw. She wore no jewelry, no ornament. She had put on this simple gray dress, beautifully made and fitted, quiet and discreet.

The Commandant felt strongly attracted by this Jewish girl. Yet there were other hard thoughts clashing in his mind at the same time. And he spoke strange words, which frightened Deborah.

"What did you say? Did you say the Jews are a strange people?" she asked.

"I'm sorry, my dear. I didn't mean it."

But the next moment he was repeating it: "The Jews are a strange people. They are religious and pious, yet they send their wives and daughters ..."

Deborah was staring at him with fear in her eyes. His words bewildered her. Suddenly something went out of her, like a blazing fire that had been extinguished. She was now dead, gray ashes.

The Commandant realized what had happened, and he tried to pass it off with a joke.

"Why must Jewish girls take love so seriously? The Polish girls don't."

Deborah went white. The blood drained from her cheeks and lips. Her fingers trembled in his.

"Aren't you feeling well, my dear?"

"I'm all right! There's nothing wrong with me."

But she couldn't face him. She turned her eyes away.

She didn't speak for a while. Then the question that had brought her there came to her lips:

"Am I going to the ball with you?"

"I'm not going to the ball!"

With quick, hurrying steps Deborah walked out through the office where the lieutenant sat. But as soon as she reached the street her legs gave way. She stood there unable to move.

The sight of people passing, and people going in and out of the office, brought her to with a jerk. She didn't want anyone asking her what was wrong. She walked away, without any idea where she wanted to go.

She only knew that she did not want to go home now. She walked slowly along the great highway, feeling quite numb; she did not feel the intense frost that lashed her face and stung her ears until she finally had to become aware of it.

She walked along, thinking of her first meeting with the Commandant. How had she been dressed that time when she went to see him? She had worn a blue skirt and a white blouse. It had been a fine autumn day. She had met Chelia, Bernfel's daughter, on the road, and had wanted to stop and speak to her. But she lacked courage. She knew that Chelia had joined the Socialists.

The sound of sleighbells behind her broke into her thoughts. She leaped out of the way, though she had not been walking in the middle of the road but at the side, in the narrow trodden path. She was scared of the galloping horses. She stumbled, just saved herself from falling, but she went up to her knees in the snow, where it had not yet been trodden down. The sleigh rushed past, pelting her with snow from the runners. She caught a glimpse of the occupants—Helena Bernfel and her lover, the apothecary's son, the landowner Jan Gnilowski. They were sitting side by side with a heavy rug over their knees. It was strange, she thought, that at the moment when she was thinking of Bernfel's daughter Chelia, another daughter, Helena, had appeared.

The sleigh vanished in the distance. And Deborah's thoughts turned again to the ball at the Krzewicki's. She pictured the whole scene in her imagination. She had never been to a masquerade ball in her life. And she wouldn't be going now either, because the Commandant had spurned her. When Panna Florentina Krzewicka had been to see him, it must have been to arrange for her to be his partner at the ball.

She visualized them dancing together; and as they danced he bent down and kissed her. Then they went off together, arm in arm, and she could see them together on that same lilac couch that stood in his office.

The tears ran hot from her eyes, and froze on her cheeks. She didn't feel it. She saw only peacocks with their gorgeous tails spread, colors, colors! And she saw bright flowers in the background. Then white stripes on a gold background. Then blackness.

13

The Ball

While Deborah's imagination was painting vivid pictures of the coming ball at the Krzewickis', everybody at the Krzewickis', not only the servants, but Madame Krzewicka, the wife, and Florentina, the daughter, were busy with the preparations for the ball, and especially the great surprise that they were arranging for the Commandant. Jan Gnilowski had given them the idea, and Krzewicki had taken it up with enthusiasm.

"An excellent idea! We'll do it. But I have another idea, and we'll do that too. Only my idea is not for the Commandant, but something for ourselves, for us Poles, my friend! Something traditionally Polish."

"You'll never guess what it is," Krzewicki said. "And I'm not going to tell you."

Gnilowski suggested that it would need a lot of preparation, and wondered if he couldn't help. But Krzewicki assured him that no preparations were needed.

Gnilowski than made Krzewicki promise him that nobody except those actually taking part in the arrangements for his own surprise, in honor of the Commandant and the other German guests, should know what was going on. The idea was to produce a play, with himself in the chief role. He said the Commandant and the other German guests would appreciate it. The only thing that worried him was whether to play it in Polish or in German. He decided that it must be played in the original language, which was German. Practically all who would be coming to the ball knew German. They had learned it at school. They spoke it badly, with a heavy Polish accent and lots of grammatical errors. But they could follow it. And the grammatical mistakes wouldn't be noticed once the guests were warmed up with dancing and with lots of hot punch with plenty of rum in it, and with masks hiding their identity.

Panna Florentina Krzewicka was the first to hear the approaching sleigh bells bringing their first guests to the ball. She thought she could recognize whoever was

94

coming by the sound of the bells.

"That's Uncle Peter with Aunt Meda and Jadzuneczka and Danilka and Tilia. Two sleighs. And a third! A long way behind!"

Florentina was deliriously happy. She hugged and kissed her mother.

The whole big house had been decorated with chains and festoons of colored paper—all the rooms, and most of all the great hall, which would be the ballroom, the small wing that had been built onto the mansion, and the long corridor. There were dimmed lights everywhere. Every door stood wide open, and the family crest was blazoned over each door. Even the four marble pillars, two on each side of the front entrance, up the few steps laid with red carpet now, were entwined with colored paper. There were flaming torches there, casting their light on the bluish-white snow that showed up through the pitch-black night. Every now and then the silence was broken by a wolf dog howling, sometimes by a hungry wolf. But over the silence and over the howling the sound of sleigh bells kept approaching the house every few minutes.

There were all kinds of bells, thin, like the silver laughter of children, and strong and loud like happy youths and maidens singing, tenor voices and soprano and bass ringing out across the silence and the black night and the snow.

The two liveried manservants, with the family crest on their gleaming buttons, stood by the steps as the guests arrived. Each sleigh, as it drove up, was lit up by the torches that the passengers, laughing and chattering, held high over their heads. The sleigh stopped at the entrance, and each gentleman helped his lady to alight. Some, who were very much in love, or in particularly high spirits, picked up their lady and carried her up the steps. The flunkeys kept bowing and scraping.

All the guests arrived in fancy dress and masked. Only the servants were not in masquerade costume.

Presentations to the host and hostess were not made by name, but by the costume—"Hunter," "Turk," "Ape," "Apollo," "Maharajah."

The girls and young women had never been so gay, so seductive, so flirtatious, so recklessly abandoned. It was New Year's Eve, with its tradition of Saturnalia. But that wasn't the only or even the chief reason. It was much more because people already sensed the end of the war, and the coming of great events in Polish national life.

The men were bold and insistent, and the women were willing and acquiescent. A good many guests had arrived, already half drunk. And they found plenty more to drink. There was a huge table loaded with bottles of brandy and cognac, wines and liqueurs—help yourself! Servants circulated among the guests with trays of drinks.

The Commandant was there, but no one would have known him in the garb he had chosen—a Polish peasant in Masurian folk dress, with long drooping whiskers, and masked of course, if it hadn't been for the way he spoke when people approached him—a few detached words of Polish, never making a complete sentence, and though he tried to disguise his voice his speech gave him away.

Bernfel, dressed as a Maharajah, attracted much atention. He was resplendent in a long blue-silk robe with gold embroidery, white-silk turban, and flashing rings on all his fingers.

His daughters, Bella in Cracow folk costume and Helena in a sailor suit, had tremendous success with the German guests.

The priest came dressed as the devil, and flirted outrageously.

Everybody got a toy trumpet, squeaker, tin whistle, and streamers that could be thrown right across the room, to hit somebody you aimed at, unawares. Each guest was serenaded on arrival with a chorus of squeaks and toots and whistles from the toy instruments, and music from the band.

It was a rollicking crowd, everybody laughing and chattering, giggling and flirting. The band played, and couples were dancing polkas, waltzes and mazurkas.

A few minutes before midnight everything stopped. All glasses were filled with hot punch, and everybody stood, glass in hand, waiting for the church bells to strike twelve. Then they all shouted "Happy New Year!", drained the glasses, and crashed them down on the floor. Couples embraced and kissed.

After that they filed in pairs into the dining room, where the tables groaned under the weight of food and bottles of champagne in ice buckets. The flunkies served fast and dexterously. The masks of course were only half-masks, leaving the mouth free to eat and drink. An orchestra played light music.

When the coffee was handed round in beautiful porcelain cups the guests began to clamor for the promised surprise. Pan Gnilowski stood up and made the following announcement, half in German, half in Polish:

"Ladies and gentlemen, we are going to give you a performance from the Edda."

He explained that they had prepared, in honor of the Commandant and the other German guests, a performance from the old German sagas about the Teutonic god-heroes. "We are only amateurs," he added apologetically, and said there would be three acts. They were starting at once.

The guests found seats on the many cushions that had been scattered about the floor. There were no chairs. People said they preferred it like that. It was like a picnic.

Then someone banged a big brass tray and the curtain rose.

The scene was a dense forest, full of darkness and fear. On the left were mountains and a stream. In the foreground a cave, and Siegfried, with a helmet on his head that was only a big copper pot, and tiger skins on his body and loins, stood holding his broadsword. He looked very warriorlike and heroic. Skulking in the background was another, less heroic Teuton god, Reigin. He had a halberd in his hand and a rusty iron pot on his head, with a horse's tail running down from it. He too was wrapped in tiger skins.

To the right was a great mass of gold, with a dragon, who was really Fafnir, guarding it. He wore a crocodile skin, and on his human face Kaiser Wilhelm moustaches. As the dragon moved slowly toward Siegfried the ladies clung tightly to their escorts. Siegfried waited till the dragon was very near and then plunged his sword right through it. Most of the women screamed, and hid their faces on the men's shoulders. A lot of men cried: "Encore!" And the Commandant and the other Germans clapped.

As Siegfried stood there, having vanquished the dragon Fafnir, the dead dragon suddenly reared on his hind legs and thrust his Kaiser Wilhelm moustaches into

Siegfried's face. Siegfried and the prompter kept signaling to him that he was dead, and must lie still, but the dragon took no notice.

Then Reigin came forward, and when the dragon saw him, he cried out: "Reigin has betrayed me. He will betray you too." Then he lay down and was still.

Reigin saluted Siegfried in Roman fashion, grounded his halberd, and cried: "Hail, Siegfried! You have conquered the dragon! Fafnir is dead! You are the greatest hero on earth!"

As he spoke Reigin raised his head higher, and his rusty-pot helmet clattered down on the stage. The audience burst out laughing. The devil who was really the priest clasped his fair neighbor round the waist, and whispered to her: "You are bright, like the sun. I am all on fire with you!"

Gnilowski's father, the apothecary, who was dressed as a fireman, sat behind the priest, and overheard. He jumped up: "Fire!" he shouted. "Fire!"

He flung out his arms as though he were working a hose, squirting water. He was terribly drunk, and the people near him saw a puddle on the floor. Two men got hold of him and led him out of the room.

On the stage Reigin had drawn a dagger, knelt down by the dragon's body, and lifted out its heart. He held it up and drank the blood from it, then said to Siegfried: "Now I am going to sleep. Roast this heart for me over the fire. I'll eat it when I waken."

Some of the blood from the dragon's heart had dripped on Siegfried's face and mouth and tongue, and suddenly he could hear birds singing and understand what the birds were saying. He raised his sword to plunge it into Reigin's body, and cried: "Now I know who you are! Go to Hell! Join your brother!"

The audience clapped wildly when the curtain fell.

The most important Polish guests, including the priest dressed up as the devil, had assembled in one of the smaller rooms.

"Now we are all Poles together, thank God," Pan Krzewicki, the host, said. "I had to get away from those Prussians! I couldn't stand them any more! They are wild beasts, like their hero-gods thousands of years ago! Blood-drinkers! Swine!

"I've got a different sort of entertainment for you," he went on. "You'll enjoy it!"

He turned to Bernfel, whom he had brought with him, and handed him a bearskin: "Get into this, Maharajah! Please, Panie Leibush!"

Bernfel couldn't understand.

"Please, only for a bit of fun!" said Krzewicki. "We want to see you dance for us, for a minute or two. Your grandfather used to, in my grandfather's time. Wearing that same bearskin."

Bernfel said he wouldn't do it. But the priest and the ladies pressed him and pleaded with him, and he finally agreed.

Krzewicki held on to the bear's chain and prodded the bear with his stick. Everybody crowded round him, clapping their hands and laughing. The women giggled. And the bear, prodded by the stick, jumped about, danced, especially when Krzewicki laid the stick about his back and shoulders. The priest-devil got very excited, tore the chain and the stick out of Krzewicki's hands, and beat Bernfel mercilessly.

Bernfel flung himself on the floor and, finding himself near a lady dressed as an angel with wings, tried to hide under her dress. She screamed and ran out of the room. Bernfel tried the same trick with one of the other women, and in trying to escape she fell, and Bernfel fell on top of her, and a crowd of men who were trying to drag him off fell on top of him.

By the time the Polish guests came back from the bear's dance, the third act of the German saga play had already started. It was the same scene as the first act, only there was now a tent in the foreground, with the entrance open. Siegfried is seen in bed inside, with his young wife, Gutrune. To the right stand King Gunther and Hagen, both in armor, with helmets on. Soldiers in the background.

"Why must Siegfried die?" Hagen is asking King Gunther. "What crime has he committed?"

"He has broken all his oaths and has betrayed me!"

"But that isn't true!" Hagen exclaims, and he goes on to tell the King that his Queen Brunhilde has been lying to him about Siegfried because she wants Siegfried killed. "She is jealous of Gutrune, because she is in love with Siegfried herself."

The King dropped his head, for he knew it was true. Then he drew his dagger, gave it to Hagen and, pointing to the tent, said "Go!"

Hagen refused. The King called over one of the soldiers, gave him the dagger, and told him what to do in the tent. The soldier grinned, moved to the tent, stopped at the entrance, and looked in. He slapped his thigh with satisfaction at the sight, went in, and stabbed the sleeping Siegfried. Then he flung himself on Gutrune's bed.

But Siegfried was not dead. He made a move toward the soldier, and the soldier ran from the tent with Siegfried after him. Siegfried hurled his sword at him but missed, amd the soldier was not cut in two as the play required. The prompter called out to the soldier: "Fall down! You're dead! You're cut in two!" Then the soldier laid down, and lay still.

The audience rocked with laughter. Nobody could hear what Siegfried on the stage was saying. In desperation the prompter had the curtain dropped. The audience clapped and laughed, then got up and went back to the dance hall.

14

Nearing the End

The town got to know everything that had happened at Krzewicki's ball—about the play with ancient German gods that had been produced for the benefit of the Commandant and his officers who had come to the ball, who had gone away feeling insulted and angry. The Commandant was fuming against Krzewicki and the other Polish landowners in his area, most of all Gnilowski, who had been the ringleader of this whole affair. The town knew by now for certain that Gnilowski, this strange landowner who was the apothecary's son, was a Socialist. People couldn't make it out. How did a landowner, one of the gentry, become a Socialist? Some ridiculed the idea: "He's as much Socialist," they said, "as he is likely to marry Bernfel's daughter."

And talking about Bernfel, they went on to discuss the story that was going around about Bernfel's having had to do the bear dance at the ball. Everybody was glad that he had been taken down a peg or two, put to shame in front of a big audience.

But the hunger and distress that winter were so great that it took away all the satisfaction the poor get (almost their only satisfaction in their bitter poverty) by talking hatefully about those better off than themselves.

There was only one consolation. Everybody felt it wouldn't be long now before the war came to an end. They had visible signs of it; the German army was in full retreat from the east, streaming back to Germany. Spring was near. The working people, especially the Socialists, were excited over the October Revolution in Russia. They were engaged in furious discussions, which were soon to lead to a split in their movement.

The town was agitated over the pogroms in the Ukraine. There was talk of Revolution in Germany and Austria. People were getting apprehensive.

The smuggling stopped abruptly. Many cafés and restaurants closed. They had sprung up like mushrooms after rain, and now they vanished overnight. Most of the Jews who had engaged in this "dirty trade" became clean again. And the workmen and artisans who had got work as a result of the prosperity brought by the smuggling were left unemployed.

That winter Gershon the linenweaver also had nothing to do. The peasants had no flax. But he had managed by then to do over his home, so that he said it was now a "palace." He had an iron three-legged stove, and a window where the hole in the wall had been. The whole place had been whitewashed, walls and ceiling. The only trouble was that the window was too small to let in much light, and the stove was mostly cold, especially toward the end of that winter. So Gershon's little boy, Velvel, his only son, the apple of his eye, got a chill. And because he was a delicate child he became dangerously ill.

It was early morning. There was heavy frost outside, as often happens in Poland when you think winter is already over. The sick child was lying on the divan where the whole family of four slept at night, because it was their only couch. Usually the boy lay next to his father, and the girl, Tzirel, at her mother's side. She was a tall, thin little girl, and terribly pale, with big serious eyes, very much like her father's.

She was now looking after her little brother, who was lying sick, because her mother had gone out at dawn to one of the neighboring villages, to see an old peasant woman who knew all the proper herb remedies for every illness. She had told Tzirel to keep a careful eye on Velvel, because he was the only brother she had, and both her sisters had died. Tzirel held a small pot of warm milk in her thin hand, that her mother had boiled up for the sick child before she left the house, and she was feeding him slowly with a spoon. Then suddenly the child couldn't take any more. Tzirel thought he was laughing and that made him splutter, one of his tricks when he was well. But there was a strange gurgling sound, and the milk came up and ran from his mouth. Tzirel pleaded: "Please drink it, Velvel! Mother said you must!"

But as soon as she put a spoonful in his mouth it came up again. Then the gurgling stopped. Tzirel was happy. She thought he was better.

"Please Velvel, drink it. Mother put two lumps of sugar in the milk for you. It's as sweet as honey. Look!"

She sipped a little milk from the spoon, and cried: "Sweet as honey! Please drink it, Velvel."

She didn't dare to take the whole spoonful, because the milk was only for her sick brother. She couldn't understand why he wasn't taking it. She climbed up on the divan, to look closely at him. Perhaps he had fallen asleep. She put her hand on his forehead, as she had seen her mother do; it was cold. She covered him up as well as she could. But the room was freezing. There was no fuel in the stove.

She was frightened. She ran to her father at his weaving loom, and asked him to come and look at Velvel.

At that moment the door opened, and Reb Isser came in. Without the usual "Good morning" greeting, he said:

"I'm on my way to prayers, so I thought I'd look in, Gershon."

"Heaven is black, and the earth is white, like a shroud," he went on. "There is a storm outside. It will stop. But now it is raging like a wild thing, smashing everything in its way, as though it wants to destroy the world. Perhaps to create a new world. Winds and storms are all God's messengers. We say 'evil messengers.' But how can they be evil? They are God's messengers! There is no evil in what God created, in what God does. Everything that happens is according to His will. Therefore it must all be good."

Listening to Reb Isser, Gershon forgot his troubles and worries, and even that his little boy was so sick. His face was flushed, not only with the exertion of working the pedals of his loom and shooting the shuttle, but also with delight at listening to Reb Isser's lofty words.

But when Reb Isser stopped, an uncanny black silence rose in the room and crept toward him. Gershon felt a cold, clammy presence. It froze him where he stood, paralyzing him. Tzirel was standing beside him, trying to tell him something. He couldn't even turn his head to look at her. But he heard what she was whispering: "Velvel is dead."

Gershon's big sad eyes grew bigger and sadder. He did not speak.

Reb Isser said: "His Will be done! Blessed is God's Judgment!"

Reb Isser stood for a moment with bowed head, then he continued:

"The Angel of Death too is a messenger of God. Death is another life in another world, and then returns to the life we can understand. If our actions deserve it we shall have the privilege of this other life being revealed to us."

The storm outside thrashed around, and merged the angry sky with the white frozen earth. There was no top or bottom or middle. Just an icy dust whirling about in the air. It was neither day nor night.

Reb Isser, with Tallith and Tephilin, continued his way to the Synagogue for prayers. He didn't walk. The gale carried him along. It lifted him up and swept him along with it. Then it suddenly went away, and left him standing there alone. And presently the sun was shining in a blue frozen sky.

"Where are you going, Jew?" an unfriendly, mocking voice asked him.

Three German gendarmes with rifles had surrounded him.

"Good morning, gentlemen," Reb Isser said. "I'm going to pray to God."

"What have you got in that bag there?"

"Tallith and Tephilin! Look!"

"Yes! All right, you can go!"

Next the German gendarmes knocked at Berl Farber's door. They were very correct about these things, the Germans. Even when they went to the houses requisitioning everything there, as now, they didn't just break in. They always knocked on the door first.

But when nobody answered they broke the door down.

"What are you making all that noise for?" Berl asked when they walked in.

Berl was standing by the one frozen window, staring at the ice ferns that had formed on the glass. His eldest daughter, Reisel, and Malka, Mirel's mother, were busying themselves with his sick wife, who had spent the whole winter in bed.

"You must go home now," Reisel was saying to Malka. "You have been up all night with us. And we are not the only people you spend your time with. You're doing this with all the poor families in the town. Go home now and rest. Or else you'll be ill as well. You are no longer a young woman."

"I'm not such an old woman yet," Malka cut her short. "The way you talk, you'd think I was a hundred. It's you who should get more rest. You still have a husband to find, and you must keep your looks. I don't need to worry about these things any more. You make too much of what I do. There are others who do more. Take Jacob, the scribe's son. He's a good fellow! He often comes in to see my husband. He says that all we do is like trying to empty the sea with a thimble. I asked him if he means that we shouldn't do anything at all. He didn't mean that, he said. But there was something else more important to be done."

Berl broke into the talk: "Yes, I know! Jacob and Hersh and Feiga, and the rest of that lot, they want every pauper to become Pan Bernfel."

While the other two German gendarmes were poking around in every corner to see what they could find, the sergeant in command started questioning Berl.

"Who's that lying ill there?"

"My wife."

"What's the matter with your wife?"

"It's her stomach! She doesn't get enough to eat, that's what's wrong with her. Because we've got to money. Because I haven't enough work to earn a living!"

"Why are there so many Jews ill round here?"

"When you don't earn enough money you don't get enough food. How would you like not having anything to eat for three days?"

"Nobody could live for three days without food."

"Then they don't live! They fall ill and die! They get T.B."

"T.B.?" said the sergeant, edging to the door. "Let's get out of here!"

He looked round the room again, and saw the children huddling by the kitchen stove for warmth. There was Black Godel, with his two-year old brother, and two sisters, four and eight. They all had a piece of black bread with garlic rubbed on it. Godel had eaten his bread and wanted more.

"Let me have a bite of your bread," he said, "and I'll let you have a whole potato each out of my share of the barley soup in that pot on the fire there. Look! It's nearly ready now!"

The older girl objected: "You never keep your promise. As soon as you get your share of the soup you gobble it all up, and you never give us any for the bread you took away from us. You even try to get some of our soup. How can you give us whole potatoes when you know there are no whole potatoes in the pot? You saw Reisel cut them all up into small pieces."

But the two-year old brother pushed his bit of bread into Godel's mouth. Godel took only one small bite out of it.

As the sergeant was leaving the room he asked Berl: "If the Jews are so poor, why do they have so many children?"

That made Berl wild. "You grudge us even that! Now you don't want us to have children either! May all our troubles and sicknesses fall on you!"

The sergeant didn't understand the rich Yiddish curses.

"Search the place!" he ordered his men. "Write down everything. Requisition the lot!"

"The lot?" Berl repeated.

"Yes, the lot!"

"Good," said Berl, mockingly. "Take the lot! Take all our poverty! Take everything we haven't got! Take the lot out of every poverty-stricken home in this town, Jewish and non-Jewish. Take all our troubles and sicknesses with you!"

"Search!" said the sergeant.

"Search!" said Berl. "Search, and I hope you find something."

"What is your occupation?" the gendarme asked.

"I'm a dyer."

"Is that what you do?"

"I used to. I don't get any dying to do now. Before the war people brought me their garments to dye. A poor man came to have his threadbare gaberdine that had gone green with age dyed black again. Or a woman brought her white wedding dress, thirty or forty years old, to have it dyed blue or red. Now they've even taken away my copper vat. The poor people who were my customers are destitute now. They haven't a shirt to their back. Poverty has dyed everything they have deep black, black as the night, black as death."

The gendarme shrugged his shoulders: "Don't know what you're talking about! How do you live?"

"I don't live!"

"But you're alive."

"If you call this living."

Berl pointed to his son Godel: "That boy of mine used to take German soldiers round to show them where they could buy ham. That's finished! My daughter Reisel is a seamstress. And Malka there is a woman with a heart of gold. She sometimes brings us a loaf of bread or a few potatoes. She sits up all night with my wife, who is ill. She does more than is possible."

But the gendarme wasn't listening any more. He was looking at Reisel.

"Nice daughter you've got," he said. "Come here, young lady. It's so dark that I hadn't noticed you before. Have you been to our sanitary department for inspection?"

Reisel went red with shame.

"I'll send someone along to fetch you," he went on.

Turning to the other two gendarmes, he said: "You haven't found anything? All right. Let's go!"

As they went out one of the German gendarmes brought the butt of his rifle down on the pot where the soup was boiling, and smashed it.

The sick woman who had kept quiet all the time now started screaming, when she saw the liquid running down on the fire, sizzling. The two smaller children were crying. Malka tried to quiet the sick woman. Then she said, speaking to everybody at large:

"I'll go now. I'll bring you another pot, in place of this. I'll be back soon."

She bent over the sick woman: "Spring is coming. The days will be nice and warm. You'll be able to get out of bed, and go out into the sunshine. You'll soon get well. I shall be back!"

When the three German gendarmes got outside, their chief turned on the one who had broken the pot: "What did you do that for?" The man looked away shamefaced.

After Berl Farber's, the three gendarmes went to Kalman the tinsmith.

They got a cheerful "Come in!" in answer to their knock.

"Anyone ill here?" the chief asked jocularly.

"Ill?" Kalman repated. "No, no one's ill here! We're all well! Strong as lions! Every one of us! Come here, the lot of you! Kibah, Shimmel, Yiddel, Chaim!"

Four strapping youngsters appeared, the oldest of them only fourteen, all working at their father's craft, hands and faces grimy, the rust clinging to them.

"Look for yourselves! Aren't they fine, strong boys? And they're only half. I've got another four. The oldest is a scholar, a brainy chap! Knows a lot of languages. He's a teacher. He's not at home.

"And these four boys here, they've got brains too. They haven't studied, but they know a lot. This little one—he's only five—can use a hammer as well as I can.

"And I've got girls too! Come here, girls! These are three of them—Gitel, Rebecca, and Yenta!"

The three girls, aged between fifteen and twenty, were just as grimy from the work as their brothers. They were all three good-looking girls.

"I have another daughter," Kalman went on. "Freidel. She's out now. Just as beautiful as these three. That's my wife over there in the kitchen, the Queen of this house. Come here, Rachel! I want to introduce you to the gentlemen!"

"And this," Kalman continued, "is my friend Mechel Politician. My best friend. He just came in to tell me the news, what's going on in the world. Mechel's got a head on him! Ought to be a Cabinet Minister in our own land, in the Land of Israel! All the Jews will be going to the Land of Israel soon. The time of the return is not far off. That's what we were talking about, Mechel and I, when you came in. You must have heard about it!"

"Yes", said one of the German gendarmes. "I read about it in the papers. The British Declaration about Palestine."

"No politics!" the chief broke in sharply.

"Tell me," the chief went on, addressing the master of the house, "why have the Jews in Poland such a lot of children?"

"Do you call my family a lot?"

"I didn't mean any harm. I only wondered about the conditions in which you live. We're ordinary working folk ourselves at home. This colleague is a locksmith. And this one is a landworker."

"My name is Greenzweig," Mechel Politician introduced himself. "You say you want to know the conditions under which the Jews live here. You mean the kind of people we are. Do you know the Bible?"

"Fairly."

"Well now," said Mechel, "the Bible says, 'A people wise and full of understanding.' God's chosen people. The Bible also says, 'a stubborn ard a stiff-necked people.' It means a people that won't give way, that won't give up. The Jewish people suffers because it is in Golus, in exile from its own land. Do you understand that? In exile for two thousand years from our own land."

"Yes, we know. In exile for two thousand years. No, not quite two thousand years, not yet.''

"You see, suffering gives strength," Mechel continued. "The more we suffer the stronger we are. I am not a religious Jew, gentlemen. I am one of the enlightened, the emancipated. I do a lot of reading. I read books of science. You wondered why Jews have such a lot of children. You'll find the answer in the Bible. God said: 'Be fruitful and multiply and replenish the earth.' And also, 'I will make your seed to multiply as the stars of heaven.'''

"Yes, yes, I see!" said the chief. "We must be going now! Good day to you all!"

But Mechel wasn't done yet. He followed the gendarmes as they moved to the door, still talking and explaining.

"Yes, yes," the chief kept saying. "We must go now. Good day!"

15

The End

The German requisitions did not stop. On the contrary, they grew more severe.

The winter came to an end. Spring had arrived. But the German gendarmes still went from house to house taking anything they found there, not sparing the poorest.

The Jews in the town and the peasants in the villages were all of one mind, that this was the sign of the end. This was the Germans' last kick.

People went mad when they saw the German gendarmes still dragging girls and young women away for the morality inspection.

"But they won't be doing it much longer," they said. Everybody knew by now about the strikes and demonstrations and riots in Germany and Austria. They knew that the German army was no longer having victories, but was wearily withdrawing from the occupied countries, retreating from the east to the west. There were fewer guns now that so many guns had been abandoned in Russia. The German soldiers who marched through the town looked dejected, conscious of defeat.

But still the German gendarmes were dragging girls and young women to the doctor for morality inspection. There were many among them whom nobody had suspected before, and some who saw them on their way said: "Serves them right! That's the sort of thing they did to get trading concessions for somebody in the family!"

There were also some innocent women among them—many people knew that the Germans did this out of spite, putting the brand of shame on them as a parting shot. Yet who could know for certain which of them were innocent? The stigma stayed with them all. They were all given prostitutes cards, and had to come to the doctor for regular medical inspection.

Deborah was one of these unfortunates. The poor girl had been ill in bed for a long time. She had collapsed on the frostbound highway after leaving the Commandant's office, wandering distractedly along the road, till she got frozen right through. She was found lying unconscious and was taken home.

Reb Yossel Fuksman had called a doctor from Warsaw, and he found bronchial pneumonia. The doctor stayed in the town till she passed the crisis; after six weeks he told her she could get up.

The day Deborah got out of bed and dressed herself was a day of thanksgiving for her parents. They vowed to give a large sum of money to charity, and to keep the laws of Judaism more carefully.

But Deborah was still very weak, skin and bones. She looked ill. She coughed all the time. And what worried her parents even more was that she hardly spoke to them.

"God will send you a nice husband, my dear," her mother tried to cheer her up. "You will be very happy. You will go traveling, and see the wonders of the world. Everything will be all right!"

Deborah's face did not change. As though she hadn't heard. She looked lifeless. Nothing seemed to matter to her. Her parents sometimes thought there was a look of reproach in her eyes. Once her mother asked her straight out:

"Have we ever done you any harm, my child? Did we do any wrong? Have you any complaint against us?"

Deborah didn't answer. But her eyes filled with tears. She put her arms around her mother and kissed her.

Another time Reb Yossel Fuksman said bluntly: "It's my fault, my child!" He sank his head, and wept.

Deborah hugged him and kissed him. She wanted to cry out: "No! It isn't your fault!" But the words wouldn't come.

With the spring Deborah's condition seemed to improve. Her parents and her older brother were delighted. Her mother started speaking of taking her to Switzerland soon. She tried to make Deborah wear her new dresses that they had brought from Warsaw. But Deborah wouldn't look at them. She wouldn't even go to the wardrobe where they hung.

Then two German gendarmes came to the house and asked for Deborah Fuksman. Reb Yossel Fuksman wasn't at home. Nor were Deborah's two brothers, Reuben and Ozer. Her mother, Brocha, was frightened.

"My daughter is ill," she said.

"We know. That's why we've come to take her away!"

"Where are you taking her? I'll come with her!"

"Nobody's allowed to come with her! There's nothing to be afraid of! We're not taking her to prison! She'll be back soon!"

Deborah felt that something terrible was happening to her. But she went with the Germans. She didn't argue with them.

She had to join a long line of women and girls, who were marched through the streets and through the marketplace, escorted by German gendarmes. Everybody looked at them as they went past. Some of the girls put their hands over their faces or tried to hide them in their coat collars. Deborah didn't. She held her head up, drinking in the Spring sunshine. She hadn't been out for so long that she could think only of filling her lungs with the fresh air.

The German doctor saw at once that she had T.B. Still in the early stages. But he wasn't there to deal with T.B. His job now was to inspect the women for V.D. And because Deborah was there, he inspected her too: "You're all right! You can go!"

When Deborah got outside she strode away vigorously, as if she had gained new strength. She walked through the back streets, not looking at any of the houses, not looking around, till she came to the open field outside the town. All the snow had gone. The meadow was green. There were no leaves on the trees, but they were no longer dry as in the winter. They already had tiny buds on them. The sky was clearer, bluer than in the town. And the sun, which was now standing directly over her head, sent its rays down, and they wrapped her round like a golden web.

But when she reached the river, she shivered. The water was full of broken ice. She hated the ice. She had never liked the winter. She loved the spring and summer. She lifted her face to the sun, drinking in the warm rays through mouth and nostrils.

She saw her mother and father as though they were standing at her side. She felt sorry for them.

She took her eyes away from the sun, and turned them on the water and the floating ice blocks, which shone and shimmered in the sun, green and red and blue. They looked lovely now. She walked into the water to get nearer to them. One big block of ice crashed down on her head, and the water round her grew red.

The town couldn't get over Deborah's suicide. Everybody felt sorry for her; they even felt sorry for her parents, though everybody said that they were the cause of her death.

Events were moving fast now. By the end of the summer the Germans were on the way out. Polish legionnaires were beginning to appear. They came on small, thin horses, galloping through the streets. Most of the youth joined them. The peasants in the villages, the Christian workers in the town, and the Jewish young men were all given rifles and bullets. Jan and Juziek distributed the arms. They were among the leaders of the revolutionary proletariat, and they armed the class-conscious workers to fight for Polish liberation from the German invaders. They harassed the retreating Germans from the rear, disarmed them, and seized their horses, lorries, provisions, field kitchens, and field hospitals, but most of all their arms and munitions. They even tore off their uniforms. They all fought together as comrades—peasants and workers, village and town, Christians and Jews, mostly in their own civilian clothes, but with rifles—and often without rifles. Krzewicki, the landowner, was the local chief.

Suddenly the news went round that the German Commandant, Major von Wolfenthal, had been seen leaving the town. He had remained there almost alone. His aides had made off during the night. They hadn't even left him his carriage. He had tried to disguise himself as a German private, and had left on foot. But people had recognized him, and ran after him. In front ran Reuben, Deborah's older brother, brandishing a revolver. Then Juziek Strzelkowski appeared, with his rifle.

"Stop!" he shouted. The Commandant went on running. Then Juziek fired, and the Commandant fell, shot through the head.

Part Three

16

After Liberation

Only a few years before, the Russians had ruled in this land. Then for a short while there had been the German-Austrian occupation. Now the true masters of the country were in control, after the long oppression under three foreign powers.

Liberated Poland was ruled for the time being by a provisional Socialist government. But it was not long before the signs of a reaction began to appear.

Jacob asked himself who really ruled in Poland, because there were things happening in the country that puzzled him. Of course, we haven't had our freedom very long, he told himself. There hasn't yet been time for the people to adjust themselves to the new conditions. So far nothing had improved. A good deal had even got worse.

Jacob wasn't the only one who felt like that. Things were bad economically too. The Jewish Socialist Party was now legalized, enjoying all the same rights as the Polish Socialist Party, which was the dominant Party in the country, with a majority of seats in the government.

Jacob, who was now a member of the Committee of the Jewish Socialist Party, realized with a pang that the Polish peole who had been liberated from foreign slavery were now enslaved to their own government. Freedom did not mean to Jacob freedom from responsibilities and duties to your fellow men. If a man still had to go hungry at the end of his day's work, or he had no work, then liberty of assembly and free speech were not real freedom.

True, he said, the conquerors despoiled the land, and had carried off everything they could lay their hands on. But they had not carried away the soil, the fields, and the forests. The war had destroyed factories and houses. That should have affected everybody in Poland equally. It was the loss of the whole country. But it had not affected the minority of people who had previously been rich. They were still rich. The people who suffered were the great mass of the poor. In this regard, as Jacob

110

saw it, nothing had changed. The mass of the people had not been liberated.

There was now more unemployment. Prices had risen and were still rising. Taxation was growing heavier. Jacob said that of course government must have money to run the country. But was it the government that was running the country? The people worked; the people ran the workshops, the factories, the shops. At least the government should see to it that the people have work to do. But they hadn't. There was a terrible amount of unemployment.

The roads and the bridges, the waterworks and the sewage were all provided and maintained by the people who lived in the area, not by the government. But the government took taxes. The schools—the people ran their own communal schools; the people ran their own voluntary social health societies. If they needed a doctor they had to pay him his fee; if they had to go to hospital they had to pay for the treatment even in the government hospital. A man had to pay for a government license to get married, or to register the birth of his child. He was not allowed to move without a passport, which would establish to the government's satisfaction who he was and what he was doing. And for that he had to pay a tax.

What about security? The police, the law courts, the prisons, without which people would eat each other up alive? Of course, if there were no poor there would be less crime, less theft and robbery. And then fewer police would be needed, and fewer law courts and fewer prisons.

Jacob couldn't make out what the government had to have so much money for— taxes on everything, stamp duties for each piece of official paper, which nobody would ever have thought of if the government didn't make it compulsory. On top of it all, the government ran its own huge enterprises, like the post office and the railways, which in private hands would have made vast profits. The government machine, the enormous number of officials, of civil servants, and the army with its stores of arms, swallowed up everything.

The head of the government at this time was Pilsudski, a Socialist, the same man who in the 1905 Revolution had been sent to prison because he had fought for freedom and justice, for Socialism, for the brotherhood of all people. He had taken his place in the ranks of the workers, with the poor and the exploited, the same Pilsudski who, when the war had broken out, had in Galicia, under Austrian rule, created a Polish Legion to liberate Poland—first from the Russians, then, though this could not be said openly at first, from the Germans and Austrians.

He had achieved more, sooner and easier than he expected. Now this Socialist heading the Socialist government of his liberated Fatherland had decided to remain the military man, the Commander of the Polish Legion, the Marshal. And his chief aim, his overriding purpose was to have a large and powerful Polish army, to defend Poland against her enemies, the Great Powers east and west, Russia and Germany.

Most of his Legionnaires were working-class people, members of the Polish Socialist Party. The inhabitants of the town received them with joy when they first appeared on the heels of the retreating Germans. Many drunk with joy kissed and hugged the Polish soldiers—kissed their uniforms, their buttons with the Polish eagle on them. The girls went mad with excitement. The boys hero-worshiped Pilsudski's Legionnaires.

The Jewish population, like the rest, thought that Polish independence and free-

dom had brought them liberty and equality. Poland after all had been their homeland for many centuries, for nearly a thousand years. The Jews had their roots here.
Here lay the bones of generations of their forefathers, fathers and sons, back to the
remote days of the tenth century. They felt that they had a part in the Polish liberation. This was their joy too. There were Jewish soldiers and Jewish officers among
the Polish Legionnaires. They also had fought in the Polish Liberation battles, just
as Jews had fought in the previous Polish Risings, under Kosciuszko, and in 1830.
Now that Poland was free, Polish Jews and Polish Christians would live like
brothers, in friendship and peace. There would be no more anti-Semitism. All
would be equal citizens of the new free Polish State.

These Jewish hopes were soon dashed.

A group of soldiers would see a Jew with a long beard, in a caftan. They crowed
round him, and made fun of him: "The Germans are gone! The poor Jews can't do
any more business with the Germans, can they, Jew!" Then one soldier, drunk or
pretending to be drunk, would stumble and fall against the Jew. If the Jew was
quick enough to move out of the way, and the soldier sprawled full length on the
ground, all the soldiers went for the Jew, because they said he had knocked down
one of their comrades. The Jew got a good beating. The Jews of the town began to
fear a real pogrom coming. It wasn't long before the streets rang with the old cries,
"Down with the Jews! Out with the Jews!"

Some Jewish optimists still argued that the anti-Semites were only a very small
minority of the Polish people. They were sure that the majority wouldn't allow any
attacks on their Jewish fellow citizens. They said all this would soon be stopped.
But most of the Jews in the town, especially the orthodox Jews, refused to accept
these comforting assurances. They knew that these were wolves on the hunt.

Then the pogroms started. It was late autumn when they began. The Jewish
newspapers reported more and more frequently cases of anti-Semitism all over
Poland, following the Liberation, with Jewish victims in this town or the other,
sometimes serious outbreaks—mobs incited and led by middle-class agitators,
students and intellectuals, invaded the Jewish quarters, broke windows, smashed
furniture, looted shops and houses, and maltreated and injured Jews, men, women
and children. Anti-Semitic newspapers printed the most incredible accusations
against the Jews, and called for war against the Jewish population. They rarely
invoked the ancient religious hatreds, about the Jews' crucifying Jesus. That kind of
accusation was left to some occasional backwoods provincial sheet. The new big
"progressive" Press of the wealthy middle-class bourgeoisie, concentrated mostly
in the National Democratic Party, used more up-to-date methods. Their cry was
that the Jews had captured all the economic positions, controlled the trade and
industry of the country, monopolized the liberal professions and dominated political life. They were an alien element with nothing in common with the Polish spirit,
exercising a destructive influence. They were Asiatics, hostile to everything Christian Polish. They said the Jews had come to Poland from Germany, and their language was German. They kept to their own language, considering Polish beneath
them. The Jews regarded themselves as the chosen people, much better than the
Poles, whom they despised.

Journalists of the kind who are prepared to provoke people to rob and kill asked
in their papers: "Who were the smugglers? The Jews! Who got all the meat and

butter and milk, so that there was none left for our children? The Jews! Who bought up the poor Polish peasants and turned their crop over to the Germans? The Jews! Who had all the concessions to send our Polish corn and flax and cattle and pigs, leather and iron and timber to Germany? The Jews! Who is responsible for the present rise in prices? The Jews! Who are manipulating the Polish exchange rates? The Jews!"

Of course, there were many true Polish liberals and intellectuals who opposed this propaganda. They argued that the Jews had come to Poland nearly a thousand years ago; they had their roots in the soil, they had fought for Polish liberation every time Poland had risen against her oppressors, they had contributed greatly to Polish commerce and industry and culture. They produced records and documents as evidence. They made lists of famous Jews in Polish history.

The Jews, they said, live a separate life. Indeed, they do. But whose fault is it? Who shut the Jews behind stone walls, in ghettos? They did not deny that there were Jews who were criminals, who had been smugglers, who had held German trade licenses and exported goods to Germany, and who were now engaged in currency speculation.

But they showed that these things were done not only by Jews. The Jews who were guilty of these offenses were a minority, and most of the criminals called themselves Christians, and Polish patriots, and worked in the National Democratic Party.

But the number of these Polish liberals was comparatively few, and their campaign had little effect. It was easier to excite the passions of the mob. So the newspapers went on reporting, "Pogrom in Pinsk!" "Pogrom in Lemberg!" The Jews were blamed for everything—for the Russian Revolution, for the Bolsheviks —wasn't Trotsky a Jew?

17

The Cobbler's Workshop

The Jews in the town were in despair. Itche the cobbler grumbled: "I thought when the war ended and the Germans were gone, we would all go back to where we had been before, the cobbler to his last, the shopkeeper to his store, the peasant to his field. We thought Poland would be free and her people would be allowed to live. I didn't expect the Christians to love us; but I didn't expect this!"

He was talking to his son Aaron and his daughter Feiga and her "Comrade Hersh," as he called him scoffingly, annoyed because he didn't get down to brass tacks about becoming officially engaged and married to his daughter. Jacob also happened to be there at the time.

The cobbler was now living in a cellar, where he had fitted up his workshop, his bench, three-legged stool, and his tools. He also had two wooden beds there, for himself and for Aaron, and an iron bedstead for Feiga, a table, a long bench, and four chairs.

Where had he got it all? If you asked him he wouldn't know what to tell you, except—"Like everybody else who came back here with nothing and somehow managed to set up home again." Like ants whose antheap had been trampled down, they had built another anthill.

Itche sat on his three-legged stool at his cobbler's bench, though he was not working; he had no work. He eyed his hammers, pincers, awls, tacks, bits of leather, rasps, and other tools of his trade, longing to be using them again. He loved the work no less than he wanted to be able to earn his bread by its means. But everything had stopped. Nobody had any work for him. His wife, Dobbe, was at the stove, wondering how with nothing in the house she could prepare a meal for seven hungry mouths. It was already noon, and none of them had yet broken their fast. What worried her most were the three little ones, who kept reminding her that they were hungry.

Hersh and Feiga sat on the iron bed, and Aaron and Jacob stood near by, against the wall, by the only window, which was really a grating through which they saw only the shoes of the people passing overhead.

They were discussing the conditions in the town, and getting worked up over their different political beliefs.

"It's a good thing," Jacob couldn't help saying, "that we have only three opinions. Since there are four of us we should have had five."

"You're wrong! Hersh and Feiga are one," her brother Aaron interposed. "So we are only three people, not four."

Hersh took him up on that: "If all the people were one," he said, "we would win."

"Or lose," said Jacob, who was finding it increasingly difficult to fight down his growing doubts.

"I am inclined to agree with Jacob," said Aaron, returning to what he had been saying when Jacob interrupted him.

"I'm in the Party administration now. As long as we were illegal I never thought of these things. I'm only a working man, not a scholar. I've read a little, I've studied Marx. It was hard going. But of course I am a Marxist. I certainly am a Marxist. But I can't help thinking. Look, Hersh and Feiga! The Social Democrats are in power in Germany and in Austria. Here in Poland too. And both there and here they have gone into partnership with the bourgeoisie. Why?"

"Because we don't want a Proletarian dictatorship! We are not Communists! We want a gradual transition to Socialism, not like in Russia. We can't do it alone."

Aaron said nothing. He didn't know what to say, though he was not satisfied. But Jacob spoke up:

"You're right there! Only it isn't as simple as that. This compromising with the bourgeoisie looks dangerous to me. As dangerous as the split in the Second International was before the war. It must bring disaster."

"What disaster?" Hersh and Feiga asked.

"I don't know," said Jacob. "I'm not a prophet. But I am sure that it is wrong to take the bourgeoisie into the government, and to want them to work with us. Isn't it absurd to expect the bourgeoisie to work with us to bring about Socialism? They'll only use us for their own ends, to save their capitalist system. And when are we doing this? When the bourgeoisie are bankrupt. When they have lost their war. No, this is no partnership. When the capitalists regain their power they won't share it with us. We've made a false step."

Jacob hadn't finished, but the cobbler broke in impatiently: "Can you tell me what is going on here? You're all so clever! You know everything! What has gone wrong? Things were bad enough when Russia ruled here, but we were able to live. We worked hard, and when there was no work we went hungry, and we owed the shopkeeper money. But when we got work again we paid off the debt—not all at once, but in time. But now! Look, that's my wife over there at the stove, with a pot on the fire. But it's only water boiling in the pot. Things are as bad as in those first days when we came back to the town after the flight in the war."

"Hold on, Reb ...," Hersh broke in.

"Reb," the cobbler sneered. "You call me Reb because you don't know what to call me.... Time you called me father-in-law! What are you waiting for? A dowry? You say you don't want a dowry. You say that when you're in love you don't think of dowries. So what are you waiting for? You're no longer a youngster, and Feiga— Feiga is of marriageable age. Are you waiting till you get rich? You say you don't want to be rich! You say that a rich man is a bourgeois, and that all the bourgeoisie ought to be killed. Shall I tell you what I think? If you should by some miracle, against your own wish, get rich, you wouldn't want Feiga any more. Would you, now? You would want to marry rich, wouldn't you?"

Feiga saw that Hersh was getting all worked up. So she went for her father:

"What do you want to interfere with our affairs for? Stop it!"

Her mother backed her up: "Keep quiet, Itche! That wasn't what you were talking about! Get back to the subject!"

"You're right, you're right!" said Itche. "I was talking about something else. Now, where was I? I was talking about the war. When things were bad we said it was the fault of the war. Whose fault is it now when the war is over? When the Germans and the Austrians have been chased out, and Poland is free and independent! When your people are running the Government! Well, now? Why are things worse now than they were in the war? No work, everything dearer, and getting still dearer, taxes so high that you can't lift your head up! And pogroms on top of everything! Not yet in our town, but they'll come here too, they'll come! They won't spare us! So what is it all about? You're high up in their councils. You should know!"

This was the question that was agitating thousands of Jews in those parts at that time. The same question, really, that Jacob had been asking himself and Hersh.

The four comrades, Hersh and Feiga, Aaron and Jacob, were at a loss what to answer. Then Hersh spoke up:

"These things are all the result of the war," he said. "And," pointing his finger at the cobbler, "it's your fault! Not you personally, but all the millions like you! What did you do to prevent the war's coming, and your sons' being sent to the battlefields to be killed and maimed? What did you fathers do to save your children? Now you come to us with your questions! You complain as if it was our doing. Adding insult to injury. Trying to put the blame on us for your sins! For your refusal to stop the criminals, your bowing your heads to them and letting them do what they wanted, unhindered! When we got together and wanted to fight them, you, our fathers, tried to stop us! Did you let Feiga and Aaron become Socialists, go to Socialist meetings? You thrashed them for it, as my father thrashed me, and Jacob's father thrashed him! Now you have the result—destruction, hunger, disease, and poverty, all the consequences of the war. That's what you brought us! And you dare to blame us!"

This was the answer that thousands of Hershes were giving at that time to thousands of parents putting the same questions that the cobbler had put.

Of course, Feiga agreed with Hersh. Aaron too.

Abish, the cobbler's younger son, standing by the stove with his two small sisters, Mindel and Zisel, nagging their mother for something to eat, had been listening to this talk with his ears pricked. He hadn't understood it all, but he had got the drift of it. Now he piped up in his thin treble:

"They're right, father. You didn't want to let Feiga and Aaron become Socialists. You hit them when they wanted to go to Socialist meetings. You won't let me be a Socialist either. But you can't stop me! I'm going to be a Socialist! As soon as I'm big enough!"

The cobbler made a rush at the boy, who took refuge with Feiga and Hersh. The cobbler went back to his three-legged stool; but he did not sit down. He stood for a while, then he suddenly burst out:

"We get pogroms because Jewish boys and girls like you get mixed up with government affairs! Why don't you leave these things alone? We don't have to interfere here any more. Not now, when we've got Palestine back again! Britain ..."

"Britain, my foot!" his wife broke in. "It's God's doing, that's what it is! God had mercy on us!"

But the cobbler wouldn't listen to her. He spoke about the Balfour Declaration, and how Britain had promised to restore the Jews to their homeland in Palestine. Now the Jews would rebuild their ancient land, and everything would be wonderful.

"What makes you think that?" his wife came back at him. "What's going to be wonderful? We'll always have trouble, no matter where we are. That's the way life is. Human beings are born to trouble. We can't get away from it! Hard times and suffering—that's our lot!"

The cobbler, who was not longer the believing and practising religious Jew he had been before the war, tried to make his wife understand that it was still possible for men and women to live happily on this earth, and that it was not necessary that they should always be poor. Then he suddenly realized that this was Hersh's argument, that Socialism would abolish poverty and put an end to war, and he shut up. He didn't trust Hersh's assurances. He was convinced that Hersh was wrong about anti-Semitism and pogroms in Poland; Hersh said it was only the rich who were anti-Semites. But he knew the common folk, and they were just as anti-Semitic, and when it came to pogroms the poor would be the mob that would go robbing and killing Jews.

Jacob couldn't agree with Hersh and Feiga, either, when they said that what was happening in Poland now was only transitional, the twilight dawn between dark night and the coming day. "Revolution is a new birth," he said. "A new era is born in blood and pain. We have no idea yet how the child will grow. He may well disappoint all our hopes. Government is only a word. We don't know how a government will work out."

"I've got to go now," Jacob went on. "We'll discuss this another time, after the meeting that Jan Gnilowski is calling. He's the big Socialist chief here now. We'll hear what he has to say. I'll see you at the demonstration! Goodby!"

18

The Demonstration

Demonstrations were nothing new in the town at that time. In the first weeks after the Liberation there had been demonstrations almost every day. There were some people, mostly the older folk, who didn't like the noise and the tumult, who scoffed: "Nothing better to do but go marching through the streets with banners and bands, shouting and singing, making a noise!"

They were mostly Socialist demonstrations, but they were all victory marches, triumphant, jubilant, celebrating Poland's independence and freedom. There was real brotherhood at first; everybody marched together, workers and peasants, bourgeoisie and proletariat, reactionaries and clericals, freethinking revolutionaries, young and old, Jews and Christians. The red flags of Christian and Jewish workers were carried side by side. There were also other flags, ultra-nationalist, and Church Catholic.

Very soon some people noticed that while the songs and the music played by the bands had at first nearly always been Labor and Socialist, and the slogans, marching cries, and speeches revolutionary, they began to give way now to nationalist hymns, and other banners were carried in front of the red flags, and other leaders in black frock coats marchd first with and then in front of the working-class leaders. They saw Pan Gnilowski walk arm in arm with Pan Krzewicki. Fewer Jews came to the demonstrations. Not because they had become less enthusiastic about Poland's liberation, but because with each demonstration they were made more aware of the growing anti-Semitism, even among the organized workers and Socialists.

Abraham, with Hersh and Feiga on either side of him, proudly carrying the red flag with Yiddish gold lettering, found himself each time placed farther back in the procession. The demonstrations were now almost entirely nationalist patriotic. The workers' songs were heard only occasionally, and then just a verse or two. All the emphasis was on the patriotic side.

When the cold days came at the end of autumn, and the chill got into people's bones, when the skies were lead, and there was a constant threat of rain and even snow in the air, a new kind of demonstration started. Small demonstrations, with-

118

out bands, without any imposing banners, as in the old days of Russian rule, when the demonstrations had to walk warily because of the Russian police. These new demonstrations were against Poland's own new "Socialist People's Government."

Only small numbers of workers marched in these demonstrations, but they were the true revolutionaries. They demanded immediate social reforms, and above all that the government should take over the land from the big landowners and distribute it among the peasants. Some of the marchers even raised Communist cries.

These demonstrations didn't march through the broad main streets, through the marketplace and along the high road, but went through the narrow back streets where the poor lived. They went carefully at first, not daring too much yet, feeling their way.

Their greatest difficulties came from the right-wing Socialists, who didn't want to be told that their leaders were working against them, that the Socialist landowner Jan Gnilowski was not concerned mostly with the interests of his own landowning class. They reminded the critics that Gnilowski had organized and led the underground movement against the German invaders. They wouldn't hear a word said against their hero, just as they wouldn't admit that any wrong had been committed by their 1905 hero, Josef Pilsudski. Hadn't he liberated the Polish Fatherland? Wasn't he, a Socialist, at the head of the government? Pilsudski wouldn't let them down!

So these small protest demonstrations didn't meet with much success. And around this time the Hallerists appeared, the soldiers of General Haller's army. They came mostly from Posen, from those parts of Poland that had been under Prussian rule. They were terrible anti-Semites and reactionaries. Not only the Jews but the revolutionary Socialists too went in fear of them, more than they did of Pilsudski's Legionnaires. If they caught a Jew with a beard they hacked it off with a bayonet, together with whole lumps of flesh. They flung Jews from moving trains, even women and children.

Any Socialist was for them a Bolshevik. While they were in the town no Socialist demonstrations could be held. Luckily, they didn't stay long in the town. They stopped there only on their way to the front. What front? Was Poland at war? With whom? With Russia? The country as a whole didn't know yet. When incendiaries set fire to a house, the occupants don't know until the flames come leaping up.

19

The Position Becomes Clear

The meeting was held in the Town Hall, which meant that it was official, sponsored by the Town Council, to get the public to put their views to the government. It was further proof that Poland was ruled by a Socialist government—the chairman of the meeting was Comrade Jan Gnilowski, with a red ribbon in his buttonhole, and a row of Socialists sat with him on the platform, the schoolteacher, the veterinary surgeon, and several others, all veteran Socialists since 1905, devoted and dedicated fighters for Socialism and for the freedom of Poland. They all were now high officers in the Town Administration.

Jacob sat with the rest of his comrades in the body of the hall. He kept staring at the platform, with all those dressed-up Socialists there. Fundamentally Jacob was a good believing Socialist, as he had in his boyhood Chedar been a fervent believer in God. But he was inclined to philosophize, and that often led him into doubts. So he sat looking at these Socialists who were now in power, and he wondered what it was that drove people to seek power and to fight for it, and what it meant to them, and what they did with their power when they got it. What was this demon urge that possessed them, that made them slaves to the power lust? He told himself that it was the nature of man, who could become like God, yet could be like the devil.

The Socialists were not the only ones on the platform. There were also representatives of the National Democrats, the Party of the rich bourgeoisie, and of the right-wing Peasants' Party and the clericalist Christian Socialists. But there were no representatives of the Radical Opposition and the left-wing Peasants' Party and the Jewish Socialists and the Jewish bourgeoisie.

All the lights in the hall were full on, including the big arc lights that were switched on only for very great occasions. Every seat in the huge hall was filled. People had come from all the villages round about. The atmosphere was one of solemn thanksgiving and patriotic dedication. There was a mood of high festive exaltation.

Jan Gnilowski, the chairman, opened the meeting. "Poland is now free," he began. "We have our own government, a truly Socialist people's government, working for the good of every section of the population. The government," he said, "is introducing very important social reforms to benefit the workers and the peasants, and to raise the standard of the poor generally. The Socialists are in a majority in the government, and Marshal Josef Pilsudski, the head of the government, is a Socialist."

The great audience burst into a frenzy of applause. They stood and cheered and clapped. The Socialist landowner Jan Gnilowski, who was in the chair, stood drinking it in, as though the applause were all for him. He stood there, a grave figure, his fat face very serious. His dark hair was well kept, as befits a member of the gentry, yet also a little untidy, in the proletarian style—a tribune of the people. His voice could soothe and charm, or when he chose it could thunder and roar.

When the applause had died down he started to explain the purpose of this meeting. They had to create, he said, a large and powerful Polish army that would, at this decisive hour, know how to defend Poland's historic frontiers.

"All Poland's sacred soil is not yet free," he cried in ringing tones. "They have three times partitioned our Polish earth. The Polish territories in the east are not yet liberated!"

Martin Ciemnowski, the accountant, was the first speaker. Everybody respected him, not only the workers, in whose Party he was a leading figure. He was a powerful speaker, a man with oratorical gifts. He swept the audience off their feet with his eloquence, with his burning sincerity, with his flaming patriotism.

When the cheering that followed his speech had died down, the chairman said he would allow questions and discussion. He wrote down on a list the names of those who said they wanted to speak. Quite a number spoke, but most of them only to say how completely they agreed with the chairman and the speaker. Each time the audience clapped and cheered.

Juziek Strzelkowski and Jacob were among those who had asked to speak. Strzelkowski had been the founder and was the leader of the Radical Socialist Opposition in the town. He was followed by a peasant who belonged to the Left Peasant's Party. Jacob, though he was a member of his Party Committee, had his own lines of thought. The Chairman decided to have Jacob speak last.

Jacob felt that Juziek had already said most of what he had wanted to say, and he didn't just want to repeat; so he spoke instead about the war, not from Juziek's proletarian angle but from the ethical point of view, the crime of killing other human beings and destroying their homes and workshops.

Then he turned to the question of anti-Semitism and the pogroms. That started an outburst of anti-Semitic interruptions whose virulence and persistence completely surprised the small group of radicals and liberals in the hall. Even organized workers joined in the cry: "Down with the Jew! Get off the platform! Jewish smugglers! Jewish Bolsheviks! Clear out of Poland! Go to Russia! Go back to Germany! Go to Palestine!"

Pan Gnilowski, the landowner-Socialist, had planned this outcome cunningly. This was why he had kept Jacob back as the last speaker. It was the finale he had worked up to.

Stash, the smuggler, who had not forgotten the smuggling expedition in the forest, had been keeping an eye on David all the time. This seemed his opportunity. He rushed at David and hit him between the eyes. It was like a signal. The mob flung themselves on the Jews. The leaders on the platform rose as one man and moving like a solid phalanx, pushed Jacob off the platform so that he fell into the midst of the struggling mass.

The mob went for the Jews, for all the Jews. They made no distinction between bourgeoisie and Socialists. Everybody got kicked—the older men with beards, the artisans like Berl Farber, Kalman Tinsmith, Mechel Politician, Itche Cobbler, and the younger people, Baruch Bernfel and Isaac Lehrman.

Most of the Jews were trying to push their way to the doors, to get out. Reuben Fuksman behaved like a gentleman, shielding Helena Bernfel with his body, all the time moving her nearer the door. Once, when she fell, he helped her up.

But the Jewish Socialists—a considerable number of them, young men and women mostly—hit back; they put up a vigorous fight, and they were aided in this by the radical Christian Socialists, with Juziek Strzelkowski at their head.

Dinah Greenzweig in particular gave a good account of herself. Chelia was for the first time feeling the power of the physical class war, in which she had once told her lover's father, the old carpenter, that she longed to strike a blow, even against her own father. Now she was fighting at the old man's side, hitting out as hard as she could. The stewards, led by Caspar Strzelkowski, Juziek's right-wing brother, and the police, whom he commanded and who were supposed to keep order, decided that they were so outnumbered that they had better stay out of it.

The chairman, Pan Jan Gnilowski, and his friend Pan Ciemnowski, with some of the others on the platform, saved the situation by striking up the Polish national anthem. That stopped the fight. Then the workers sang the "Red Flag", and dispersed.

20

The Scribe

A great deal had happened since the scribe's quarrel with his son Jacob. His little girl who had been born in the field during the second flight from the town had died, and his wife, Jochabed, had had another child, also a girl. But infant mortality at that time was very high. Mirel, who kept the restaurant, also lost a child at the same time.

There had been a remarkable change in the scribe. He remembered that when he was a young boy he had not always found it possible to believe what he was told. Trying to frighten him with stories of devils and ghosts had no effect. He laughed at them. When he was thirteen or fourteen—he was exceptionally scrupulous at that time about his religious observance—he began to have doubts about the Creator. It made him so miserable that he wanted to die. He kept it to himself, and then his doubts disappeared, and he forgot all about them.

Then came that difficult summer in the war, the temptation of field and forest—he hadn't been able to resist it. He had said: "How lovely is that tree, how lovely is that field!" He had been punished for that immediately. He had caught a chill, and since that time was ill. Now he was very ill.

He couldn't understand how it had happened that the Tempter had overcome him, who was usually so strong to resist. After that first time the Tempter had found it easy. He hadn't been able to take his eyes off the beauty of field and forest, the corn in the field, the leaves on the tree, the grass, the worm on the ground, the birds as they flew by, or as he heard them singing, the sky, the sun by day and the stars at night. How could it have happened to him? Because he had always loved beautiful things. He had always admired the ornaments in the Synagogue, a fine building, good furniture, a beautifully printed and beautifully bound book.

He wrote a beautiful script; people came to him from distant towns to have him write a Torah Scroll for them. They paid him more than they paid others, because he did it so beautifully. When they arranged the match for him with his wife, Jochabed, it was enough for his mother to say that on top of all her other virtues she was beautiful, and he agreed at once to the match.

Yet till that summer he had never succumbed like that. It says, "One sin leads to another." It want so far that he had tried to find excuses for his conduct, for transgressing the prohibition in the Ethics of the Fathers: "He who is walking by the way and studying, and breaks off his study and says: 'How lovely is that tree, how lovely is that field!' Scripture regards him as if he had forfeited his life!"

He argued with himself—"God created beauty to delight the eye of man, so that by appreciating beauty man praises God. Only one mustn't break off one's study, because study is more important. One mustn't let oneself be carried away by one's delight in beauty, which is only a fraction of God's greatness!"

Reb Isser had said the same when he brought up this question with him. Since then he had softened in his anger at his son Jacob's disbelief. More than that, he had felt that he was coming nearer to some of his son's ideas. There too Reb Isser had been of help, for every time he had spoken to him about Jacob's heresy, Reb Isser had defended Jacob, sometimes even when Jacob was present, arguing with him. He couldn't suspect Reb Isser of being a heretic! On the contrary, he often wished that he himself was of such pure faith as Reb Isser, as free from doubts, and able to serve God with the same complete and utter selflessness.

The scribe took down from the bookshelf that the carpenter had made for him a heavy volume with the Hebrew inscription "Holy Scriptures" on the leather back. He put it down on the table, and sat for a long time pondering whether he should open it. He hadn't opened the Bible for a long time. About two years before his marriage he had begun to make a thorough study of it. Then he had stopped at Ezekiel and had gone on to Proverbs, Job, and Ecclesiastes without finishing any of them. He felt that he was not yet worthy of them. He had tried again several times, and each time had stopped. He didn't trust himself. He went on pilgrimage to the Rebbe about that time, and told the Rebbe about it. The Rebbe had said: "If one fears to climb a mountain lest one may fall, one shouldn't climb." He had added: "There are many other scribes, Saul."

Since then he had felt powerfully attracted by the Prophets, but because they attracted him so powerfully, he realized that the Rebbe had been right.

Weeks passed, and the scribe did not dare to take the Bible in his hands. He was afraid. Yet his desire for the Bible was now intense, more intense than even that summer in the forest when the Tempter had made him take delight in the beauty of the trees. His desire burned in him like a fire. Yet each time he put out his hand to take hold of the Book, his heart began to thump wildly. Now he forced himself to take it in his hand, in spite of the fear in his heart.

It was his son Jacob who had fired him with this desire by quoting those verses from Isaiah to him during their quarrel.

The pious scribe read the Prophets quite differently now from the way he had in those early years before his marriage — he read them now without commentaries, without the interpretations that had been read into them, without the deep probing of every word in the text, though he did glance at Rashi's commentary now and again.

He started with "The vision of Isaiah" and went on to the last words of Malachi.

He pondered for a long time over those last words: "And He shall turn the heart of the fathers to the children, and the heart of the children to their fathers; Lest I come and smite the land with utter destruction." And "Behold I will send you Elijah the Prophet, before the coming of the great and terrible day of the Lord."

For weeks on end the sick scribe sat thinking. Perhaps the Rebbe had been right, he concluded, when he had said that one who feared to fall should not climb. Of course, the Rebbe had meant falling into temptation, ceasing to believe in Him who is Eternal. But that had not happened. "God forbid!" he had cried out aloud. He had on the contrary become a firmer and a stronger Jew.

He felt that he was growing stronger in every way; he was becoming a different man from the one he had been all his life. His piety, his Jewishness, was gaining new significance. It seemed to him that he was growing inwardly, growing higher. He felt that he was getting well now, gaining new strength. Had a miracle happened to him? His heart leaped up with joy. His eyes sparkled, his face was radiant. There was a happy smile on his lips.

Jochabed thought that her husband was looking better. Jacob saw it too. Everybody was overjoyed—he had got better without going for a cure to Otwock or Switzerland.

Jochabed didn't speak to him about it, of course. No pious woman like Jochabed would consider herself worthy to discuss such high matters with her learned and scholarly husband.

Jacob was full of joy. If he were not ashamed to admit his belief in such things, he would have said that a miracle had happened.

The scribe did not speak to anyone yet about the change in him. His face, which his illness had made pinched and irritable-looking, began to soften. He grew milder generally, more mellow. He was kinder to the children. Jochabed often felt her husband's affectionate glance on her, and dropped her head modestly and blushed, until one day he said to her, quite unexpectedly: "Great is God, and greater God's mercies to the people of Israel, whom He has chosen!"

Then she knew that something tremendous was happening to him. But she still didn't ask him what he meant with these words. She interpreted them in her way—that God, whose Name she was not worthy to mention, had sent healing to her husband. "Thank God!" she whispered to herself.

When he had grown more calm the scribe asked himself: "Why didn't they teach me the Prophets at Chedar?" When he was five they had started him—as in every Chedar in Poland at that time—on Leviticus, difficult reading for a five-year-old. He couldn't understand all those laws about the sacrifices that a man must offer for his sins. When he was six they began to teach him Rashi, then Gemara and Tosefot, which is much harder than the Prophets. And as he grew older, when he was nine and ten, they had taught him the Psalms, the Song of Songs, Ruth, Lamentations, Esther, even Proverbs and Ecclesiastes. Afterward, under the biggest teachers, he had studied the Talmud Tractates Zeraim and Mo-ed, even Nashim. And Ezra, Nehemiah, and Chronicles. But not the Prophets.

He recalled a story he had been told about a great teacher who had come to one of the small towns in Poland from Lithuania, and had taught his pupils the Prophets. He was chased out of the town.

When he himself had started to read Isaiah, Jeremiah, Ezekiel in the Beth Hamedrsh, he had done it furtively, not to be observed. For Ben Zion, who was also studying the Bible, had warned him to be careful: "If they catch you they will brand you as a heretic!"

He hadn't been able to understand why. Surely God had spoken through the Prophets to His People Israel, as He had spoken to them through Moses. Then why did they teach the Pentateuch, and not the Prophets?

Now that he was studying Isaiah, Jeremiah, and the other Prophets, it seemed to him that he was climbing up a high mountain, as the Rebbe had said to him. He kept climbing higher and higher, hearing God's voice speaking to Isaiah, Jeremiah, Ezekiel, Hosea, Amos—all of them. "Thus hath the Lord said unto me." "And the word of the Lord came unto me."

Now the scribe never ceased hearing God's voice: "For I the Lord love justice. I hate robbery with iniquity." "I will come near to you to judgment. And I will be a swift witness against false swearers, and against those that oppress the hireling in his wages." "Hear this, you who would swallow the needy, and destroy the poor of the land, falsifying the balances of deceit, and saying that we may buy the poor for silver." "Cease to do evil. Learn to do well. Seek justice. Relieve the oppressed. Judge the fatherless. Plead for the widow."

The scribe thought—every Jew, just as he says his prayers three times a day, should read a chapter of the Prophets every day, not just once a week, on the Sabbath, at the Reading of the Law, Maftir.

There was a sudden fear at his heart: he was placing the Prophets higher than the Pentateuch, the Mishna, and Gemara! He was beginning to think like his son Jacob! All rich people now appeared to him wicked. He saw injustice in the oppression of the poor and the weak.

The scribe was seeing the greatness of Judaism as no longer so much faith, prayer, and observance of Kashruth, as God's word demanding justice. And God's message was for everybody, not only Jews, but for the whole world, for all peoples! "Have we not all one Father? Hath not one God created us? Why do we deal treacherously every man against his brother?" "And many nations shall say, 'Come and let us go up to the mountain of the Lord, and to the House of the God of Jacob. And He will teach us His ways, and we shall walk in His paths. For out of Zion shall go forth the Law, and the word of the Lord from Jerusalem. And He will judge between many peoples and shall decide concerning nations. And they shall beat their swords into ploughshares, and their spears into pruning hooks, nation shall not lift up sword against nation, neither shall they learn war any more.'"

Now that he was feeling better, the scribe began to go to the Beth Hamedrash again to join in communal worship. He couldn't go to his Rebbe's bethel, which had been in Reb Mordecai Goldblum's house, because the house had been destroyed.

He did not push his way forward to the top seats by the east wall. He stayed at the back, with the common folk, the artisans, the carriers, and the carters. As soon as these saw him they made way for him to go up higher to the top seats. But he never went, because the prosperous people didn't make room for him to pass. They didn't even look at him. He knew them, the new rich, people who had been poor before the war, and were still coarse and unmannered and unlearned. On the other hand, there were many who had been well-to-do before the war, who came of a good family, with a tradition of learning and respect for the learned; these all stood now at the back, among the poor.

Reb Isser too stood there at the back, among them. And when he saw the scribe he came up to him: "Welcome back, Saul. Glad you're well again! Stand next to me. Over there! Where Reb Mordecai is!"

At the Reading of the Law—most of the Jews in the front rows were seated—the scribe standing up could see right to the top, where Bernfel and Fuksman, the new leaders of the community sat against the east wall beside the Rav, both well-fed and ruddy, like Esau. Both had their beards cut short. The scribe could not help seeing that when Bernfel said something to the Rav, the Rav put on a sycophantic smile.

A little lower down sat the less wealthy. But it was wealth that determined their status and where they should sit. It didn't matter how they had made their money. The richer they were the higher up they sat by the east wall.

The poor scribe was all this time standing on his feet, and it was too much for him. There were no seats where he stood, and he began to feel his legs giving way.

The scribe now saw with his own eyes what he had previously refused to believe—that even in God's House the honors go not to the God-fearing, not to the man who studies Torah, but to the man of wealth. Worse still for him was the fact that he couldn't pray with proper devotion in the Beth Hamedrash because people kept talking all the time, mostly during the Reading of the Law, even talking about their business.

So he went back to saying his prayers at home. His health became bad again. He coughed and ran a temperature. Jochabed called the doctor, who told him not to go to the Beth Hamedrash again. "You mustn't go out of the house! You must stay in bed! God will hear you praying at home too."

That was what the doctor, a notorious disbeliever, said to the pious, believing scribe. He wrote out a prescription, refused to take his fee (he always refused it), wished the sick man a quick recovery, and left. The Christian apothecary made up the prescription, wouldn't charge for it, and teased Jochabed:

"Your God won't help your husband to get better! Your Messiah is not coming yet! They're all up in heaven, ever so far away."

When he gave Jochabed the medicine he put a few coins in her hand as well, and said: "Get a chicken for him, and get him some butter; they'll do him more good than this colored water."

The scribe was well aware that his relapse had been caused mostly by grief and annoyance at what he had seen happening to Jewishness. His son Jacob was right! When Reb Isser came to see him, he said: "You were right, Isser, when you always spoke up for Jacob and the other sinners. For they are sinners!"

Reb Isser smiled. But he spoke very earnestly: "You mustn't use that word *sinners*, Saul. A believing Jew must never condemn others. A Chassid must understand God differently from the rationalist Mithnagdim, even if the Mithnagid happens to be pious and knows the whole Torah by heart.

"But I want you to know this, Saul, that when I spoke up for Jacob and the others I was not saying that they were right. All I wanted to tell you was that no man knows enough to be able to judge."

The sick man sat up abruptly in bed. "Isser!" he cried.

Reb Isser put his hands on the scribe's shoulders and settled him gently back on the pillows.

"You mustn't jump up like that, Saul. You mustn't get excited. I know what worried you. You thought I was taking away your power of judgment. God forbid! But you know that God is the Creator of everything—evil as well as good."

"So that we can choose," the scribe broke in.

"Yes, that is true," Reb Isser admitted. "But evil too has strength, not a little strength. Therefore good must wage war against evil. That war is necessary for the shaping of man, of his heart and his soul, his mind and his will, to purify himself, so that in his purification he can better recognize God and His actions and His ways, which are still very much hidden. Only then can man turn completely away from evil. God did not complete the Creation in those six days. He created only the beginning, and that creation was enough, because till then the idea of creation did not exist at all. But God Himself existed, because He existed always. He created His messengers, and through them He creates the world and man all the time, continuously. You know what I mean. You understand it well enough. For you are a better scholar than I am, and you have read it all in your studies. The only difference is that you always studied more Gemara, while I studied more Caballa. That always seemed strange to me—a Chassid! But it has nothing to do with our present subject. You must never say that someone is a sinner, because everybody is God's messenger. Even the Tempter, even Satan himself. Else why did God create him, if not to do His will? Is that clear, Saul?"

The scribe smiled:

"I wish I knew your road, Isser, your road in study."

"I'll tell you. But you must first listen to something that happened to me. A true story. I was on my way to Selichot one night when I met your son Jacob. We hadn't long come back here after the flight. It was around midnight. I asked him several questions. This and that. Then in the midst of it a cow came along, and stood looking at us with its eyes that spoke of utter honest simplicity. I saw in that cow the greatness of God's creation, how deep are God's mysteries. I said that to your son Jacob at the time. But the cow," Reb Isser went on, "is no saint. Because the cow knows no temptation, has no desire to do evil. It just lets man slaughter it."

Reb Mordecai, Reb Henoch, and Reb David Joel with his game leg also came to visit the sick man at the same time. So they fell to discussing with the scribe the theme that was occupying his mind most just then—the Prophets.

But Reb Isser saw it one way. He saw the Prophets as the revelation of God's mysteries, that justice, truth, and righteousness are the essential qualities that God requires from man, His creature. He again recalled his talk with Jacob, and what Jacob had said to him, that we never know whom Providence chooses as its Prophet.

Reb Henoch saw it differently. He saw the greatness of the Prophets as proving God's might against all the gods of the nations, as proving that God is the One and Only God, and that Israel alone could comprehend Him. "That is why," he proclaimed, raising his voice, "we are a Chosen People! From the Holy Scriptures we know almost everything about the Children of Israel in those times, not only the period when they dwelled in the Holy Land, but also previously and after." Reb Henoch did not speak of justice, truth, and righteousness.

Again the scribe rose from his bed. He was feeling better again. And again he questioned Reb Isser about his way, about his road in study and learning. Reb Isser tried a little shamefacedly to explain:

"I know what you will think at first, Saul. But think it over after I have gone. I haven't read very much for a long time. I've done little studying of late. I sometimes don't look at a book for weeks and months. But it's just then that I learn most. You can't get over it, Saul, because you once transgressed what the Perek says, that you should not delight in the beauty of a tree. But then you came to realize that it was no transgression. I had told you that right away. So let me tell you now, that I still stop to admire not only a tree or a plant that I have seen with my eyes, but even a stone, even a grain of sand. Because I learn from the least thing. It reveals to me—not always, I admit—God's mystery. I learn much from these things. About heaven and about the heavenly bodies, the sea and the woods, the mountains and valleys, the winds and the storms, the birds and beasts—the whole earth is full of the glory of God. There is Torah in all that God has done and does, both the revealed and the concealed.

"Now listen to me a little longer—and this may astonish you even more. When I walk through the streets, especially late at night, and especially outside the town, and also when I lie sleepless on my couch, the deepest thoughts come to me. Then I hear them, yes, I hear them in the air. Only I don't know if I hear them with my ears or with my heart, with all my soul. They enter into me—so it seems—through my whole body, through every limb. I hear their voice. Yes, I hear their voice. And I know that they are the great truths, the eternal truths that come straight from God Himself. They have no need to go through any messenger or intermediary; therefore nothing of them is lost or diminished, as happens with thoughts that come through an intermediary, as would happen if I were to tell you what I hear. I am not going to tell you what I hear. I couldn't do it. I am not worthy to transmit to others the thoughts I hear. They are for me only. Yet I think that every mortal man could hear those thoughts if he would lend his ear to them. For if God's voice hovers between heaven and earth, then we must be able to hear it. If only we forget the body. And then we no longer know any anxieties or sorrows or fears. Then the world is all glory, the world is all song, all joy. Every son of man must come to that, and he will come to that."

When the scribe told all this to Reb Mordecai, he said: "I can't tell you anything about Reb Isser's deep thoughts, Saul. But this is true, that when the body loses its hold, then one no longer feels anxieties or sorrows or fears. Then one serves God with a full heart."

21

The Light of the Simple

That winter when his youngest child died was a very hard one for the scribe. But when spring came he felt a little better; he coughed less and breathed more easily. As soon as the days grew milder he started going out. He felt that the warm rays of the sun would do him good.

It was then that Jochabed confided to him that she was pregnant again. It consoled him a little for the loss of the other child.

Reb Saul had been contemplating for some time separating himself from his wife, having Reb Isser in mind. But he found it difficult. It was not in his nature to be a Nazarite. Each time he said to himself: "It would mean leaving home. Reb Isser's wife died. So he didn't remarry. That's different. But when you're living in the same house with your wife. And when your wife comes back from the bath of purification ..."

In his heart, though, the scribe knew that his desire was still strong. When he had fallen ill he had thought this was the time to separate himself from Jochabed. What happened was the very opposite. His desire increased. He was not so modest now when he looked at his wife and saw that she was still lovely. Her face was so gentle—and what was beauty if not gentleness of face? His mother had said so when the match with Jochabed was being arranged. "It all passes," his mother had said, "rosy cheeks, the delicate form of the body, but not the gentleness of heart and soul, that shines out through the eyes and sheds light on the face. It is like good wine, which improves with age."

"My mother was a saintly woman," he reflected, "and she was very beautiful too." He knew that he had inherited many of his good qualities from his mother. "His mother's eyes," Jochabed used to say, "may he live longer than she did. His mother's mouth, and her whole majestic appearance. Her beautiful, gentle hands." He had inherited his love of beauty too from his mother. When he was a boy he had a way of rolling little pellets of dough when he was eating bread, and modeling figures out of them, the head of a man or an animal or some grotesque creature without any reality. He always got annoyed with himself because of it, because it was breaking the Second Commandment—and he crumbled up the figure he had made. But the week before Shevuoth he had cut out paper ornaments for the whole town. Before he was married the women used to come to his mother to get him to make cut-outs for them. When he was married they came to Jochabed. The things he had cut out with colored paper and scissors! He had become a scribe because his fingers wanted to make beautiful shapes. His calligraphy was beautiful. His lettering was beautiful. The things that came into his mind when he sat down at the table with his parchment, and held his goose quill in his hand! Heaven opened to him, and he saw the Throne of Glory and the host of angels!

But since his illness he had written no Sepher Torah; he had felt that he could no longer write with the same purity and holiness of mind as before. He now wrote only parchments for mezuzas and Tephilin—if anyone still ordered them, and he didn't have to stay in bed. Even now, he was filled with great joy every time he held the goose quill in his hand, and the characters he was writing shone before his eyes. But now he saw not only the Throne of Glory and the angels in heaven, but also the fields with golden grain, and the green forests, and the silver streams, and the varicolored butterflies—all that he had seen that summer when he was a refugee in flight from the army that had occupied his town, and he was wandering with his wife and children along the roads and fields and forest.

He no longer drove those pictures from his mind, from his memory. He accepted them, with his new thoughts about the Prophets.

He was feeling better now, and he was working and earning a little money. There were some pious Jews among those who made their living by smuggling, and they came to the scribe to get him to examine their mezuzas and their Tephilin, and they bought new mezuzas and Tephilin. Some even wanted him to write charms and talismans for them, to bring them luck in their deals. But Reb Saul wrote no charms and talismans.

It was late summer, in the month of Ellul, when Jochabed gave birth to her child. A seven-month baby. From that moment his illness grew worse. And with the liberation of Poland there had been an end of the smuggling, and people stopped coming to him for mezuzas and Tephilin.

Jacob fell out of work. Anti-Semitism increased, and the Jews in the town went about in fear of a pogrom.

The scribe no longer spoke calmly and tolerantly to Jacob about his thoughts and ideas. He had suddenly grown frightened of his own heresy.

The severe frosts had started. Benjamin, the scribe's younger son, was standing by the window in the half-room occupied by Gronem, the melamed. His big dreamy black eyes in his thin pinched face, with the long earlocks dangling over his ears were fixed, entranced, on the frost ferns on the panes. He was as much attracted by beauty as his father was. He forgot that it was winter and that he was indoors. He was imagining himself in an orchard, among fruit trees, with a blue sky, the sun shining, and birds singing.

Benjamin sometimes made drawings of things he had seen in his imagination, and he wrote captions to say what they were supposed to be. His small brother

Meir, who was playing with the Hebrew teacher's boy Leibel, came over to him and disturbed his thoughts. He said that Leibel and he wanted to make money. Benjamin knew what they meant. They wanted to press a few small Russian and German coins they had picked up against the frosted window panes. He didn't want them to do that, because it would spoil his ice ferns, and the whole landscape that he could see etched on the windows, sky and trees and birds. He tried to frighten them out of the idea by saying that the pressure of the coins would crack the windows.

His mother and the melamed's wife came into the room just then from the street, where they had been shopping, and they brought the gray frost with them. Jochabed had bought a few potatoes and half a loaf of rye bread. The melamed's wife, Henne (she was pregnant again), had brought a bundle of firewood.

Meir and Leibel forgot about the coins and eyed the bread hungrily. So did the melamed's older boy, Yoske. Jochabed turned to Henne: "Cut a few slices of bread, and let the children eat, yours and mine. We'll straighten things out afterward." She turned to the youngsters: "Have you said your prayers? Say the blessing for bread!"

Henne asked Yoske: "Has your father come back?"

"No."

"Where is Hersh?"

Yoske looked important: "Hersh went out with Jacob!"

"Ah!" Henne sighed. "The things that are happening in the town!"

Jochabed went to the cradle in her half-room, and muttering to herself, "My poor little baby," turned around so that neither her sick husband in bed nor the young boys should see, and with her thin bony fingers felt first one breast and then the other. Both were empty.

"I have no milk for you, my poor baby," she murmured to the infant. "I haven't touched a drop of warm water all day!"

Yet she leaned over the cradle, lifted the child out, and put it to her breast. The child sucked greedily, but getting no satisfaction, cried.

Jochabed covered up her breast again, took a small piece of bread, bit off a crumb, chewed it, and fed it to the baby. At the same time she warmed its red frozen hands with her breath. She hoped that Mirel would come soon to suckle the child. For Mirel was suckling her own child, and she was very glad to do it, first of all because her mother, Malka, had told her to, because it was a good thing to help the poor, and also because she had too much milk and it needed drawing off; besides, Jochabed was almost one of the family, for wasn't her sister Rabeh going to marry Jochabed's son Jacob?

Jochabed was very happy to see Mirel, who apologized for being late. "Such goings-on in the town!" she said. "We're going to be put on our feet again. There's a Committee coming all the way from America. They are going to give money and food and clothing to everybody who needs it!"

Mirel rubbed her hands to warm them, went over to the cradle, and spoke to the baby:

"You're hungry, aren't you? Eh, baby? I've kept you waiting today, haven't I?"

She bared her breast, which was like a full jug of milk, bent down to the child, and gave it to feed.

Henne didn't like Mirel. She was jealous of her good looks, and she envied her good fortune. Mirel wasn't poor, as she was. Mirel had everything of the best. Look at her, how well-fed she was! Strong and healthy!

"I'll soon be able to feed your child, Jochabed," Henne said spitefully. "When my child is born I shall be able to feed both."

"That's right!" said Mirel cheerily.

Jochabed noticed a movement at the partitioning curtain dividing the room into two; it told her that her husband had finished saying his prayers and was ready to break his fast. She was afraid that he might draw the curtain aside and see Mirel with her breast exposed.

So she called to him: "I'm coming right away, Saul!"

Mirel realized at once what she meant. "Hurry up, baby," she said to the infant. "Finish your feed, so that your father can have something to eat."

The child slipped the brown nipple out of its mouth. It had had enough. Mirel covered up her breast. Jochabed laid the table.

Mirel still couldn't help marveling at the scribe's noble appearance, his fine features, his delicate, gentle hands, his deep black beard. He had kept his good looks despite his long illness.

The scribe had hardly sat down at the table when the old carpenter Mateusz, his landlord, came walking in with a sack full of firewood, bits and chips left over from his work.

It was two days after the fight in the Town Hall, and Mateusz's face was still bruised. He put the sack down by the stove. And when he saw the bundle of firewood there he shook his head. "Silly women!" he muttered to himself, "buying firewood when I can give them plenty."

He walked with slow unsteady steps toward the table where the scribe sat. Reb Saul stopped eating, and the two men looked at each other. The carpenter felt kindness and compassion in the Jew's eyes. But he also felt that the Jew was worried and disturbed. Indeed he was. Since that change in him his mind had kept hammering away all the time: "What about the Gentiles?"

He could of course, with all the anti-Semitism there was, have dismissed the question—"The Gentiles are wicked; they can only fight and rob and kill!" But as he looked now at his Christian landlord and neighbor he pushed such thoughts out of his mind. He saw the bruises on Mateusz's face and asked: "Did you fall?"

"Yes, I fell!" Mateusz answered savagely. He was furious, because he couldn't get out of his mind what he had been saying to the scribe when he put up the shelf in this very room for his few sacred books, that when Poland was free the Jews would be happy in Poland. Instead of that there was anti-Semitism striking at the Jews in free Poland. It made him angry.

The carpenter had not come just to bring the sack of firewood. That was only an excuse. He had really wanted to have a talk with the scribe; not only with the scribe, but with all the Jews in the town, with all the Jews in Poland, about the way they were being treated now by the Poles, beaten up in the streets, and pogromed. He couldn't bear it. He kept talking to his family about it, and to his friends, and to the peasants from the villages round about. There were some who said he was right. But most of them said the Jews had bought him. He was always quarreling with his son Caspar about it.

Mateusz felt ashamed. He couldn't look a Jew in the face. He wanted to speak to every Jew individually, and ask for forgiveness, not for himself, but for the Polish people as a whole.

He couldn't help feeling that even the scribe, though he looked friendly and kind, was angry with him, and despised him, as he despised all the other Poles, as he despised all Christians. The Jew would be right, he told himself, because the Jews had always suffered at the hands of the Christians. His son Juziek said so. And Jacob said so. It was all the fault of the big Polish landowners, the Krzewickis, the Zarembas, and even Jan Gnilowski, who called himself a Socialist. Why did they allow such things to happen in the town?

"Yes, I fell," he repeated. "Your son Jacob fell too. So did my son Juziek, and Hersh, and Pan Bernfel's youngest daughter—a very nice girl! We all fell, all of us at that meeting in the Town Hall. But we stood up to the hooligans who were going for the Jews. They didn't have it all their own way. We saved a lot of Jews! I too, hunchback as I am! We went for those beasts! By God, we let them have it! I'm no weakling, Pan Saul! Look at my muscles—! If I hit a man on the head he feels it. I hit my own son Caspar, who is in the militia, because he didn't come to the aid of the Jews, but stood by and let the hooligans hit them. He was there to keep order. He should have drawn his sword and used it on those s.o.b's.

"I know what you're thinking, Pan Saul. Every time I come in you look at me and you think: 'Those Gentiles are a rotten lot! There isn't a decent man among them! They're all wicked! All they can do is to go about hitting Jews and making pogroms!' Panie Saul, all Jews hate Gentiles, and I know why they do. Because we're bad. But not all Gentiles are bad. Not all Jews are good. There are good Christians as well. There are good Christians and there are good Jews. I have two sons, Juziek and Caspar.

"It's the fault of the rich that the poor peasants don't understand these things. They're not educated. So they let themselves be led astray by the Krzewickis and the Zarembas and the Priest in the church, who tells them that the Jews are to blame for everything that goes wrong. It won't be like this always. There are different times coming! Then all men will be brothers! Please believe me when I say that, Pan Saul! You're a religious man, always studying the sacred writings, God's Holy Law. You know that God created all men, that we are all His children. A father has good children and bad children."

The scribe remembered that he had heard all this before, from his son Jacob. Yet it worried him: "God created all men. We are all His children. A father has good children and bad children."

He took Mateusz by the arm, and said to him: "Please sit down."

Jochabed had not finished eating. But she stood up, with her piece of bread and cup of chicory in her hand, and said: "Meir, Benjamin, you come with me!"

Meir followed his mother immediately, but Benjamin didn't move from the table. His eyes were fixed on his father's face. His cup of chicory stood untouched. It had already gone cold, like his father's. He bit into his bread twice, each time that his father did, following his motions. He was drinking in every word that came from his father's lips.

The carpenter's words were like a burning fire in the scribe's mind. Everything he had experienced in these last five years since the war broke out stood before his eyes now—the way the Jews in all the towns they came to had treated the refugees; how they had left him out in the street, with his wife and children, when they returned to this town, and if it weren't for this Gentile he wouldn't have a roof over his head now. He had been living here for four years, paying rent for it less than a year. This Gentile landlord of his never worried him for his rent and never asked him for payment for all the things he made and did for him. He brought firewood, chips and shavings, and potatoes. The Gentile apothecary not only didn't charge for his medicines, but even gave his wife a little money when she went to fetch them.

But the Rabbi and the heads of the Synagogue took no notice of him. He had made his wife, Jochabed, take an oath that she wouldn't go to them for charity if they didn't trouble about him.

And that time he had gone to the Synagogue—what he had seen there.

Yet he couldn't accept the idea that there were good and bad Jews, as there were good and bad Christians. It was different! Jews didn't kill! Jews didn't make wars! In the days of the Jewish Kings Jews had fought in self-defense, when Judea and Israel were invaded. But in every Gentile state there were pogroms and massacres of whole Jewish communities; they burned Jews at the stake, tortured them, and drove them from their homes. And it wasn't only the rich who did it!

He sighed: "All men are the children of God!" The Gentile carpenter's words had sunk deep. Other words flamed up in his mind: "At the end of days!"

"Yes," he said to the carpenter, "God created all men. He is the Father of us all. There is much evil in the world. But God will help! He will punish the wicked. The day of justice will come! It must come!"

The carpenter jumped up from his chair: "It will come! It must come! And if they start anything here against the Jews I'll split their heads with my axe! I'll stand with you, Pan Saul, and I won't let them get anywhere near you! I'll split their heads like so many blocks of wood! So help me God!"

22

An Argument

Jacob came home late. His mother and Henne, the melamed's wife, started questioning him about what was going on in the town. He tried to calm them. He said everything was quiet. But the melamed suddenly asked him: "Where's my son Hersh?"

Jacob was shaken. "How should I know?" he answered.

"You went out with him in the morning," Hersh's mother, Henne, reminded him.

There were three adults and four young boys all at Jacob, wanting him to give them information about the disturbing news going around in the town. But he was anxious to get away from them, to go into the other half of the room and see his father.

His father was in bed, teaching Benjamin Gemara, and Benjamin was begging his father to teach him the Bible.

When Jacob came over to him his father said: "Well?"

Jacob gathered from the tone and the inflection that his father was not really asking for news, but wanted him to know that he had been waiting for him, that he had something to discuss with him.

He was right. His father wanted to tell him about his talk with the carpenter. He motioned to Jacob to sit down by the bed. "Our Gentile landlord has been here," he began. "He was saying the same sort of thing that you say. That all men are the children of God. It's true. The Holy Torah says so. God created one man, Adam, and we are all descended from Adam, we Jews like the rest. Cain and Abel were brothers. Jacob and Esau were twins.

"But that isn't the point. We have to consider what Jacob was and what Esau was. The Jews are the seed of Jacob, and the Gentiles are the seed of Esau. God took His Torah to all the nations, and they wouldn't accept it. The Jews didn't accept it at once, either. But they did accept it, and they keep it. Not all Jews keep it as they should, completely. There are enough Jews who commit terrible sins. But tell me, when did the Jewish people make pogroms against other peoples, murder children, rape women, burn and loot, burn people at the stake! Of course, there are

136

righteous men among the Gentiles. I agreed with you about that several times. I have also considered, especially today, what has become your faith, and of which there is so much in the Jewish Torah, that all nations will join together in one brotherly bond. But it will be only at the end of days, through God's hand. Not before the time, and not by the hand of man. The hands of the Gentiles are now red with blood. They are out to kill us. You see it with your own eyes. There was that fight in the Town Hall. They tell me that most of the Gentiles who were there were your people, those who share your beliefs. Well?"

It wasn't the first time that Jacob had listened to such talk from his father. But never with so much grief and mortification. What could this Socialist son answer his religious, pious father? Read him a lecture on political economy, on historic materialism? Give him a lesson in Marxism? He was feeling anxious about his father's health. He didn't want to have the sick man getting excited.

His father didn't wait for Jacob to answer. "You say that you want justice, my son!" he said. "But your justice is not the justice that our holy Prophets wanted. You and your crowd don't want to call the wicked to repent and to return to God; you don't want to show them the right road, that they should stop thinking only of the flesh, wanting to live well, to eat and drink and indulge themselves, which must lead to sin and degradation! You only want the things of the flesh, except that you want them, instead of others having them. You want the same things that the wicked want. You don't think of cleansing and purifying yourselves, and ridding yourselves of lust and sin. Your justice is to have everybody able to indulge in sin and lust, in the same earthly pleasures. To me that means away with God! No God in Heaven! No God in your hearts! And you seek to achieve it through violence, with weapons in your hands. You say that afterward there will be justice on earth, no more poor and rich, that all will be equal, that everybody will have all he needs. The Redemption will have come!"

The scribe wiped the perspiration from his face, and continued:

"Is it any wonder that such people have no God in Heaven? What need have you to pray, to keep the Commandments, to observe Judaism? So far as you are concerned there are no sins, no transgressions. You are all equal, all of you the same, Jew and Gentile. You have no faith! You sneer and scoff at the Torah, you laugh at our prayers, you make fun of all that was revealed to us through Abraham, Isaac, and Jacob, through Moses, through the Prophets and the Rabbis, the sages and the saints. You wage war against everything that made a man out of the beast, because what made him a man was religion, and the ethics of religion. You say there is no God. That everything created itself! Life and death, reason, wisdom, the power to comprehend God, the soul, everything created itself! You say the world is a machine, a vast machine. And man is a little machine. All right! What made the machine? Do machines make themselves and go on reproducing themselves? Changing themselves? The beast machine transformed itself into a man machine?"

The scribe had a feeling that Jacob was laughing at him inwardly.

"You said," he went on, "that Nature created the different species. Nature created the flea, and Nature created the Vilna Gaon! I can't make it out!"

"I thought you had more sense, Jacob, my son! I thought that you who had studied in the Beth Hamedrash till you were sixteen—and you had a good brain. It's those books you read that led you astray. Where are your hopes now? Your face is bruised, you've got a black eye. You had several teeth knocked out. That's what your friends did to you."

Jacob said nothing. He felt that his father hadn't essentially changed his attitude. Why should he have expected him to? How could a man with a firm faith based on a thousand-year-old tradition be expected to abandon it for something new and utterly alien to him? To abandon his belief in his religion for a new belief in a new world built on Socialism? His father was a sick old man, almost on the threshold of that heaven for whose peace and bliss he longed. How could he suddenly say it didn't exist?

Jacob remembered something his father had once said to him during one of their discussions: "The ship on which I sailed has struck a rock. Many of those on board have been drowned. The rest are struggling with the waves. You, Jacob, are building a new ship. I warn you that your new ship will sink long before mine does. Because the materials you use to build it with are poorer in quality. Faith in God is a lifebelt that will bring you safely to harbor. The whole voyage over the sea is so short that it doesn't matter compared with the eternal bliss on the other side."

"Do you suggest, father," Jacob said after a pause, "that everything should stay as it is, injustice, exploitation, robbery, and violence? One war just ended, and another already begun?"

The sick man sat bolt upright in bed:

"God forbid! 'The Heavens are the Lord's, and the earth is for the sons of men.' The Torah and the Commandments were given to men to fulfill them. All these troubles have come because we don't keep the Torah and fulfill the commandments. Man doesn't observe a proper relationship with his neighbor because he has ceased to believe in the Ruler of the Universe. Man is twisting and distorting God's eternal truths; he interprets them as it happens to suit him. He throws away the core and eats the husk."

The scribe saw the door opening slowing and quietly, and he broke off. Everybody in both half-rooms was paralyzed with fear. But Benjamin called out: "It's Reb Isser!"

Reb Isser wasn't alone. He had two others with him, Reb Mordecai and Reb Henoch. Each stood back to let the others go in first, but in the end Reb Henoch pushed his way into the room. He was so precipitate that he almost forgot to kiss the mezuza. All three in unison said: "Good evening!"

Reb Mordecai continued: "We've just come from the Beth Hamedrash. There was hardly a minyan. Everybody is afraid to stir out of the house."

"Afraid?" Reb Isser repeated the word, dismissing the idea. "How can a man be afraid? I'm not afraid even of God!"

"How are you feeling, Saul?" Reb Mordecai asked.

"Thank God!" the scribe answered. "Good of you all to come. Please sit down."

Jacob and Benjamin brought two chairs to the bedside, and were going into the other half-room to fetch a third. But Gronem, the melamed, who lived in the other half-room, arrived with two stools. He sat down on one of them himself.

The scribe called to his wife, who was in Gronem's half-room: "Could we have some tea, please?"

Cheered by the sight of the visitors, the scribe told them about the argument he had just had with Jacob.

But Jacob wasn't going to leave things like that. Their visitors must not think the great vision of justice and equality was simply materialism.

"Do you think, father, that everything has been revealed to you from Heaven?"

"God forbid!"

"Then you must say—perhaps the road my son is traveling now is one of God's hidden roads, leading to His justice! Yes, father, we are going the road of sacrifice for the sake of God's Name! We are being tortured for its sake! Many are condemned to death for it, and executed. Gentiles too! Because there are more of them than of us. Doesn't it say—'Whether it is Gentile or Jew, man or woman, slave or handmaid, who does a good deed shall find the reward'"?

Reb Isser cried, his eyes shining, "Your son knows what he's talking about, Saul. The fact is that we know very little of God's hidden ways. God told Jonah to go to Nineveh, and when Jonah didn't want to go he was punished. Is it possible that we are being punished because we, Israel, God's messenger, are not carrying out His mission? I sometimes think that we have completely forgotten our mission. Now having said so much, let me add that I often feel that the Judaism that the great mass of Jews keep is not Judaism at all, is certainly not the essential Judaism! But it's getting late, Saul; we must go. Good night! Come along, Reb Mordecai. We mustn't stay any longer! Good night!"

It was indeed late now, and the people who lived in both half-rooms prepared for bed—the scribe, exhausted by his bouts of coughing all day, Jacob who in his mind was still arguing with his father, Jochabed worn out worrying about her husband's illness, and Benjamin, his imagination fired by all the talk that he had been hearing.

But they were no sooner asleep than they were wakened by a tremendous bang. Everybody jumped up, scared. Nobody knew at first what had happened. There were bits of glass in their beds and all over the room. An icy blast was blowing through the shattered windows. The women screamed. They thought the pogrom had started. Even Jacob and Hersh were confused and bewildered.

Then suddenly flames were shooting up outside. Now they were sure the house was on fire. The next moment there was another terrific bang, worse than the first, because now they were awake and took in the full impact. They all flung themselves flat on the floor. In the light of the flames Jacob and Hersh saw glass all over the floor. The women screamed: "It's the pogrom! They've thrown a bomb!"

Jacob and Hersh tried to calm the women and the children. Jochabed was at her husband's bed. "Are you all right, Saul?"

"Yes, thank you!"

Jacob wanted to light a match, but there wasn't a match in the place. Every now and then someone trod barefoot on a piece of glass, and cried out in pain.

"That was an explosion!" said Hersh.

"Yes," Jacob agreed. "It couldn't be anything else. But we have no more factories here. What could have caused the explosion?"

They were all shivering in the cold wind coming through the broken windows. The gray dawn was just beginning. Benjamin was the calmest person among them. He had no understanding yet of the fear that had gripped the older people. He stared eagerly through the gaping hole where the window had been. It was the first time !.e had seen the dawn. His imagination was bright, and he was watching a huge brush painting color over the black-gray sky.

23

Business Is Business

The town was bursting with excitement. People stood around in groups, discussing what they had heard had happened, particularly in the poorer parts of the town, in the narrow little streets, especially where the poor Jews lived. They were doubly afraid, because any trouble might set the mob on them. But there were knots of people standing about also outside the church and the Town Hall in the market square. Not only the Jews were excited about the explosions. Everybody knew now that the explosions had been in what used to be a German munitions store, two or three miles outside the town. The population hadn't known of its existence before. Now there were all sorts of fanciful tales being told about it. Somebody said the munitions store had been all underground, stretching for miles and miles. It was a great arsenal, so big that even these two explosions hadn't destroyed it. Only two of the storerooms had been blown up. Two bangs. The Germans hadn't had enough time to explode the arsenal before they left the town, and it had fallen into the hands of the Poles. The story went that the Polish soldier on guard had been blown to bits.

Was it an accident? Or a conspiracy?

"It was the Communists, of course," some said. "The Bolsheviks did it!"

"No!" said others, more cautious, reluctant to spread alarm without having more definite information. "It could have been an accident. Someone passing may have thrown away a cigarette, not knowing this explosive material was there!"

"Impossible! There was a sentry on guard all the time. He would have seen it in time to put it out."

"Perhaps the sentry did it," someone ventured. "He was there all by himself, cold and miserable, so he lighted a cigarette, and that's the result!"

"It was the sentry, all right," said another. "But it was not an accident. He had been bought by the Bolsheviks. He started the fire and made off. That's why there isn't a sign of him. It's all nonsense about him being blown to smithereens. There would have been something left. The buckle of his belt or the iron tip of his boot. But there's nothing at all! He vanished into thin air! You bet he got away in time!

He knew when the place was going to blow. Because he set light to it himself. They say the police are searching among the Bolsheviks!"

The police were indeed conducting house-to-house searches. Every window in the town had been smashed. In some houses the walls had cracked.

As they moved along the police broke up the gossiping groups.

"Home you go! Don't stand around in the streets!"

It was an offense for more than two people to be together in the street. The word soon went around that there were spies in the town. They were listening to everything that people said and reporting it to the Bolsheviks. "You must be careful what you say. Some people have been arrested on suspicion."

One of the people under arrest, they said, was Chelia Bernfel.

Bernfel was lucky again. The explosion had burst only a couple of windows in his house, and the glazier had come immediately and put in new panes.

It was still breakfast time in the Bernfel home. Bernfel's wife, Rivka, didn't count breakfast as a meal.

"You get up in the morning with an empty stomach," she said. "and you have a little hot milk and water with a piece of cake, or a roll and butter, and two eggs. Just to keep going till we have our meal." (The mid-day meal was about two). Breakfast in the Bernfel house went on from nine or ten till eleven or twelve—because everybody didn't get up at the same time, so they didn't all finish together.

Rivka was the first to rise. She got up very early. She waited for her husband, who never got to the table before nine or half past. While she was waiting she had a glass of hot milk and water with a piece of cake, not to feel faint till her husband joined her. Then when the family or most of them were already eating, she took a glass of tea with two or three fried eggs, half a roll and butter, and a cup of cocoa with cake to follow.

The same for the husband and the daughters. Except that she ate hers in the kitchen, and the daughters had theirs in bed. The maid took it up to them so they could stay in bed longer.

But the two sons got up early (not so early as their mother) and went straight to work in the office. The maid brought them tea and cake there, and afterward she called them to breakfast.

Chelia now got up before everybody else, even before her mother. She went straight into the kitchen, got herself something to eat (she wouldn't let the maid or her mother do it), and went back to her room to read for a few hours. She did not come down to breakfast. About nine she went out, usually returning for the midday meal, but sometimes not till supper. She often came back only to go straight to bed.

Since the day she had run away Chelia no longer considered herself part of the household. She felt and behaved like a stranger there. She hadn't meant to come back, but Juziek had persuaded her to—he had taken her back himself that same evening. He had surprised her by his attitude. She had pleaded with him: "Let me stay with you! I'll sleep on the coffer, or I'll sleep under your father's work-bench."

He admired her for wanting to give up her wealthy home and come to him. But when it got dark he decided that she must go home.

"It would get us both into trouble if you stayed here," he said. "I am a Socialist, and they know me as such, and the Germans are in occupation. The German gendarmes would jump at the chance to get me out of the way. Your father is a rich man, on the best of terms with the German Commandant. He need only say one word to him. There are a number of things I dislike intensely, Chelia."

"For instance?"

"Sentimentality, carelessness, weakness."

Chelia went back home. The maid, who was the first to see her, threw her arms around her, and ran to tell everybody that Miss Chelia had returned.

"I told you she would come back," said Baruch.

"You must be hungry!" her sister Bella suggested spitefully. "You discovered that your workman-lover hadn't any money to give you a decent meal, eh?"

Her father, at the head of the table, tried not to show how relieved and glad he was. He threw a sharp reproving glance at Bella, and she shut up. He wanted no reproaches that would lead to fresh quarreling.

Chelia had changed completely in that one day she had been away from home. She had become calm and thoughtful. She didn't fly into a temper so quickly as she used to. She spoke very little. She didn't even answer when she was spoken to, when she was asked a question in the most friendly way. Bella stopped talking to her altogether. What was the use of talking to her if she didn't answer? Under her breath she sneered at her—"Stuck-up little bitch!"

When the meal was finished Bernfel asked Chelia into his study. He had come to realize that she was not spoiled because she was bored, with an indulgent father who gave her everything she asked for. This was more serious. She was really in love with that Christian fellow, the carpenter's workman son. Bad enough that he was a Christian! But he was a pauper as well. His father hadn't a penny to his name and neither had he. And on top of it all he was a Socialist and a revolutionary, a dangerous character, with the police after him!

He begged Chelia to give him up. But she wouldn't budge. She said that she had made up her mind to go her own way.

And now, though she was living at home, she didn't belong there. They hardly ever saw her. She never sat down to a meal with her father. She stayed in her own room. She went out in the morning before anyone was up, and she often didn't come home till they were all in bed.

Even her mother felt that Chelia had become a stranger. And her mother was the only person for whom Chelia still retained any affection.

But the person she gave most of her time to was the maid. She made a friend of her. She took her to her room, she read to her, she told her stories, she helped her with her work in the kitchen. The result was that the maid was dismissed. The same happened to the maid who came in her place. Her mother and Bella got rid of them very quickly.

Her father took her behavior more to heart than any of the others. But he still hoped that he would win her back—even now, after several years. He thought the explosions would give him a chance to talk to her. And he had another card up his sleeve. He had that same week received a letter from his brother in America.

He decided to speak to her immediately after breakfast. That was why he had asked her up to his study. He was standing with his back to the big tiled stove, warming his back. This helped him to think. And he was busy now thinking, working out his plan for rescuing Chelia. His brother's letter from America would play an important part in his plans.

He had hinted to his wife, Rivka, and to Bella what was in his mind.

"No, Chiel! No!" his wife cried out. "You mustn't! I'm going up to her room now to talk to her. Perhaps I can do something with her. I know she treats us like a stranger. But she still is our daughter. You and the other children will call me an old foolish mother. That's what I am! Chelia is my daughter! I won't let you do it!"

Bella jumped up from the table in a temper: "I'm getting out of here. I'm not staying in this house. We do nothing else but worry about that good-for-nothing sister of mine! It's just mad! I'm not standing for any more! Let her go to her proletarian friends! She wants nothing to do with us? All right! Let her go! We shouldn't have allowed her into the house when she came back! The only thing she comes here for is to eat, because she would starve there! I'm not putting up with it any more!" And she ran out of the room.

The next minute she opened the door and poked her head in: "You do what you said you would, father!"

Rivka found Chelia in her room, looking very tense and on edge.

"You haven't slept, Chelia!" she said reproachfully. "I know, we were all upset by the explosions. But we did try to get some sleep afterward, when things got quiet. But you've been awake all the time. You didn't go back to bed. There's something wrong. You're trembling!"

Chelia was indeed shaking all over. She clenched her fists, and told herself: "Get hold of yourself!"

Her mother was right. She hadn't slept all night. She had come home earlier than usual, before ten. She had spoken to the maid in the kitchen, and had asked her to let her have some supper in the dining room, which was quite new for her, because these last few years she had always got her own meals in the kitchen, or had taken them up to her room. Last night she had joined the family at the supper table. She had been in high spirits, had talked and joked with her father, with her sister Helena, and with her brothers. She had sat with them till midnight. Then she had said goodnight and gone up to her room. She had switched on the light, to read. But she couldn't read. She had undressed and got into bed. But she couldn't sleep. She lay awake all night, her ears pricked and her nerves tense.

"You got no sleep at all last night," her mother repeated reproachfully. "The explosions didn't take place till five in the morning. What was wrong before? What is the matter with you, child?"

Chelia flung her arms around her mother:

"I did sleep, mother! The explosion woke me. And after that I couldn't get back to sleep. I couldn't compose myself. Don't worry! I'll be all right!"

"I must talk to you, my child," her mother said. "I may be a very silly woman, and you won't listen to me! But I must say it! I'm so afraid for you, Chelia! You're going such a dangerous road! God knows what may happen to you! It's those explosions last night. They say your people are responsible. They're arresting your friends. I'm afraid they'll come to arrest you, too. Take my advice, Chelia, drop your foolish ways! Promise me that you will, and we'll see that you come to no harm. Your father has influence, you know. One word from him to the police, and they will leave you alone. But only if you promise to keep away from those people in the future. Otherwise he won't lift a finger to help you. That's what he said. You know your father. He doesn't want to get mixed up with any troublemakers. Take my advice, Chelia; give them up!"

Chelia felt the blood rush to her head. She realized what it was her father was trying to do. And suddenly she was no longer afraid. She stared composedly at her mother. She was feeling a little annoyed with her, because she had lent herself to her father's plan. But when she saw the grief and love in her mother's face, her annoyance vanished, and in its place there was a great pity and compassion for her mother.

"Sit down, mother!" she said. She sat down beside her, and held her hands, and stroked them. They were so hard-worked! Just like the maid's hands, she thought to herself. Real proletarian hands. Her own hands were not like that. She had never done any work. She had always been spoiled.

Chelia reproached herself: "I didn't realize! I didn't know how hard my mother works; I know so little about my own mother."

"Were you religious when you were young, mother?"

Rivka stared at her daughter uncomprehendingly. Since her husband had become rich she had felt like a stranger with her children and with her husband as well. She was not at home in these rich rooms. She walked about in them as though they were not hers, as if she were one of the servants there. And now suddenly Chelia was talking to her like her own child, showing interest in her, asking her about herself, what she had been like when she was young, what she had felt like, had she been religious?

"Was I religious when I was young? I don't know, Chelia. I tried to observe Judaism. I don't so much to-day. Why do you ask, Chelia?"

"Because if you were really religious, mother, and you believed in God, you would understand me."

"Do you believe in God?" Rivka asked, with her eyes wide open.

"No, mother, I don't! That wasn't what I meant. I'm thinking of something else. There are people like father, and Bella and Helena, and Baruch, who never consider anyone except themselves. Nobody else matters. So long as they are all right, they don't bother about the rest. I couldn't live like that. I always worried about the poor and the unfortunate. You're not happy here, mother, are you? Don't you feel out of it, all this rich living, this smugness? Do you feel at home here?"

"Perhaps I don't, Chelia. One doesn't get used to new ways at my age. It doesn't matter! My life is nearly over, my child!"

Chelia jumped up from her chair. "You mustn't talk like that, mother!"

"Why not?"

"Doesn't it matter to you what people do in your own house, what people do in the world outside? The war, the destruction, the want, the suffering! Weren't you poor yourself once? Weren't your parents poor? Didn't you start as a servant girl!"

"What if I did?" Rivka said, uncomprehending. "Your father wasn't a rich man either. When I married him he was a worker in an ironmonger's shop. And he worked very hard. God prospered us!"

Chelia felt that there was no point in talking any more with her mother. She gently helped her up from her chair, and led her to the door. "It's no use, mother," she said.

She sat down again, and told herself that if the police came to arrest her now she would welcome it.

But it wasn't the police who came into her room now. It was her sister Helena.

Chelia sprang at her with blazing eyes:

"What do you want? Get out! I don't want to talk to you!"

"Stop screaming at me!" Helena said. "What's all the excitement about! Calm down!"

"I'm not excited! I don't need you to tell me to calm down! I don't want to talk to you! Get out!"

"Look Chelia! I've never poked my nose in your affairs. I never told you to lay off that silly Socialist business of yours. It doesn't suit you! You're a bourgeois, with a bourgeois father and a bourgeois home, with a bourgeois upbringing and bourgeois tastes. You're not such a fool to think you could live in the way your Strzelkowski is living. Don't make me laugh, Chelia. You're not going to risk your freedom for such a stupid thing! Don't you know you're in danger! The police will be here any minute to arrest you!"

"It's none of your business! Get out of here! Father sent you to frighten me! He'll be coming here himself next. But nobody is going to scare me!"

"You're behaving like an idiot, Chelia! This is not a joke! You're going to be arrested!"

"Why should I be arrested? It isn't a crime now in Poland to be a Socialist. Haven't we got a Socialist government here? Aren't all the top people in the town council Socialists? With a Socialist police chief? Your Jan ..."

"My Jan...," Helena laughed. "What will you do, Chelia, when your Juziek chucks you?"

Chelia hadn't expected that question. The possibility had never entered her mind. "Juziek will never chuck me!" she cried. "You're talking rubbish! Not when two people share the same ideal as Juziek and I do. We're not like you and Jan!"

Rivka had gone to her husband's room, to report the result of her talk with Chelia. When she walked into his room he looked at her in a way that made her drop her head. He still lusted after her. His lips moved sensuously. His reddish whiskers danced as he whinnied at her. This sort of thing had disgusted her for a long time. But most of all now, when she was feeling dispirited after her talk with Chelia. Yet her fingers went to her corset, to make sure that she had pulled it tight, because he didn't like her to look flabby. He kept telling her that a rich man's wife must look after herself, and be presentable in his circles. He cut her short when she started telling him about Chelia. He had already learned all he wanted to know from her face when she walked in. He wanted to talk to her now about the letter that had come from his brother in America.

"We'll give your American guests Chelia's room and Helena's room. The two girls will share the big bedroom. This is no small matter! Delegates from America! Representatives of big Jewish organizations! My brother—he is Mr. Burnfield in America—is one of the members of their Committee. He's got a very distinguished name, Burnfield. It carries weight. It speaks of money. Like Rothschild! I wish I could change my name to Burnfield! It isn't so easy in Poland!"

"There's no need to talk to me about Chelia. I saw it as soon as you came into this room—you got nowhere with her. Leave her alone. I'll deal with her myself. Now let's talk about this American business. My brother writes to me that the American delegates' names are Mr. Green and Mr. Silverstone. 'Give them your best rooms,' he writes. 'Rooms'—meaning more than one room. 'They are going to investigate conditions among the Jews in Poland for our Relief Committee.' They will be distributing relief funds. Lots of money. They will need advice from somebody like me, who knows the people and the conditions and can tell them who should be given help and who shouldn't. I'll give them this room as their office. We'll do up the whole house, to make it fit for the headquarters of an American delegation. I don't want the maid to wait on them; Bella and Helena will look after them. Remember, they're an American delegation!"

The door opened, and their son Notte came in. He looked worried. His thick, lips were quivering. He stood stock still for a while, trying to speak, but no words would come.

"What's the matter with you?" his father said testily. "Have you lost your tongue? What have you got to tell me?"

"Bad news!" Notte stammered.

"What bad news? Tell me, man!"

"I've been to Pan Krzewicki. You told me to go. To ask him to leave the things you bought with him till the town quiet down. You know what he said to me? You bought nothing from him. He doesn't sell to Jews! It means things are bad, father! It's because of that explosion. They're saying the Jews did it. I tried to see the police chief, Pan Caspar Strzelkowski. He refused to see me."

"That nobody!" Bernfel fumed. "He's not the police chief! He's only a police sergeant. He doesn't mean a thing. I'll go to the mayor. He's a Socialist. And I'll see Pan Ciemnowski. He's also a Socialist."

Helena came into the room, and before she could shut the door behind her, Bernfel said: "Helena, I'll want you to go to Pan Gnilowski for me!"

"What about?"

Before Bernfel could answer Notte burst out:

"I haven't told you everything yet, father. Pan Strzelkowski wanted to know if Chelia slept at home last night."

"Meaning what?" said Bernfel.

"Meaning that it looks black for Chelia," Helena said. "But Chelia won't mind. She says she wants to go to prison for her beliefs."

Bernfel entered Chelia's room just as she was speaking to her brother Baruch:

"You really mean it? You're not trying to fool me? Because I hate lies. Is it true that this is your great ideal? That this is holy to you?"

"My great ideal!" Baruch cried indignantly. "It is the great sacred ideal of the whole Jewish people! I am a Jew, a son of my people! What are you?"

"I asked you," Chelia broke in, "if this ideal, Zionism, comes from your heart, or—"

Baruch wouldn't let her continue:

"What are you getting at? I tell you Zionism is my ideal; it is holy to me, it is the ideal of the whole Jewish people, redemption from the Galuth, which has lasted for two thousand years, our return to the Land of Israel, to Palestine, to become a nation again, to restore our land. We shall be a nation again like all the nations—with our own state, Jewish state! We have suffered enough! We want no more pogroms and expulsions! You see what is happening to us here in Poland now!"

"Stop!" cried Chelia. "Stop this talk of yours about anti-Semitism and pogroms in Poland. That isn't Poland! That is capitalism! As long as there is capitalism it will be the same everywhere. In Palestine as well! But I'm not going to start an argument with you about that. I'm not going to discuss your ideal or mine. All I wanted to know—and you've told me now—is whether Zionism really is your ideal. Are you ready to give your life for it? Will you go to prison for it, stand up for it in the face of death? Will you go to Palestine as a Chalutz, and work the land with your hands; will you go hungry, will you live in poverty, to drain the swamps and plant the desert, to dig the earth, to draw the plough?"

"Stop cross-examining him, Chelia!" Bernfel said. "What do you expect him to say? You go now, Baruch. I want to talk to Chelia."

"I came to warn you, my child," Bernfel began. "You know what it's about. Nearly all your crowd have been arrested. Your Gentile boy friend, too, and the scribe's son, Jacob."

He saw that Chelia had gone white, and there were tears in her eyes.

"They'll soon be here to arrest you," he went on. "The new police sergeant, your Juziek's brother, just asked Notte if you slept at home that night."

"I did! You know I did! I've been sleeping at home every night, haven't I? I was home last night before ten!"

"That's true! But it won't help you. They will arrest you all the same."

"So what? They've got nothing against me. They'll have to release me!"

"Not so soon, my girl! They can keep you in prison for years. These are not ordinary times. There's another war around the corner. Things like this have a dangerous smell about them in wartime. Your Gentile boy friend may be sentenced to death. Some of the others as well. I'll do what I can to get them off. Juziek too. But I can't do it if you don't promise to give up this stupid business. They led you off the straight path. You didn't know what you were doing. You were only a child, not seventeen when they got hold of you."

"You say they led me off the straight path! It was you," she screamed at her father, "who wanted to lead me off the straight path!"

"How do you make that out!"

"Didn't you want me to go to the German Commandant? I would have been like Bella, if I did what you told me to, only ten years younger. Afterward you would have sent me to the Polish Commandant, or to the rich landowners, to promote your business. I might have ended up like Deborah Fuksman! Juziek didn't lead me off the straight path! He gave me an ideal, a purpose in life! Something you never did! You gave your children nothing! And if one has nothing to live for, one becomes what my sister Bella is! Or one does what Deborah Fuksman did!"

Bernfel stroked his finely trimmed little beard, and said very calmly:

"That's what your Gentile boy friend with the torn trousers taught you! I'm a Jew! I've always helped the poor as much as I could. Now the Committee from America that is coming to help the people here will be staying as my guests in this house. Baruch is a Zionist. And I'm a Zionist. Bella is becoming a Zionist. So is Helena."

Chelia laughed: "You're a Jew, all right, father! You danced the bear dance at Krzewicki's fancy-dress ball. And now you're a Zionist. And the American Committee to help the poor is going to stay here in this house with you. So you've got two new businesses!"

There was a ring at the door.

"That must be the police come to take you away!" Bernfel cried wildly. "Chelia, my child! Save yourself! Do what I tell you!"

"No, father! Never! Jacob Lichtenberg, the scribe's son, told me how the Jews of old went to their death, but did not deny God! I am ready to suffer for my belief. If you had brought me up as a religious Jewess I might have been prepared to die for Judaism. But now my cause is the cause of the poor, of all oppressed and exploited people, Jew or Christian. If my friends have been arrested, I must be arrested too. I don't want you to do anything for me, to try to get me out of it!"

Baruch came into the room: "It's for you, father! A delegation to see you—Reb Henoch, the Shochet, Mechel, Mirel's husband, Nachman, and a few others."

"We have come to you on an urgent matter," said Reb Henoch, acting as the delegation's spokesman. "Our whole community is in danger!"

"I know, I know! Do please sit down. Rivka," he called to his wife, "tell the maid to bring in some tea."

"Help yourselves to sugar," Bernfel invited them. "Take as much as you like. We've got plenty. As for the danger that threatens—God will help us!"

"Yes, God will help us!" the others echoed him.

"I hear the American delegation are going to stay here with you," Reb Henoch ventured.

"Where else should they stay?" Nachman put in his word, licking the rich man's boots.

Mechel went one better: "Why, of course! If it wasn't for Pan Bernfel there wouldn't be an American delegation here at all. It's only thanks to him and his brother in America that the delegation will be coming to our town. We owe it all to Pan Bernfel!"

There was another ring at the door. Bernfel stood up in great agitation, but he pulled himself together:

"I'm expecting a visit from the authorities," he said. "You must excuse me now. I promise you I shall do all I can."

24

The Troubles Start

The police had made a lot of arrests, not only townspeople but also peasants from the surrounding villages. From the members of the Left Opposition.

Pan Czapski, once a hot revolutionary, and now the Commandant of all the security forces in the area, felt uncomfortable about it. True, his Socialism had never been more than auxiliary to the insurrectionary Polish nationalism, which had adopted Socialism as an adjunct, and after the Polish Liberation, he and thousands like him had dropped the Socialism and revealed themselves as out-and-out nationalists. All the same, it was awkward to order the arrest of people with whom he had only recently been plotting and working. Nor was he quite happy about the legal position. He knew someting about the law. He had been for years second secretary in the District Law Court under the Russian administration. He had been wakened that night by the explosions, like everybody else in the town, and he had come rushing to his office in the Town Hall, beside himself with anxiety and fear. The watchman had reported to him that the military commandant, Captain Minkowski, had already gone to the scene of the explosion. He got into his car with two subordinates, and followed him. There he found the chief of the political department, his old friend Martin Ciemnowski, and the three of them, Czapski, Ciemnowski, and Minkowski immediately set out on a tour of investigation.

There were two big holes in the ground, about eighteen feet deep. Czapski was about to jump down when Captain Minkowski stopped him, warning him that there might be unexploded bombs there; he said it would be better that he, the military man, go first.

So Minkowski, in full uniform, with his sword in his hand and his revolver in his holster, jumped down and searched around. Then he said the others could follow. Czapski, Ciemnowski, and the subordinates jumped down, and nothing happened. They all scrambled safely out again.

But it wasn't good enough, because they hadn't found anything. So they started searching again, and they found a few bits of metal on the ground, quite plainly fragments of bombs and grenades.

They would have questioned the soldier who had been on guard that night, but he had vanished. Had he been killed by explosion? There was no dead body. There was nothing of him there at all, no legs or arms blown off, not even the metal buckle off his belt, or his rifle. Had he blown up the arsenal himself, and then escaped over the frontier to Russia or Germany.

Ciemnowski, as the Chief of the Political Department, wanted to know if he vanished sentry had been a Socialist—was he a member of the Party? Captain Minkowski laughed at the idea: "A Socialist? No!"

"Was he a German spy?"

"He was a peasant, a clod. He couldn't have understood such things!"

But the saying is—"Seek and you shall find!" And one of the militiamen poking around came across a piece of electric wire.

"That's it!" Ciemnowski cried. He had experience from his revolutionary days of how explosions were arranged.

"We must find where the wire came from," said Czapski.

So they set out on a fresh search. They found nothing. They came to the conclusion that the explosions were the work of the Bolsheviks, the Communists.

They called a small meeting of a few of their chief people. Jan Gnilowski was in the chair. They met in Ciemnowski's office. Only five people were present. All five agreed that it was the work of the Communists.

Jadenusza Slamowa, the schoolteacher, asked: "Whom shall we arrest?"

"Everybody!" said Jan Gnilowski. "The whole Opposition! And first of all the Jews!"

Slamowa, the schoolteacher, and Jendrek Kapusta, the veterinary surgeon, both asked together: "On what charge?"

Czapski asked: "Is it necessary?"

Kapusta, who was the secretary of the Town Administration, explained that they must have a charge against people to arrest them. "We don't know," he went on, "Who the Opposition is. We don't know everybody there. And as for those members of the Opposition we do know, they are all still members of our Party. We haven't expelled them. We have no right to arrest comrades who hold different views from ours, even if we are the majority. We are a democratic Socialist Party, not a dictatorship.

"That's right!" Slamowa agreed.

"Furthermore," Kapusta continued, "we have no instructions from the Party Central Committee to proceed against members of the Party who are in the Opposition. We can't do these things on our own."

"Bravo!" Slamowa cried.

Kapusta went on to argue that the arrests would give the Opposition a halo of martyrdom. He also took up Gnilowski on what he had said about arresting the Jews first.

"We can't make any distinction between Jews and Christians," he said. "We mustn't discriminate against any of our national minorities."

Jan Gnilowski answered Kapusta: "First of all," he said, "we do know who are in the Opposition. All those who had at the Town Hall meeting grouped themselves around Juziek Strzelkowski. Membership in the Party doesn't give them immunity to carry out acts of treason. They will be arrested not because they hold different views, but because they had committed acts of treason. If they can prove their innocence they will be released."

Czapski and Ciemnowski agreed with Gnilowski. But Slamowa persisted in her opposition. "How do you know," she asked, "that there are not Communists in our Party whom we don't even suspect? Because their instructions are to make us think that they are loyal members, to win our confidence, so that they can transmit information?"

All five looked at each other wonderingly. Slamowa had let loose a frightening thought. No one spoke for a while.

Then Czapski said: "Nonsense! If there is anything like that going on we'll get it out of those under arrest."

That concluded the meeting.

The prison was a small building, with only two large rooms and a small cell for dangerous prisoners. Czapski, the Police Chief, found himself faced with a very serious technical problem. He had more prisoners under arrest than his prison could hold. All the men in one room, all the women in the other. He couldn't get one more person into the space unless he used the small cell.

Stash, the young smuggler, came to see Caspar Strzelkowski, the police sergeant.

"I know where you can find several Communists," he said.

"Where? Who are they?"

"David Soroka, Abraham the tailor's son, Bluma Spitzman, Itzik the carter's daughter, Mechel Greenzweig, Berl the dyer and his daughter."

Caspar Strzelkowski went in to report this to his chief, Czapski.

Czapski wrote down the names. "David Soroka", he said—"absolutely unimportant! He's a member of the Jewish Socialists. Panna Spitzman isn't a member even there. Her brother Abraham is a member, on their Committee, in fact, but if they were all like him we could sleep quietly in our beds. Mechel Greenzweig? No! Never! His daughter? Yes! I don't know the other two. Send Stash Badilio in to me!"

Martin Ciemnowski, the head of the political department, had the whole dossier in front of him on his desk, with all the particulars about the political prisoners. Not only the name, birthplace, age, and such like, but also a long report by the police on the political activities of each of them, how the prisoner had behaved on arrest, and what answers were given to the police interrogators.

Ciemnowski wondered if he should start questioning the prisoners now, or whether he should wait till late at night. This was going to be his first official interrogation. He had never done it before. He used to be a bookkeeper in one of the big factories in the town. But people learn with practice, he told himself. Even the great Marshal Pilsudski wasn't trained to be a soldier.

What Ciemnowski did have was personal experience of Russian prisons. He had spent two years as a political prisoner in the Warsaw Citadel and four years in the Fortress of Schluesselburg. He had undergone numberless interrogations himself. And he remembered that the most effective interrogations had been those late at night, when his resistance was low.

But wouldn't that mean leaving the prisoners together for a long time, while they could work out a plan of what each of them should say? There was a way of overcoming that difficulty—putting one of his agents among them, supposed to be a prisoner, to report what they said. The trouble was that the prisoners knew everybody in the town and would suspect a trick like that.

He decided to start his interrogation at once. He rang his bell, and ordered David, Berl the dyer, and his daughter to be brought in, all three together. He had already made up his mind about the three of them. The girl's father was a rebel, but he was no revolutionary and no Socialist. The daughter had her father's temperament, but she was naive and cowed. The young man was an artful one. He would leave him to the last.

He let the three stand there for a few minutes, pretending that he hadn't noticed them. Then he looked up at the dyer, and said: "Your name is Berek?"

"Berl—that's the name I was given when I was circumcized."

"Not Berek? There was a Jew in Poland named Berek, a great Polish patriot, a Colonel in the Polish army. He organized a Jewish regiment that fought for Polish independence."

"I know nothing about that," Berl said. "My name is Berl. But it is Berek on my passport."

"Your surname?"

"Sharfman."

"Why do you look so sorry for yourself?"

"Because I'm so happy. Because everything is going right with me."

"What are you getting at?"

"I mean, I've got too much money. You can't be happy with too much money."

"Shut your jaw! I'm not going to let you poke fun at me. You're not in a position to make jokes!"

Reisel ran over to her father, but Ciemnowski ordered her sternly back to where she had stood before.

"You're feeling sorry for yourself," he went on, speaking to Berl, "because you know what is coming to you!"

"Yes, I know!" said Berl.

"That's good! Tell me the truth now. It will be better for you if you tell me the truth. The truth about yourself, and the truth about the others. Tell me all you know!"

"What I know? I know that I am a poor soul without a penny to my name. There isn't anybody in the town as poor as I am. And I know what is coming to me. I shall die of hunger. That's the truth, the whole truth. That's all I know. Nothing more! You say that I mustn't joke about things. If I didn't joke about my misery I would have been dead long ago. It's bitter jesting, gall and wormwood! Especially now!"

"Why especially now? Because you're afraid!"

"Afraid? I'm not afraid even of death!"

"Then why did you say—especially now?"

"Because I was arrested early this morning. And it's getting dark already. I haven't had a bite or a drink all day. My wife is in bed at home, ill. She can't get up to see to the children. And I have no idea why I have been arrested. Why?"

"You don't know why?" Ciemnowski asked sarcastically.

He indicated David: "Do you know him?"

"Yes!"

"Do you know Jacob Lichtenberg?"

"Yes!"

"You know Aaron Mickenshleger, Itche the cobbler's son?"

"Yes!"

"And Dinah Greenzweig, whose father is Mechel?"

"Yes!"

"Do you know Chelia or Chaya, the daughter of Pan Bernfel?"

"Yes!"

"And Juziek Strzelkowski, the son of the carpenter?"

"Yes!"

"And you still don't know why you have been arrested?"

He rang his bell, and told the militiaman who answered to take out David and Reisel.

Ciemnowski went on: "Now tell me what you know about them."

"About whom?"

"About all these people you know. You just told me that you knew them. Don't keep anything back! I know everything! If you tell me the truth about them your punishment and your daughter's punishment will be much lighter. I may even decide to let one or both of you go free. What do you know about them?"

"I know that they are Socialists. The whole town knows that!"

"Were you at the meeting at the Town Hall?"

"Yes! I got beaten up."

"Why did you go there?"

"Because everybody went!"

"That's a lie! Only the Communists went! The Jewish Bolsheviks!"

This outburst bewildered the poor Jew. He didn't know what to say. In the end Ciemnowski decided to let him and his daughter go free.

He called in David next. He asked him in the friendliest way to take a seat. He asked him how long he had been a Socialist, and what he understood by Socialism. "Don't be afraid to speak," he said. "Poland is a free Socialist country. The head of the state is a Socialist. He played a great part in the 1905 Revolution. Most of the members of our government are Socialists. The days of the Russian gendarmes are over. Cigarette?"

He offered David his cigarette case and lit a cigarette himself.

Having worried out of David all the answers he wanted, Ciemnowski offered David another cigarette.

"You must be hungry," he said. "I'll have some food brought in for you. I hope we won't have to keep you here much longer. Just answer my questions. How well do you know Comrade Lichtenberg?"

"I know him very well." And David told Ciemnowski all he knew about Jacob.

"And Aaron Mickenshleger?"

"I know him well, too!"

And David told Ciemnowski what he knew about Aaron.

And the same with Dinah Greenzweig and with Chelia Bernfel.

"Chelia Bernfel is a Communist, like her lover Juziek Strzelkowski, isn't she?"

the interrogator prompted him.

David did not give a direct answer. But it satisfied Ciemnowski, who rose, and said:

"You can go now. You are free. I think I can rely on you. By the way—how are you finding things materially? You're a tailor. There's no work in tailoring now, I know. A good citizen who helps his country mustn't go hungry. I'll see that you'll be all right! Sign here. And remember, all that we have discussed in this room must remain absolutely secret between us."

Ciemnowski decided that he would again draw on his own experiences as a Russian prisoner under interrogation. It meant questioning the prisoner after midnight, when he was worn out and sleepy. He decided to start with Chelia. It was nearly two o'clock in the morning when he had her brought into his office. He started by putting her into a state of embarrassment and confusion by playing a powerful projector on her, on her bosom, then lower down, on her lap and her knees, staring at her fixedly, till she dropped her eyes and blushed.

After that he went straight to the attack:

"Your lover led you off the path in a double sense! You are not yet twenty. You were under seventeen when you ran away from home to join your lover!"

"I didn't run away to my lover. He was my friend. I had only just got to know him."

"But you knew he was a Communist."

"He isn't a Communist! He was a Socialist and he is a Socialist."

"You were in love with him."

"No!"

"Then why did you run away from your rich home and your devoted parents?"

"I think you should understand why a Socialist runs away from a bourgeois home!"

"Were you a Socialist then?"

"By instinct!"

"And now you are what your friend is?"

"Yes."

"A Communist!"

"I told you that my friend is not a Communist! I am not a Communist!"

"You're very naive. You just said you are what your friend is. We know what he is! And he isn't such a friend of yours if he involved you in last night's outrage! You knew of course what he was going to do! That's why you were so confused and frightened when the police came for you!"

Chelia laughed: "I wasn't the only one who was confused and frightened. Everybody was. My mother was, and my sisters were just as confused and frightened as I was. We heard the two heavy bangs, and we didn't know what had happened. We were afraid that a pogrom had started. When the police arrived we wondered what they had come about, and we were disturbed and frightened."

"You knew the police had come to arrest you! Why did you expect them to arrest you if you didn't feel guilty? The police are not such rare visitors to your home.

Your father has quite a lot to do with them. Why were you suddenly frightened of them?"

"Because my father said they had come for me! And because he was frightened."

"Why did you go white in the face when I put the question to you?"

"Because I had to control myself not to slap your face!"

"So you wanted to slap my face, did you? Why?"

"Because you have been very insulting to me the whole time!"

Ciemnowski didn't get anywhere with Dinah Greenzweig either. She led him quite a dance by using all her womanly wiles on him. The old revolutionary was sure that she was laughing at him, and he didn't know what to do about it. The end of it was that he lost his temper and had her put in the separate cell. He had the big prison room divided into several small rooms, and he put Chelia into one of them.

Next he had Juziek Strzelkowski brought in. He felt very embarrassed confronted with his former colleague in the Socialist Party. He knew from experience that Juziek could give as good as he would take, that he would be a hard nut to crack. He expected Juziek to reproach him and call him names.

But Juziek saved him that embarrassment. He treated Ciemnowski as though he had never seen him before. He behaved like any political prisoner facing his interrogator. He agreed that he was a Socialist. He contended that he had been arrested only because he refused to accept the new policy of his former colleague, the landowner Jan Gnilowski.

When Ciemnowski told him that both Chelia and Dinah had confessed that he and they were Communists, and were in touch with Russia, Juziek stared him straight in the face, and didn't say a word, till Ciemnowski dropped his gaze.

"Do you deny that you are a Communist?" Ciemnowski demanded.

"Emphatically!"

"Aren't you ashamed of yourself?" Ciemnowski tried a new line. "In my time a revolutionary on trial proudly proclaimed his faith—he did not deny it!"

"I am a Socialist," said Strzelkowski. "That's what I was, and that's what I am! And that I will proclaim before any judge!"

"I have witnesses who will tell the Court to your face that you are a Communist!"

"If you have a new definition by which every Opposition Socialist becomes a Communist! The government in Warsaw would then have to arrest a lot of people! And then what would happen to our democratic Socialism, and to our free speech, and the right to express a contrary opinion?"

"God forbid!" said Ciemnowski. "This has nothing to do with freedom of speech and the right to express a contrary opinion. This is sabotage! This is blowing up a government arsenal, to assist the Bolshevik enemy! This is treason!"

He produced the piece of electric wire that had been found on the scene of the explosion.

"What is this?"

"Wire."

"What sort of wire?"

"I am a bricklayer. I can tell you what bricks and mortar are, but I don't know much about wire."

"Have you never seen an electric wire? Here! Take it!"

Strzelkowski fingered it, and said: "Electric wire? You mean for wiring electric light?"

"What else?"

"All sorts of electric connections."

"Correct! This electric wire was used to blow up the arsenal. We have caught some of the gang, trying to escape to Russia. We have also caught the sentry. He pretended to be a country clod. But he was a cunning devil. If he had got away to Russia they would have made him a commissar. But we caught him at the frontier!"

The next day Ciemnowski had Jacob, Aaron, and some of the others released.

"It was all a mistake," he explained to them apologetically. "Sorry to have given you so much unpleasantness."

The reason was that Comrade Hersh Krumholz had gone to see Comrade Jan Gnilowski, and Comrade Jan Gnilowski had telephoned the chief of the political department. The rest were also released soon after. There was no real evidence against Juziek or any of them.

Chelia was doubly fortunate. On the one hand there was her father, who kept worrying Czapski and Ciemnowski to release his daughter, and they couldn't refuse Bernfel. On the other hand, Helena kept at her lover, Jan Gnilowski—"Let my sister go!" till he decided to tell Ciemnowski to set her free. But what really decided it was the government's decision to play down the explosions on political grounds. The government wanted the country to appear united behind it, and a trial of alleged terrorists among its own Socialist people would have defeated that purpose. So the order went out that the explosions had been an accident. And all the accused were freed.

25

Helena's Eyes Are Opened

Helena felt very angry at Jan Gnilowski over the way he had behaved at the big meeting in the Town Hall. They had arranged to meet afterward, but she hadn't kept the appointment. She had got out of the hall without being caught up in the fighting; she was only pushed around. But she was full of resentment at the way the meeting had been conducted from the platform, and particularly the way Jan had conducted it. She had gone straight home. Physically she had suffered no harm, but her spirit had been badly wounded.

She told herself that Jan hadn't stirred up the crowd. The Communists had started the whole trouble, that Juziek Strzelkowski, the ragamuffin bricklayer, who had lured away her sister Chelia, and that stupid Beth Hamedrashnik Jacob, with their silly speeches. Jacob especially had sickened her with his ungrammatical Polish.

Yet she couldn't get it out of her mind that Jan had spoken at the meeting like a real anti-Semite. She felt outraged and humiliated.

Helena had an underlying love of Jewishness. She respected her mother's pious ways. She liked to see her brother Notte saying his prayers every day. She had been delighted when her brother Baruch became a Zionist.

It did not mean, however, that she herself bothered much about being Jewish. It had never worried her that Jan was a Christian, as it had never worried her that he was a Socialist, though she detested Socialists. She loved him. They never discussed Socialism, as they never talked about her being Jewish and he Christian.

But the things she had heard him say about Jews at the meeting rankled. And when the fighting broke out in the hall she had felt ashamed that Strzelkowski and other Christians had fought for her and the other Jews, while her Jan sat on the platform and did nothing to defend her.

She hardly slept all night, so great was her annoyance. Yet in the morning she found herself wishing that he would come. He did come, around eleven in the morning, when she had just finished dressing.

She greeted him coldly, though she was very glad inwardly. She wanted him to see that she was angry; she wanted him to ask her forgiveness. He did. He said he was sorry about the disturbance at the meeting. It had been impossible for him to leave the platform. He hoped she had not been hurt. He kept excusing himself.

Driving with him afterward in his sleigh, she forgave him. He asked her to join him in a hunt on his estate the following week. He arranged to call for her, to take her there. Helena loved hunting. She was always very happy when they went hunting.

The first few days on the estate Helena was very happy. The hunting lodge where they stayed was a small wooden structure with a big verandah. It stood in the middle of a big orchard. The ground was thick with snow. The trees were covered with snow. The fruit bushes, raspberries, gooseberries, blackberries, looked like fantastic white gnomes. Wherever Helena looked the world was white.

The estate manager with his wife and children occupied a wing of two rooms and a kitchen. The workers on the estate lived in a thatched hut near the stables.

The house had once been the home of Jan Gnilowski's grandfather. Now it stood empty all year round, except for the occasional days or weeks when he decided to go hunting there. All the furniture, and the oil paintings, mostly bad ones, engravings, and photographs were from his grandfather's time. Gnilowski didn't bring his servant here from town. The estate manager's wife looked after him and Helena.

Helena sensed hostility in the woman's attitude; plainly she hated having to wait on a Jewess. The workers on the estate hated her being there even more.

Though they were supposed to be there for hunting, there were whole days when Jan and Helena never took a gun in their hands. Some days they never even left the house. Two people in love find enough ways of spending their time agreeably.

Helena loved all winter sports. She enjoyed walking for hours in the snow. But Jan tired at last of the long monotonous white stretches of snow-covered ground.

Helena was fond of sitting indoors, playing cards with Jan, or reading, or having Jan read Polish or Russian poetry aloud to her.

But her great passion was horse-back riding. She interested herself in the stables, in the animals, the horses and cows and pigs. She spent hours with them. She wanted to know everything about the agricultural implements used on the estate. Gnilowski got worried. He thought she was beginning to consider herself the mistress of the estate.

"She has made up her mind to turn Christian," he said to himself, "to make me marry her!"

That evening, after a good meal, they sat down, she in a Chinese silk kimono and he in a red silk dressing-gown and slippers, on the red leather couch in the small salon. Against the walls stood several bookcases full of books beautifully bound in leather, with gold lettering on the backs. There was a finely carved cabinet with French and Chinese porcelain and Venetian glass. The carpets on the floor were Bokharan and Persian. A small round table stood in the middle of the room with

four chairs. And there was a clavichord in the corner. The furniture was French
rococo. Heavy double curtains hung at the windows. A log fire burned in the big
grate, spreading a comfortable warmth through the room.

The estate manager's wife had lighted the big center chandeliers, but Helena
turned them out and lighted instead the two small wall lamps in silver sconces. It
gave the room a romantic mood. If there had been a piano in the room she would
have played Chopin, though she was no great pianist. But she didn't like the
clavichord.

She started looking through the books. Jan said that his grandmother had been a
great reader. Most of the books were in French and German, which Helena didn't
understand. Her languages were Polish and Russian. In the end she brought out
Pushkin's *Eugene Onegin*. But the next minute she saw a slim volume of translations of Tu Fu. "This is what I want," she said, hugging the Chinese poet. "They
are the loveliest poems! Listen!"

> Where the streams wind and the wind is always sighing,
> From the flutes of the forest come a thousand voices.

Jan stroked Helena's hair, and felt that he loved her now more than ever. She
fascinated him. She had a strange Jewish charm that captivated him. Her hair
gleamed in the firelight like copper. He pressed his lips to her hair, and inhaled the
perfume. He took her head in his hands, and kissed her lips. He kissed the tips of
her fingers, her arms, her breasts.

Helena closed her eyes with rapturous joy. But inside worrying thoughts kept
disturbing her. The memory of the meeting in the Town Hall came into her mind.
She wanted to speak to Jan about what had happened there. He called himself a
Socialist. She wasn't a Socialist, but she wanted him to talk to her now about Socialism, to explain it to her. And to talk about Zionism. She was not a Zionist; she had
never given Zionism a thought. But today, when she had been in the cow-shed,
while the cows were being milked, she had suddenly remembered something her
brother Baruch had said to her about the Kibbutzim in Palestine, about the young
Jews, the Chalutzim, who worked the land and milked the cows.

But Jan was not in a mood to talk about such things now. He wanted love-
making. And she wouldn't let him, and kept talking serious talk about Socialism
and about Zionism, he suddenly blurted out: "Why must Jews always be so dead
serious! Always worrying about world problems."

"Because the Jews are an old people, and have suffered so long and so much," he
added.

A sudden fear caught at Helena's heart. The word "suffering" frightened her. She
hadn't thought any more about her sister Chelia's warning: "Wait till your Jan casts
you off!" But now those words came back to her and frightened her. She flung her
arms round Jan's neck and kissed him passionately.

The next day they spent on horseback, but they had no sooner got back, had not
even stabled the horses, when Jan's servant arrived from the town to say that an
important visitor was waiting to see him there and he must return at once. They got
into the sledge and drove to the town.

They did it at top speed, in just under two hours. During the whole journey Jan didn't say a word to Helena. His mind was completely on his driving. And she made no attempt to speak to him either. She couldn't quite understand why, but something had snapped in her relations with Jan. Her mind was confused.

And she spoke no word to anyone when she reached home. She went straight to her room, locked the door behind her, and sat there with her eyes closed.

When they had got back to town Jan had asked her when he could see her again. She had rushed away without answering.

Now she sprang up and ran out, to go to see him. He was in the salon with he priest, with Krzewicki, and with a man she had never seen, a man of about twenty-eight, with a straw-colored mustache and short, flaxen hair. he looked to be a man who wouldn't say a word more than he absolutely had to, a hard, taciturn man with cold eyes and duel marks on his face.

Jan seemed embarrassed by Helena's arrival, but he greeted her, as did the others whom she knew. Then he introduced her to the stranger, whom they all treated with tremendous deference. Jan blundered by introducing Helena as Panna Bernfel, so that the man realized that she was Jewish and didn't offer to kiss her hand. He only bowed to her stiffly, out of politeness, in his friend's house. Helena felt his hostility to her, and she reproached herself for having come.

They had been talking when Helena entered the room, and broke off as soon as they saw her. There was tea on the table. The priest invited Helena to sit next to him, so that she had Krzewicki on the other side of her. The priest brought a chair over for her and started a polite conversation, made a few jokes, tried hard to dispel the embarrassment that she had brought into the room, and also to keep off the serious subject they had been discussing.

Krzewicki and Jan laughed at his jokes. Even Helena smiled. But the stranger remained cold and distant.

Then the priest turned to the Bible. He talked about the Old Testament and the New Testament. He was trying to mollify their important visitor by throwing out a hint that even if Helena was a Jewess she was on the way to becoming a Christian.

Helena felt more and more embarrassed. She didn't know which way to turn. She looked at the pictures on the walls, the paintings and engravings of Polish kings and patriots, already including Pilsudski, of Polish landscapes, and of ancient cities like Cracow and Lublin. She had seen these pictures many times, but she didn't know where else to direct her eyes. The priest kept talking at her about Jesus and salvation, and she was getting angry. She had never liked the priest, with his fat pink cheeks. She was working up a fierce hatred of him, and of everybody else there, including Jan. She suppressed the desire to get up and tell them all what she thought of them, and to run out of the room. She hated the lot of them. But most of all she hated herself for having put herself in this predicament.

She suddenly thought of a way of getting out of this place. She told Jan that she had come only to borrow one of his books, to read in bed. She went to the bookcase, selected a book, and left.

26

Fear

Fear was spreading among the Jews in the town, fear of a pogrom, like the pogroms in other towns all over Poland. There were reports of an agitator traveling from town to town, stirring up the people against the Jews. It was the young man Helena had seen at Jan's house. He was in their town now, spending a lot of time with the priest and with Krzewicki. There were stories about his close contacts with the authorities. They said his father was a member of the government in Warsaw. They said he was telling the Christian population to have no dealings with the Jews, to establish their own Christian cooperative trading organizations; he was preaching a boycott of the Jews, working up hate against the Jews.

It was a gray misty day. The snow had lost the blue glimmer it had when the sun shone. In spite of their growing fear, there were a number of Jews out in the streets. Their poverty drove them out of the gloomy homes. They wanted to meet people and talk things over, to find out if there was anything happening that held out some hope.

Across the street, chatting happily together, came Mechel Politician and Kalman Tinsmith.

"They must have good news!" one Jew said to another. "Let's go and find out what it is."

"Good news?" Mechel echoed. "I should say it is! All the papers are full of it! The Jews in America are coming to our aid. There are American committees already at work in Warsaw, Lodz, Lublin, Bialystock, in all the big towns; artisans are getting new Singer sewing machines, tools, all they need to restart their work-shops, and small traders are given credit loans for their business. And most important of all—we've got Palestine! Britain has given Palestine to the Jews! There's an official agreement, called the Balfour Declaration, that was made three years ago. The King of England, the greatest monarch in the world, the only King in Europe who has kept his crown, not like the Czar of Russia and the German Kaiser and the Austrian Emperor, said that the Jews should go back to Palestine and reestablish the Jewish Kingdom! We will soon hold a celebration for the third anniversary of his Declaration, and there will be meetings in every town where Jews live. Big celebrations everywhere! The Balfour Declaration!"

"It's a wonderful thing!" Kalman proclaimed ecstatically. Some women came and joined the group, listening to the good tidings with joyful hearts.

"When will we go to Palestine?" some wanted to know. "When will we be saved from this anti-Semitic inferno? When does the Redemption begin?"

"The Redemption has begun!" Kalman answered. "Baruch Bernfel is starting to distribute collection boxes today, with big Hebrew lettering on them, 'Keren Kayemeth'—the Fund for the Jewish People, for the settlement of Jews in Palestine! Every Jew, Zionist or not, will get a box and will put in it as much as he can spare, so that we can rebuild our Holy Land, the Land of our Fathers!"

"Look!" Kalman added. "There goes Baruch with my son Isaac distributing the boxes."

Actually, Kalman was mistaken. From that distance he had misjudged who the two young men were. They were not Baruch and Isaac, but Jacob and Aaron.

Jacob was feeling bitter. He was speaking about having been arrested.

"It was nothing in itself," he said. "They kept me only about twenty-four hours. But it was everything connected with it. The way Czapski and Ciemnowski behaved. They had been our comrades, fellow Socialists. It makes the whole thing look like a lie! This Socialist government of ours! It's make believe! How can you trust such people?" Aaron agreed with him:

"And talking of people you can't trust, I can't trust Abraham! I've spoken several times to Feiga and Hersh about him! How can you have a man like him on our Committee? They put his name forward, and that got him elected. Hersh said he is a good representative of the masses, a man of the people. What about Hersh himself, Comrade Krumholz? He's our chairman. He's a fighter. Agreed! He's been dedicated to the Party since he was a boy. He is a good platform speaker for the general public. He can keep discipline and carries out the instructions of the Central Committee faithfully. The rank and file adore him.

"But—I don't know how to explain it to you. The whole Party—Hersh, my sister Feiga, Abraham, it all seems to be only on the surface, a lot of phraseology, lies, like the Polish Socialist Party, like German Social Democracy. All party politics. And worst of all—treachery."

"I have my suspicions of David!" he went on. "I told Hersh and Feiga that. They won't listen to me! They think he is honest, and a good Party member. He does their various jobs for them, sticks up posters, hands out leaflets. Gives up a lot of time to this work. And it's that which makes me suspicious."

"What have you to go on?" Jacob asked. "Anything besides the feeling you've got about him? You never did like David!"

"No, I didn't!"

Aaron thought for a moment. Then, "What about you, Jacob?" he asked. "You seem to be out of step, too. You've gone silent since the arrests. Your mind is somewhere else."

"No, I'm not in step," he said. "I think it would be right if the Party expelled me from the Committee."

Aaron was pleased to hear that. "I have been thinking the same about myself," he said.

"I don't know whether I still belong to the Party," Jacob went on. "But I can't agree with Strzelkowski, with Communism."

"Why not?"

"There are a lot of reasons."

"Aren't you for a Revolution?"

Jacob didn't answer.

"I am for direct action!" Aaron burst out vehemently. "But I can't agree with the Communists, either. I am beginning to realize that what is wrong is government. Any government will do the same—will use force and violence and oppression. Ordinary people like me will always have to do what we are told, say what others will allow us to say."

"You've turned Anarchist?" Jacob asked, puzzled.

"No! What gave you that idea?"

"What you've just said."

"I don't know, Jacob! I was thinking aloud."

"I've also been thinking," said Jacob. "I don't like the way things are going. When we start building a new world we mustn't pull the foundations to pieces—the ethical and moral foundations on which our whole life stands. How can they build a new world without sound foundations, without truth and justice?"

The cobbler sat at his bench, in his cellar. Looking up he could see only snow, and people's feet passing. Having to do with feet all his life, he had learned to distinguish by the tread if it was a man, woman, or child; He could even tell if it was someone rich or poor, happy or sad.

But now he saw something very strange, very unusual. Men's feet dancing in the snow.

"The pogrom's started!" he said to himself, feeling terribly frightened. "Dobbe, where are you?" he called, and got up to look for his wife. "Dobbe! Feiga! Aaron! Abish! Mindel! Come here! We must keep together!"

He couldn't see his wife; and the older children were not at home. So he got the two younger children, Mindel and Zisel, and held them close. The children struggled to get away from him, crying, "Mother!"

"Yes," he said, "where is your mother? Where is Feiga? Where is Aaron?"

He wanted to find a hiding-place for the children. There was nowhere to hide here in the cellar. Frantic with fear he tore open the door, to seek safety outside. He collided at the door with his son Aaron, who was coming in.

"Where have you been, Aaron! Where can we hide from the pogrom?"

"There's no pogrom, father! There's nothing to hide from!"

"Then what are they dancing for?"

"Oh, that! That's Kalman Tinsmith and Mechel Politician and some other madmen like them dancing with joy because they've been given Palestine, and they're all going out to live there!"

Itche Cobbler's eyes went mad. He took hold of a big heavy wooden last, the length of a man's arm, and rushed into the street with it.

As Aaron had said, Kalman Tinsmith and the other Jews were dancing and singing the Hatikvah.

"Come along and join us, Itche!" Kalman greeted him. "Put away that club! I know! You thought the pogrom had started, and you were going for the pogromists with it! Self-defense! Good for you, Itche! Jewish self-defense! But there's no pogrom yet! We've got wonderful news! Come on, Jews, let's all sing! 'Od lo ovdu!'"

At the same time, the Committee of the Jewish Socialist Party was holding a meeting. It had its own building now, with a library, a reading room, and a big meeting hall. When Jacob arrived he told them of the funny scene he had witnessed outside Itche the cobbler's house—all those Jews dancing and singing because they had been told that Palestine had been given to the Jews.

"Aren't we a strange people, we Jews," he said. "For days no Jew dared to show his face in the street, afraid of a pogrom. And to-day they're dancing and singing Hatikvah in the street. Your father too, Dinah! And we sit here, having a meeting about Socialism and about the school."

The big question on the agenda was the pogrom, which everybody expected, and the organization of a Jewish self-defense. Hersh and Feiga were against the use of firearms. "We'll defend ourselves with sticks and iron bars," they said. "No shooting! Shooting would only provoke them!"

"That's rich!" Comrade Dinah Greenzweig laughed mockingly. "They pogrom us, and we mustn't provoke them! Perhaps we shouldn't use iron bars either! Just stand still and let them kill us!"

Aaron sided with Dinah.

But Hersh called the meeting back to the agenda. He reminded them that the first item on the agenda was the school. Jacob then opened the discussion, repeating his point that a Jewish school must teach the Bible—its poetry and mythology and its ethics, and the early history of the Jewish people, even if much of it was only legend. And the Prophets! Naturally, in Yiddish! It was not only Jewish national, he said, but also Socialist. The Prophets, beginning with Moses, were the first Socialists. The Patriarch Abraham, the father of the Jews, had started as a rebel who had overthrown the idols of his day.

Everybody there, except Aaron, who didn't join in the discussion, spoke against Jacob. Abraham more than all the others. Hersh and Feiga agreed that they must teach Jewish history, especially Jewish working-class history, and the history of the Yiddish language, and Yiddish literature. But not the Bible! Definitely not the Bible!

The second item on the agenda was the cooperative, which had been started in the first year of the German occupation, but had soon been closed down for a number of reasons—the inexperience and the incompetence of the comrades who had been elected to run it, and their constant quarreling among themselves about how to run it, everybody wanting to be boss. They hadn't lost much over it, because it had never grown big enough to incur heavy losses.

They decided that there was no time now to go into these matters. They had two important questions to deal with that could not be delayed. The first was the Self-

Defense. The other was whether they could continue to have confidence in the government, and go on supporting it, or come out in opposition.

The speeches went on—on and on—; just then the door burst open, and Motte Katz and Lemel Gaver, the two thieves who had turned Socialist and become honest workmen, rushed in.

"It's started!" They shouted.

Frightened Jews were hiding behind the big stove at the end of the long passage in Kalman the tinsmith's ruined house. Men, women, and children lay there with fear in their eyes, and dread in their bellies. The older men muttered "Shema Yisroel!" "Lord God in Heaven, help us!" The women prayed. The young children clung to their mothers, who held their hands over their mouths to stop them from crying out and calling attention to them.

Jews were running through the streets, looking for a place to hide—a cellar, an attic, a refuge. And Christians were running after them, throwing stones that sometimes hit them on the head or caught them in the back. Most of the pogromists were young boys, town lads and villagers, and young girls with sacks in which to put the loot they would collect from the Jewish houses. Windows were being smashed all over the town. Hooligans smashed Gershon the weaver's loom, and ran off with parts of it, breaking the wood to fragments as they ran, and flinging them about in the road. Gershon had been beaten about the head with sticks and iron bars because he had tried to stop them. Blood was streaming from his face.

The members of the self-defense arrived—Hersh, Feiga, Jacob, Abraham, Dinah, Aaron, Motte Katz, Lemel Gaver, with a crowd of carters, carriers, butchers, bakers, locksmiths, cobblers, and some intellectuals led by Isaac Lehrman. They were armed with iron bars. As soon as they arrived the pogromists made off. Only Stash, their leader, drunk with blood lust, stayed, shouting defiance.

Just then old Mateusz arrived, carrying his big plane, and crashed it down on Stash's head. Stash staggered; he was covered with blood. Then he bent down, drew his knife from his top boot, and stuck it in the old man's chest. The same moment Juziek, Mateusz's son, came on the scene with a crowd of his comrades. He had a revolver in his hand. He shot Stash dead.

Part Four

27

In Between

The bad doesn't last for ever, any more than the good. Nothing stays the same. Only sometimes people think good times have started when in reality things are getting worse.

The severe winter had gone. And the Jews in the town thought their troubles were over. The spring sun began to shine, and they became hopeful and optimistic.

Old Mateusz, who had died defending the Jews, and his murderer, Stash, had been buried quietly. There were people in the town who had wanted to give Stash a big patriotic funeral, but both police chiefs, Czapski and Ciemnowski, had prohibited it, mostly because they feared a counterdemonstration by the Socialists, who had wanted to give old Mateusz an imposing funeral.

Juziek was not arrested, nor charged with the killing of his father's murderer. The fire seemed to have been put out, but actually it was still smoldering.

It was the first mild day. Children who had been kept indoors all through the winter frosts came tearing out of the cold, damp, stifling houses, as if they had been set free from prison. They went whooping along to the marketplace and the open highway. They didn't know what to do with all their pent-up young energy.

They found great joy in the streams and rivulets that were growing swollen with the melting snow. The youngsters had a fine time, digging channels for the waters to run through to the river behind the town. They put up a dam of stones and mud to make a sea, on which to sail ships all the way to America.

There were Kalman the tinsmith's three sons, Itche Cobbler's Abish, Reb Yossel Fuksman's Ozer, Gronem the melamed's two boys Yoske and Leibel, Abraham

Tailor's Noah, even dreamy Benjamin, the scribe's favorite son, who said he had come only to keep an eye on his younger brother Meir. Berke Petzer and Osher Lekech were as always the ringleaders, and Black Godel, Berl the dyer's son, was their adjutant.

Godel showed great expertise in the building of the dam—he was quite an engineer. He worked hard at it. Not like Ozer, who did very little himself but kept telling everybody else what to do.

The small fry jumped and splashed about and got themselves sopping wet and all covered with mud. There were several little girls among them, like Gershon the weaver's sad-eyed only child, Tzirel. Water was running from her plaits. The little girls lifted their skirts to the knees. But they made no attempt to help their "menfolk" at their "work." They only splashed about.

The "workers," using bits of tin, and sometimes only their bare hands, scooped out a big hole and made a "sea" in the middle of the marketplace.

Suddenly the Jewish children found that they were surrounded by a gang of Christian boys and girls. They were no older and no bigger than they were themselves, but except for Berke, Osher, and Godel, the Jewish children were scared. "Dirty Jews!" said one of the Christian boys. "We didn't kill you that last time. We'll get you next time!"

The Jewish children ran away, followed by stones and jeers: "The circumcised!"

Then Berke Petzer punched the leader of the gang in the mouth, and the situation was completely changed. Osher Lekech, Godel, Yoske, and even Benjamin all went for the gang, who made off. The Jewish "heroes" held the field.

"Thought we'd be scared! They forgot how our Jewish Self-Defense gave the pogromists a beating!"

The boys who had fled now came back, and got a good talking to for being cowards, and Ozer got a clip on the ear into the bargain, because he had led the flight and the others had followed him. Benjamin put on a very serious face and chided Ozer. Yoske jeered at the lot of them, said they were lousy cowards. Yoske was like a real revolutionary, jeering at Ozer, the rich man's son, as a good example of bourgeois timidity. "That's what they're all like!"

Then everybody set to work again building the dam. The Christian boys had broken down parts of the wall.

"Over here, all of you!" Yoske suddenly called out.

"What's up!" Godel wanted to know, very much unmoved by Yoske's excitement.

"Look! If we cut through here all the waters will come rushing to this spot! Like a revolution! All power to the proletariat!"

They all watched intently while Yoske worked feverishly to bring about his "revolution." When they saw he was right they all came to his assistance. The last bit of wall was torn down by the rush of water, which now flooded in from all sides.

"The great sea! The ocean!" they all shouted excitedly. Yoske was triumphant. Young Leibel was proud of his big brother's achievement. Everybody believed him now that his eldest brother, Hersh, the famous Socialist, had helped to make the revolution in 1905, and had single-handed killed a hundred gendarmes, governors, and ministers with his revolver and with the bombs that he had thrown. Godel was the only skeptic who still refused to believe it.

The "sea" expanded, grew much bigger. And two of the smaller children who had gone paddling in it were nearly drowned. It was Tzirel who jumped in to the rescue, with Godel, Yoske, and others after her. Berke gave them all a good telling off when the two youngsters were brought in to safety. "What did you think you were doing," he shouted at the two little ones. Tzirel put a protecting arm round them, and told them not to be frightened.

Other youngsters were sailing "ships" on the "ocean." "Hurray! We're going to America!"

A few stuck sticks with rags on them into the water, and shouted: "We've conquered the sea!"

Then everybody started work again, building a bridge across the sea, and a fortress in the middle of the sea. When they were tired they sat on the ground to rest. But they did not stop chattering.

The gang of Christian boys suddenly came marching back, with rakes and spades like rifles over their shoulders, singing soldiers' songs. They were following a stream that had suddenly started running toward their "sea" in the marketplace. "They've opened the wall of the dam, and they're sending all the water here to flood us out."

When the flood came both gangs, the Jews and the Christians, set up a wild whoop. It was a grand sight.

Then the ringleaders of each gang began exchanging hostile looks, spoiling for the fight.

But Benjamin saw that the water was gathering height and spreading, threatening to break into the houses. And he suddenly cried out: "We've got to divert the water, we've got to send it to the river! All of us together! Or else we'll flood the houses!"

The ringleader of the Christian gang gave his followers an order, and all the boys, Christians and Jews, set to work with their spades and rakes to turn the water to the river outside the town.

28

Preparing for Passover

The sun was already warm. Jews and Christians were preparing for Passover and for Easter, Jews to celebrate the deliverance from bondage in Egypt, Christians to rejoice that Jesus had risen from the dead. Moses and Jesus; both were Jews, who had come bringing God's message to the Jews.

The Jews washed and scoured and kashered their utensils and their tables and chairs, made their homes clean and tidy. The Christians did the same. Both had their dwellings painted or at least whitewashed. Both baked—the Jews matzoth, the Christians cakes.

The high water from the melted snows and the rains had subsided. The town looked clean. The chestnut trees and the lime trees spread their branches up toward the spring sky and the radiant sun. The trees were filling themselves with sap, with new life, and were forming buds. The brass cross on top of the church tower sparkled in the sun. The Virgin at the entrance to the Church was kneeling before her son. She looked lovely in her freshly painted red and blue garments, her head bent in adoration and supplication to the God of mercy and love.

The rebuilt Beth Hamedrash was grateful for its new roof and doors and windows, and thanked God for His mercy. The birds chirped and twittered. The seed planted in the fields was beginning to sprout.

But the newspapers were full of the war between Russia and Poland, which was now flaring up with the spring. Yet it didn't stop the Jews from going on with their preparations for celebrating the Liberation, or the Christians from rejoicing in their savior's resurrection.

There were again a lot of women standing about outside Kalman the tinsmith's ruined house, where he had managed to put one room into decent living condition. Again the big stove was burning, and huge pots of water were boiling on it. Only now the hot water was wanted for kashering their things for Passover. The women had their sleeves rolled up, busy scrubbing and scouring, without stopping their chatter for one moment.

They were talking about the American delegates staying at Bernfel's house; they were swearing and cursing at Bernfel, and his sons, especially Baruch, and also Nachman, Mirel's husband, who had made himself a big boss at the Committee. They spoke about Palestine, and about the Socialists, and gossiped about all the sinful things that people were doing in the town. Their faces lit up talking about them.

Kalman's wife, Rachel, was doing the work of three; her face shone happily. She kept adding water to the pots and putting more wood on the fire.

"You're not getting on too well with it, are you, Braina?" she said to Samuel the orchardman's wife, an elderly woman who found the work hard.

"Let me give you a hand," said Rachel, taking over from her, "We're none of us getting younger."

The woman sighed. "I can't get to sleep at night," she complained. "In the summer I sleep in the loft in the orchard. Plenty of air there. But in winter, in our tumble-down hut, it's impossible to breathe. Eleven of us sleeping in that pigsty. My husband and I and Hannah, our youngest, that's three; Koppel, his wife, and their four children makes nine. Then there's the newly married couple, who are already talking of a divorce."

"You see!" said Mechel Politician's wife, with a note of triumph in her voice, "you see what we're coming to nowadays, what happens to our modern love affairs!"

"Rubbish!" Rachel protested, "modern love affairs, old time love affairs—it's always been the same!"

"No, it hasn't," Mechel's wife insisted. "It was different when we were young."

"You know Tzippe," she went on, her face beaming over the spicy story she was going to relate, "the one who was raped by the Cossacks and the soldiers ... now she's pregnant. Guess who! Hersh, Gronem the melamed's son. Everybody says so. But he won't marry her! He's going to marry his comrade Feiga, Itche the cobbler's daughter. He's been going around with her long enough."

The other women pricked up their ears. But Rachel said reprovingly: "You mustn't say such things! It isn't right!"

Itte, Abraham the tailor's wife, shook her head sadly. "That's what's happened to our Jewish life. Not a decent Jewish girl left in the town. All the doing of those Germans ..."

"Yes, it was the war," the other women agreed. "It has killed our Jewish life."

Their hands went slack. All this scouring and cleansing of pots and pans, this kashering, seemed meaningless now; what good was it, when Jewish observances and Jewish decencies were being flouted? Wasn't it all futile?

But they went on mechanically scouring and cleansing all the same.

"God will help! Things will improve!" the tinsmith's wife tried to cheer them up. "We've gone through worse times. God saved us from Egypt. He will save us from all our troubles."

"Wonderful words!" old Braina cried. "That's how it always was! And that's how it will be now! God will help us! I can see it in myself. Things are looking up! We've been through terrible times. But now my husband has rented an orchard again, and we'll be able to make a living."

29

Time Breaks and Time Makes

Passover was always the loveliest, the most precious festival to Jews. For thousands of years, year in and year out, the whole Jewish people rejoiced with childlike glee over the Liberation from Egypt. The poorest made his home look nice, scrubbed and scoured and washed, everything clean as a new pin. In the night before Passover, when no suspicion of leaven was left in the house, the Passover pots and pans and dishes, the crockery and the cutlery that had been stored away all year, were unpacked and brought out, with glassware, with cups and goblets, sometimes good cut glass, sometimes colored glass, with ornamental designs. The finest cup was left for the Prophet Elijah. There was china and glassware that had come down in the same family for generations. And illustrated Hagaddas printed in Amsterdam. The house was fragrant with the smell of fish and meat. There were matzoth enough for the whole week of the Festival.

Husband and wife and children, even the poorest, managed to get something new to wear, at least a new hat, or a pair of trousers or a skirt, a pair of shoes, even when it was impossible to get a whole new suit or a new dress. Because renewal was a symbol—the Children of Israel had come out of Egypt to a new life.

The finest Passover celebration in the town had always been in the home of Reb Mordecai Goldblum, the wealthy manufacturer and devout Chassid. He had kept up the old patriarchal way of life. All his married sons and daughters with their husbands and wives and children had lived on the factory. On Sabbaths and Festivals they all sat together at one table. There was a festiveness about the Seder. It was like a great banquet in a royal palace. As soon as the sun set the house blazed with light, and there was an air of expectancy over everything. Big and small wore new clothes. The women wore their jewelry. The maids too had new dresses. The host had given everybody handsome Passover gifts, including the workers in his factory.

The Seder started early, so that the little ones could stay up till the end. The long oak table was extended at both ends, and additional tables were attached to make it longer. Silver candlesticks and menorahs and beautiful vases of flowers were set along the whole length of the table. The flames of the lighted candles flickered in the red and golden wine, and broke into rainbow colors against the crystal glasses. The Amsterdam and Padua Hagaddas were open at the pictures of Jews doing slave labor in Egypt, building Pithom and Rameses, Moses standing before Pharoah, Moses turning his staff into a serpent, Moses slaying the Egyptian, Moses bringing down the ten plagues, dividing the Red Sea, and the Egyptians drowning in it with their chariots and horses.

A glass of wine stood on a small silver dish beside each Hagaddah. Counting the poor who had been invited as guests and the servants of the house there must have been several minyanim seated at the Seder table.

Reb Mordecai, the "King" of the Seder, sat reclining at the head of the table, leaning against his raised pillow as on a throne. He wore a white linen mantle, a kittel, with a silver braid collar, a gold-embroidered white skull cap and a broad silk girdle round his loins. The Seder dish with the symbolic matzoth, the shank bone, the roasted egg, the maror and cheroset stood before him, covered with an embroidered white satin cloth, which Serel, the Seder "Queen" had made when she was fourteen. The embroidered flowers and leaves looked as though they had grown, they were so natural. And her Shield of David with the two Hebrew words that meant "For Passover" shone like bright lights.

After he had inspected the Seder dish, satisfying himself that everything was correctly set out, the master of the house smiled a welcome to the poor who had come as his guests, and to the servants, threw a loving glance at his wife and children, then "commanded" all the glasses to be filled. His Kiddush was a song.

The servants brought in big brass basins with two-handled copper cups for pouring, and pitchers of water and white towels for washing the hands.

The service proceeded in the usual way, with the solemn recital of the verses "This is the bread of affliction", till it came to the turn of the youngest little boy to ask the Four Questions. Then the older boys repeated the answers and explanations they had learned in chedar, and the King on his "Throne" recited: "We were slaves in Egypt," with all the participants repeating after him.

They went through the story of Israel's sufferings in Egypt and the deliverance. They rendered thanks to God for His miracles and His mighty deeds. The great legend came true for all who sat there at the table; for most of them the poetry of the ancient narrative was living and real, as though it was all happening before their eyes. The patriarch on his white-cushioned throne led the others in the dramatic recital of the Hagaddah, declaiming and singing it louder, with more emphasis. He raised his voice to an agonized shriek when he came to relate how on Pharoah's command all the new-born male children of the Hebrews had to be cast in the river and drowned, as though he were himself witnessing and suffering from this despotic edict. Everybody at the table, the children too, raised their voices as he did, so that it became a chorus of the children of Israel crying aloud to God to help them and save them. And salvation came: "Therefore," they sang, "we thank, praise, laud, glorify, extol, honor, bless, exalt, and reverence Him who did all these miracles for our ancestors and for us."

When the second cup of wine had been drunk the servants brought in again the big brass basins, the copper two-handled pouring cups, the pitchers of water and the towels, and carried them around to each guest to wash—this time before starting the meal.

Everybody chattered happily—the children, with more than half the Hagaddah said and released from the strain of the solemn service, were dancing with excitement on their chairs. They were hungry now, and the food was very welcome.

The young women, Reb Mordecai's daughters and daughters-in-law, served fish out of the huge fish bowls in front of them. Reb Mordecai kept telling everybody to eat, and he hoped they would all meet again round the table next year for the Seder.

After the first course the women and children each took a glass of wine, but the men drank good strong Austrian Sliwowitz. The young women giggled and said they wanted some of the strong stuff as well. But after taking only one sip they pulled faces and spluttered and coughed. Pearl was the only one (she was a big girl now) who drank a man's drink like a man. Her cheeks flushed and her eyes sparkled. She looked radiant.

Everybody was now very merry. The daughters and the daughters-in-law flirted with their husbands openly, and Pearl laughed and joked with her brothers and brothers-in-law, but mostly with her father. Reb Mordecai told everybody that the limitation to four glasses was lifted. They could drink as much as they liked. And when they drank their hearts opened in song. They sang the Rebbe's melodies, and Pearl broke the rule that women should not sing these songs by joining in with the men. Reb Mordecai gave his judgment that on the Seder night women with a good singing voice ought to sing.

His wife, Serel, the "Queen" of this feast, hadn't the heart to say no. She herself enjoyed the singing. She looked up shyly at her husband, the "King." She kept fingering her long diamond earrings, the rows of pearls round her neck, and the emerald brooch on her dress.

When the meal was finished the master of the house told the little ones to search for the hidden Afikomen, and said there would be a reward for the finder. Then they said grace. The third cup of wine was drunk, and the fourth cup was filled. Reb Mordecai filled Elijah's cup himself. He asked for the door to be opened, and all stood to receive the Prophet. Reb Mordecai went quite pale with awe and reverence as he pronounced the welcoming words, "Baruch Habo!" Everybody felt a shiver of pious fear run through them, and all joined in the chorus: "Pour not Thy wrath upon the nations that know Thee not!"

When the door was shut again, at the closing words, "Destroy them from under the heavens of the Lord!" they reseated themselves and continued saying the rest of the Hagaddah. As soon as the fourth cup of wine had been drunk the little ones were sent to bed. The real merriment started then. The Rebbe's melodies were sung again. Till the Seder ended with that lovely and profound song, "Had Gadya"—"One only kid that my father bought for two zuzim."

All rose from the table. The guests said goodbye and left. Those who were tired went to bed. But the young women, Pearl among them, went out on the verandah to get some fresh air. They looked up to the moon and longed for the love of which their husbands spoke when they repeated the words of the Song of Songs.

The war had changed all this. Reb Mordecai Goldblum kept this Passover like the previous five Passovers since the war and the German occupation in quite a different fashion. On the eve of the Festival he said to his daughter Pearl:

"You know what it used to be like in the old days, my child. Our Jewish life has been destroyed. Mine no longer exists. I could perhaps do what people like Bernfel and Fuksman and others are doing. I could be rich again. I could at least make a living. But ..." He flung out his arm despairingly.

Pearl had prepared for the Passover festival as well as she could, as she had been doing all the years since the destruction. There was only the one habitable room now. The holes and gaps in the walls and ceiling had been mended more or less, otherwise the room would have collapsed. Pearl was now earning a little money, giving lessons to the children of the newly rich. She had made the room look as nice as possible, and she had bought matzoth and wine, fish and meat.

Returning that night from the Synagogue service, Reb Mordecai tried to put as much Festival joy into his "Good Yom Tov" greeting as he could. The tablecloth was not expensive, but it was clean and fresh. There were no massive silver candlesticks now, only two small tin ones. Reb Mordecai put on the white kittel with the silver braid collar, and the skull cap, and the broad silk girdle round his loins. These and his Tallith and Tephilin and a few other ritual articles were all he had saved from his former state.

He took his seat on the cushioned "Throne" like a "King" and started the Seder. But when he came to the words "This is the bread of affliction," and set his hands on the embroidered cloth that covered the Seder dish that his wife, Serel, had embroidered when she became his betrothed, he wept. And Pearl, seeing him weep, wept also.

30

A Different Kind of Festival

The intermediate days of Passover came, and brought a happier mood to many Jews in the town. The Zionists were having their Balfour Day celebration now. And the Jewish Socialists were opening their secular Jewish school.

It was night. In their houses the people were getting ready for these two big celebrations. Not only in the rich houses, like Bernfel's and Fuksman's, but also in the homes of the poor. All wore their best for the occasion. The streets were full of people streaming in two directions, the Zionists to their meeting, and the Jewish Socialists to theirs.

The Socialist hall was not very festive-looking. It had no bright lights. But the people who came there, most of them with their children, looked very happy. This was a great occasion for them.

All the members of the Committee were busy on the stage behind the drawn curtain. Other comrades were in the hall, the stewards with red armbands and red ribbons on their dresses or in their lapels. A bell rang, and the curtain opened. On the stage stood a mixed choir. All the girls in the choir wore white blouses with red ribbons on them. Bluma stood out among the rest; she was the best singer in the choir. Tzippe, a new comrade, was also in the choir. (Hersh had brought her into the Party himself.) Dinah, who had selected the choir together with Abraham, had discovered that Tzippe had a good voice. So this poor young woman, who had been raped by soldiers and Cossacks and had for so long been an object of pity and scorn in the town, found herself now accepted by the Socialist section of the Jewish population.

The male members of the choir stood in a row behind the women, all with stiff white collars and black bow ties, and red ribbons in their buttonholes. Abraham was the conductor.

He raised his arms, and the choir sang, not at all badly, "Brothers and sisters of toil and want." The people in the hall stood. Then the choir left the stage, and Comrade Hersh Krumholz, in a sober black suit with a red ribbon in his lapel, walked on, and announced that the Polish Socialist Party, meaning the town administration, had sent an official delegate to their meeting, the schoolteacher Jadenusza Slomova. He presented her to the audience, praising her work for Socialism and for humanity and for their town as head of their educational department. Everybody applauded, and Comrade Slomova delivered a brief but warmly worded message of greeting.

Next, Comrade Hersh Krumholz spoke about the importance of a secular Jewish school, and about the freedom and the rights the Jews had now obtained from the Socialist government of liberated Poland.

Everybody clapped and cheered. The curtain was drawn, and when it opened again Comrade Feiga and Comrade Abraham had arranged a dramatization of Peretz's poem "The Three Seamstresses." It was at the same time a commemoration of the fifth anniversary of Peretz's death.

There was a sewing machine on the stage, and a table and three stools. Feiga was at the machine. Two other girls sat sewing.

Feiga was declaiming:

> I sew by day and I sew by night,
> But no wedding dress to make my own life bright.

A lot of girls in the audience, no longer young, sighed with feeling. And when Feiga went on, "There is no food and no sleep for me," the older women groaned and moaned: "Poor thing! She's not the only one."

One of the other girls took up the song:

> I sew and stitch like this all day,
> And I only stitch into my hair more gray.

And when Feiga declaimed the closing lines:

> I shall soon forget the past.
> The town will give me a shroud at last,"

most of the women were wiping tears from their eyes. "The Three Seamstresses" was a tremendous success.

Then Isaac Lehrman and Pearl Goldblum, the teachers, came on the stage with little Abish, Comrade Feiga's young brother, and he recited Reisen's

> A family of eight
> And beds only two.
> And when the night comes,
> What can you do?

Again people sighed and groaned: "That's how it is! Some of us haven't even the two beds, and we have to sleep on the floor."

After that Black Godel came on. He wore a short jacket much too tight, that his sister Reisel had made over from an old coat, not so much for Passover as for the school, which he had joined against his father's wish. His shiny black hair was combed back. His eyes sparkled mischievously as he bowed to his audience, and started reciting in a squeaky voice:

> Children all alike we are,
> Forming one company.
> We know no rich and we know no poor,
> And our own world build we.

The children sitting in the hall with their parents cheered and envied the children on the stage.

Then another group took the stage, led by Tzirel, Gershon the weaver's only surviving child, in a blue dress that the school had given her.

"Children, will you do what I say?" she sang.

The other children nodded their heads, "Yes!"

> Then see how fresh the fruit trees grow!
> Hold hands, and let us dancing go!

And the children danced on the stage, around and around, and Pearl stood clapping her hands and keeping time. The whole audience cheered and clapped. Then the children, with Lehrman conducting, sang:

> And though the day
> Is far away
> When love and peace prevail,
> Yet we will wait,
> For soon or late
> Our dream will never fail!

Balfour Day was being observed in a much larger hall, the largest and finest in the town. It was hung with hundreds of small blue and white flags, and the place was packed. The hall was brightly lighted. The best Jews in the town were there, with Bernfel, his wife, his two sons, and his daughter Helena in the front row. The Bernfel women were well dressed and wore jewelry.

Madame Fuksman was there too, also in the front row, with her sons Baruch and Ozer. She had not really wanted to come, because her husband had refused to go, insisting that Zionism was irreligious. He had stayed stubbornly at home. Besides that, she did not like to show herself in public since that terrible tragedy with her daughter. But her son Reuben had made her come.

Now she was glad of it, because Reuben seemed to be quite a big man here. He was talking to Bernfel and his wife and Helena. He mixed with all the big people. They consulted him about things, and he had his say.

She saw Mirel and her husband, and Reb Henoch Malach sitting far behind her, in the fourth row. Reb Henoch Malach had found that Zionism was in accordance with Jewish religious belief, was part of the hope for the restoration of Zion.

All the rich businessmen were there, all those who had made fortunes out of the latest developments, and also the people who had been rich in the old days and had not managed to reestablish themselves in the new conditions. A lot of poor people too had come—plain, simple folk like Itche the cobbler and Fishel Shmulevitch, the Jewish militiaman, who had been dismissed from the force after the pogrom. They all came with joy and hope in their hearts, expecting to be liberated from the anti-Semitism around them. Shimmele Loterinek was in raptures. Kalman the tinsmith and Mechel the politician felt on top of the world. Many people wore a blue-and-white ribbon in their buttonhole or on their dress.

The stage was draped in blue and white, with a great Shield of David over it. A large gold-framed portrait of Herzl stood on a pedestal in the center of the stage, flanked on each side by palms in green tubs.

The meeting opened with everybody standing and singing Hatikvah. Some were so moved by it that they had tears in their eyes.

Then Bernfel spoke, very briefly. Nobody knew what he said, but everybody clapped. He went on to announce that the authorities had sent a representative to this meeting, and he introduced the Vice Chairman of the Town Council, an elderly Christian who was received tumultuously. He told them that this was a great occasion—it was a tremendous thing that one of the Great Powers, the mighty British Empire, had interested itself in this way in the destiny of the Israelites, an ancient people who had suffered terribly through the centuries, but God had preserved them alive, because they were His Chosen People, and now after they had been punished for their sins, God was going to restore them to their Land, as the Bible had foretold. He said that the Polish government and the Polish people shared the hopes of the Jews to return to their own land, and would do everything to further this noble Zionist aim. There was another outburst of applause at the end of his speech. Then Bernfel read a long telegram of good wishes from the American relief committee now in Warsaw, signed by Mr. Silverstone.

After that Baruch Bernfel spoke. It was a good speech, sincere and full of Jewish emotion. He spoke particularly to the young, calling them to join the Hehaluz and go out to the Land of Israel to restore it, to build it. He appealed to all Jews to join the Zionist movement. "The great two-thousand-year-old dream has been realized," he cried. He spoke of the Jewish sufferings through the ages, the Inquisition, the auto-da-fés, the expulsions, and the pogroms. Then he spoke of Herzl, and of the Balfour Declaration, and he concluded: "It depends on you whether we remain in exile and continue to suffer, or return to our Holy Land and build a Jewish state, and become again a nation like all the nations. You have our future in your hands."

It was a good speech, and he deserved the applause that followed. Then troops of boys and girls went around with blue-and-white boxes, collecting for the Jewish National Fund.

After that came the artistic part of the evening. Helena Bernfel made a hit reciting Yehuda Halevi's Hebrew poem in Bialik's Yiddish translation:

> Do you still long for your children, Mother Zion,
> Who, scattered and dispersed, long for you?

The people in the hall held their breath listening to her, hearing her voice tremble, like a woman in love weeping to her lover:

> I long for you! My heart goes out to those places
> Where the Patriarchs met with angels,

Where the Shechina rested, where the Creator
Opened the holy gates.

She continued:

Where shall I take wings, that I might fly
And lay my broken heart upon your shores?
I would fall down upon your earth, and kiss the ground,
Kiss every footstep, kiss each separate stone.

People wouldn't stop clapping when she was done. They wanted her to come back on the stage, but Helena had disappeared.

The choir came on and sang Hebrew and Yiddish songs, some of them gay and rollicking; then with hands on each other's shoulders they danced the Horah.

31

Jacob with Diogenes' Lamp

Both demonstrations made a big impression on the Jews of the town. The Zionists gained many new members. So did the Socialists. Both movements grew in strength, the Socialists particularly, because as the war against Russia spread, the Polish government became more concerned to accede to many of the demands of the workers and peasants, and promised that after the war it would realize the full Socialist program—distributing the land among the peasants and nationalizing the factories and the mines, everything. It started a sudden great burst of activity. Manufacturers whose factories were still standing, even if they were badly damaged, put them into quick repair, adapted them to war production, and the machines were kept going twenty-four hours a day. Small industry also picked up. Workers and artisans were in full employment. Anti-Semitism disappeared overnight. There were government orders enough to keep everybody busy. Smuggling too revived, as in the time of the German occupation.

Gronem the melamed was busy teaching children in his chedar, as in the old days. Attendance was large, even though there was now a Yiddish secular school in town. He taught the youngsters Pentateuch—"The nakedness of your father's wife you shall not uncover." He taught them to translate the Hebrew words into their vernacular Yiddish: "The nakedness of your sister, your father's daughter, you shall not uncover." "What does it mean?" he asked. The eight- and nine-year-olds didn't know what to say. Those who knew didn't dare say it. Again Gronem asked what it meant. Getting no answer, he boxed the ears of the nearest boy. He pulled another boy's ear, and the boy screamed. Hersh was in the room at the time, packing his things. He had found a place to live, a room of his own. He was busy at his trade now, and earning enough. He was going to open a small workshop in the room, with two or three workmen.

It infuriated him to hear the way his father was teaching the young boys, and

181

hitting out at them. He held his father's hands, and said: "Leave the boys alone! Aren't you ashamed teaching them such things at their age? Stop hitting them!"

Gronem couldn't keep his temper back: "You want me to be ashamed of teaching God's Torah! I know the sort of things you do with your Socialist clique! You and your girls!" He pointed to Tzippe, who was helping Hersh to pack. "Wait! You'll rot in prison again, like you did before!"

Hersh tried to keep calm, but his face went white, and his fingers tightened on his father's wrists.

"Let go!" his father screamed, kicking out at Hersh. "He has lifted his hand against his own father!"

Hersh let go, and Gronem fell back on the floor. Tzippe lifted him up, and said reproachfully: "You have no right to say such things about Hersh and me. You should be ashamed of yourself! It's a dirty lie!" Then Hersh and Tzippe left the room, with Hersh's pack of his few belongings.

Gronem put his hat straight, drew his fingers through his beard, sat down again in his seat, and went on with the lesson: "The nakedness of your sister, your father's daughter, you shall not uncover."

Gronem's wife wasn't at home then. The curtain that divided the room in two was drawn right across, shutting out the other half, where the scribe was in bed. He was very ill, and couldn't get up any more, not even though the weather was much milder now. The death of the new-born child—the third in five years—had depressed him. He was very weak.

Isaac said he was going to see Pearl, so Jacob said he would go with him.

"We must have our own country, like every nation," Lehrman said, as they walked along together. "Because we can't possibly assimilate utterly. We have been assimilating all the time, from the beginning, since we first became a people, and we are still here, the Jewish people. I believe it is because we are more firmly rooted in the source of life-understanding. Leaves fall, branches break off, but the tree remains, renews its green and brings forth fresh fruit. All the Great Powers tried to destroy us—Assyria, Babylon, Greece, Rome, the Crescent and the Cross, the Crusades, the Inquisition, Chmielnicki, the Russian pogromists. All failed. We are the burning bush that is not consumed. Yet we draw our sustenance from everywhere, from the cultures of all peoples. We are a tree that takes sun and water from all around us, and we give our fruit freely to all."

"I never said that the Jewish people should assimilate," Jacob said. "I belong neither to the Left nor to the Right, who both insist that the Jewish people ought to cease to exist as a people because we have no country of our own. But I am not so sure as you are, Isaac, that neither wind nor sun will make the Jew fling off his cloak. The sun may yet succeed in doing that. There are no everlasting laws. The sun has never warmed us enough yet.

"But the question is a different one. You say it is because we are more firmly rooted in the source of life-understanding. There I agree with you. All the peoples of the earth will have to accept the message. Then, my friend, we shall indeed remove our Tallith, and the Christian will remove his crucifix."

"Is that why you are against Zionism?"

"I never said that, though I do belong to a Party that is combating Zionism. But it is my conviction that as long as this mission has not been fulfilled we shall be in

Galuth, even in our own country, the Land of Israel. Even if the land becomes completely ours, as in ancient times, there is Jewish blood being shed in Palestine now. Wars are still going on. How many wars were there in the short period in which the Jewish state existed? Didn't the land split in two, and Israel and Judah murder each other? There must be a reason.

"We have spent two-thirds of our existence in exile. That is destiny. How can you stand up against your destiny? Our destiny is our mission, or our mission is our destiny. It is the law, God's or nature's. And we can't escape it. I am a Jew. Therefore I am a Socialist-Internationalist and not a Zionist."

Jacob paused. "It wasn't this I wanted to talk to you about, Isaac."

"It is a terrible thing," he went on, "to see how the conscience of man is almost dead. Yet most people are religious, and have God in their heart, and pray to Him."

"The masses have nothing to do with God," Lehrman objected. "What the masses have is superstition, which has nothing to do with God and religion. They have no God in their heart. The masses are not interested in Socialism, as you understand it, Jacob. All the masses are interested in is getting more wages and better conditions. You won't admit it, because you won't face the truth. Your Socialism was born in your soul, out of your religious feeling. The Socialism of the masses was born in their stomachs. You don't live on this earth, Jacob. You float in the sky."

"How can you say such things! The masses always fought, always sacrificed themselves!"

"Never for an idea! Always for the fleshpots. They never understood a God in Heaven. They preferred a god of wood or stone or a golden calf here on earth. They always rose against God's messengers and stoned them."

They had got so absorbed in their discussion that they had gone on walking along the high road till they found themselves at the forest outside the town. There, coming out of the forest, they saw Fuksman's son Reuben with Comrade Dinah Greenzweig. When Dinah caught sight of Lehrman and Jacob she left Reuben Fuksman and ran back into the forest. Fuksman came toward Lehrman and Jacob with a welcoming cry.

"Isn't it a wonderful day! Look at it! Look at the sky and the bright sun and the green trees. Listen to the birds! What were you talking about? Socialism, I suppose. I'm a Socialist, too!"

Isaac looked at Jacob and laughed: "I was going to see Pearl, and you were coming with me, and instead we've landed up here! We must go back. I shall need you to explain to Pearl why I am late."

Reuben Fuksman took this to mean that Isaac and Jacob wanted to get rid of him. "Am I in the way?" he asked.

Before they could answer him, Dinah, coming out of the forest, answered for them: "Yes, you're in the way!"

Fuksman looked sheepish. But he tried to put a brave face on it, pretending that he hadn't seen Dinah before: "Oh! Panna Greenzweig!" he cried, with a gallant gesture.

"Don't pretend, Comrade Fuksman!" Dinah said. "I come from the forest, where we have been together. Why has your face gone red, Comrade? You won't get very far now with your plans to make a rich marriage with Pan Bernfel's daughter Helena, now that she's turned Zionist after her Christian lover sent her packing. She'll soon know that you've been to the forest with me, the red firebrand! You won't be able to fool Bernfel any longer with your stories about being a Zionist, and having nothing more to do with the strikers!"

Noticing Isaac's and Jacob's embarrassment, Dinah turned to them with a brazen smile: "What's all this modesty come over you two! What's wrong with the pleasures of the flesh? Don't be such hypocrites! I'm not a bit ashamed!" She put her arm through Fuksman's: "You're no comrade of mine!" she said. "You can't fool even Comrade Jacob Lichtenberg! Everybody knows that you're a swine! But when it comes to being a male, then you're just what I need." She laughed shamelessly.

"Suppose Comrade Aaron comes along!" Fuksman said, thinking to frighten her. But she only pressed closer against him.

"Comrade Aaron is at work now," she said. "Besides, he knows all about me! I'm not deceiving him. I'm not one of those women who deceive their men!"

The four of them walked back together to the town, talking very earnestly about love, which had then become a most important problem for the young people—there was this new idea spreading that love was only physical satisfaction.

Peasant carts loaded with red bricks came along the road from the brickworks near by—a whole caravan, one behind the other.

"We're right in the midst of a new building activity," Jacob said with bitterness. "We're putting the ruined factories back into shape, and we're building new factories, to turn out more war material, to make arms and munitions. The workers don't care what they do, as long as they get their wages. That's true even of our Socialist comrades."

"Listen to the idealist!" Dinah Greenzweig sneered. "What do you suggest, Comrade Lichtenberg, the workers should do?"

"They shouldn't do war work!"

"You're a bloody fool!"

Jacob was shocked. "But we said so, at our last meeting! You, Comrade Greenzweig, and Comrade Aaron too, you all spoke—just as I did—against the war, especially because it is a war against Russia!"

"Of course, I am against the war, especially because it is against Russia, the one country that has made a real Revolution, where all power belongs to the workers and peasants. But that doesn't mean that you can tell the Polish workers not to work in the factories against the instructions of their own organization. What we have to do is to organize sabotage, to incite them to revolt, to start a mass uprising. That is different. But what you are talking about is conscience! Individual conscience! The conscience of a pacifist!"

"Yes," Jacob agreed. "Refusing to do anything to help the war!"

"I won't go!"

Comrade Dinah Greenzweig burst out laughing: "If you won't fight, you're against the Revolution!"

"Revolution is different," said Jacob. "That is defending ourselves. If a serpent has its coils round you, you must defend yourself."

"What! Each of us separately!" Dinah sneered again. "Is that what you mean?"

They had now come to Goldblum's ruined factory. The walls still stood, but there were gaping holes everywhere and weeds were growing where the floors had been. It was a place of desolation.

Jacob wanted the others to go with him through the ruins. "This is what war does," he said. "Look at it!"

But the other three refused to go with him. They continued their way without him, and left Jacob standing alone. Suddenly he saw Lozer, the war cripple, come limping toward him on his crutch. "What brings you here, Comrade Lichtenberg?"

Jacob felt embarrassed. But he had no need to explain, because Lozer was trying to explain his own presence there: "It's habit. I used to come here in the old days when I was a sound man; I came here every day to work, when the factory was in full swing. It still draws me. I'm not the only one. I often meet others here who used to work in the factory in the old days. Look over there!" he whispered. "See him? That's Reb Mordecai Goldblum. He is always here! Every time I come! Let's get out of here, Comrade Lichtenberg. I wouldn't like him to see us. It would embarrass him."

When they were outside Jacob asked Lozer: "If you could, Lozer, would you go to work in a munition factory now?"

"Yes!"

Jacob was shocked by the unhesitating answer.

"Have you thought about it?"

"No! But if I had I would have given you the same answer. I know why you ask me that question."

"Yet you would go?"

"Yes!"

"I am surprised at you, Comrade Lozer!" There was scorn in Jacob's voice. "I consider you an intelligent person."

Lozer winced at the word *intelligent*. Jacob softened his voice a little. "I didn't mean to be sarcastic. An intelligent person need not be educated. I mean it, that you are an intelligent person. Reading good books is important. But that is not intelligence. Intelligence is inborn. You don't say much, but you have common-sense. And I know you are an honest, sincere man, devoted to the Socialist idea. Aren't you?"

"Yes."

"And you're not only an emotional, but a conscious Socialist. I know that, though you never speak in the discussions to express your views."

Lozer smiled like a bashful girl. "I don't know about conscious," he said. "I've read very little on Socialist theory. I don't really understand Marx."

"I don't really understand Marx myself," Jacob reassured him. "He needs a lot of hard study; it isn't everybody who can do that. Let's return to my first question. I think none of the comrades suffered as much as you did from the war. You lost your parents. You don't know whether your brothers are alive or dead. And you lost an arm and a leg in battle. I was sure that your answer to my question would be a very different one. You're not one of those who believe the lying propaganda of the so-called Socialist government about the war."

"No, I don't believe it."

"Yet?"

"Yes! Because what difference would it make if I didn't go into a munitions factory, or even if a hundred or a thousand others didn't? You wouldn't find more than about ten thousand like us in the whole country. Perhaps nothing like so many. There isn't one in this whole town. They are not only ready to make munitions. They are going into the army voluntarily."

Jacob hung his head. Then he silently put his arm around Lozer's shoulder and walked away.

32

Things Look Up

The town came back to life. Lots of people were earning good money. There was more work in all branches of occupation than there had been even before the Great World War. There was feverish building activity. Government orders and the smuggling trade, which was renewed, made people rich overnight. Their experiences in the war had destroyed their trust in the stability of the banks and in the value of money, even foreign currency, so they put their money into buildings; they bought up the war-damaged houses and had them restored or completely rebuilt. It wasn't easy to get building workers or building materials. The government wanted everything and everyone for war work. But there's nothing you can't get for money.

The whole country was looking up because of the war. There was work for everybody, even old people and children. It was a golden time for workers and artisans and for the peasants. Those peasants who had no land of their own got good pay for their farm labor. The air rang with the sound of hammers, with the noise of machinery, and the babble of traders and shopkeepers. It was a golden time too for people who had any business connected with getting married. There were never so many brides and so many pregnant young wives.

The biggest government orders in the town went to Bernfel. But the others got plenty. Comrade Krumholz couldn't supply enough saddles and other leather goods to meet the demand. David had also started a workshop of his own. He became an employer of labor, and with a recommendation from Ciemnowski, the Chief of the Political Department, he got government orders for military trousers and tunics.

Reb Yossel Fuksman was now the only one in the town who refused to exploit the golden opportunity. He had not forgotten the heavy punishment that had followed his chase after wealth during the German occupation—the tragic death of his only daughter, his dearest child.

But his son Reuben couldn't sit still and watch his father letting all these wonderful chances slip. He talked to him until he finally persuaded him. His most effec-

187

tive argument was that he, Reuben, would attend to everything. "You need have nothing to do with it, father!"

His mother added her pleas, and Fuksman agreed.

Reuben's next step was to speak to Bernfel; he asked him for his help to get a license for supplying cloth for military clothing. He took his mother and his sister Helena to Bernfel with him; they added their appeals, and together they got what they wanted.

The chink of gold and the crackle of notes can bring gladness even into houses that sit in mourning. Money is a more powerful intoxicant than wine. It can make people forget their sorrow.

At the Fuksmans' there was always a bottle of wine on the table at meals, and heaps of gourmet foods.

Reuben ate fast and kept talking the whole time. That was his way.

"The government," he was saying, "doesn't worry much in wartime about the quality of the goods we deliver. What difference does it make to the soldier who is killed in battle if he has a uniform of wool or sacking? Currency speculation is no good now, not unless you can buy foreign money cheap and sell it immediately at a profit. It isn't worth holding on to. It's different with goods. We must buy a lot of stock and keep it, because the prices are sure to rise."

"He's right!" his mother said proudly. "He's got the makings of a big businessman!"

The big businessman in the making had now begun to read his father a lecture:

"You've got to get into the swim of things, father. You still consider Zionism a heresy. That won't do! Lots of religious Jews, fervent Chassidim, have now turned Zionist. Reb Henoch is a Talmud scholar, and I've heard him say that the Love of Zion is a duty binding on every Jew. That's how he interpreted 'Uvo l'Zion'— 'When you come to Zion you will be redeemed!'"

"He interprets as it suits him!" his father cried angrily. "I stand where I stood on this question. A believing Jew has faith, and waits for the Messiah for the Redemption!"

"Careful!" his son warned him. "It's wartime now. People are glad to get the things they want without asking too many questions. But the war won't last for ever. And then, with everything back in normal supply, Zionists won't buy from an anti-Zionist. And most Jews will be Zionists, I tell you! After the war, anti-Semitism will come back too. Worse than before! We shall have to depend on Jewish customers. Then there is the American Jewish delegation here. It's important for you to be connected with it. And you can't be as long as you refuse to become a Zionist!"

"Isn't he absolutely right!" his mother exclaimed dotingly.

Reb Yossel Fuksman groaned.

Things were considerably harder these wonderful days for Abraham the tailor; he still earned his bread for his wife and family by the sweat of his brow. He did not own the tailoring workshop that was busy turning out army uniforms for the government, but was only a very minor partner to his son David, but it still worried him. It was heavy on his soul. There were six sewing machines now in his work-shop, and ten more workers in addition to the members of his own family.

"So much work and so much money to be earned," he said ruefully. "It's never happened to me before. Not even when I got a wedding outfit to make. This is some wedding outfit now! So many bridegrooms to be fitted—hundreds of thousands of bridegrooms all at the same time!"

His wife Itte sighed heavily: "Our Getzel was one of those bridegrooms! Who knows what the end of these big earnings will be? If we don't have to flee again from the enemy armies!"

His wife's reminder of their oldest son, who had fallen in battle, moved Abraham to tears. He was cutting out military trousers, and the big shears fell to the floor with a clatter, and the two halves flew apart.

"You're a silly woman!" he grumbled at his wife. "The papers say that there were ten million like our Getzel killed in the last war, and about thirty million wounded and crippled for life like Lozer! Whole countries were devastated! Why did we let Getzel go into the army? That's the question! Why did all those fathers and mothers let their sons go into the army? Why did the women let their husbands go? Why did the people allow the war to happen? Why didn't they stop it at once! Who wants war? What good does it do? Why should we go and kill other people? Even if we win the war what do we poor people get out of it? The worker and the artisan still have to work hard for their living. I've been thinking about these things since our Getzel was killed. What do you say, David? You're a Socialist! So you must be against war!"

His wife, Itte, wiped her eyes with a corner of her apron. She had never in more than thirty years of married life heard her husband speak such a lot. The same thing had happened to him as to Balaam's ass in the Women's Pentateuch.

Noah, too, busy with the pressing iron, was surprised at his father, surprised to hear him talking like a Socialist. All the others, working the sewing machines won-dered what David, the boss, would answer his father. None of them spoke. They had strict orders not to talk at work, not even to sing. Not even Socialist songs. David wouldn't allow it. He said that they must put all their energy into their work. Because they were working for the army, and this was war! They were helping the Socialist government to defend the homeland. That was David's answer now to his father.

"All right," said his father, "defend the homeland! God knows what we poor folk get out of the homeland. You say it's a 'Socialist government.' All right! But they still drive us working people like sheep to slaughter. And we've got to keep quiet!"

He picked up the two broken halves of the shears, took another pair of shears and went back to his cutting. The machines rattled on. The workers sat silent.

Comrade Hersh Krumholz had many more people working for him than Com-rade David Soroka. His workers included comrades of his own Party who looked up to him as their chairman and leader. Tzippe was one of his workers.

Hersh was very different from David in his attitude to his workers. At first he hadn't been able to look them in the face when he handed out the work—especially when the worker was a Party comrade. He spoke to them so gently, so quietly that he was almost inaudible. He found it hard to be an employer. He tried leaving the supervision to Tzippe. After all, he told himself, he had not engaged her as a worker like the others, but as someone he could trust to keep an eye on things, to watch that there shouldn't be any bits of leather left lying around, to get swept up with the waste. He found her amazingly good at that. She had behaved from the start like the mistress of the factory, as she insisted on calling his workshop. He marveled at the way she knew how to keep the workers at it, how to make them work faster, how to get the most out of them.

But she wasn't left in command very long. Feiga saw how things were developing, and she started coming in to the workshop very often. She didn't call it a factory.

Hersh felt uncomfortable when Feiga came. "You mustn't spend so much time here," he argued. "You must be losing a lot of money by staying away from your own work. I'm sure you must be very busy at your own trade."

"I'm giving up my trade," Feiga announced calmly. "I'm tired of dressing other women's hair and making wigs."

So Feiga took over Tzippe's job as Hersh's supervisor. She did it very cleverly. She won the workers by calling each of them "Comrade." And she delivered little pep talks to them. "We are all working for the defense of our Socialist Fatherland," she kept repeating. In a way, she relieved Hersh of his sense of embarrassment at having become an employer of labor.

But she also kept an eye on Tzippe. "She's an attractive woman, isn't she?" she remarked slyly to Hersh.

Hersh didn't answer. He realized that she had outwitted him, and he felt it would be better not to say anything.

Feiga was also clever in quieting his conscience about becoming an exploiter of labor. She quoted to him instances of Socialist theoreticians and leaders who had been manufacturers and businessmen. After a couple of months Comrade Hersh Krumholz lost his scruples, and became quite a taskmaster himself. He always used the same argument—they must work faster, and produce more, to save the Socialist Fatherland!

"Our war," he said, "is not an Imperialist war. It is a defensive war. This government of ours is a Socialist government, our own comrades. Our comrades are fighting on the battlefield against the counterrevolution. The Bolsheviks in Russia have shot hundreds of thousands of our comrades. If the Bolsheviks should win and occupy Poland they would shoot every one of us!"

Feiga was very much in love with Hersh, and she was happy to be so near to him now in the workshop. Everybody in the workshop saw it, Tzippe most of all.

Both Feiga and Hersh began to fill out and look prosperous. It didn't escape the notice of their workers; some of them made sarcastic remarks about it among themselves.

Hersh's output kept increasing, and the checks he received from the government for his work became fatter. Now Hersh realized that Feiga was the woman for him.

Hersh and Feiga didn't like it when David tried to stop their workers' singing, especially when they wanted to sing Socialist songs. They encouraged it, particularly when they were the kind of Socialist hymns that went with a swing and a quick marching tempo. It speeded up the work. Even the "International" did that.

They very often started them off by singing themselves. They struck up the Bundist "Oath":

> Brothers and sisters of toil and of need,
> All who are scattered and spread like the seed.

Or Edelshtat's "Last Testament":

> Oh, my good friends, when I shall die.

Then Hersh and Feiga led the chorus with:

> Arise, all who must toil as slaves do,
> Who live in hunger and despair.

And the workers, several Communists among them (though neither Hersh nor Feiga knew that) joined in:

> The spirit seethes, and calls to battle,
> To arms, brothers, everywhere!

Mirel's restaurant was busy again, as in the old smuggling days of the German occupation. The buffet was loaded with good things. But now Mirel stood at the buffet herself, because her husband was working with the American Jewish Committee. He had a higher post there now. "All Mirel's doing," people said, shaking their heads wisely. "Mirel's looks and Mirel's brains. Mirel knows how to talk to Bernfel."

Mirel knew what they were saying; she consoled herself with the knowledge that she was innocent, and that this was all so much slanderous talk. But she had no intention of denying anything publicly. She was too proud to go around telling everybody that her husband's post with the American Jewish Committee and his promotion there had nothing to do with Bernfel, and that he owed it all to her brother in Warsaw, who was a famous writer in the Polish Press there, under the pen name Felix Wislawski. Mirel was very proud of her brother in Warsaw.

She managed the restaurant very capably by herself, even the sidelines, the gold and currency exchange, dealing with all kinds of ,merchandise, besides being a housewife and a mother with a new baby on top of it.

Rabeh was giving her a great deal of assistance in the restaurant now. Mirel found her very useful.

It was jolly in the restaurant. Every table was occupied. Mechel Politician had grown in importance since Zionism had become a big force in the life of the town. He kept going from one table to another, from one group to another, dropping a word here and a word there; he was the man who set the tone.

To Shimmele Lotterinek, sitting with a group of Jews at one of the tables, he said meaningfully: "We shall soon start packing again."

"For Zion?" Shimmele asked.

"Yes," said Mechel, and went to another table.

"Mechel meant that things are getting bad again here, and that Jews will have to run away," Shimmele interpreted his remarks to the others at the table.

"Rubbish!" said one of the people at the table. "Let's have a drink to seal the bargain," a reference to the deal that he had just been negotiating, that as far as he was concerned it was settled.

David sat at one of these tables with Reuben Fuksman. Every time they met—David to deliver the finished trousers and tunics and Reuben to hand over a fresh supply of material—they stepped into Mirel's restaurant for a bite and a chat, not about business but about Socialism. Reuben was very much interested to find that David still regarded him a Socialist.

"You ought to play a bigger part in the Party, Comrade Soroka," he told David. "I have heard you speak at the meetings, and I found you more to the point than Comrade Lichtenberg. Why shouldn't you be on the Committee? You're just as good! I can understand Comrade Krumholz being there. He is a first-class speaker and a fine organizer. Look at the way he's built up his business! He's got over twenty people working for him."

"I'm employing fifteen people myself now," David boasted. "I'll soon catch up with him if the war lasts much longer."

They went on to discuss the progress of the war. Each made a point of emphasizing the fact that he had been exempted from military service because he was doing work of national importance. They didn't say how much it had cost them in bribes to get the exemption.

Some Jewish musicians and their comedian sat at a table nearby. The musicians too were having a wonderful time. There were so many weddings now! The comedian was trying out one of his songs:

> There's a bustle, and it's plain
> That the wheel has turned again.
> There are weddings all day long,
> Music, gaiety and song.
> Everybody wears a happy face.
> The world is such a lovely place!

His companions laughed and applauded, and shouted their orders: "Quarter duck!" "Half a chicken!" "Chopped liver with onions!" "Two brandies!"

Rabeh was busy taking orders and passing them on to the waitresses.

The comic had made up some new rhyme and declaimed it:

> At the head of the festive board,
> The wealthy guests are seated.
> They get served with the fattest fish,
> For that's how the rich are treated.
> They throw the poor a bone or two,
> Just to keep them quiet,
> With their tails between their legs,
> Not to start a riot!

When the hubbub had died down a bit Reuben Fuksman called Rabeh over to his table. He liked showing off to her, playing the intellectual, and at the same time having a sly dig at her Jacob, and at her too.

"Socialism takes a lot of understanding," he said. "Is Comrade Lichtenberg really a Marxist?"

"Of course, he's a Marxist!" Rabeh sprang to Jacob's defense.

But Reuben Fuksman knew that Rabeh had no idea of what Marxism was. To his mind she was quite ignorant. So he tried pulling her leg, pretending to discuss these things with her seriously.

"How can he be a Marxist if he doesn't follow Aristotle or Plato?"

Rabeh knew very well that Reuben was getting at her, but she kept a straight face:

"Surely, Comrade Fuksman, it isn't as simple as that! There are big differences between them. Perhaps you would tell me a little more about Plato in the light of Marxism?"

Fuksman went red in the face, and tried to change the subject. But Rabeh wouldn't let him:

"Jacob has spoken a lot to me about Plato and Marx," she said. "As a matter of fact, he does follow Plato, and he finds much in him that runs in line with Marx."

Fuksman became confused, and tried to turn the conversation in a different direction. But at that moment the door was flung open and Czapski, the chief of the militia, came in with Caspar Strzelkowski, the sergeant, and several militiamen.

Mirel was a little alarmed; not because it was a police raid, for she was used to such, but because she was usually warned in advance by the militia that they would be coming, and they hadn't warned her this time.

Caspar Strzelkowski, the anti-Semite, fixed Mirel with a cold, hostile stare, and rapped out orders to his men:

"Guard the doors! Everybody stay where you are! I'll shoot anyone who tries to escape!"

Czapski addressed the customers at their tables:

"Bring out your dollars, pounds, gulden, and Swiss francs. And the gold you're smuggling out of the country or hoarding. Put it all on the table in front of you! Empty your pockets! Give me your keys!"

He turned to Strzelkowski: "See that nobody gets away! Look out for those who are evading military service, and for the Bolsheviks!"

Mirel remained calm. She smiled seductively at Czapski, and moved so near to him that her full breasts touched his arm. She had felt instinctively that her womanly appeal would be the most effective way of softening him. She was right.

"Panie Police Chief!" she said to him. "This is a restaurant. My customers come here to eat. There is no trading here in gold or currency. We don't harbor people evading military service, or Bolsheviks. Examine them all! You won't find one! But I can tell you where you will find them! Not in front of everybody here! If the Pan Police Chief will come into the next room with me, I'll tell you!"

Caspar Strzelkowski lost his arrogance. He realized that the Jewess had got the better of him.

"I'll pay her out yet!" he swore to himself. "Her and all the other Jews in the town."

Czapski had a quick search made of Mirel's customers; he found nothing, as she had assured him he wouldn't, and he soon left with his men. Mirel had told him privately that if he was looking for anything he could find plenty at Krzewicki's. "She knows!" he said to himself. "She's devilishly clever, this Jewess!"

But how could he make a police raid in the house of his own close friend Krzewicki?

33

Jacob Perplexed

Jacob had not gone back to work yet, though he had promised his parents that he would, even if it was military work, which meant helping the war. He felt that it would be hypocritical to do that and to maintain his pacifist attitude. What had affected him most in this connection was not Comrade Dinah Greenzweig's sarcasm at his expense, but Lozer's simple honest answer to his question whether he would have done war work.

Jacob had decided to go to work, but he kept putting it off like a man who has made up his mind unwillingly to commit a crime but delays it as long as he can.

He wanted to talk it over again with Isaac Lehrman. He knew that Lehrman would be at Pearl's now, so he went to her home. Lehrman opened the door to him.

"It's you, Jacob!" he cried. "Come in!"

Jacob followed Lehrman into the house. The sun was shining outside, but the house was in darkness because the curtains were drawn. Lehrman made a move to pull the curtains apart, but Pearl stopped him: "The sun is too bright, Isaac!"

Lehrman sat down beside Pearl on the chaise longue, and they held hands. Jacob recognized the chaise longue. It had been cleaned, and the bricks that had been scattered on the floor had been cleared away.

"Come and sit down here, Jacob!" Lehrman said. "There's enough room for three."

"I'd rather stand, thank you. I came to talk to you."

Jacob spoke about conscience and about responsibility. His voice was grave, with a note of pain in it. Pearl felt it, and said: "Why must you torture yourself, Jacob! Why must you keep thinking all the time about things you can't change? About problems you can't solve? Do you know, Jacob, my father is opening his factory again."

"What!"

"Yes, Jacob! He has found a partner with money, and he is going to put the place back into running order. I think my father is doing the right thing."

"You too!" Jacob gasped.

"Don't you see, Jacob," Pearl tried to explain. "My father hasn't lived these past five years. He was like a lost soul, spending all his time wandering through the ruins of his devastated factory. He wasn't doing anything. He was not engaged in any activity. And I don't know any other man to whom activity means so much as to my father. He hasn't anybody left of his whole family, except me. He must do something, he must work, to keep his mind steady!"

"But don't you remember, Pearl," said Jacob, "what you yourself told me—that when your father came back here from the flight and found his factory in ruins, he lifted his arms to heaven, and thanked God that he had been freed from the yoke of riches, and could have more time now to serve God!"

"That's true," Pearl admitted. "But—you know, all these five years my father spent most of his time in the ruins of his factory. The ruins drew him there."

"I can't understand it!" Jacob cried. "That your father is rebuilding his factory, now in the war, to help war production! Your father! Reb Mordecai Goldblum! Everybody! My father too! Everybody is for the war!"

"Sit down, Jacob," Lehrman tried to pull him down beside him on the couch. "It isn't right that we should sit while you are standing."

Jacob fetched a chair and sat down.

"You remember our talk about the masses, Jacob," Lehrman began. "The people are behind the war. They are against Russia, where the workers and peasants are in power, establishing Socialism, fighting for the liberation of the proletariat of the world. Why have the masses of the Polish people flung themselves like this into the war against our Russian comrades? I'll tell you! Because it gives them the comforts they want!"

Jacob jumped up from his chair: "No! I answered you on that point before! The masses lack critical understanding. The whole thing is a tragic contradiction! I can't make it out."

Jacob was now speaking to himself more than to Isaac and Pearl:

"God or substance... There is a certain force in man that drives him toward something higher, ethical, divine, in the same way as a plant seeking the sun."

Isaac rose and forced Jacob back in his chair.

"But you're terribly wrong, Jacob," he said. "You don't deny death, even if you assume that life is itself eternal, which I don't. Be that as it may. He who created life also created death. This force that creates is the same force that destroys. Man, created in the image of God, the creator of the idea of God, love, beauty, and nobility, is also the carrier of all that is contrary to it."

Jacob jumped up again:

"But it is man who will create the harmony for which we strive. He will bring about the brotherhood he desires."

"You are a greater believer, Jacob, than all those who believe!"

Pearl's father just then came in. He was in a good mood, and was glad to see Jacob.

"How is your father?" he asked him. And when Jacob kept silent he realized that things must be bad with his old friend, and he looked sad.

After a while, he said: "It must have surprised you, Jacob, when they told you that I am opening up the factory again."

Jacob felt that it was stifling in the room. He made his excuses and hurriedly left.

Jacob felt sad; he needed a warm affectionate hand and heart. So he went to Rabeh. He entered by the back door, through her parents' room, not through the restaurant. He wanted to avoid the restaurant frequenters, all the people who were doing well from the war. He didn't want to see Rabeh in those surroundings, serving these people, running at their beck and call. He knew it was like that, but he didn't want to see it with his own eyes.

He found her father, Reb David Joel, as always at the table, studying one of the holy learned books. His wife, Malka, was there too, still busy with the old garments that she had collected in the town for the poor. But she dropped everything when she saw Jacob. She made signs to him not to disturb her husband at his studies, to take no notice of him and come straight to her corner of the room.

She took him by the hand and looked him up and down with affectionate concern. He felt the affection and, suddenly bending down, he snatched his intended mother-in-law's hand to his lips and kissed it.

Just then Rabeh came in:

"Oh, hello Jacob!" She came over to him, and drew her fingers through his hair. Malka pretended not to see when their lips met. But Joel David, bent over his book, saw what was happening behind his back, and coughed discreetly:

"I didn't see you come in, Jacob! How are you? How is your father? What's the latest news about the war?"

Jacob answered only the last question: "I'm afraid we will have a third flight from the town. Not right away, but..."

"God forbid!" Reb David Joel cried. "How could I run now with my leg swollen as it is! And the other one beginning to swell! God will help us! For the sake of His people Israel! The Russians will be defeated, as they were in the last war! Poland will be victorious!"

Malka passed Jacob a plate of fruit: "Have some, Jacob. See that he has some fruit, Rabeh! Sit at the table, Jacob!"

"I'll go and get changed," Rabeh said to Jacob. "We're not busy in the restaurant now. Let's go for a walk."

34

Hot Blood

A lonely field outside the town, the road to which leads past the barbed-wire cemetery of the soldiers who fell in battle here in 1915, forms a huge triangle with the Christian and the Jewish town cemeteries. The river runs through the middle of the triangle. There are orchards along the riverside, which Jews like old Samuel Sudovnik rent each spring for the fruit picking. Narrow, muddy paths lead to the surrounding villages scattered about the countryside, yet all near enough to the great high road that cuts through forests to link the towns together.

This small field is like a forgotten corner in this big expanse, like a secret pocket tucked away in a greatcoat. The grass is greener here, and grows higher, and is softer, for rarely a human foot treads on it. Even the herdsmen don't bring their cattle to graze here, as though the spot were haunted.

There is a local legend about this field, about the great chestnut tree standing in the midst of it, said to be hundreds of years old. The story goes that a boy climbed the tree one day to pick chestnuts. A figure appeared and told him not to pick chestnuts from that tree. The boy ignored the warning, but when he wanted to draw his hand back he couldn't. He lost his grip and fell, and hung among the branches head down for a long time, unconscious. The tangle of branches kept him from falling to the ground. Somebody passing by saw him and brought him down. When the boy recovered he told the people about the figure he had seen. The legend says that this figure is the spirit of a saint who lies buried under the chestnut tree, and who doesn't like to be disturbed. People therefore avoid this spot.

It was here that Jacob came with Rabeh. The sun was setting. The big chestnut tree seemed on fire. Jacob and Rabeh sat on the ground close together with their backs against the tree. The high grass was like a cushion under them.

Jacob held Rabeh in his arms. "You're not afraid of being here?" he asked her jestingly. "You're not afraid that the ghost of the saint who is buried under this tree might suddenly appear to us?"

Rabeh shivered. Why did Jacob have to talk about such things?

But Jacob hadn't done yet. He flung his arm out toward the three cemeteries.

"How many dead do you think lie there?" he asked her.

"Jacob dear, why must you talk about the dead now?"

She tried to change the subject by telling him about all the things she had been buying in preparation for their marriage—dresses and coats and nightgowns, tablecloths and towels and lengths of linen. She spoke of the wedding arrangements, how her father and mother wanted the wedding as soon as possible. She too!

"Good!" said Jacob laughing. "As soon as you like."

"And you don't have to worry about going into the army, Jacob. Mirel has arranged all that!"

Jacob sprang up: "She mustn't! I don't want her to interfere! Whether I go into the army or not is my business!"

"Yes, of course, dear!" Rabeh agreed. "But you must do something soon to know how you stand about the army. Speak to Abraham-Moshe about it. He'll do it for you!"

"I'm not going to discuss these things now, Rabeh," Jacob said. "I don't want to talk about them. Look over there!" waving his arm toward the barbed-wire military cemetery. "There are eighteen thousand soldiers buried there. Hundreds in one common grave. Do you remember people telling stories a few years ago of meeting the dead soldiers marching at night, whole regiments come out of their graves, marching along the high road. The crippled, too, armless or legless ..."

"Stop it, Jacob! If you don't stop it I'll go home! What is the matter with you, talking about the dead!"

"I'm sorry, Rabeh. I don't know what is the matter with me. Please don't go. Please stay with me!"

Rabeh sat down again. She stroked his hair and nestled against him.

"Would you like me to read you some poetry, Jacob?"

"What poetry?"

"My brother Felix's poems, Jacob. This is his new book of poems. I brought it with me to show you. They say in Warsaw that he is one of the best young poets today. He sent me the book from Warsaw. Listen to this poem, Jacob."

> When I see you walk in the avenue—
> You don't walk! You soar as the angels do!
> Divine thoughts in my spirit rise.
> My soul goes winging to the skies.

She read him poems about flowers, hymns to the morning star, odes to Venus, and intimations of immortality. Jacob couldn't take his eyes off her. She looked so beautiful when she was reading. Her eyes were full of feeling. He stroked her knees, and passion stirred in him strongly. Rabeh gently drew his hand away. That only made her more desirable. He smothered her face with burning kisses. Then it happened.

He felt terribly ashamed afterward. But Rabeh comforted him. "You are my husband, even if our wedding is still to come," she said. "We are getting married soon. Don't reproach yourself, Jacob."

"I should have waited, Rabeh! Now we must get married as quickly as possible. Arrange it as soon as you can, Rabeh. And if there is a child this time, have it, my dear. I want you to have my child. If you can fix it, let's get married next week."

As soon as the warm weather started, pairs of young lovers began going for walks on their days of rest, Sabbaths and Festivals, along the roads leading to the lonely field by the cemeteries. Though they were tired out after a week's hard work, they rose early, before their fathers rose to go to the Synagogue.

Abraham had overslept a bit this Sabbath, and was now hurrying over his toilet. He was combing his thick brown hair at the same broken mirror with some of the silver worn off where his sister Bluma was also combing her hair, the same brown hair, and just as thick as his. She too was in a hurry, knowing that David was already waiting for her at their appointed meeting place.

Abraham was meeting Hannah in the orchard that her father Samuel had rented for the season. Both her parents must already have been in Synagogue, for she was by herself, waiting for him.

Abraham passed several young couples on his way to Hannah. The girls were lightly dressed for the summer weather, white skirts and red blouses, and the young men wore white collars and smoked cigarettes openly on the Sabbath, without any fear of the religious Jews whom they would meet on the road. They were all busy chattering and laughing.

Abraham had on a light summer suit, light brown shoes, and a white straw hat. He greeted the girl comrades like a comrade, but when he passed a girl who was not in the Party he swept off his hat with a flourish and bowed to her like a Warsaw gentleman. Abraham was earning good money now, and was on good terms with the whole world.

As he passed the barbed-wire military cemetery it didn't even enter Abraham's head, as it would have done Jacob's, that there were eighteen thousand young soldiers lying here, and that, with another war on now, more young soldiers would be killed. Besides, Abraham was too busy thinking of getting to Hannah as quickly as possible. All the same he kept remembering the nice smart girls he had met in Warsaw while working there. Those Warsaw girls certainly knew a thing or two! He decided that as soon as the war was over he would go back to Warsaw to live there. The army didn't worry him any more. He had his exemption papers. So he went along, whistling and thinking of Hannah. "She's not a bad girl! She's quite good looking."

Abraham quickened his step. He hadn't broken his fast at home and he was beginning to feel hungry. He knew that Hannah would offer him some food. He was passing the Jewish cemetery now. It was partly fenced and partly walled, and there were gaps both in the wooden fence and in the brick wall, so that he could see the gravestones inside. He saw two figures moving among the gravestones. For a moment he was scared—what if they were the spirits of the dead!

Then he recognized them—his sister Bluma and David. He saw them pass out of sight behind a gravestone. Abraham didn't like David. "Beast!" he swore to himself. "Couldn't find any other place for his love-making but among the graves!"

Here was the door leading to Samuel's orchard. Abraham opened it and went inside. The air was cool and fragrant with the smell of apples and pears and cherries.

Hannah was there, barefoot, without a blouse on, and her apron lifted high to gather in it the fruit that had fallen to the ground overnight. Her father was doing the same a long way off, but instead of gathering the fruit in an apron he was collecting it in one of the ends of his long Sabbath caftan.

His wife was in the caravan where they lived, getting ready to go to the Synagogue, and trying not to think of her husband and daughter desecrating the Sabbath by picking up the windfalls from the ground. She knew speaking to them wouldn't be of any use. They paid no attention to what she said.

Hannah blushed when she saw Abraham, and let her apron drop, so that all the fruit scattered on the grass. Now her knees and thighs were covered. But her breasts and her bare arms still showed. She had on only a low sleeveless slip.

Abraham put his arm around her waist, and drew her close to him. She found him a bit too rough.

"Don't, Abraham! My father's here! And mother hasn't gone yet!"

Abraham let her go. She looked at him affectionately. She kissed him. Then she led him to a big apple tree: "Wait here for a few minutes. They won't see you behind this tree. I'll be back soon."

She picked up the scattered fruit from the ground, and disappeared with it.

Abraham didn't stay behind the apple tree. He came out and hid among the mulberry bushes, so that when Hannah returned in a short-sleeved chintz dress, her thick black hair under a flowered scarf, but still barefoot, she couldn't find Abraham.

"You can come out, Abraham," she called. "It's all right now. They've both gone to Synagogue!"

"Do you think your father didn't see me?" Abraham teased her, appearing from among the mulberry bushes.

"I'm sure he didn't see you. He would have told mother, and mother would never have left me alone with you."

He fixed his eyes on her hungrily: "I don't know! Your parents have a pretty good idea that we're in love. They're expecting us to get married."

"Oh! You think they're all set to welcome you as their son-in-law!"

"Yes, I do! Don't you?"

He drew her toward him. At first she yielded happily. But suddenly she tore herself free.

"I'm sure you haven't had any breakfast at home. Come into the caravan and I'll get you something to eat!"

"Carry me to the caravan, Abraham!" she whispered. And as he bent and lifted his precious load, she smiled happily.

When they came out of the caravan the sun was already high in heaven. Not a leaf stirred on the trees, not a blade of grass moved. The birds were silent. The air felt hot even in the shade of the orchard. But it was pleasantly shady under the trees.

Abraham and Hannah sat down in the shade of a tree, and she leaned against him and very softly sang her favorite song:

> I lay my little head
> On my mother's bed.

"Not that one," Abraham objected; "sing a Socialist song! You're a worker, aren't you?"

Hannah stopped singing. His reminder had wakened her out of her dream. After a short silence she said: "All right! If you will sing too."

Then she started:

> In the smithy, by the fire,
> Stands the blacksmith at the anvil.

This song didn't suit Abraham either.

"It's hackneyed," he said. "I keep talking to you about Socialism, trying to make you understand, so that I can show you among my comrades. And you ..."

Hannah dropped her head.

"I ought to go now!" Abraham continued. "My father will be coming home from Synagogue and he will expect me there. Your parents will be back soon too."

"Don't go yet, Abraham! Please!" She looked up to the sky. "It's no more than half past eleven. They won't be leaving the Synagogue till twelve. Stay a little longer!"

Abraham pulled away from her: "I must go now. I'll be back right after dinner. With some of the other comrades. Like last week."

"Please don't go yet, Abraham! Don't leave me by myself. Supposing thieves break in, to steal the fruit!"

That persuaded him. He stayed. Hannah was so glad that she kissed his hand. But Abraham was still angry with her:

"I can't make you out, Hannah. Tzippe and others like her didn't know a thing about Socialism, but they put their minds to it, and they know about it, and they are now members of the Party. But not you! I bring you books to read. Do you read them?"

"I don't understand them, Abraham. There are such funny words there. I don't know what they mean. 'Accumulation.' 'Appropriation.' 'Socialization.' 'Co-operation.' And that other book you gave me. I threw it away. All about free love. I can't understand free love. I know what love is—it means loving one man, always! As I love you! But not free love. How could I love another man?"

Abraham was moved by that. He stroked her hair and he spoke more gently to her:

"But you must learn at least the ABC of Socialism. You must know about the class war. I want you to be able to join the Party!"

"I will, Abraham, I will, to please you! I'll read your books about Socialism, if you will help me with them!"

After that Abraham left. On his way home he met Comrade Aaron Mickenshleger, arm in arm with Comrade Dinah Greenzweig. They looked happy.

"Talking about love?" he asked.

"As far as I know you, Comrade Spitzman," Dinah answered coldly, "you are not one of those who talk about love. You talk only about Socialism!"

35

Sabbath Joy

After his Sabbath meal old Samuel got into bed under the covers. He did that even in the hottest weather. Breina, his wife, wanted to settle down with the Tze'enu Urenu. But she didn't know what the Portion of the Law for the week was. Samuel didn't know either, so he pretended to be asleep. Breina wasn't taken in, though.

"You're not asleep! You're only pretending. Because you don't know what the Portion for the week is. You're an ignoramus! You didn't even say grace properly after the meal. You just mumbled something. No Zemiroth! And you think you can get away with it?"

Old Samuel pretended to be snoring. That made Breina very angry. But she knew that it would be wrong to start a quarrel on the Sabbath day. So she grumbled to herself:

"Poor me! That's the kind of man I had to marry! No sooner had he opened his eyes this morning than he was out in the orchard gathering fruit. On the Sabbath! He didn't read the Portion of the Law! He didn't read a Psalm. He didn't even say his prayers. You're just an Esau!"

She took her Tze'enu Urenu to the steps of the caravan, and sat down there, to get more light. But she still didn't know what the week's Portion was.

"Why don't you tell me the Sedra?" she cried.

Samuel stopped snoring, and mumbled "Balak" and snored again.

" 'Balak?' I don't know whether you're right. But let's say it is 'Balak.' All right!"

She put on her glasses and began reading: "And when Balak, the King of Moab, saw that the two powerful Kings Sihon and Og could not stand against Israel ..."

She saw a group of young people coming into the orchard, Abraham among them.

"Get up, Samuel!" she called to her husband. "The guests have arrived. We've got to keep an eye on them. That scamp Abraham, the carter's son, is after our girl again! God knows how far she's gone with him! For all I care they can get married to-morrow. So long as they don't mess around, and do things properly!"

The young people kept away from the caravan. They were in a merry mood, laughing and carrying on—as long as Hersh and Feiga hadn't arrived. Only with many of them it wasn't so much youthful exuberance as a feeling of determination to get as much as possible out of life now, quickly, before everything came to an end.

Some of the crowd played catch and hide and seek. The orchard was big enough to run in and hide in. Every time a young man caught a girl he exacted a kiss from her. The older ones walked about sedately, discussing politics. But even they had more frivolous things on their mind. Bluma was singing softly, dreamily: "I go out on the balcony." And as she sang she drew nearer to where Aaron was standing talking to two comrades, and continuing her song, "Above me flies a little bird," she put her hand on his shoulder. "Not so much his beauty as his high flying," she sang.

Aaron didn't like Bluma, and he didn't want to be diverted from his serious talk with his comrades. He moved away. Bluma had no great liking for Aaron either, but she detested Dinah, and she was trying to make Dinah jealous. So she moved nearer to Aaron again.

"Please," said Aaron impatiently. "I'm busy!"

David joined the group, apparently to take part in the discussion, but really to put his arm around Dinah's waist. Not that he was fond of Dinah, but because he wanted to make Bluma jealous, and Aaron too, because he couldn't stand Aaron. And also because he knew that Dinah was game for anybody. She had already had Abraham and Reuben Fuksman and now she had Aaron. He felt pretty sure of himself now—he was making money. He wore a white silk suit, a silk shirt, silk socks, and a white panama hat.

But Dinah wasn't having any. "I'm sorry," she said, disengaging his hand. "You've made a mistake."

The next moment Dinah was calling excitedly to the crowd: "Here comes Fuksman! See what I'm going to do with him!"

"Hello, Fuksman!" she greeted him. "I want you!"

She stretched out both arms toward him, and as he came near she held him by the hands and spun him round and round. Faster and faster she whirled round with him, her skirt billowing. "Faster! Faster!" she cried. "You're a man, aren't you!"

He was breathless by now, but she wouldn't let him go. His knees were giving way. He tottered. Then suddenly Dinah let go, and he went flying and fell.

Almost everybody—even Bluma, who hated Dinah—laughed, pleased with the way Dinah was dealing with Fuksman.

"Now get out!" Dinah shouted at Fuksman when he had got on his feet. "And don't come near us any more! We don't want you! Stay where you belong! We don't want people who have a foot in each camp!"

36

Strzelkowski's Goodby

After his father's death Juziek Strzelkowski felt that he couldn't go on living in the old home, with his mother, and above all with his brother Caspar, who behaved as though he were the sole heir to everything his father had left. He also couldn't stand his mother's religious piety. She objected to his living with his Jewess, Chelia, under her roof, without having had a proper Church wedding.

When Chelia came out of prison she had refused to go back to her parents' home. This time Juziek accepted her decision, and they took a room of their own and lived there together. He was working now, getting good pay. He had suggested to the owner of a small brick house that he could build himself an additional room on the roof, and let the landlord have it, in return for only one year's free rent. They had got the barest minimum of furniture; Juziek had made most of it himself. Chelia had added a few womanly touches, and the room had become a pleasant, livable home.

They had just finished supper. Their one and only white tablecloth was spread over the oilcloth. Chelia had washed it the night before, before they went to bed, and had ironed it just before supper.

Juziek was not going to work any more this week, because he had a lot of things to do before setting out on his journey. But Chelia had gone to work as usual. She was working hard, and she didn't want to miss a single day at her work. Before going home she had paid a visit to the meadow where in earlier days she had gone walking with her lover, and had picked a bunch of flowers, which now stood in a vase on the table with a bowl of fruit beside it.

As soon as she came home she had washed and put on her best dress for the occasion. There was a slim book of poems by Maria Konopicka on the table. Her eyes were bright with love and pride as she held Juziek's toil-hardened hand in hers.

"Do you know what poem I want to read to you? Maria Konopicka's 'The King went out to War!'"

"You mean the poem 'Stash?'"

There were tenderness and grief, and also teasing and jauntiness in his voice, the kind of happiness revolutionaries sometimes feel when they go out risking their life for their cause. He stroked her hair.

"No, I am no King! Nor am I Stash! No trumpets will sound gladly now when I depart, nor will the gates open gladly when I return, nor will the grass in the field weep for me."

Chelia clapped her hand over his mouth when he said "weep." "Don't say that!"

"All right, I won't!" he laughed, and kissed her. "I'm a bad patriot, according to Pilsudski's conception. Blowing up the arsenal didn't do much good. We must try other ways. The best way is our propaganda among the soldiers in the battlefield. But the sabotage in the factories must not be stopped. Do you hear that, my dear?"

"Yes."

"And you mustn't be sad. No sadness! Sadness dampens your spirits. The wheels of revolt and revolution are kept turning by gaiety. Everything must be sacrificed. Even love, the dearest of all!"

Chelia found it hard to keep back her tears. "But love can't be sacrificed. Love stays in the heart always! What shall I do without you? I am a woman! A woman's love is different, more realistic!"

"More realistic? More realistic than a man's? Than a man's when the man is a Marxist-Leninist!"

"I should have said, more earthy. Even at its most romantic. When the woman longs and dreams. Or am I expressing myself badly?"

Juziek burst out laughing. He laughed so loud that she dropped her eyes abashed. He cupped her face in his two hands, and looked into her eyes.

"Longing ... dreaming ... romantic.... All that old stuff of moonlight and night-ingales and the shepherd's reed."

"Now you're laughing at me!" She had tears in her eyes.

"Don't cry, my dear," he kissed away her tears.

"I cried, thinking of your father," she tried to explain. "Your father was a good man. You remember what he said to me one night?—that I would go with you, that I would carry a gun, and I would shoot! I am glad it was you who killed his murderer. Why didn't your brother Caspar and his militiamen arrive sooner! They might have saved him!"

"We'll deal with them all just as they deal with us! Without mercy! We will use their own weapons against them!"

37

Patriots

The Committee of the Jewish Socialist Party had been busy for weeks preparing a public meeting. Notices had been put up in their Club Library, a large hall where the comrades met most evenings to read and discuss, or to play dominoes. There was a buffet there. Lectures were held there regularly on the history of Socialism, the development of the working-class movement in the different countries, on Jewish and general history, political economy, popular science and literature. The lectures were usually arranged for those evenings when there would be no work to go to next morning.

The public meeting was to be held in this hall. Not only Party members were invited. The organizers wanted to get the general Jewish public there. One attraction was the announcement that the meeting would also deal with the question of the American Aid Committee, which had now become one of Bernfel's businesses.

In the midst of the preparations came disturbing news of Polish reverses on the Russian front. The government and the press played down these reports, speaking rather of "the brave struggle of our heroic armies." but the people knew that things were going badly. It was thought that this news would reduce the attendance at the meeting, but it didn't. The hall was packed, including many people outside the movement, like Berl Farber and Itzik Carter. The pupils of the Yiddish secular school came, Noah, Yoske, Abish, Godel, Osher Lekech, Berke Petzer, Kalman Blacksmith's two lads, Benjamin, and Tzippe. The youngsters were nearly squashed in the crowd, but they didn't mind. They were too proud to be there in the ranks of the fighters for the cause.

Abraham Spitzman was in the chair. Comrade Hersh Krumholz was the chief speaker. There were only two other members of the Committee on the platform, Feiga and Jacob. Dinah and Aaron sat in the body of the hall.

Hersh read out the agenda: 1. The American Committee, 2. The situation in the country, 3. Our attitude to this situation. He had something to say on each point.

Should the American Committee remain the private affair of a few individuals, or be made a social institution, run by a democratically elected administration, representing the whole Jewish population? Big funds, he said, were being raised in America, largely among the Jewish working class. The American Jewish trades unions were taking an active part in the work. A lot of money came from American Jews who wanted to help their relatives in Poland. "We want a proper control over the distribution of this money," Hersh said.

On point 2: "I want you to say in the discussion that will follow whether the war in which our country is engaged is an Imperialist war, as the Communists allege in their lying propaganda, or are we defending ourselves against the aggression of the enemy?

"The Bolsheviks want to plunge Poland into civil war. They have confiscated everything the people possessed."

That started a row. Dinah jumped on a chair, and shouted: "Lies! All lies! It isn't true! Russia didn't attack Poland! Poland attacked Russia!"

She pointed a finger scornfully at Comrade Hersh Krumholz on the platform. "Look at him! There's a Socialist for you! A proper Proletarian! Tell me, Comrade, how many workers do you employ in your factory? How much money have you made out of government war orders?"

Dinah had been shouting at the top of her voice, but the Chairman's bell and the protests of a lot of Hersh's supporters drowned her voice, so that few people in the hall really heard what she said. But she was glad she had spoken now, instead of taking her turn in the discussion later.

38

The Scribe Dies

When Jacob came home he found his father very ill, running a high temperature. He was no longer coughing; he was struggling for breath.

On Friday the end seemed near. But Jochabed made her preparations for the Sabbath. She tidied their half of the room, and put down yellow sand on the floor. When the sun, orange red and immense, set in the west, saying goodbye to the town, she lighted eighteen candles, eighteen being the numerical equivalent for the Hebrew word for "Life," twelve more than every Sabbath eve. In addition she lighted the lamp that hung suspended from the ceiling. She added kerosene, and turned the wick low, to keep it burning through the night. She laid the table with the Sabbath-Festival cloth, and put the embroidered challa cover over the challes, the Sabbath loaves. She had polished the brass candlesticks till they reflected the bright candle flames.

All those candles, all that light gave a solemn air to the room, as on the Eve of Atonement, as on Kol Nidrei Night, as in the Synagogue at Nielah.

The scribe was almost sitting up in bed. Jochabed had propped all the pillows she had behind his back. He had asked her to dress him in his black-satin caftan, with his shtreimel on his head, and his loins girded with his silk sash. The candle flames shimmered against the satin caftan, and lighted up his pale face. His eyes were larger than usual, and there was a strange fire in them, deep, like a well in the moonlight. His long curled earlocks hung down to reach the white collar of his newly ironed white shirt. His prayerbook lay open in front of him on the clean fresh white bed cover, though he knew all the prayers and a great deal of Talmud by heart. But he had never in all his life relied on his memory. He would have considered it presumptuous pride. He kept his long white fingers all the time on the open pages of the prayerbook; he had opened it at chapters 3 and 4 of the Song of Songs. The table had been moved up beside his bed.

Benjamin and Meir said their prayers at home this evening. Their mother had said they were not to go to the Synagogue, but to stay with their sick father and pray for him. She had put on her white wedding dress, which she had saved with all her other precious treasures in their flights during the war. She used to wear it only on Rosh Hashonah, and she hoped to wear it to welcome the coming of the Messiah, together with her husband and her children and all Israel.

She held her own prayerbook in her trembling fingers, and was reading out loud with great fervor, "O sing unto the Lord a new song; for He has done marvelous things." She had Benjamin and Meir standing on either side of her, each holding his own prayerbook, and repeating the Friday night prayers with her. They welcomed the Sabbath bride, and prayed for their father's recovery. There were tears in their eyes, but they did not weep, because it is forbidden to weep on the Sabbath. So they sang aloud: "Come in peace, crown of your husband, with rejoicing and cheerfulness."

But Jacob could not pray. He stared at the eighteen lighted candles, looked at his mother and his two young brothers praying, and envied them their ability to pray. They were praying for his sick father, and he couldn't. They had a God, a mighty God in heaven, and they believed that He could restore his father to health.

"I believe in man," Jacob told himself, "in a world of absolute justice, in a future where truth and righteousness will prevail, and love. I believe in the spirit of man, in his striving to liberate himself from evil and wrong. I believe in a kind of divinity, in a divine Power that drives man to the divine. But I do not believe in the God in whom I once believed, the God to whom one can pray, and who can restore a man when he is dying because he has no lungs left, as the doctor said."

He looked at his father, who seemed radiantly white, as though he had now become a part not of death but of eternity, the eternity to which he was returning, his eternal home—to God, to his Father in Heaven.

Jacob burst into tears.

When Jochabed came to the end of the prayers she shut the prayerbook and kissed it. So did her two young sons. They waited a few minutes for the scribe to finish, till he said "Good Shabbos!" Then all four, Jacob as well, went over to his bed, and said "Good Shabbos, father!" His wife, Jochabed, also said "father". She added, "my dear husband—may God send you healing . . . for the sake of the Holy Sabbath!"

The scribe began to say: "Shalom Aleichem, ministering angels, angels of God!" And they all, even Jacob, who was swept up with them, responded, "Shalom Aleichem, ministering angels, angels of God!" Their voices rose to the crescendo, "King of Kings, the Holy One, Blessed be He!"

In the other half of the room Gronem had just come home with his two boys from the Friday night service in the Synagogue. When he had finished Kiddush he took to telling his wife all the gossip he had heard in the baths and in the Synagogue.

The scribe felt that he was dying, but he believed he had with his prayer succeeded with God that he would not die on the Sabbath, would not have to lie waiting till the Sabbath was over before he could be buried.

His singing voice was weak and a little husky—his lungs were gone, so that his voice came out of an emptiness. That grieved him. But he collected all his strength and started singing Zemiroth. As he went on his voice cleared and took on a ringing quality. Benjamin and Meir sang with him. And the singing of the Sabbath hymns and the solemn Sabbath joy dispelled the gloom.

The sick man ate hardly anything. He barely touched the fish (tiny pieces for everybody) and the other dishes (very small portions of everything)—just a few things for the sake of the Sabbath.

Gronem presided over the table in his adjoining half of the room. They had big portions of gefilte fish and large plates of soup with barley and huge chunks of meat. The cheapest kind of everything—but that was the point—that they should have a lot, plenty. A big challa, a huge loaf of bread, and an enormous black radish. There was also a little brandy. And a tremendous dessert of sweet stewed carrots. Gronem sang Zemiroth lustily, his boys assisting him at the top of their voice.

The scribe didn't like having to live under one roof with these loud-voiced people—actually in the same room, with only a partition between them.

As he started saying grace Reb Mordecai Goldblum and Reb Isser came in. "Good Shabbos! Good Shabbos!" both said twice over, and asked: "How are you, Saul? The good God will help you!"

"Have you finished your meal?" Goldblum asked apologetically. "Said grace already?"

"No, we haven't said grace yet."

"But I heard you singing Zemiroth."

"Zemiroth can be sung again and again."

"Yes, of course," said Reb Mordecai. "Very well, you start, Reb Isser. 'Boruch El Elyon.' We'll all join in. You too, Jacob. As you did when you came to my house as a boy with your father."

The Rebbe's melodies rose again in the air, one Zemirah after the other. Then Reb Mordecai repeated something he had once heard the Rebbe say:

"He once said at table that sadness can be dispelled only with song, even a song that is almost weeping. Because in song there is no sadness, as there is no sadness in prayer. What to some people in song is sadness is really earnestness. Song is all gladness, gladness in all its degrees. Song is pure holiness and the highest form of prayer. Song that is sung in a voice pleasant and beautiful and with devoutness reaches the world divine."

"Yes, but there is a difference in sadness," said Reb Isser, "There is sadness of a very high level, through which one can attain elevation of the soul. But this is the holy Sabbath, so it is better we should continue singing."

Both Reb Mordecai and Reb Isser saw that the sick man was exhausted. The effort he had made had been too much for him. They pretended not to have noticed, and went on singing softly for a little while longer. Then Reb Isser said:

"Let's sing Shir Hamaloth, Saul, and then say grace. We mustn't forget that you're a sick man."

It was on the tip of his tongue to say "a dying man." For that is what the scribe looked now. He found it very hard to breathe. His head had fallen back. "We oughtn't to go away now," Reb Isser thought to himself. Aloud he said: "Wouldn't you like me to stay the night with you, Saul? To relieve your wife and Jacob, so that they can go to bed tonight. I'll stay up with you."

"I'll stay with you too," said Reb Mordecai.

"No," said the sick man. "Thank you for coming. But please go now."

He had a very bad night. When the candles had burned out, the room was left in almost complete darkness. There was only the faint glimmer of the tiny kerosene lamp over his face. Benjamin and Meir insisted on sitting up with their father, but they dropped off to sleep sitting there in their clothes, and Jacob picked them up and put them down on their mother's bed in their clothes.

Jochabed and Jacob sat all through the night by the sickbed, full of anxious fears. As dawn broke the sick man fell asleep. He awoke at eight, looking much better. He asked for a little water to pour over his fingers, and said "Modi Ani." Then he asked to be washed, and to have his Tallith put on. He repeated the whole Sabbath morning service, even the Portion of the Law, but very quietly, hardly moving his lips. He sipped with difficulty his glass of hot water and milk. He couldn't eat; but he made an effort to taste a fragment of the food for the sake of the Sabbath. The others couldn't bring themselves to eat at all. Not even little Meir.

The sick man said Zemiroth—he could no longer sing. The two boys made an effort to sing, to please their father, but they too said most of it instead of singing. The meal didn't take long. When the scribe finished saying grace they were just starting the Reading of the Law in the Synagogue.

Then the scribe said he wanted to be alone with Jacob. When his wife and the two boys had left the room he motioned to Jacob to sit on the bed beside him.

"My mind is clear," he said, "receptive for the great Torah mysteries. I have in my life been only rarely privileged to such high elevation of the soul. I know that I shall soon stand before the Glory Seat of God, to give an account of my life on His earth, of all my actions. It is God's will that my soul should part from the sinful body. I accept it lovingly. There is no doubt that I have committed many sins. But I never for one moment ceased to believe in Him, in all His deeds, and in His Torah, which is mostly hidden from man, from such a simple mortal as I am. I therefore hope and trust that God will forgive me much. I did what I could. I kept His commandments, and I resisted the Tempter as much as my strength let me."

He stopped for a moment, to take new breath. He was speaking very quietly, but each word was clear and distinct. Jacob waited till his father spoke again:

"I know that I did not depart from the faith by a hair in that I came to see that you are right in many things you said and keep saying. It is God's Truth. God Almighty said it all to Moses and to all his Prophets after Moses. Therefore in fundamentals, Jacob my son, you are a Jew. Of course, it would be better if you were a Jew in other matters as well, if you kept all the observances, with piety and with belief in God, saying your prayers and doing His will. But this must all come from the heart. Judaism is in the heart. Therefore I make no demands on you, and I ask you for no promises, not even that you should say Kaddish for me.

"But this one thing I do say to you, I leave it to you as my last Testament— Remember, my son, God's Word and His ways of righteousness and justice we can only learn and seek and teach to others. But first and most of all you yourself must observe what you want to teach others. You must not turn aside to the right nor to the left from the Truth. The Truth is fundamental, and lies do not lead you to the

Truth. You do not get justice by committing injustice. No injustice that is committed gets lost. Every injustice is a spark that smolders and is not extinguished. And when many sparks have collected, they burst into flame. Then you get a fire that burns down houses and towns.

"Of course, good deeds don't get lost, either. They earn their reward, just as wrongdoing brings punishment. Both are weighed at the trial. It depends which scale rises and which falls. Forgiveness follows when the good deeds weigh heavier. But punishment for sins is God's own prerogative—He Himself judges and He executes judgment, with His own hand or through His messengers."

The scribe said no more. The terrible flame that had burned in his eyes last night had lighted up there again. His head was no longer so clear. When his wife, Jochabed, returned with the two boys, and with Reb Mordecai Goldblum and Reb Isser, who had arrived to see their sick friend, he no longer recognized anyone. He didn't respond to their "Good Shabbos." He was muttering words that were intelligible only to Reb Isser and to Jacob. He said: "With the ultimate bitterness begins the sweet. With the ultimate sweet the bitterness. Before the True Life there is a high threshold of long pointed knives. And everyone must pass over this threshold."

Then the death pangs began. The scribe breathed his last as the Sabbath ended, as the first stars appeared in the sky.

Reb Mordecai Goldblum had things to attend to when the Sabbath was over, and rushed away. He was very busy these days, since his factory was being rebuilt.

Reb Isser stayed with the widow and the children. It was now nearly midnight. The dead man lay on the floor, covered right over. Candles were burning. The melamed's wife had taken Benjamin and Meir into her half of the room, and had put them to bed.

Jochabed couldn't wail and weep any more. She swayed to and fro, moaning. Reb Isser was reading the Book of Job. Jacob stared with unseeing eyes. Then he flung himself on his dead father, uncovered his face, kissed his hands and cried: "Father!" "Father!"

39

The Last Hour

It was some weeks since the scribe had died.

In spite of the denials by the government and the press, the rumors of Polish reverses on the battlefront were causing increasing anxiety and fear in the town. Proclamations were posted on the walls of the Town Hall, in the marketplace, and on hundreds of houses warning deserters and spies that they would be shot, and calling on citizens to defend the Fatherland to their last drop of blood. They only added to the apprehension.

The leaders of all Parties, from the most reactionary and clericalist to the Socialists—all except the Communists—the representatives of the Christian and Jewish religions, the notables of the town, and those active in the cultural field all tried to rouse the patriotic ardor of the people.

The Rabbi delivered a flaming exhortation in the Synagogue on the Sabbath after the Reading of the Law. He was a striking figure in his satin caftan and velvet cap, his long beard reaching to his waist, wrapped in his Tallith. He took his text from that week's Portion of the Law—"And the Lord thy God will go before thee, and will fight for thee."

He sang Poland's praises—it was the land that had let the Jews in when they were hunted and murdered everywhere. "We were as beasts of prey fleeing from the slayer," he cried, "and Poland took us in, gave us food to eat and water to drink and a place to rest our head.

"This Poland," he went on, "was partitioned and enslaved. Now it has been freed; it is a land reborn. Now the enemy seeks to enslave it again. This enemy is the enemy of our religion, of our faith, the denying spirit, Satan himself! With God's help we shall overcome him. 'The Lord thy God will go before thee, and will fight for thee.'"

The country was swept by a wildfire of patriotism. Young and old volunteered for military service. Woman and children, even the sick and the old, put their names down for war work.

At the same time the police tightened their hunt for Communists and other opponents of the war effort. The previous fear was replaced by patriotism run mad.

On Sunday the great church bell tolled. Not the deep bass which usually summoned the Christian population of the town and surrounding villages each Sunday to worship, but a loud alarm, as when it warned people of a fire. The sound struck terror through the air, which was fragrant with the smell of ripe corn and ripe fruit in the fields and orchards. The earth rocked under the hurrying feet of old and young on their way to church. They knew this was a fateful hour.

The peasants came in crowds from the fields in top boots and coarse linen blouses with blue and red buttons and ribbons, with big floppy straw hats or four-cornered fur hats, though the sun was already burning hot. The peasant women wore wide-gathered, gay, cotton and chintz skirts, with striped blouses, and colored scarves over their heads, tied under the chin. The colors were loud and flaming, red and green and yellow, striped and flowered, or with large and small dots.

As they made their way across the paths and the footpaths, the thought came to some of them that the ripe corn in the fields was not so much afraid of the scythe and the sickle, already sharpened for reaping, as of the bitter fate of 1914–15. The corn does not fear the scythe and the sickle—it hardly feels their gentle touch before which it falls and is then gathered in sheaves and stored in the barns. But it is afraid of heavy military boots and iron horseshoes and the wheels of gun carriages trampling it down, and shellfire burning it to ashes.

The bells stopped ringing. The church was packed. Many had to stay outside because there was no more room inside. They stood on the wide steps of the church, surging all the way down, right into the street. The great high church doors were wide open so that those outside could follow the service and join in the prayers. They prayed earnestly and devoutly to God, to Jesus, the Son, and to the Holy Ghost, and to the Virgin Mary in her red and blue and white draperies.

All the worshipers prayed fervently for their Fatherland which was in danger, and for their heroic army fighting on the battlefield. The church was full of lighted candles, not only on the altar but in all the niches where the stone figures of the apostles stood. The organ was playing, accompanying the singing of the choir boys. Thousands of fingers counted their beads.

When the service ended, all who were in the church sat down in their places. They included all the big shots of the neighborhood, like Count Zaremba, Pan Krzewicki, and the high local civil authorities. They all wore formal black frock coats, with medals and ribbons. But they were quite outshone by the few military officers present, and by the two police chiefs, Czapski and Ciemnowski, in gala uniform. The priest had put on his finest vestments. He was an imposing figure, with a big crucifix on his chest. His sermon from the pulpit was devoted to Poland's fateful hour.

Then the great bell boomed again, but this time accompanied by two smaller silvery bells, which if the heavy bass notes carried solemn warning, they cheerfully promised victory and implanted hope.

This was the signal for the procession to form behind the priest. The whole congregation fell in. The procession marched three times round the church.

There was a solemn meeting afterward in the Town Hall, to which the heads of the Jewish religious community were also invited, with the Rabbi, and Bernfel and Pan Yossele Fuksman. They came straight from the Synagogue, where there had been a special service of intercession for the success of the Polish arms.

Thousands of Christians standing outside the Town Hall when the Jewish representatives arrived gave them a tremendous welcome, and forgot all about anti-Semitism, about the anti-Jewish boycott, and about the pogroms.

On their heels came the members of the Committee of the Polish Socialist Party and of the Committee of the Jewish Socialists, both together, one fraternal group, Comrade Jan Gnilowski with Comrade Hersh Krumholz, Comrade Jadenusza Slomova with Comrade Feiga Mickenshleger, Comrade Jendrek Kapusta with Comrade Abraham Spitzman.

A barrel was upended to make a platform, and Comrades Jan Gnilowski and Hersh Krumholz addressed the crowd, Christians and Jews, about the things they had in common, which united them—the Socialist ideal, the fact that they both belonged to the International Proletariat, their joint struggle for the cause, for the Polish soil, for their Socialist Fatherland, which was now in danger. They were both brief, and both concluded with "Poland will never be enslaved! Poland will be free!"

Christians and Jews embraced and kissed: "We'll show the dirty Muscovites! Down with the Bolsheviks!"

The meeting in the Town Hall did not last long. They came out again with the priest arm in arm with the rabbi and Pan Krzewicki arm in arm with Pan Bernfel. The rabbi and the priest and Pan Czapski made short speeches in response to the cheering. They spoke of Kosciuszko, Mickiewicz, Chopin, and other great names in Polish history. Then the crowd joined lustily in singing the Polish national anthem.

Suddenly Jacob appeared on the improvised upended barrel platform. There was a mad look in his eyes. He started telling the crowd that war was a terrible crime, that shedding blood, murder, and destruction were a sin. In a few minutes there was a rush at him by a howling mob of Christians and Jews, wanting to lynch him. He was knocked down, and if Hersh and Feiga hadn't rescued him he would have been trampled to death.

"He is out of his mind!" they shouted above the noise. "He has gone crazy since his father died."

Caspar Strzelkowski and two of his militiamen took charge of Jacob and shoved him, bruised and bleeding, into a prison cell.

All the way to prison he kept shouting: "Down with war! We want peace! We want brotherhood of all the peoples! Long live Socialism!"

Caspar Strzelkowski punched Jacob in the face. "Stop that, you dirty Jew!" he cried. "You're going to get it for this! And you're a deserter. You didn't appear when you were called up for the army!"

Jacob went on shouting, "Down with war!"

But this honest patriotic fervor among the people did not improve the military situation. The Polish armies withdrew from one position to another all along the line. The news went around (not officially) that the enemy was already near Brest-Litovsk and Kovel. "The Reds are leaping ahead like tongues of fire," people said.

Many construction works, even ones of great importance for the war effort, were stopped. The crops were left standing in the fields because there was nobody to reap them. The peasants had all been called up to the army, even the young peasant lads. Industry and commerce were short of labor. Everybody was in the army. Prices shot up terribly, so that only war profiteers could afford to buy. The militia and the military police were kept busy searching for spies and deserters.

The American Committee at Bernfel's closed down. Mirel's restaurant kept being raided, and people were arrested there. Rabeh was almost out of her mind after Jacob's arrest. They had told her that he might be sentenced to death.

It was near their wedding day; the date had already been fixed. And the whole population went about in fear of a third flight from the town before the invader.

On the night of Tisha B'Av the religious Jews read Lamentations in the Synagogue, weeping not only for the destruction of Jerusalem, but for the present destruction in Poland. Next morning some went to say Lamentations in the cemetery. They gathered at the graves of the venerated dead, the saints of old, whose ancient tombstones were already settling down into the ground and the lettering was half obliterated. Reb Isser and Reb Mordecai Goldblum were among those saying Lamentations in the graveyard. Their wailing and sobbing carried through the whole cemetery. Reb Mordecai Goldblum was a grief-stricken penitent. He could not forgive himself because after the destruction of his fortunes he had wanted to build up his factory again. It was wrong of him to have listened to the Tempter!

Then the Posnanskis arrived, Polish troops from the Posen area, on their way to the front. They made an immediate dash for the Jewish streets; soon Jewish women and girls and old men were running panic-stricken through the town, with the soldiers in pursuit, shouting: "Kill the Jews! They're all Bolsheviks! Trotskys!"

The Christians in the town, who had only the other day been fraternizing with the Jews, made no attempt to defend their Jewish fellow townsmen. Some in fact joined the Posen soldiers, and shouted with them: "Down with the Jews! They're the enemies of Poland! They're Bolsheviks! Spies!"

Then the pogrom started. Again there were no police in the Jewish quarter when the trouble began.

The first two who were attacked were Samuel, the old orchard man, Hannah's father, and Kalman the tinsmith.

Samuel had just come into the town from his orchard, with two big baskets of fruit he had hoped to sell, one slung over his back and the other in front. Kalman was out for a walk. The two met and continued on their way together.

It was the night of Tisha B'Av, and most Jews were in the Synagogue reading Lamentations.

"You don't hold with Lamentations any more than I do," said Kalman.

Before Samuel could answer he heard hurrying footsteps behind him, and looked around. "Soldiers after us!" he said to Kalman, in a frightened voice. "Let's get out of here quick!"

There were only two soldiers, but they had already caught up with them. One punched Kalman in the belly, so that he doubled up and collapsed on the ground.

The other took Samuel's gray beard, and tugged and tugged till half the beard came out in his hand. The fruit rolled on the ground, and the soldiers kicked it and trampled on it.

Samuel tried to run away. His face was bleeding where the beard had been torn out with the flesh. Kalman was in agony. He had a stabbing pain in his stomach. But he tried to run. The soldiers let him go and stood watching him, guffawing.

The third victim was Berl Farber. He was still more unlucky, because the soldiers got him on the ground and kicked him with their heavy boots till he was dead.

There were ten Jewish dead. The soldiers were still hunting and beating up Jews. They caught children, and tossed them like balls from one to the other. One soldier told the rest that in one town they had passed through they had hung up a Jew in the marketplace. He thought they should do the same here.

40

The Executions

A few days later the pogromist soldiers were gone; the Red Army was marching through Poland. The Jewish population of the town had fled—their third war flight. They were again refugees, wandering through fields and forests.

They passed through town after town, where the people had already fled or were preparing for flight. The roads were all taken up with lorries, troops, guns, ambulances, field hospitals, field kitchens.

One day they came to a large county town, and found a huge crowd, thousands of people waiting outside a big building, with an iron fence round it. The local Jews told them it was the district law court, and the crowd was waiting for two condemned men to be brought out for public execution.

Both were Jews—one, Moshe Talismacher, a boy of seventeen, was a deserter. He had run away from the front, with a horror of bloodshed. He was an only child who had been living at home with his mother. The father was in America.

The other, Ezekiel Freedman, was an altogether different person. He was a Bolshevik. Born in Warsaw and brought up there, he had been in Russia for a long time, had served in the Red Army, and had joined the Polish army on instructions to work among the Polish soldiers to get them to mutiny.

A guard of Polish soldiers with fixed rifles was stationed at the iron gate of the law court. There was a military van in the courtyard, with another armed guard with fixed bayonets. The van was draped with some black material.

The crowd kept getting bigger. They filled the whole roadway. Then suddenly a terrible cry burst out through the law court door. It made people shudder at the sound. The cry rose again, like the cry of a wild beast in torment. It was followed by a hysterical burst of laughter that struck fear at people's hearts. Then the door opened, and a figure like a rolled-up bundle fell out. People whispered among themselves: "The poor boy's mother!"

The woman picked herself up. Behind her two men in black frock coats, with grim, solemn faces, came out, and tried to hold the woman up under the arms. One of the court officers brought her wig, which she had torn off her head in her anguish.

The woman struggled not to let herself be led away from the door; she tried to push her way back inside again. The porters shoved her back, and she fell down the small flight of steps. She picked herself up again and rushed back to the door. The two frock-coated men took her again by the arms, and tried to lead her away. They spoke to her, but she wouldn't listen: "I want to see my son!" she cried. "My only child! All that I have in the world!"

She tore at her clothes; she banged her fists against her head; she clawed at her face till it bled. But they wouldn't let her go inside again. In the end she allowed them to lead her away.

Some of the people in the crowd felt sorry for the woman. But most of them made fun of her, jeered at her.

The soldiers sprang to attention. An officer came out through the door, followed by two soldiers, then the two condemned men, in chains, and then two more armed soldiers behind them. The officer led the way to the black-draped van.

One of the condemned men was a slim young man, just over average height, with a pinched white face, and eyes that stared far into the distance. He didn't seem to see the soldiers and the crowd and the black van that was waiting for him, as though it all had nothing to do with him. There was a strange smile on his lips.

The other prisoner didn't walk by himself as his companion did. The soldiers were pulling and pushing him. His eyes rolled wildly, and his head kept jerking convulsively.

The iron gate opened, and the black van with the two condemned men inside drove out. The crowd divided to let it pass, and thousands of people followed behind. Then something unexpected happened—one of the wheels of the van came off. The horses stopped.

"They're saved!" people whispered to each other. "They mustn't execute them now! God doesn't want them to die!"

The crowd included some Socialists. But they were all split into two camps. One held that the Bolshevik deserved to die. The other lot were furiously indignant that a Socialist government should want to execute a man for being a Socialist. But they didn't dare to say so aloud.

The officer examined the wheel that had fallen off, found the screw, ordered the soldiers to keep guard over the prisoners, and went back into the law court.

He came out presently behind a colonel and two other officers, who inspected the van and the wheel on the ground, examined the screw, and then returned to the law court with the officer who had brought them there. He soon came out again, with an official document in his hand. He gave an order to two of the soldiers, and they fixed the wheel back on the van. Then the van drove off again, amid a loud muttering from the crowd.

The van stopped in a field, hard by the forest, beside two poles, the height of a man. The ground had been freshly dug there. The fields had not been reaped. The smell of the ripe corn and the unpicked fruit in the orchards was heavy on the air.

The armed soldiers pushed back the crowd that had followed the van. At an order from the officer they ranged themselves in two ranks, each side of the van. The sun was high in the sky; its golden rays broke up into many bright colors against the gleaming bayonets.

Moshe Talismacher rolled his eyes wildly when they tied him to the pole. When they bandaged his eyes his head dropped forward, and he looked like a child falling off to sleep. He didn't hear the officer ask what his last wish was.

Ezekiel Freedman answered that question unhesitatingly—take off my chains, don't tie me to the pole, don't bandage my eyes. He also wanted a cigarette—the last smoke I'll have.

The officer considered it. There was admiration for Freedman in his eyes. All right, he said, agreed! He offered him his packet of cigarettes, and when he took one he struck a match and lit the cigarette for him.

Freedman thought back, as he puffed at the cigarette, to the past, to the first Socialist pamphlet that a friend had given him to read. He had been an apprentice then in a shoe factory. He recalled his parents, his brothers and his sisters. He saw the streets of Warsaw, where he was born and brought up. He was enjoying this smoke. He took the cigarette out of his mouth, and looked at it. More than half smoked. Time was drawing short. A shudder ran through him. So this was the end.

The thoughts in his mind began chasing each other, faster, wilder. They got mixed up, confused. He didn't want that. So he dismissed his childhood memories, the thoughts of his family, and he tried to concentrate on what he remembered of his work in the Party. First in Poland, then in Russia, in Charkov and Berditchev and other towns, because he had to go from town to town to escape the police who were searching for him. He had been in the October Revolution. His friends Kolko and Yevroshin had once said to him, when he was in the Red Army: "Comrade Freedman, the world is now an ugly place, a pit of filth and misery and pain. But we Communists will clean it up. We shall change the world into a lovely place, so that people will be glad to live in it. We won't live to see it—but the future generations will."

Comrade Freedman saw red poppies and blue cornflowers growing where he stood. The cigarette was almost burned out. He gave one more puff, then threw away the stub. Then he stood straight up and waited.